Siobhán MacDonald was born in the Republic of Ireland. She was raised in Cork where she learned to read and do joined-up writing, and in Limerick where she first had notions of becoming a writer.

Siobhán studied engineering at University College Galway and had a successful career writing for the technology sector in Scotland and the south of France before returning to Ireland.

Growing up in a large family, there was a premium attached to being able to spin a good yarn. Siobhán's mother taught speech and drama and was a proficient storyteller – a talent she encouraged in all her children.

After writing many short stories and scripts, Siobhán published her first novel, *Twisted River*, in 2016. She followed this up with her second novel, *The Blue Pool*. *Twisted River* won an AudioFile Earphones award in 2016 and *The Blue Pool* has been a top ten bestseller in the Kindle charts. *Guilty* is her first novel for Constable, Little, Brown.

Siobhán lives in Limerick, where she is married with two sons.

Instagram: siobhan.m.macdonald

Facebook: Siobhan MacDonald

Twitter: @SiobhanMMacD

Also by Siobhán MacDonald

Twisted River
The Blue Pool

SIOBHÁN MACDONALD

GUILTY

CONSTABLE

CONSTABLE

First published in hardback in Great Britain in 2020 by Constable

This paperback edition published in 2021 by Constable

Copyright © Siobhán MacDonald, 2020

1 3 5 7 9 10 8 6 4 2

The moral right of the author has been asserted.

A CIP catalogue record for this book is available from the British Library.

ISBN: 978-1-47213-413-4

Typeset in Caslon Pro by SX Composing DTP, Rayleigh, Essex
Printed and bound in Great Britain by Clays Ltd, Elcograf S.p.A.

Papers used by Constable are from well-managed forests
and other responsible sources.

MIX
Paper from
responsible sources
FSC
www.fsc.org
FSC® C104740

Constable
An imprint of
Little, Brown Book Group
Carmelite House
50 Victoria Embankment
London EC4Y 0DZ

An Hachette UK Company
www.hachette.co.uk

www.littlebrown.co.uk

For Neil, Jamie and Alasdair.
And for my parents, Pat and Catherine,
who came before.

Now

Luke

Saturday 13 April

Something told Luke not to watch, to turn away, that he'd be sorry if he looked. But his eyes were drawn above him where he stood. A white flash seared overhead. It gathered mass and started falling. It tumbled, spinning ever downwards, ever brilliant against the darkening sky. In a drunken pirouette, it cast a spinning shadow as it fell towards the earth. Luke was in the creature's path. He stepped aside just in time. There was a sickening thud as it hit the ground.

The creature quivered, inches from him. It was mangled, its neck was broken and its blood-soaked feathers splayed as if reaching out. It blinked with a glazed eye and he shied back. The creature shuddered and gave a long, low, piteous moan.

Luke bolted upright against his pillow convinced that he'd cried out.

'Sophie . . .'

The woman beside him was breathing gently, her long hair tousled, tired from the night before. Luke sat shaking, a cold sweat prickling his brow. He stared nervously into the dark, listening to the sound of the water lapping outside. It had been a while since the white bird called to see him.

3

Last night's shift was heavy going. The girl had been critical. According to her friend she'd taken some pills at a party. She was young – fifteen – three years younger than Nina. It had taken hours to get her stable. Everyone called him a hero.

Wide awake, he sat and waited for the dawn. When light streaked the sky, he dressed quietly and slipped downstairs. Through the kitchen, out the heavy door and down the glass corridor to the boathouse. The air was damp and it was cold for April. His breath formed in ghostly clouds as he stepped into his boat. It felt good to be up and about.

Checks complete, he steered the cruiser out into open water. Powering up the engine, he planed slowly through the waves before picking up speed. It was the first Saturday in a month he wasn't on call. He'd left his mobile in the glove compartment of the car and his laptop in the boot. He was under orders.

The sky was bruised and sullen, and rain was in the air. He'd head first for Carey's Island then cruise across to Lisheen Bay before heading back to Kilbawn Pier. Out here, alone, Luke could think. He often thought about escaping, of floating off to somewhere safe. As he watched, a bank of trees sheared away from the pine-green stubble of the hillside down towards the lough. The rain had been relentless. Mudslides had closed roads all around Lough Carberry and the forecast warned of further flooding.

The surface of the water wrinkled as the breeze picked up. On the northern hills, turbines were staked in the ground like giant white crucifixes, their long arms turning in the rain-soaked wind. In the distance, Luke saw folds of starlings swishing one over the other, dispersing then coming together in great bisecting arcs of flight.

Something had disturbed these starlings. He scoured the hillside for a bird of prey. Luke's days were driven by reason and logic. Birds of prey were driven by instinct and impulse alone. He envied their simplicity, the pureness of a kill to sate an appetite, not cursed by doubt or conscience. There were things in life he couldn't control and Dr Black was helping him with those. There were also things he couldn't accept. Things that lay between him and sleep. Things so dark no one would want to know.

The wonder of the starlings lingered as he approached the house. Seeing his home from the water made him feel sad. It was a project he and Alison had worked on together. Locals had dubbed it the Glasshouse and the name had stuck. Three large cubes of flat-roofed, glass-panelled walls, off-set slightly from one another. They linked to the boathouse by a long glass corridor over the lawn. The house had won several design awards. That had made Alison happy. His wife liked beautiful things.

But there was something else. Foreboding. As he looked out for the inlet marked by a rocky outcrop and an old bench, he sensed that something was out of place. He spotted what it was. Something painted on the lough side of his boathouse. Drawing close, he made it out.

Six white letters in fresh paint:

GUILTY

Classified

Luke guided the cruiser into the boathouse and sat in the silence, trying to think. Low drifts of fog swirled across the water. It was the first time in a fortnight he'd been out on the lough. He checked his watch. Sophie would be up by now expecting him back. She was coming to his place most weekends now. He told himself not to worry, that she couldn't have seen it. It was on the lough side, and couldn't be seen from the house. He'd clean it later.

He had to move. He couldn't stay out here, shivering. Stepping off the boat and onto the steps, he grabbed the handrail. There were five steps clear of water instead of the usual eight or nine. He'd never seen the water as high. The result of all the rainfall, combined with run-off and the opening of sluice gates up the river. He stopped at the security camera by the door, and waved.

'Hello,' he mouthed and smiled. 'I'm home.'

It was a one-way system and he didn't know if Sophie was even watching but he'd behave as if she was. Yanking the door open, he started to hum as he dragged his legs through the glass corridor on towards the house.

OK, showtime.

I'm a normal guy with a normal life.

At the sound of footsteps in the kitchen, the dog raised his head.

Luke bent to rub him. 'What's got into you, little man?'

No reaction.

'He's jealous, pure and simple,' said Sophie. 'He doesn't want to share you.'

Sleepy-eyed, she handed Luke a coffee.

'I dunno, he's not the jealous type.' He took the mug. 'I'll tell you one thing though. He's not the same since giving up the fags.'

Sophie laughed.

'Can't believe you used to smoke. A bad boy in your day?'

He tapped the side of his nose and looked at the dog. 'Hey pal, you're going to have to straighten up. Cos if it's a toss-up between yourself and this gorgeous woman . . .' He turned to Sophie. 'We're together how long now?'

'Two months and twelve days, to be exact.'

'Really? You hear that, Duffy? So pull yourself together, because I'm hoping the lovely Sophie's going to stick around.'

He wrapped an arm around her waist and kissed her neck. She smelled warm and musky. He was trembling but she didn't seem to notice. The animal watched them closely. Sophie pulled away and returned to the hob with a smile playing on her lips. Luke headed for the table.

'The paper man buzzed a while ago,' Sophie said.

'Oh yeah?'

He sat down.

'Said this place was as far as he could go, that further up the road is flooded.' She twisted the peppermill over the pan. 'How bad is it out there?'

She fetched two breakfast plates and, leaning over, she set them onto the table. She was wearing nothing under the white

7

cotton nightdress – usually enough to get a reaction but right now Luke's mind was elsewhere. Anyway, Sophie didn't like it when he took the lead. That was her domain.

'It's like some enormous bog. Floods, muck, sludge, trees uprooted. I witnessed a mudslide right in front of my eyes . . . a whole bank of trees just ripping away. It's a godawful mess. They'll have to close more roads and as for driving, well, that's going to be even more of a pain in the arse . . .' He was speaking way too fast. His mind was racing.

Sophie set the cafetière on the table. 'Eggs all right?'

He'd started without her, not out of hunger but keen to occupy his shaking hands.

'Perfect. The dog's bollocks, in fact.' He cast an eye in Duffy's direction. 'Sorry, pal.'

No reaction.

'A pity about all the kids making first communion today.' Sophie sat down. 'Imagine, all those pretty white dresses in the wet.' She looked up from her plate and across the table at him. 'You OK? You seem a bit off.'

'Fine.' He held her gaze. 'It was great to get out on the water. It's been a while.'

Her eyes stayed on him as she reached across the table for the paper.

'You're pale though.' She peeled off the plastic covering. 'Sleep all right?'

'Tired, that's all. It was rough in the ER yesterday. I didn't want to bother you with it last night but we had a young girl in. For a while there we didn't think she'd make it. Same age as Nina, more or less. But it worked out all right in the end.'

'I don't know how you do it,' she murmured.

He was still getting used to being asked how he felt. Alison had never asked. He watched as Sophie opened the paper. She spread it across the table at the entertainment pages.

'*Jersey Boys* is on up in Dublin.' She fixed him with her soft brown eyes. 'We should go. It got great reviews.'

'So I believe,' he said. 'Some of the guys at the hospital have been. I'll check my diary.'

He'd spotted the ad for U2. He fancied that as well. Maybe he could swing it that they'd do both. The thing about Sophie was that she enjoyed entertainment for entertainment's sake. Not like Alison. Not to fundraise. Not to lobby. Not to grease a palm.

'Top up?' She held the cafetière.

'Please.'

She came close to pour. This time Luke reached out and stroked her leg.

She pushed his hand aside. 'Chancer.'

'Spoilsport.' He pulled a face.

Settling into his chair, he pulled the paper towards him. It was a treat to sit with the weekend papers and a cooked breakfast. If only he could relax. He started to turn the pages but it was impossible. His mind kept returning to the scrawl along the boathouse wall.

Something in the paper caught his eye. He stiffened.

'Luke, you all right? What's the matter? Luke . . .?'

He was staring. Sophie stood. He felt her eyes on him, watching as he read and re-read the classifieds, his finger pressing down hard on the paper. He angled the paper towards her, his finger drawing attention to one particular entry. He turned his gaze up to her.

The private rooms of Professor Luke F. Forde (Paediatric Cardiothoracic Surgeon) will remain closed on Monday 15 April and Tuesday 16 April due to the tragic and untimely

9

> death of Nina Forde-Thompson, beloved only daughter
> of Professor Luke Forde and Government Minister Alison
> Forde-Thompson. May she rest in peace.

Sophie was saying something but he couldn't make it out. Her hand was squeezing his shoulder. He felt light-headed. A knot formed in the pit of his stomach. Sophie sat on the chair beside him and turned the page over. The listings were alphabetical. She traced her finger down through the death lists.

There it was, again:

> Forde-Thompson, Nina, 18 years of age. 12 April.
> (The Glasshouse) Tragically and untimely. Only child
> of Professor Luke F. Forde and Government Minister
> Alison Forde-Thompson. To the inestimable grief of her
> parents and her loving grandfather Senator Cornelius
> Thompson. House private. Family cremation at a later
> date. Ashes to be scattered over Lough Carberry in
> County Clare. A bright star gone for ever. May she rest
> in peace.

Luke looked at Sophie in horror.

'Oh, God, no.'

He jumped up from his chair and rushed to the hall, grabbing his car keys from the hall table.

He had to get to his phone.

A Few Months Earlier

Doctors

January

'So then, Luke – you don't mind if I call you Luke?'

Luke shook his head. He just wanted to get this over with.

'Better to dispense with titles, I always think.' The guy was softly spoken. He pointed to a green upholstered armchair. 'You were referred to me by your GP?' The therapist was rustling through a sheaf of papers.

'No.' Luke sat down awkwardly. 'I was given your card by . . . a friend.'

'Ah, that explains it. I can't see the referral and I like to keep my paperwork together.'

Not making a great job of that, thought Luke, as three more sheets floated off the desk. His secretary Fran, however, had recommended this guy and she didn't recommend lightly. 'Doctor Black's good to talk to, so I hear,' she'd said. 'Helped my brother when he went through his marriage difficulties. Men are such rubbish at talking about their feelings.'

Yet another article of faith, another incontrovertible fact from long-serving, officious Fran, gatekeeper to his consulting rooms, custodian of his business affairs. She had placed the business card on the filing cabinet. 'One of those that left the priesthood,' she'd said, raising an eyebrow. 'Married now, so I believe.' Fran was nothing if not thorough.

The therapist abandoned his paperchase. 'Right then, Luke, what would you like to talk about today?' he asked, settling himself into the armchair opposite.

So that's how this was going to go? A series of open-ended questions when a few pertinent ones could put an end to all of this? Luke rubbed his chin. He contemplated making his excuses there and then, and leaving.

'In your own time . . .' Terence Black nudged a box of tissues in his direction.

Did this guy think Luke was going to become emotionally incontinent on demand? He'd regretted coming as soon as he'd set foot in the waiting room. All those crappy photos of waves and mountains and Buddhist temples. He should have acted on instinct, finished his take-out coffee and crossword in the car, and driven off.

'Would you like a glass of water?' Terence asked.

'No . . .'

Luke was floundering, vainly trying to think of an excuse to get out of here.

'Oh well, OK, maybe I will then . . .'

Jesus. Why had he ever thought that this would help?

'Don't worry. It can be hard to start.' Terence poured from a jug into a plastic cup and set the water in front of Luke.

Luke checked his watch. 'It's just that I'm due back at two-thirty.' He was doing a valve replacement that would be assisted by his senior registrars.

'My fault. I was late,' Terence apologised. 'Look, a lot of the time, people come to see me because they feel that, for some reason, things are not quite right. Finding out the cause can be something of a . . . process.' He drew quotation marks with his fingers.

Luke winced. It set his teeth on edge.

'However, we have a good twenty-five minutes today, so why don't you start by telling me a little about yourself. Who you are—'

Luke looked at him askance.

'Oh, of course I've seen you on TV once or twice,' Terence responded quickly, 'talking about your work for children with heart defects, and your involvement in various trusts and charities.' He leaned in. 'But let's imagine I know nothing at all about you. You tell me about yourself.'

What on earth had Luke walked himself into? There was no easy way out of here. He might as well say something.

'OK . . . well, you probably also know that I'm married to Alison Forde-Thompson. She's running as an independent candidate in the local elections.'

Terence nodded.

'And we have one child, Nina.' He paused. 'Since campaigning started, things have been . . . well, difficult for us all.' In the run-up, Alison had been doing her utmost to link her election aspirations to Luke's success.

'I'm sure something like an election campaign would put a stress on any family.'

Luke gave a wry smile. He'd known it was a matter of time before Alison followed her father's footsteps into politics. It was a natural progression from her PR world. She freely admitted to relishing nothing more than turning people to her way of thinking.

Terence sat blinking, waiting for a response. Disclosure did not come easily to Luke. 'I guess it doesn't help that my wife's been spending quite a lot of time at Crow Hall. Her father's place,' he volunteered.

15

'That's Cornelius Thompson, the senator?'

'Correct.'

A number of years earlier Cornelius had been forced to retire from office. Found drunk in parliamentary chambers, he added to his transgression by fondling a female colleague, and was abusive to the policewoman who'd tried to stop him leaving in his car.

His reputation had been rehabilitated since then by none other than Thompson Consulting, his daughter's PR firm. Cornelius currently enjoyed the position of senator in the upper house – all courtesy of Alison's persuasive powers. 'I create myths and I make the ugly truths go away,' she'd say.

'So, the campaign has been hard on your daughter Nina?' Terence probed.

'She and her mother don't see eye to eye.'

'She gets on better with you?'

Luke thought carefully. 'Yes . . .' He hesitated. 'That would be true to say. Alison says we're thick as thieves.'

Terence made a note. 'I'm sure I don't need to say that what you say in here is confidential. I'm here to help. What you say in this room remains between the two of us.'

Luke shifted in his seat.

'I'm not sure exactly,' he started, 'but I think . . . I think my wife may have left me.' He rubbed his chin. He felt like a prize idiot.

'I see. Why do you say that?' Terence blinked slowly.

'At first I thought Alison was spending quite a bit of time at Crow Hall, getting campaign advice from her father,' Luke explained. 'She'd sleep the occasional night there. But I noticed recently that there are large gaps in her wardrobe, like many of her clothes are missing. And she can be gone for days at a time.'

The therapist looked at him thoughtfully. Luke had a sudden insight into just how ridiculous he sounded. How could any fool not know whether his wife had left him? And why would he not simply confront her and ask?

'Can I ask you something, Luke?'

He tensed. 'Ask away.'

He'd answer if it wasn't incriminating.

'Do you love your wife?'

Luke exhaled.

Easy question.

'I'll tell you one thing,' he replied. 'I'm pretty certain Alison doesn't love me. And to tell the truth I wonder if she ever did.'

Later that afternoon, back at the hospital, Luke grew increasingly ill-tempered. He kept spotting deposits of hair and dust along the corridors. The unkempt floors were symptomatic of a greater malaise at St Matthew's University Hospital.

Luke encouraged a higher standard in the cardiac surgery unit. The cleaning rota he'd organised for the staff sitting room was working well, undertaken by the staff in the unit themselves without the help of slipshod cleaners.

Making his way towards the scrub room, he ruminated on the session with Terence Black. He'd had a plan of what he'd wanted to say going in there, but he'd been thrown off course. He'd wound up talking a load of old nonsense instead.

As he stood at the taps washing his arms, he glanced about the scrub room at his team. He frowned. Which one of them had betrayed him to Fran? A theatre nurse? One of the registrars? A senior house officer? They wouldn't dare. If there was one thing he couldn't stand, it was a snitch.

Each time it had happened, there was alarm from those around him. Increased blinking, an exchange of glances, suspicious looks. Eyes questioning his and air sucks of alarm through the porous gauze of facemasks. He'd be breathless, paralysed, unable to function. And after what would seem like for ever, the feelings would subside. His pulse would slow to normal. He would breathe. Bit by bit, snippets of hushed conversation would return.

The last time it had happened, he had been concentrating on manoeuvring wire from a defibrillator. All of a sudden he'd gone rigid. Perspiration had trickled from his forehead. He'd floundered, unable to proceed. The whole terrifying episode had probably lasted only seconds but it was long enough for people to notice. The time before that, it had happened when he was making an incision into an artery for a catheter. Again, Luke had frozen, closing his eyes, trying to smother the host of unwanted images flooding his head.

It was clear to him that someone had voiced concerns about what was going on. And Fran had somehow surmised that Luke's out-of-character behaviour was down to problems with his wife. Fran had never been a fan of Alison. As far as Luke was concerned, if his secretary chose to believe his behaviour was due to stress within his marriage, he wouldn't disavow her. The one thing he couldn't do was fool himself. He'd noticed a pattern.

Luke had been careful in choosing his secretary. In spite of that, an informality had found its way into their working relationship. Fran's familiarity could be tiresome. And she saw too much. She definitely said too much. Luke was still annoyed at an exchange they'd had earlier in the week.

'Not backwards in coming forwards, is she?' Fran had remarked about Alison. 'Making excellent use of *your* name.' Her eyes were fixed on her computer screen.

Alison had double-barrelled Forde to her maiden name for the election. Prior to that she'd gone by Thompson.

18

'Yes, indeedy, has her notions, that one.' Fran reached across her desk for a pen.

Luke bristled. 'Branding is key in politics and PR.'

Fran snorted. Her typing grew more vigorous. 'Perfect timing also.' Her voice was smooth, her fingers furious. 'With your name splashed all over the newspapers.'

Of late there'd been a flurry of articles detailing Luke's volunteer work in the broadsheets. Fran was right. The timing had been fortuitous. Though he tried to dispel the thought, he found himself wondering if his wife had somehow been behind those articles. He found it disconcerting to see the Forde name on every pole and hoarding in County Clare. What Fran had said struck home. His secretary had an uncanny knack of pointing out unwholesome truths.

It was late when Luke left the hospital at the end of his shift. He was relieved the procedure on the thirteen-year-old boy had gone well. He was strolling down to his reserved space in the hospital car park when he heard the electric whirr of a nearby car window.

'Hey there, Luke!'

It was Johnny Whelan, a consultant in emergency medicine.

'Johnny, how's it going? A&E was mental today, so I heard.'

'Like a zoo,' said Johnny.

'What we do for kicks,' Luke said drily.

'I've been meaning to ask.' Johnny leaned out his window. 'You on for Thailand this year?'

'Maybe . . .' Luke was caught on the hop. 'I'll need to check my rosters. The usual suspects?'

'Yeah, same select bunch. You, me, and Hugh Smyth. The same old reprobates.'

'I thought Hugh was out . . .' Luke lowered his voice, 'after last time . . .?'

Johnny grinned. 'Miriam doesn't know.'

Miriam was Hugh's wife. They had three young kids.

'What goes on tour stays on tour?'

Johnny winked. 'Too right.'

Luke slapped the roof of Johnny's car. The window was purring up when Johnny appeared to think of something else. He froze the window.

'Maybe we could have a get-together in your basement? To kick things off?'

'Sounds like a plan. I'll be in touch.'

'Top man,' said Johnny.

For the first time that day, Luke felt a glow of pleasure. He was pretty self-sufficient. Although he had to admit he enjoyed the camaraderie of those Thailand trips. As he swung out of the car park to head for home, he tried his best to hold on to the warm glow.

Sebastian

'Nina?'

Someone was home. Luke had seen the house lit up from the road above. Light bounced and danced off the glass walls.

'Alison?'

Duffy came scudding and sliding across the marble hallway. Luke's nostrils filled with the warm scent of baking and something else. Definitely not Alison. He'd seen her wear an apron once. For a photoshoot to launch a charity event.

His stomach rumbled. Apart from a few snatched mouthfuls, he'd been too busy to grab a proper bite to eat all day.

'In here,' a voice called out.

Luke followed the voice down the hall to the kitchen at the back of the house. It was Nina in the garden room adjoining.

'Well, this is a hive of . . . of . . .'

He was about to say 'industry' but realised it didn't fit. Industry suggested order, control, planning. What he saw was none of these things. He scanned the kitchen. Flour and cooking debris sat on the island among election posters and glossy pamphlets. Paint-splattered newspapers were strewn over the floor in the garden room. All Luke could see of Nina were two bare legs underneath the easel. His daughter was on a gap year, working part-time, and taking a night class in life drawing before heading to college in the autumn.

'It's my day off.' She poked out her head from around the easel. She was wearing her glasses and a black T-shirt. It was covered in flour. 'I've been painting.'

'You don't say.'

She stuck out her tongue.

God knows how his daughter ever got that part-time job in Spillane's bakery in town. She always managed to look dishevelled, as if she'd been dragged backwards through a bush.

'I guess it's just the two of us this evening. Have you heard from Mum today?' asked Luke.

'I have. She wants me to order a birthday cake for some old dear at Inishcloon who's going to be a hundred.'

Inishcloon was the local nursing home.

'That's all she wanted?'

'Don't sound so surprised, Dad. If it's not about the election, she doesn't want to know.' Nina peeked out from behind her easel. 'She's too busy canvassing the incapacitated and the bewildered. She's Election Bridezilla.'

Luke headed for the cupcakes, the dog at his heels. 'I'm starving. I'd eat the twelve apostles.'

'No!'

Luke stopped in his tracks.

'I don't think you'd like them.' Nina scrunched up her face.

'They look grand to me.'

'No, really . . . I overdid the raising agent. Give me a minute and I'll fix you an omelette.'

An omelette would do fine. She could hardly make a bags of that. 'Let me see what you've been painting . . .'

Luke ruffled the dog's head as he walked around the easel.

22

'What on earth . . .?' Luke felt the blood drain from his face.

'It's a first attempt.' Nina sounded disappointed. 'I can do better.'

It was crude. It was primitive. A novice's attempt at life drawing. The subject: a bony dark-haired youth draped over what looked like their leather sofa, legs sprawled wide, genitalia on display, a knife and fork criss-crossed the concave stomach, eyes rimmed in black. In the bottom right-hand corner, she had titled the work, *Eat Me?*

'What, no eyebrows?' It was a ridiculous question but he could think of nothing else to say.

'He shaved them off.' Nina giggled.

Luke was looking at a real person. Not a creature conjured from her rich imagination.

'Who is this . . . this person?'

'A guy from my night class. His name is Sebastian.' Nina angled her head to the side, surveying her work. 'He's really gifted. Look.'

She directed Luke to the kitchen table. There among the mess was another painting.

'He's so talented. Don't you think?'

Luke pretended to examine the work, as if he were genuinely considering its merits. It was a good likeness. Some of the essence of Nina had been captured. That clever vulnerability. That blend of intellect and innocence. Her lovable goofiness. Agreeable Nina. Luke offered no opinion.

'Aw, c'mon, Dad. You're not going to come over all censorious on me, are you?' She looked pained. 'It's a bit late for all that now. You're the one who always encouraged me to experiment.'

'Not exactly the kind of experimentation I had in mind, Nina.'

His daughter was eighteen. The fact that she chose to pose half-naked for some crude life drawing was her prerogative.

This young fella, whoever he was, probably couldn't believe his luck. Luke wanted to shake her but she had to be handled with care.

'Wait 'til you see this.'

She danced across the floor to grab her tablet.

'He's *really* clever.'

She swiped her finger across the screen.

'There,' she said, her breath coming in excited bursts. 'Isn't it genius?'

Genius wasn't a description that immediately sprung to mind. Adolescent and derivative, more like. Although the construct itself was good. It appeared a biblical homage at first. The expression on the face chilled Luke. Two manic, black-lined eyes were staring out at him from a plate. Unlike John the Baptist's head, this youth's head was flanked on either side by a knife and fork. The same bony, dark-haired youth as before. Nina's new friend, Sebastian. Behind his head was the bloody, butchered head of a cow set on a pole, its tongue lolling from its mouth.

'Powerful, isn't it?'

Nina's cheeks flushed with excitement.

'Doesn't it look like the cow is about to eat Sebastian? It does, doesn't it? And you've no idea how long it took us to drill a hole through that old table. Ages. But it was worth it. A statement like this would make people think twice before they ate meat, don't you think?'

'I'm starving, Nina. What was that you said about an omelette?' That was quite enough about this guy Sebastian. But Nina hadn't heard. She was too busy admiring the freakish work of her newfound friend.

It was to be expected that there'd be a boyfriend some day. But did Luke really want someone like this in his daughter's life . . .

this weirdo? He eyed the cupcakes with suspicion. Too much raising agent, my arse. Did she think he was soft in the head? Luke thought back to the strange smell when he'd come in. He'd play along for now. But he wasn't stupid.

Tanya

Luke made a second appointment to see Dr Black. Instead of getting better, things were getting worse. Most nights the white bird came to him as he slept, and each time he would explode into waking. His heart would hammer violently against his chest and cold sweat would slither down his face. He'd noticed a deterioration in his performance at the hospital, and if he had, others had as well. During the day he was too tired to be alert, at night he was too scared to go to sleep.

Terence Black's clinic was close to St Matthew's University Hospital. Luke would never have bothered going to see him otherwise. On this, his second visit, he sat in the waiting room doing a crossword instead of skulking in his car outside. He was against the clock and he hoped the therapist was keeping time.

Screwing up his eyes, he focused on the empty crossword boxes. He bit his lip. He was struggling with a clue. He texted Nina. 'Clandestine,' came her prompt reply. His mouth eased into a smile. They were alike in many ways.

At the nearby sound of a door opening, Luke looked up. Terence appeared in the doorway opposite. 'Come on through,' he beckoned. Luke got to his feet. On time today. A better start. The therapist glanced beyond Luke to speak to the woman at the reception desk. 'Could you possibly mail through those attachments again?' he asked.

Luke followed him through to the office and sat down in the same armchair as before. Terence was clearing the remains of a sandwich into the waste basket. 'I'm glad you came back,' he said. He proceeded to open the drawer of a filing cabinet under his desk. Retrieving a folder, he came to sit in the armchair opposite.

'I'm anxious to get this sorted.' Luke cut to the chase.

'No problem.' Terence cleared his throat. 'All righty, last time we spoke, we touched on your wife and daughter.' He settled back. 'So, how are things there?'

This time Luke was ready.

'Fine. Nina seems to be enjoying her gap year, trying out new experiences before going to college.' He filled Terence in on the paintings and on Nina's new friend. He took a moment before continuing. 'Her mother dismisses her efforts a lot, unfortunately. In as much as Alison has time to think about anyone else's endeavours.'

'And how do you feel about that?'

Luke immediately regretted opening up. He sounded needy, petulant.

'I suspect Nina's behaviour is driven by a craving for her mum's attention,' he said hastily. 'And I wonder sometimes whether her newfound interests are really genuine—'

He stopped himself, again surprised at sharing so much. He hadn't expected to give voice to this latest concern. He needed to be careful not to head off on a tangent again.

'Please, go on,' said Terence.

Luke settled back. The line of questioning appeared to be safe for now.

'The way things are at the moment, Alison is totally absorbed with her campaign. And of course there's all that wind farm carry-on up on Lough Carberry.' Luke shrugged. 'The thing about Alison is that she has to be at the centre of every shindig, big or small – fundraising for a local playground, birthday parties at retirement homes . . . you name it, Alison's at the heart of it.'

'You feel left out, is that it?'

Luke shook his head.

'It's Nina really,' he said. 'She's the one who feels left out—'

Luke was suddenly distracted by a flashing in his peripheral vision. The flashing often heralded the beginnings of a migraine. The conversation looked like they were going down the same dead-end route as the last time. 'Can I suggest something here?' said Luke. 'You're the professional in this situation, Terence, but I have to say I think we're heading off on a wild goose chase with this.'

Terence blinked, bemused. 'Yes, I agree it may seem like that. You're an intelligent person, Luke,' he said. 'I don't discuss theory with every patient, but I'd like you to understand what it is we're trying to do here.'

Luke didn't have time for the scenic route. Why could the guy not just get on with things?

'Something has happened to you, Luke,' Terence continued sombrely. 'With your cooperation we can discover what that something might be. Or at the very least to acknowledge it, and to bring it into awareness.'

'Look, I know that this is only my second session,' Luke responded, 'but I need to fix whatever it is that's happening to me. And urgently. With this in mind I'd like to come to what I think the event is.'

Terence leaned back considering this request. 'All right then,' he said. 'I'm listening.'

Luke swallowed. He felt clammy. The seat underneath him suddenly felt very hard. He cast his mind back to a night six weeks earlier. It was time. The time had come for him to talk about Tanya.

It had been busy that night. He wasn't usually called to the Resucc room but the hospital's one emergency paediatrician had gone off duty. The girl's injuries were extensive. She had a blunt rupture of the aorta. Most victims died straightaway, but this girl, his patient, was somehow still alive when they brought her in.

There were pelvic, rib and open ulna fractures along with facial lacerations and contusions. Even if they saved her, she would never be pretty again. Her face would stop and shock. Luke focused on the task in hand, blocking out her youth and all that potential hanging in the balance. It didn't make a difference. He couldn't stop the bleeding. The girl arrested.

There were moments that stood out in Luke's career. He knew, standing there, that this was such a moment. It would be with him for ever. The deadly hiatus. That deafening hush, that sacred silence before the team dispersed to treat another patient.

'How can this happen?' the mother whimpered. She leaned against a wall on the corridor, blood and matter congealing on her blouse. The girl's father had an arm around her shoulder. He too was sprayed in the girl's blood.

'How could anyone do this?' the father asked, his voice thick with emotion.

'I'm so very sorry,' said Luke. He always felt inadequate in dealing with the bereaved. 'Her injuries were . . . well, they were catastrophic.'

The mother moaned.

'Tell me,' said the father. 'Tell me *exactly* what they were. I want to know.'

The mother turned, burying her head against the father's chest. Luke told them about the thoracic injury, the fatal injury. There was no need to tell them everything. That was for the police. They didn't need to know just then. He spoke as gently as he could, all the while horror was welling up inside him.

His voice shook as the words coming from his mouth stuck on the dryness of his tongue. His compassion for the parents was supplanted by alarm. The mother lifted her head and looked at him strangely, an extra layer of confusion and bewilderment on her ravaged face. The father clasped her even tighter. The tattoo on his forearm spelled out the name of the child. TANYA.

'She was a little girl,' said the father. 'I am going to kill the monster who did this.'

The mother went deathly pale.

Luke was struck by an urge to run. His eyes darted up and down the corridor looking for someone, anyone to take these people off his hands. From the corner of his eye he sensed a movement. When he turned to the couple again, the mother had crumpled onto the floor. She was slumped in a heap against the wall. Thankfully, a passing nurse happened by and Luke scurried back to Emergency to immerse himself in the commotion of another trauma.

It was amid these events that Luke was convinced his unravelling had started. As he finished recounting the episode to Terence, he wondered if he'd come anywhere close to describing the debilitating fear he'd experienced that night. The feelings of shame, of loathing, the slipping gravitas.

'We're on to something now, all right,' said Terence. 'We're cutting through the thorns.' He drew quotation marks.

Luke wished he wouldn't do that.

'However, you do this kind of work all the time, Luke. This is your profession. Sometimes things go well, sometimes they go wrong. Perhaps what you're telling me about this girl is indeed at the heart of it. But then again, what if it's a symptom rather than the cause? I'm not saying there isn't something in what you've just told me. But I think we should explore things further.'

Luke crossed his arms. He said nothing more. He'd been in this position before. In the headmaster's wood-panelled office at boarding school, being exhorted to rat on Nathan Nolan. Nolan had been the ringleader in an initiation rite involving a first-year.

Old Froggy refused to believe that Luke had any direct involvement, suspecting him only of witnessing the incident. The first-year had been blindfolded, laid on his back, tied to a plank and was told he was being levered out the top-floor window of the dormitory block. Unknown to the boy, the plank was levered on a bed and not out of a window, but that was immaterial to the kid.

A nice lad like Luke Forde would never be a willing participant in an incident like that. That's what all the teachers said. Forde was a decent guy who'd never cause a lad to lose control of his bowels and shit himself in fear. Happily for Luke, Old Froggy agreed.

Luke got away with murder at St Aloysius School for Boys. Everyone felt sorry for him after what had happened to his parents. Though it was true that Nolan was one hell of a prick, there was no way Luke was ratting on the guy. First rule of boarding school: no snitching.

'You've done really well so far,' Terence coaxed.

But Luke was done. He tapped his foot. He was saying nothing further. He wanted to be free of this room, free of the rumbling cadence of Terence's voice, free of his forensic stare.

'I think what you've described here, Luke, the incident with the child in the hospital . . . Tanya . . . it's only a symptom. I think the real problem, what it is that's really bothering you, lies further back.'

Luke shook his head. 'I don't think so. I think you're wrong about that. For me, that is when it started.'

Terence waited. The therapist had the ability to administer silence like a truth serum. But Luke had made his mind up. This was a mistake. This therapy lark would make things worse. He had shared as much as he was going to.

Terence leaned towards him. 'You know what? I'm sensing that's enough for today. Perhaps next time we'll go back and talk about Nina?'

Luke considered this a moment. Maybe. Maybe he could do that. But it would require a much longer session. And where would he start?

Family Dinner

'What a head wreck of a day.' Trudging into the kitchen, Luke pulled off his scarf. That latest session with Terence was heavy going.

'An election campaign is no joke either.' Alison was sitting on a high chair at the island. 'Nine more days to go.'

Despite her complaint, there were no signs of flagging that Luke could see. Her dress looked neat, her make-up fresh, and she smelled of perfume.

'Nina's making dinner,' Alison whispered. 'Lentil stew.' She pulled a face. 'Smells delicious,' she said loudly. She held up her glass of wine. 'Want one?'

Luke declined.

Nina was busy at the hob. 'As I keep saying, Mum, it doesn't have to be all about meat, you know.'

'It's a good source of iron, sweetie.' Alison threw her eyes to heaven.

Alison was a carnivore. Luke remembered an occasion in their flat in Edinburgh early in their marriage. The arrangement was whoever was home first would cook the evening meal. If Luke suspected he was in danger of landing the job, he'd park out of sight up the hill and wait for Alison to get home. He wasn't fond of cooking and preferred to use his time to study.

On the occasion in question, having waited half an hour, hunger got the better of Luke. He gave up, went into the flat, and set to preparing dinner. Alison turned up shortly after. In the tiny kitchen, with his back to her, he talked about a procedure he'd be observing in Great Ormond Street. A film of oil was sizzling in the pan.

'So we're off to London now, are we?' she asked. 'And what about the senior reg post here?'

It had been Alison's suggestion to move to the UK from Ireland where his prospects of promotion seemed speedier.

'You must be in with a chance of that, surely?'

'Let's wait and see.'

He turned to get the rounds of steak. To his surprise, one remained, a damp red stain where the other had been.

'Where . . .?'

She giggled. 'I got carried away,' she said, grinning. Her square, prominent teeth were coated in blood. Luke shook his head, calling her a cannibal. It became a joke between them.

These days, since the election campaign had started, he saw very little of his wife. It had been a while since Alison had joined him and Nina for dinner. 'Fancy a walk afterwards, Alison?' he asked. 'We could catch up.'

'Oh, Luke, I'm so sorry. Roddy's collecting me shortly. We're heading to Crow Hall to go over stuff with Dad. As you know, election strategy is one of Roddy's things.'

Luke shrugged. Each rebuttal stung a little less. Roddy Gilligan was Master of the Scarigell Hunt and his estate bordered Crow Hall. Roddy was also partner in Alison's PR firm, Thompson Consulting. He would be running the PR firm if Alison got elected.

'Pity you weren't at the hospital when I popped by today,' said

Alison. She was texting. 'Fran said you were out and your phone was off.'

'In that case Fran must be mistaken.' He was just as casual. 'I don't recall having left the hospital at all today.' He turned to Nina. 'Maybe you'll come for a walk with me?'

'Sorry, Dad. I'm heading out to see Sebastian.' She came towards the island with a steaming pot of lentils.

Alison set her glass down on the island with a clatter. Her eyes flashed at the very mention of Sebastian.

'I'll go for a walk with the dog,' Luke said quickly. Their fragile peace took effort. 'I need a walk to clear my head. The junior doctors are threatening to strike. I've got to think about contingency.'

'The very idea of junior doctors on strike . . .' Alison picked up a cautious forkful of food. 'Dad was saying a strike would never have happened in his day.'

'Is that so?' Luke too picked up his fork. 'Why should the young bulls have better working conditions than the old bulls? Why shouldn't the junior doctors be up to their necks in muck and bullets like they were? That the gist of it? What about patient safety, Alison? What about duty of care? Shit happens when doctors are tired.'

'Thanks, Mum,' Nina groaned. 'You've set Dad off on a rant again.'

Alison was examining her phone. 'You're right, Luke. You're absolutely right,' she said, distracted. She hadn't really been listening.

Nina's stew was vile. It was an effort to swallow. Nina was studying them both. Luke made appreciative noises. He'd slip his plate to Duffy when she wasn't looking.

'Maybe Mum could agitate for better conditions if she gets elected,' Nina offered. She was trying hard.

'*When* I get elected, sweetie,' Alison cautioned. 'You'll be there for me – both of you – on election night?' She dropped her knife and fork and took Luke and Nina by the hand. She looked from one to the other.

'Sure, Mum. I'll be there. I'm looking forward to it.'

'Thanks, sweetie. I want things to go OK.' Alison looked at Luke. 'I want everyone to know what a nice ordinary family we have. That's what the electorate wants. People like themselves.'

She turned to Nina. Her expression changed.

'And on the night, Nina, you might wear something a little less, a little less . . .' Alison searched for a word.

'Boho? Alternative?' suggested Nina, smiling.

'Well, sweetie, maybe something a little less . . . *lesbian*.'

Nina opened her mouth but no words came out.

A flash of light flared at the bottom of the garden, breaking the tension. It was at the water's edge. Duffy skidded to the window, going berserk. He snapped the air, patrolling the length of the glass, barking into the dark at the unknown menace.

'Come here, you daft animal.' Luke bent to soothe the dog. Duffy enjoyed a cuddle as much as Luke. The animal didn't check up on Luke or cause him grief.

'Bloody hacks,' Alison muttered. 'They must have had at least twenty shots of me today. Why do they insist on pursuing me in my home?'

Luke and Nina looked at one another. Alison adored the spotlight and her protest lacked conviction.

'Probably a passing cruiser,' Nina said. 'It's not all about you, you know.'

'Well, actually, it is, sweetie. At least for the next nine days.'

Luke shot a look at Nina, advising her to leave it. Nina got down from her chair and headed to the magazine rack in the garden room. Returning, she handed her mother a medical journal. 'This arrived in the post. Have you seen it?'

Luke cringed. He'd seen the journal in the hospital. Alison put her phone aside. 'Wow,' she said, scanning the cover. 'That's fantastic.' Luke could see the speeding neurons. She was thinking, twisting, manoeuvring, slotting ideas into place.

There was Luke on the cover, surrounded by hordes of smiling children. It had a cheesy caption. The only blessing was that he wasn't grinning like a pompous dick. He looked decidedly dour. He hated having his photograph taken. *Professor Luke Forde, Cardiothoracic Surgeon With a Big Heart* read the caption. Inside the journal was an article about his part in a rheumatic heart-disease prevention programme in Sudan.

Alison pulled a face. 'Pity the press covering this election can't come up with any decent soundbites for me.'

'You're not exactly making it easy for them,' Nina said.

Luke tensed. Alison glared.

'Apart from your dad and your grandpa serving in government, what do they have to go on?'

'I really don't know what you mean, Nina.'

Nina's eyes narrowed. 'What do you stand for, Mum? What are the issues you feel passionate about?'

Alison looked at Nina as if she were crazy.

'I would have thought that was perfectly obvious, to any thinking person at least. I stand for the people of County Clare,' she said. 'The people of Gortnashee, Kyledurka, Tullabrack, and all the towns and far-flung reaches of this large constituency.' Her voice grew shrill and indignant. 'Our friends and neighbours around Lough Carberry, the people I grew up with. That's who I'm passionate about. Is that good enough for you?'

Nina's eyes glinted.

'Ah, yeah, but that's hardly an election manifesto, now is it? Where do you stand on hunting, for example? OK, forget that. We know your take on that. Ripping an animal limb from limb is A-OK. So, moving on, let's take the proposed extension to the wind farm. What's your take on that?'

'Sweetie, I think we all know that clean energy is the way to go.' Alison's eyes flashed dangerously, her voice dropped.

Nina shrugged. 'I'm only trying to help you out here. I'm talking about the farmers bordering Roddy Gilligan. You think they'll give a rat's ass about clean energy if they can't sleep a wink for the turbine noise at night?'

'That's what they're saying in the town?'

'In town and all around the lough. The dogs in the street know Roddy wants those turbines. Everyone knows he's been bending the ear of Zephyr Energy.' Nina was triumphant.

'And that Roddy is my business partner in Thompson Consulting . . .' Alison looked thoughtful. 'Well, Nina, I must say I think you have a point. It may be that I should call an emergency meeting in the town hall to allow local people to debate the issue. Yes, I think that's a good idea.'

Nina was taken aback.

'Thanks, I guess,' she said, unsure. 'I was just curious about your agenda.'

The intercom buzzed, interrupting them.

'I'm just as curious, sweetie,' said Alison getting to her feet. 'Since you started seeing Sebastian, I'm not at all sure of your agenda either.'

Nina went stock still.

'Have the last word if you must, Mum. It's so pathetic.'

'Oh, there's nothing pathetic about *me*, my dear.'

Luke couldn't tell if Nina was going to explode or not. He held his breath. He laid a hand on hers. Wisely, she said nothing.

38

He followed Alison into the hall where she picked up her laptop and what looked suspiciously like an overnight bag. She proceeded briskly to the front door, slinging her coat over her arm.

'Staying over?' he asked.

'I think it's best, don't you? I don't feel particularly welcome here at the moment,' she said loudly. 'Anyway, it'll be late by the time we wrap up. And I'm not sure about tomorrow yet – if I'll come back here after my meetings or if I'll head straight to Crow Hall. Either way I'll be in touch.'

'Whatever suits.'

She pulled at the hem of her short black dress, smoothing it over her legs. She glanced in the mirror above the hall table. 'I bought this yesterday. I'm still not sure. What do you think?'

'Is it a little short?' he asked innocently. 'A bit "mutton dressed as lamb"?'

Some of her own medicine wouldn't go astray.

'Oh, I don't know about that, Luke. A lot of women my age have spare tyres and cellulite. I think I carry it off all right.'

Opening the door, she turned to him, 'Oh, before I forget. Glenda Wallace on the Tidy Towns committee? Her child with Down's syndrome has been on a waiting list for months. She'll be contacting Fran for an appointment. I said you'd see them shortly.'

Luke didn't have a chance to respond before the door slammed shut. He stood listening as Gilligan's two-seater revved and skidded out of the driveway. He gritted his teeth. Luke hated patients jumping the queue because they knew the right people. He had a private as well as a public practice. Despite that, he was convinced that equal access was the way to go, that care should be single tier. But life, politics and circumstance had got in the way of any ideals. He'd forfeited those years ago.

Nina joined him in the hall. 'You think Mum will win?'

'You kidding me? Of course she's going to win. You off to see that lad now?' he asked. 'I'm a proper Johnny-No-Mates this evening.'

'Aw, Dad, I won't be gone too long. When I get back maybe we could watch that Everest documentary on Netflix, if you're still awake?'

'OK, you're on.'

He felt a momentary lift. He may not be able to rely on Alison. But there was always Nina. She would always be his girl.

A Proposal

Despite his scepticism, Luke found himself making and attending repeat appointments with Terence Black. If he overlooked some of the guy's more annoying personal habits, he was easy enough to talk to.

'Where did you and Alison meet?' Terence asked, settling back and loosening his tie.

'At a charity lunch,' Luke responded. 'It was a fundraiser for the cardiac surgery unit at St Enda's Children's Hospital in Dublin. We needed a heart–lung bypass machine and I was chosen to stand in for Professor Wilkins to accept the cheque on behalf of the unit, say a few words, shake a few hands, keep the goodwill flowing. The sort of thing I hate, to tell the truth.'

Luke had definitely drawn the short straw that day. He was missing an arterial switch. To make matters worse he was being taunted by his colleagues. Wilkins only chose him because the charity needed a pretty boy for their photos, so they said.

'It was an upmarket hotel,' Luke recalled. 'Lots of fizz and frocks. The way I remember it, this tall, slim woman approached me after I had spoken. "You're a young professor," she said. She'd missed me saying I was standing in for Wilkins.'

They'd laughed at her mistake.

'I'm sure you'll be a professor someday though.' Her eyes twinkled and he felt himself relax. She'd held out her hand, studying him intently. 'I'm Alison Thompson. It's lovely to meet you.'

She looked an outdoor type. Her long, lean arms were tanned and he imagined she'd look good with the wind in her hair.

'Nice to meet you too, Alison. And now I'd better head back to the hospital. Enjoy the lunch.'

'I didn't come for the lunch,' she said quickly. 'I work in PR but I volunteered for this fundraising gig. Judging by the size of the cheque, I'd say my efforts were successful, wouldn't you?'

'For sure. A great success indeed,' he agreed.

'Why don't you let me get you a quick bite of something? It's a crab dish for starters. I could sneak into the kitchen and pinch a plate for you,' she said mischievously.

He laughed. 'Thanks but no. I'm not a fan of seafood and anyway I wouldn't want to get you in trouble. We need all the fundraisers we can get.'

'More needs to be done though.' She touched his elbow and looked at him in earnest. 'The fact that parents have to sleep on floors by their kids' beds because there are no proper facilities, I find that shocking.'

'We junior doctors have no say on how the money is spent,' he said. 'I'm only the errand boy today.'

'Oh, I imagine you're a little more than that.' She tilted her head and smiled. Her front teeth were prominent and overlapping. But it was an attractive smile in spite of that.

'So you found yourself attracted to Alison from the outset?' Terence asked.

'She had a magnetism. And yes, she was attractive.' Luke remembered thinking her face too long and thin at their first

42

encounter, but pleasant for all that too. 'She had an energy I found compelling.'

Terence signalled for him to continue.

'I was busy and Alison didn't cross my mind again. I was a Registrar and researching RHD—'

'RHD?'

'Rheumatic heart disease,' Luke explained. 'I'd volunteered for a programme in Tanzania and headed out that summer. That was when I came across Alison again. She'd volunteered with the Equal Hearts Foundation. There she was, right in the thick of it. Lobbying NGOs, seeking funds from the WHO, organising visas, and tackling all the admin to get paediatric cardiac surgery expertise into the country.'

It all seemed such a long time ago now. A different life. Luke described how one night Alison had come looking for him. She had some infected mosquito bites and he was arranging antibiotics. She'd leaned across as if to kiss his cheek in thanks, or so he'd thought. Her lips had landed on his. He was unprepared, startled. She pulled away, blushing, and the moment had been ruined. Luke had cursed himself, feeling like a fool, unable to navigate the rudiments of a simple kiss.

After that night, unsurprisingly, nothing further happened in Tanzania. On arriving home, Luke realised that he missed her. He missed their discussions about the programme, who she might lobby, which government officials she might meet in person.

Alison contacted him once or twice to go for a drink, but on each occasion he was working. He expressed dismay at not being able to meet. He was surprised she bothered with him at all, given their last encounter.

'I suppose you could say it was a neat confluence of events that Alison ended up volunteering in Vietnam the following year,' Luke concluded.

'You're saying you don't think it was a coincidence?' Terence raised his eyebrows.

'I thought so at the time.' Luke shrugged. 'Oh, I was excited to see her, don't get me wrong,' he said. 'Alison was right at the centre of things. She'd managed to secure a sizeable tranche of overseas funding. Alison seemed able to unlock doors that had been shut. To be fair, all she was ever doing was pushing on an open door—'

'What do you mean by that?' asked Terence.

'If you recall, Cornelius Thompson was in government back then. Teflon Thompson, that's what they used to call him, remember? Nothing that smelled ever stuck to the guy. And you can just guess what Cornelius's portfolio was . . .'

'Overseas aid?'

'Bingo.' Luke gave a sour smile. 'I'd taken extended leave of absence from my post at home,' he continued. 'I wanted as much exposure as possible to children with congenital abnormalities.'

'I take it you and Alison were going out together at this stage?'

'Not quite. But things began to happen quickly in Ho Chi Minh.'

Around the hospital, Alison's name was linked with his. He'd hear mention of Dr Luke and Miss Alison in the same breath. Staff assumed they were a couple, yet they'd never been on a date. He decided to broach the subject. In a clumsy fashion, he blurted it out without ever considering the consequences.

'So, Miss Alison,' he'd joked, 'word around the hospital is that we're going out together.'

'And tell me, Dr Luke, is that suggestion so repugnant to you?'

She looked up from her computer where she was sorting out work permits. She pulled a sad face.

'No, erm . . .' he stumbled, 'no, actually. Not at all.'

It was as if the idea had suddenly revealed itself to him.

'Well, that's good to know,' she said, merriment in her eyes. 'How about we go out tonight for dinner? You work hard and need some fun. How about Le Chat Blanc, two blocks down? My treat. When you finish your list, of course.'

Alison had gone back to typing with no suggestion of coyness or embarrassment. Afterwards, Luke realised the dinner at Le Chat Blanc that night had been the culmination of a courtship he'd been unaware was even taking place. Sex had followed too that night, but try as he might, he couldn't remember a thing about it. The experience must have been adequate because from that point on Alison assumed they were a couple.

'I'm guessing you proposed marriage sometime after?' Terence clicked the top of the biro.

'Not exactly.'

'Oh?'

'The way I remember it, Alison was folding T-shirts into a suitcase, getting ready to fly home. She looked up and asked me if I intended returning the following year. I'd already committed to doing a charity climb on Kilimanjaro. Alison has this way of doing T-shirts, you know, sleeves in, and then folding into three parts. She's quite particular like that. Then she said, casual-as-you-like, "That's fine. Time is precious and we should use it wisely. We'll kill two birds with one stone and do Kilimanjaro on our honeymoon." And that, Terence, was the way it happened.'

Terence nodded, allowing himself a little smile.

Sitting in the green upholstered chair in Terence's office, Luke cast his mind back to that time. The marriage had seemed as good an idea as any. As for the wedding day itself, Alison made all the decisions. Luke had gone along with all the plans. A recipe for an easy life, so his married colleagues said.

Luke made critical decisions every day in his professional

life. He was more than happy for Alison to take care of matters concerning their personal life. It left him free to concentrate on his work. In finding Alison, Luke counted himself a lucky man indeed.

Making his way back to reception, Luke reflected on today's session. Terence was good. The guy's clothes might bear testimony to his last meal, his shaving might be haphazard, so what? He put Luke at ease. And Luke needed reassurance if he was going to risk any journey back to the dark.

He'd never spoken to anyone as freely about his wife before. How could he? Her name was synonymous with children's charities. Along with her Thompson Consulting profile, Alison's public image contrived to put her beyond the reach of any criticism. The woman was beyond reproach.

Hugh Smyth and Johnny Whelan were friends as well as work colleagues. The three of them could speak frankly to one another. They had shared experience. But this stuff with Alison was different. Luke couldn't share that stuff with them. There were times he wondered if Hugh knew. Did he suspect? And for some unknown reason he was keeping quiet?

At reception, the Buddhas gazed serenely from the wall. Luke tilted his head to the picture of the footsteps in the sand. 'Now there's a thing . . .' he said to the woman on the desk. 'A walk on a sunny beach, wouldn't that be nice?'

Outside the rain was hammering down.

'Oh, I wouldn't go dusting off the bikini just yet.'

'Me neither,' he said.

He made his next appointment. He chose the last slot of the day. It was tough returning to the hospital after a session, to a waiting room of patients, to the scrutiny of students.

'See you soon,' said the woman at reception.

Things were improving slowly. Now, in the middle of the night when the white bird came to see him, he could usually wake before it started screaming.

The Mask

Putting his key in the door, Luke was dismayed to hear raised voices coming from inside. It had been a busy day and all he wanted was peace and quiet. He took a breath, turned the key, and went into the house. The voices grew louder. The spats between his wife and daughter were growing tiresome. If he moved quietly, they might not hear him. He edged towards the basement door. He might be able to slip down there, unnoticed.

Duffy barked and rushed to greet him. Luke groaned. He'd been rumbled. Alison had started to shout. Resigned, he went through to the kitchen.

'He's a total scumbag. Nothing but white trash. Trailer trash.' Alison was in full throttle.

'You wouldn't want people to hear you use pejorative, emotive language like that, now would you, Mum? I thought the representative of the people was standing on a ticket of inclusivity – *all* colours equal?'

Nina glowered at her mother through a curtain of hair and over the top of her glasses. Earlier in the week, she had pointed out Alison's social media posts and he had balked. On the surface, Alison's campaign was honourable. On closer scrutiny, he was uneasy with her tactics. They made one thing clear though.

Whatever was going on between his wife and that weasel Gilligan, Luke still had his uses.

'Damn, she's good, isn't she?' Nina had remarked.

Luke had scrolled through the tweets. Alison had been peppering her Twitter feed with photographs. Him in surgical scrubs cradling an infant. A black infant. Him at an outpatient clinic surrounded by a swarm of faces. Asian faces. Him with a surgical team in Tanzania. There were links to articles about his overseas charity work prefaced with 'So proud of my husband, Professor Luke Forde.' Another read, 'Luke Forde, a doctor for all hearts and colours.'

Luke had been appalled. Mortified that Alison would try to make political capital out of the projects that were dear to him. That she would so brazenly appeal to the immigrant vote by hanging onto his coat-tails. He'd felt deep embarrassment and disgust. Nina stood in front of him now in the kitchen, eyes blazing, and she thought she knew it all. She had no idea.

'Mum, get over yourself – it's only banter.'

'If that's your sense of humour, Nina, then you're more delusional than I thought. You're as sick as he is.'

'What's going on?' asked Luke, reluctantly.

Alison spun around like a marionette. 'I'll tell you what's going on, Luke. Nina's lame, misguided, yobbo boyfriend has only been defacing my election posters, that's what's going on.'

'Sebastian has to stand by his convictions too,' retorted Nina.

'That so? By the looks of him, I'm sure he has plenty of those. The drunk and disorderly kind and God knows what else.'

'People in glasshouses shouldn't throw stones.'

'And what's that supposed to mean?'

'How many times has Grandpa been caught for drunken driving?'

'Your grandfather has never been convicted of drunken driving.'

'*Convicted* being the salient word, Mum. And only because you know people. Only because you *fixed* it. Grandpa is a drunken old pisshead.'

'Don't you dare speak about my father like that!'

Nina was a great kid but she didn't know when to pull back.

'Well, I passed a bunch of election posters on the way home,' said Luke. 'They all looked fine to me.'

Alison shot him a filthy look. 'It's the ones over by town that I'm talking about, up from their grubby encampment. That's where they're defaced.' She planted her hands on her hips. 'You know my byline is "Alison Forde-Thompson, a voice for the people", right?' Luke nodded. 'This clever-arse yobbo has only superimposed a photo under my byline with a text that reads "Who's a voice for me?"'

'What's the photo of?'

'A masked head and torso. It's revolting. Depraved. The torso is all slashed up and . . . uuugh, there are bleeding flaps of skin.' She shuddered. 'Coward's tactics, of course . . . wearing a mask like that, afraid to show his face. Pathetic.'

'What kind of mask?'

'A ridiculous fox mask.'

Luke glanced at Nina. She nursed a gleeful smile. Nina had always refused to hunt, proving a disappointment to her mother. When Nina saw a hare or fox she saw something cute. When Alison saw a hare or fox, she saw something she could kill.

As a child, Nina had tried to persuade her mother not to hunt, not to kill. But Alison would shrug off her tearful pleas and leave the sobbing child behind. Cornelius too would shake his head, pronouncing Nina the oddest child.

'Was defacing the posters the work of your friend?' Luke turned to Nina, disinclined to leap to her defence. He'd had a bad feeling about this character from the outset. This guy whose pubescent animal-rights paintings Nina so admired.

'I don't know why you bother to ask,' said Alison. 'Of course it was Sebastian. The little shit was caught on CCTV in the town.'

She turned her fury back to Nina. 'This guy must be thick into the bargain. Interfering with posters right next to the police station? Did he not think that I'd find out?'

'Sebastian isn't to know you know every bloody policeman in County Clare.' Nina flicked a curtain of hair over her shoulder.

There would be no apology. Alison looked like thunder. Luke knew his antagonism towards Sebastian was fuelled by a desire to protect his daughter. He knew his opinion was skewed, his impartiality impugned. What bothered him was not the fact this tosser had defaced Alison's election posters, but the lengths to which he was willing to go to make his point. Nina's so-called boyfriend.

It was puzzling that Sebastian was drawn to Nina. Surely Luke and Alison represented all that he reviled? They were Establishment. Some might commend the guy's stance on blood-sports. It was his attitude, however, sullen and dismissive, the latent sarcasm, the lack of respect – these were the things that pissed Luke off. The smugness of his smile. The knowing glint in his eyes. The thought of him pawing his daughter made him queasy. Luke imagined his hands around the guy's neck, slowly, deliberately, pressing his thumbs against his carotid artery, cutting off the blood supply.

To learn that the guy had deliberately cut himself and peeled back flaps of his own skin, well that just confirmed his fears. The guy was a nutjob. A disciple of disorder. These were not the actions of a balanced person. And certainly not the kind of company he wanted for his daughter.

'Is this *sabotage*, Nina?' Alison wasn't letting it go. 'Do you really want to wreck my chances of election before I've even started? Because that's what it feels like. Where's your loyalty? Do you want to pull the whole Considine encampment down on top of me?'

'Oh for God's sake, Mum, stop calling it an encampment. It's a mobile home and caravan. They're just there until the planning permission comes through.'

'*Considine?*' asked Luke. That name sounded familiar.

'Don't tell me you don't know who this scumbag, Sebastian, is?' Alison's laugh was bitter. 'Your precious daughter is only screwing the bastard son of Lucy Considine, that pain-in-the-butt activist. "Friend of the earth and friend of the people", or whatever bullshit name she calls herself.'

Lucy Considine was at the centre of the wind-farm controversy that was dominating the local airwaves. That's where Luke had heard the name before.

'You know what you can do now, sweetie? You can show me some support. You can come down to the community hall and be there for my first public meeting. You too, Luke. Instead of sneaking off to the basement. A show of support from both of you would be nice.'

Nina glanced at Luke with dismay. She shrugged her shoulders as if to apologise for what she'd walked them into.

'Why do you want me there when I'm such a disappointment to you?' She eyeballed Alison.

'You're not wrong there, sweetie. But here's some useful news. Folk don't trust politicians that don't have children. Especially female politicians. So slap a smile on that face, because you're coming.'

So much for a quiet evening. A political broadcast by his wife in a dusty town hall was the last place Luke wanted to be. He thought by now Nina would have learned when to keep her mouth shut.

The Gathering

A crowd had gathered on the steps outside the town hall. Luke, Alison and Nina arrived in Luke's car, a picture of family solidarity. Gilligan was on the kerbside, ready to open the door for Alison.

'Thinks he's FBI,' muttered Nina. 'What a dick.'

Alison emerged to claps and cheers. Swarthy-looking characters in heavy overcoats clapped her on the back as she ascended the steps towards the paint-peeled doors. Luke and Nina left her to it as they drove off to park the car. By the time they returned, the crowd outside had swollen in size. Luke was surprised to see so many on a cold winter night. Alison was busy pressing the flesh of those milling about her on the top steps.

'Who *are* all these people?' Luke muttered. Some of the faces were familiar but he didn't know from where.

'Think, Dad.' Nina was impatient. 'You know . . . it's the guys from the scrapyard at Crow Hall and their families. Grandpa's employees.'

Of course. Behind the house at Crow Hall were stables along with a hotchpotch of brick and stone outbuildings where Cornelius ran his scrapyard. His father-in-law was an enterprising man.

'Alison!'

A voice rang out behind them. Alison turned at the top of the steps, waving delightedly at the cameras flashing in the dark.

'You didn't think they'd leave anything to chance, did you?' Nina asked. 'Grandpa's got everything covered.'

Inside the hall it smelled of wet coats and bleach. A harsh white light flickered from a single-tube fluorescent light. It made a zapping sound. A steward with thick black hair and jawlappers jerked his chin, indicating that Luke and Nina should go to the front. Luke ignored him. He directed Nina to the plastic chairs midway down the hall. He didn't want to be conspicuous in the front row.

'You've upset Elvis, Dad,' Nina whispered. The guy was wearing a hi-vis vest with 'Thompson Metals' on the back.

'One of Grandpa's lads?'

'He sure is.'

Cornelius was patrolling up and down the aisles, a word for those he knew, eyes clocking and processing those he didn't. He pulled at his cap. Indoors and out, he wore the deerstalker like a Roman emperor with a crown of laurels. A look of displeasure crossed his face as he noted where Luke and Nina had chosen to sit. He stopped to speak to the woman in front.

'How's Sean doing? Did he get that stairlift fitted?'

'We're on a waiting list.' The woman coughed.

'Give me your number, Lou. I'll pass it on to Alison. Ali is a great woman to get things done. Just imagine all she could do if she wins.' Sliding his glasses down his nose, he punched the woman's number into his phone and recommenced his walkabout.

The hall was filling up. Nina looked over her shoulder, her long hair swishing into Luke's face. He didn't mind. He liked the smell. Turning round he spotted what had caught Nina's attention. Who had caught Nina's attention. He bristled.

Sebastian Considine.

There he was, threading his straggly hair across his cheek and through his mouth. He leaned back, making a right-angle triangle against the hard back of his chair. It couldn't have been comfortable. Yet the guy managed to look both slothful and indolent. Beyond, the Elvis impersonator closed both doors. He lifted a heavy metal bar into place, locking them. The hall was packed, every chair occupied. It was just gone 8.15 p.m. Luke turned back, straightened up, and redirected his attention to the stage.

Alison stood to welcome the gathering. There were two tables on the stage. One for the landowners, the other for Lucy Considine. The opening address dispensed with, she returned to her chair at the apex of tables. A hesitant Lucy Considine took to the floor. The hall fell silent.

'I'm in favour of clean, green energy.' Her tremulous voice wavered across the hall. 'But it has to be delivered in a way that's not detrimental to the health of those living near these sites.'

Straightaway, Gilligan cut in. 'There's no scientific evidence showing a link between wind turbines and ill health.' He was seated with his neighbouring landowners.

'With respect,' she responded, '*Noise and Health* has just published a study showing a *direct* relationship between wind farms and clinical indicators of health such as sleep and mental health.'

Gilligan muttered something behind his hand. There was a titter at his table. The activist carried on. She referenced notes and trotted out facts and figures. Low conversations sprung up around the hall. The audience grew bored. So did Luke. He could be in his basement. He had stuff to do. His eyes wandered, taking in the naked unlit bulbs on the side walls, some broken with jagged edges. A basketball hoop was pushed against the wall.

'We have anecdotal evidence too.' Two clown-like circles of red had sprouted on Lucy Considine's cheeks.

Gilligan shook his head.

The woman grew increasingly agitated. 'The evidence doesn't make it into the public domain because people settle out of court. They are bound by confidentiality clauses. Hush money, if you like.'

Out of nowhere, someone clapped. The sound rang out like gunshot. All went still. Ahead, in the front row, Cornelius turned. A pall of silence descended. There wasn't a rustle, not a whisper. Cornelius reached for his glasses. He took them off and pinched the bridge of his nose. Pulling a handkerchief from his pocket he wiped the glasses. Right lens. Left lens. He settled the glasses back on his nose. Putting the handkerchief back in his pocket, his head swept slowly like a minesweeper, right to left, left to right, scouring the hall.

Where was the lone applauder?

Who was the lone applauder?

Zzzz zap. Zzzz zap.

The only sound was the faulty fluorescent lighting.

There came a low murmur. Luke's attention was pulled across the aisle. His eyes followed those of the crowd. He zoned in on the source of the clapping. A guy in leathers with a motorbike helmet on his lap. He was staring ahead, defiant. There came another sound from a skirting board nearby. A scrabbling sound. A mouse perhaps.

'Will there be construction jobs for locals?' a man next to Cornelius called out.

Cornelius nodded his approval. The tension lifted. A collective exhalation followed. Cornelius turned back to face the stage.

'Now you're asking the right questions.' Gilligan beamed from the stage. 'Almost certainly there will be jobs.'

'That is *not* the case.'

The crowd held its breath again.

Lucy Considine's earrings swished. 'I have it on good authority if the project goes ahead, most of the construction work will be done off-site in another country.'

'Perhaps you'd like to share the name of that authority with us?' Alison pulled the collar of her cream shirt upright. She crossed her long, shapely legs, sitting at the apex between the two opposing sides.

'I'm not at liberty to say,' the activist replied. 'But rest assured I've done my homework. The guidelines on the siting of turbines are out of date. Infrasound will come through the roof, in through the walls, it can shake the organs in your body.'

'Isn't it the case you're just peddling fear, Miss Considine?' asked Alison.

Nina stopped craning over her shoulder at Sebastian. It was too embarrassing, her mother doing battle with her boyfriend's mother.

'Surely it's not all bad?' Alison asked. 'There's a sizeable stipend payable to those willing to site the turbines on their land.'

'You're happy for people to be bought off? I thought you were supposed to be *chairing* this meeting, you're hardly *impartial* in this matter . . .' the activist's earrings were swinging like windchimes in a breeze '. . . your business partner, Roddy Gilligan, has been seen with Zephyr Energy in the Lakeland Hotel. Is it not true that he stands to gain hugely from these proposals?'

'All this from the same authority you get all your information from, Miss Considine?' Alison asked. 'I must say this nameless authority has been a very busy little bee.'

Ripples of laughter sounded in the airless hall. More blotches appeared on Lucy Considine's neck above her scarf.

'Let me spell it out for you. Twenty-five turbines on one site requires planning permission. Zephyr plans twenty-four. All on Gilligan's land. So, if any of you,' she jabbed a finger at the audience, 'think you'll profit, you're mistaken. It's *all* going to Mr Gilligan. It's simpler for Zephyr to deal with one individual. Especially an individual that has the ear of Cornelius Thompson, who's moved in government circles for years—'

Cornelius stood up, scraping his chair. 'These are scurrilous allegations, Miss Considine. All I've ever done is try to help my friends and neighbours in this constituency.'

Alison held up a hand, signalling him to stop. 'Let's all call a halt to this lively and informative debate before things get too personal.'

A ripple of approval followed. Loyalty to the Thompsons was so entrenched that, whether the invective was warranted or not, no one liked to see them harangued. Lucy Considine had miscalculated. A newcomer to Lough Carberry, she'd attacked the Thompsons. Instead of the support she'd expected, she'd cast herself as villain. It would take more living in these parts to figure that was one flawed strategy.

Alison brought proceedings to a close. 'If Zephyr decide to go ahead and extend the number of turbines, I'm going to make it my number-one priority to see that all your concerns are addressed.' She gave a studied look about the audience. 'And one last thing.' She put up her hand, sincerity paining her face. 'Where there is disruption like this to a community, there should be a social dividend. If elected, I will talk to Zephyr to see what they might do for communities around Lough Carberry. That dividend could come in the form of enhanced facilities like a new swimming pool and extra playgrounds.'

Cornelius led a cheer. The clapping grew more thunderous. Alison had sounded the perfect note. She was queen of *le mot juste*. Luke and Nina joined the queue towards the door. They were directly behind the guy with the motorbike helmet.

'Do I know him?' Luke asked under his breath.

Nina shook her head. 'I don't think so. I've no idea who he is.'

The Elvis impersonator was manning the door. As Motorbike Guy approached, Elvis's demeanour changed. A guttural noise sounded in his throat. As Motorbike Guy passed by, Elvis let rip and gobbed up a foamy lump of spit shy of his boot.

'Bad move earlier, pal,' said Elvis.

'Fuck you,' said Motorbike Guy.

Outside, Luke and Nina stomped on their feet and blew on their hands, waiting for Alison. Nearby, Cornelius faced the street below, watching. A pocket of people stopped to chatter. Most disappeared quickly into the cold January night. At a whispering behind, Luke turned to look. Lucy Considine emerged from the doorway. She ignored everyone, her head bowed as she picked her way down the steps.

Cornelius tutted. He went back to talk to the man beside him. Luke was within earshot.

'Tests go OK, my old pal?' Cornelius asked.

'They found something all right. About the size of a pea. But early stages, so they said.'

Cornelius clapped a hand on his friend's shoulder. 'Not a problem if they catch it early. Cut out any badness before it spreads.' He was watching the woman with the swinging earrings heading up the street, followed by her son, Sebastian. 'It's when the badness spreads that it's a problem,' he added. 'That's when things get tricky.'

Next to Luke, Nina shivered in the cold. 'Sebastian's mother was right,' she said. 'Mum was supposed to chair that debate, not take part. It's clear that there was only one winner here tonight. And that was Mum.'

The bells chimed out the hour. Luke craned up to look at the town hall clock. 10.00 p.m.

'Here I am! Sorry to keep you all waiting.' It was Alison. She linked Luke and Nina. 'That went well, I think,' she gushed. 'You know, I almost felt sorry for Lucy Considine.'

'Yeah, Mum. That really came across.'

'Oh, did it? Good.'

Nina looked at Luke in disbelief. He said nothing. His wife had more faces than the town hall clock.

Cornelius drew up alongside them and rubbed his daughter's back. 'That's my girl.' He gave her a proud, gold-fillinged smile. 'A chip off the old block.' He turned to Luke. 'Where are you parked?'

'Down by the courthouse.'

'Excellent. That's where I am too. Sly is waiting to drive me home. We can walk together.'

Excellent indeed, thought Luke.

The small family group headed down the steps, proceeding to the courthouse parking bays. As they passed a side street, Cornelius was distracted. He stopped, his attention pulled to a car that was parked in the shadows.

Squinting into the dark, Luke followed his gaze. He could make out two people. Lucy and Sebastian Considine standing at a car, leaning over and examining something on the windscreen. They stood a moment, watching them.

'Would you credit that?' Cornelius shook his head and tutted. 'So much for the environment.'

'Can we go? I'm freezing,' Nina said. She was reluctant to be seen.

Back at the courthouse car park, Luke and Nina bade Cornelius goodnight. Alison walked her father to his car. Sly Hegarty, his foreman and odd-job man, was waiting in the car to drive him home. Alison exchanged some words with Sly, before the Jaguar took off.

When Alison returned, Luke started the engine and pulled out of the parking bay.

'Where are we going?' she asked, when he didn't turn left for home.

'Small detour.' Luke was curious.

He drove into the side street where the Considines had been, his eyes peeled. Then he saw it. There, discarded on a white parking line. He thought he'd seen Sebastian pick something from the windscreen. He opened the driver's window for a look. It was a flower of some kind. A single long-stemmed flower. Luke looked closer. He was looking at a rose. A black rose.

Banished

'I saw you all on the news. Congratulations.'

Terence was pointing his key fob out of the office window trying to turn off his car alarm. Intermittent wails sounded from the car park.

'The outcome was never in any doubt,' Luke responded.

He realised this remark might sound ungracious to an innocent bystander. Despite his caution at the outset, he now considered Terence in his inner circle. Terence left the window and made towards his chair, the siren silenced for now.

'Do you think Nina will follow in the Thompson family tradition?' he asked. 'Is she interested in politics?'

'She is. But at this juncture, her mother's views and her own couldn't be more divergent.' Luke paused. 'I suppose I should mention at this point that Nina's away for a bit.'

'I take it that her relationship with her mother is still quite . . . difficult?'

'I guess that's one way of putting it, yes. We've had a bit of trouble with a boyfriend.'

'I see. Would you like to elaborate?'

With a sharp taste in his mouth, Luke began. He hated the fact that he was even talking about this guy. Crossing and uncrossing his legs, he went on to describe the Svengali-like influence that Sebastian had on his daughter. He took care to explain that Nina was an idealistic eighteen-year-old, who was going to change the world. But she was impressionable.

He remembered that feeling – the unassailable integrity of ideals at that age. Things were right or they were wrong. They were black or they were white. He hoped in Nina's passage to maturity, she'd be spared the choices he'd been forced to make.

Luke told Terence how he'd suppressed his initial misgivings about the boyfriend. He described what Sebastian had done to deface Alison's election posters. But it was what Sebastian did afterwards that revealed he was far more than just a prick and a nuisance. The incident had shaken them all. And it became pressingly clear that Nina would have to be removed from his influence.

Luke explained that he and Alison had both agreed on the urgency of extricating Nina from the relationship. In fact, Alison had given up an entire evening to discuss a plan to send their only child away. Luke couldn't help but feel that Alison's motivation in removing Nina was less about their daughter's welfare than Alison's new career. As he sat now in the green upholstered chair, it pained him to recall their conversation with Nina.

'But this is crazy,' she protested. 'I'm eighteen.' She looked up from her cornflakes, incredulous. 'I'm an adult. You can't go around telling me what to do. You can't pack me off like a forced rendition. I've done nothing wrong.'

It was slowly sinking in that her mother was deadly serious.

'Tell her, Dad.' Nina pointed at Luke with her spoon.

Luke let Alison do the talking.

'You're still my daughter, sweetie, and while you're under my roof, I can and I will tell you what to do. You're going away until you get this scum out of your system.'

'I'll see whoever I want.' Nina shoved the bowl of cornflakes away. 'I'm not six years old any more. You can't lock me away like Grandpa did at Crow Hall, under the stairs with the ghost of Marigold Piper.' Local legend had it that in times gone by a young child had disappeared near Crow Hall and that her ghost roamed about the house at night. 'You can't hide me away like it's the fucking eighteenth century!' She sprang up from her chair.

'Make no mistake, Nina. It is happening. It's all arranged.'

'What a pity the Magdalene Laundries are all gone,' Nina said. 'You could have told the nuns to keep a hold of me, make sure I never got out. Make sure I never tell about your's and Grandpa's secrets.'

Alison's face went dark. 'I think you're losing the run of yourself, Nina.'

'Really? All those times when you were in a huddle in Crow Hall? You think I didn't listen? I had no one to play with in that house. What else was I going to do?'

'It's decided.' Alison wasn't budging. 'You're going. When you see sense you can come back and knuckle down to college. Your dad and I have discussed this.'

Nina glared at Luke accusingly.

'I can't believe you're siding with her. I can't believe you're actually making me do this.'

She turned back to Alison.

'And as for you, you're a fucking control freak.'

She picked up her bowl of cornflakes and launched it against the kitchen wall. The bowl cracked and soggy cornflakes slid down the pristine paintwork.

'Not cool, Nina,' said Alison calmly.

Early the following morning, Nina bent to cuddle Duffy. She

straightened up, walked right past Luke, and proceeded through the front door with her suitcase. She got into Alison's car without ever turning around.

Luke went to the front door with the dog. He watched as Alison slipped into the driver's seat and applied mascara in the rear-view mirror. Reversing towards the door, she wound down her window.

'Get on to Sly, will you, Luke? He was supposed to do a few jobs around the house. And while he's at it, ask him to touch up the kitchen wall.'

Sly Hegarty did a host of odd-jobs for Cornelius as well as working in the scrapyard. He also did general maintenance and looked after the garden at the Glasshouse.

The gates opened and Alison drove off. Duffy gave a plaintive whimper. Luke felt like part of him had wrenched away. Nina had to go, he told himself. It was for the best. Things were getting messy. He would get on with things here at home and busy himself at work. There was no shortage of that and he had a paper on prosthetic valves to make some headway on.

Nina would get over this guy with distance and time. This would all blow over. And in years to come she would thank them for what they'd done. With a little luck it wouldn't be that long until she was home again.

'I hear how much Nina's going has upset you,' said Terence. He was at the office window again. The car alarm was wailing. 'It's a textbook conflict, you and Nina.' He checked in on Luke over his shoulder. 'You're bound to miss her.'

'I do. It's mostly me and the dog.'

The wailing stopped. Brushing against the rubber plant, Terence sat back down, crossing his legs. He made church steeples with his hands.

'Tell me more about Nina,' he said. 'The arrival of children changes every marriage.'

And there it was. The time had come. 'You two are like teeth in a zip.' That's what Alison said. If he did a persuasive job, he might be able to get Terence to understand. Terence might be able to see things from Luke's point of view. He might not judge too harshly.

Luke had gone through it all again in his head. He knew he was taking a risk by even talking. How could he be sure Terence wouldn't go straight to the police? That was the crux of it. He couldn't be sure. The outcome was uncertain. All he could do was make a calculated guess. Which he had. He'd thought it through.

Terence must have heard countless confessions in his former life as a priest. He must have winced, recoiled and shuddered at things that he had heard. All Luke could hope was that the seal of the confessional was so ingrained that the therapist was unlikely to rush with tattle-tales to the police. He could only hope that old habits die hard.

Luke opened his mouth to speak, but it was difficult to know where to start. The early days of his marriage, perhaps? Yes, that was as good a place as any. That was probably where the story of Nina started. Clearing his throat, and hoping that he wasn't making a terrible mistake, he began.

'Before I talk about Nina . . .' he paused, 'you need to understand a bit about myself and Alison. About what it was like in the beginning.'

In the Beginning

The short Kilimanjaro trip doubled as their honeymoon just as Alison had planned. Before Kilimanjaro was the wedding. Luke recalled being on call right up until the night before, driving down from Dublin, not arriving at the lough until shy of midnight.

'Sixteen years ago, Alison and I were busy with our careers. It was a hectic time . . .' Luke hesitated, still unsure. He circled his thumbs.

'Go ahead,' Terence coaxed, pointing his steepled hands in Luke's direction.

Luke closed his eyes and cast his mind back. He'd been looking forward to the day. The reception was to be in a large white marquee on the front lawn at Crow Hall. His share of the wedding-guest list was small: his sister Wendy, Aunt Christine, another widowed aunt, and a handful of pals from school and university. Unlike the Thompsons whose share ran from senators, politicians and police, to the CEOs of children's charities. Luke assumed many of the unfamiliar faces wandering through the house and gardens belonged to the hunting set and people of influence in the county.

Alison was disappointed that only one of her friends from school could make the wedding. Nicola Mitchell. If Alison's schoolfriends were anything like Nicola, Luke was relieved they couldn't make it. Alison had described Nicola as a 'gas woman'. In Luke's opinion the woman was brash and attention-seeking. Several times during the ceremony she roared 'hear hear', standing to toast them with her naggin of vodka decorated with a white ribbon.

'It was an odd sort of day, to be honest,' Luke confessed.

'What do you mean?' asked Terence.

'Well, I pretty much felt like a guest at my own wedding.'

It was the first time in years Luke had thought about that day. He remembered Cornelius's speech. That memory made him squirm. He remembered the nervous feeling as his father-in-law stood to speak.

'Esteemed friends,' boomed Cornelius, 'you see before you here today a proud father. I'm sure Alison's dear departed mother, Marguerite, is also looking down with pride. Alison is a credit to us both. I'm sure you'll all agree I schooled her well.' There followed murmurs of approval. 'And now the bold Luke Forde has gone and hitched his wagon to my star.'

Cornelius droned on, thanking any dignitaries for coming, naming them all individually. Luke felt superfluous to proceedings. Cornelius thanked the local caterers before turning any further attention on him. And then, what Cornelius delivered in supposed compliment proved to be acutely embarrassing.

Cornelius gave a detailed account of Luke's résumé. Someone had filled him in on Luke's career and had told him that Luke had been the top-performing student in his year. Luke sat, mortified, wanting the ground to open up and swallow him whole.

It was Alison's turn to be embarrassed when Cornelius spoke of continuing the Thompson line. She turned to Luke and winced. Quite how that was supposed to work, Luke couldn't fathom. Any children from their marriage would bear the Forde name. As the speech rambled on, it began to feel like a political manifesto more than a blessing for Luke and Alison's life together.

'Interesting man, your father-in-law,' Wendy remarked afterwards.

Cornelius seemed to find Luke's sister, Wendy, equally curious. He gawked darkly at her as she sat a table away, her arm around her girlfriend at the time. Later, when the music started, Cornelius slung an arm around Luke's shoulders. The two men were standing on the marquee dancefloor and watching as Alison did the macarena with the flower girls.

'Welcome to the family, Luke,' Cornelius said. 'You're one of us from today.'

'You're stuck with me now.' Luke grinned.

Cornelius's expression changed. 'Listen here, lad, don't misunderstand when I say this.' He lowered his voice. 'We're tight here at Crow Hall. The thing is, the way it is, lad . . .' he paused to puff on his cigar, 'if you're not with us, you're against us.' He didn't look at Luke but continued to survey the dancefloor.

Luke blinked, searching for a response. In the end he said nothing. It seemed a strange wedding blessing. His new father-in-law now turned to him. 'And Luke, I expect you'll look after my daughter,' he said. 'I've taken very good care of Alison up to now. You'll do exactly the same.'

'Of course.'

Cornelius made a smacking sound with his cigar.

'Mmm.' He looked at Luke. 'She said you'd fit in nicely,' he said, puffing. 'That you were suitable. I guess we'll have to see.'

Luke found the words unnerving. Suitable for what? It was his wedding night and he should be celebrating. Though not a fan of dancing, he left Cornelius and made off into the thick of the dancefloor.

Despite the mention of children in Cornelius's speech, Luke couldn't recall having any discussion with Alison about a family of their own. There never seemed the need. Alison's interest in children was implicit in all she said and did. Just like most couples, Luke assumed they'd get around to having them at some stage, at some point in the future, when the time was right.

From the outset, Alison had supported Luke, often to the detriment of her own career. My turn will come, she'd say. It was Alison who'd encouraged Luke to take up the post in Edinburgh when it looked like promotion wouldn't happen speedily at home. There's no point in hanging around here, she'd said. It was she who organised the flats, the drinks parties, and the beer and chilli nights to break the ice with new colleagues.

Outside salaried fundraising, Alison volunteered on fundraisers with colleagues' wives. And when Luke got a posting to Great Ormond Street, she moved from Edinburgh to London without complaint. She set aside friendships she'd made, sidelining her own ambitions so his might flourish. Plans for children were always somewhere in the future.

All that changed when Cornelius had his heart attack. Alison was in tears. Luke remembered how strange it looked to see her like that. He'd never seen her cry before. Upset about her father, she fretted about the running of Crow Hall.

Spotting a vacancy for a senior reg position in the new cardiac surgery unit in St Matthew's University Hospital, Alison suggested Luke put himself forward for the job. How fortuitous, she said. A job in Ireland, close to County Clare and Crow Hall. An indication that the economic climate had changed, she said. They should take it as their cue to return and progress Luke's career back in Ireland. Once home at Crow Hall she could help Cornelius back to health and oversee things until he got better.

Luke was cautiously optimistic about his chances of getting the position. At the same time, he had to manage his wife's expectations. Of course he would get the job, she declared. She looked at him, bemused. He knew some day her unerring faith in him would lead to disappointment. But not on this occasion. Luck was in his favour. Luke was delighted when, after the interview process, he was offered the job. Of course you were, said Alison. I never doubted you, she said. Alison headed back to County Clare and Crow Hall. Luke followed a number of weeks later, having finished his notice period.

He felt uncomfortable moving into Crow Hall, however temporary the sojourn might prove. He put the unnamed feeling of unease down to the transition between countries, jobs and houses. The truth was he disliked being a guest in another man's home, even if that man was his father-in-law. He accepted that Alison wanted to be with her father to oversee his recovery, however, and she had suffered upheaval enough at Luke's hands. He would put up with the transient discomfort to see her happy.

'You know, Luke, I no longer feel immortal or that our lives are infinite,' she said one evening in the kitchen at Crow Hall. It had once been the great hall with an open, cavernous fireplace. A range cooker now sat in the recess. The rest of the staff had gone home for the night. Cornelius was sleeping with a rug on his lap next to a crackling fire in the damp drawing room at the front of the house. 'Dad's heart attack has made me think.'

'Maybe it's time we thought about children of our own?' he put it to her. It seemed natural in the circumstances to think about the next generation. At times such as these, the instinct for survival made its presence felt.

That's when Alison told him. That night in the kitchen in Crow Hall. For the briefest of moments, he wondered if he'd misheard. It was so unexpected, so shocking, that he'd stared at her, dazed and wordless.

Marfan syndrome.

'What's Marfan syndrome?' Terence asked. He looked lost.

The query confirmed Luke's suspicion that Terence was not from a medical background. His title had likely come from a doctorate in psychology.

'Can you elaborate?' Terence asked.

Luke obliged. 'Marfan syndrome is a disease of the connective tissue affecting the heart and the skeletal frame.'

'That sounds serious.'

'It can be,' Luke explained. 'Marfan sufferers often have mitral valve damage and enlarged diameters of the aorta.' He tried to simplify the explanation. 'This can sometimes lead to aortic rupture and cardiac arrest.'

'Not good.'

'Not the best, no,' Luke agreed. 'Some patients have aortic root replacement to reduce the possibility of that occurring. But that all depends on the diameter of the aorta, and whether the aorta is considered to be under pressure.'

Terence's eyes glazed over. 'And your wife Alison has this . . . this syndrome?'

Luke wondered how much of this Terence was following. There was little point in burdening him with medical jargon. He'd try to put it as simply as possible.

'Yes, she does,' he replied. 'Marfan syndrome requires lifestyle changes. And it does of course have some far-reaching consequences.'

His mouth was dry and his tongue was sticking to the roof of his mouth.

Terence noted his discomfort. 'Can I get you another glass of water?' He poured without waiting for a reply.

Luke reached for the glass. The air in the office was dry, heavy and a fraction too warm. Unlike the damp chill that had gripped him in the lower back that night in the kitchen in Crow Hall.

Raymond Grogan

Luke gripped the wooden table to steady himself. His thumbs were squeezing white against the oak. He knew by Alison's expression that she was deadly serious. She didn't do preamble. She didn't tread softly towards unpleasantness. She locked horns with it. She was looking at him, following his expression, gauging his reaction. Observing the effect of her words as they struck home.

'Are you telling me . . .' he had to be absolutely sure.

'Yes,' she confirmed.

Christ.

Sitting there, the seconds ticking by, he felt a fool. A prize idiot. How had he not noticed? Or even suspected? How could he have overlooked, in the one human being he was closest to, what was obvious now? As he sat, dumb and paralysed, he realised the signs had been there all along. He specialised in cardiothoracic surgery and yet he'd missed it. The old adage was surely true. Love was blind and lovers could not see.

He tried to rationalise his blindness. This striking, vivacious woman had swept him into her orbit, fooling him with her drive and energy. And yet he knew he'd have spotted the syndrome if Alison had been an ordinary patient. He'd never before experienced such an acute sense of failure.

In the high-ceilinged, oak-beamed kitchen, he scrutinised Alison as if for the first time, examining her as if she were an exhibit in a natural history museum. She waited, appreciating he needed time. She remained still and silent, allowing him to go through an internal checklist. He took in her long face, shifting his scrutiny to her long thin arms, moving to her long slim legs, travelling up again, fastening his eyes on those prominent crowded teeth. His gaze dropped to her stockinged feet. He'd never noticed before how flat her feet were. All the outward markers of Marfan syndrome. None of these peculiarities were life-threatening or remarkable in themselves. But it was what they'd pointed to that concerned Luke most. The effects of Marfan syndrome on Alison's heart.

Some people had aortic root replacement to reduce the possibility of aortic rupture and cardiac arrest. Alison had no thoracic scars and no outward indication of heart surgery. Marfan syndrome was not an area that Luke specialised in. There was only a handful of specialists in the country qualified to diagnose and manage it.

'Who are you attending?' he asked eventually.

'Raymond Grogan. You probably know him.'

Luke nodded. 'I know he's a leading authority on the syndrome.' Grogan was a brusque individual where male colleagues were concerned, but less harsh with his female colleagues.

He slipped his hand over the table's rough oak surface, gathering himself after the shock. He covered Alison's hand with his. He had no idea what to say, or how to say it. This was not unusual. Alison told him often enough he was poor at expressing his feelings.

As Luke covered her long thin fingers with his, he considered all the difficulties she must encounter with the burden of the syndrome. Opening his mouth to say so, it struck him that the last thing Alison would want was pity. He leaned in to kiss her. She remained still as his lips rested on hers. Then pulling back, she exhaled as if she'd been holding her breath. She rested her head on his shoulder. They sat like this a while, his hand still covering hers.

He thought back to all the clues he'd missed. Their honeymoon on Kilimanjaro. It made sense now. At the time he'd thought her behaviour was related to altitude sickness.

He remembered noting her colour change and realising she was struggling. Even so, he'd been surprised at her reaction when he suggested that they stop. He'd fully expected her to protest. She never backed down from a challenge. Instead, she'd agreed with him that he was right – she didn't feel so good. She was holding back the rest of the team.

She'd insisted that Luke head on to the summit without her, despite him arguing it was a honeymoon, that they should stay together. No, she said, you go. Take photographs, lots of them. And so he'd left her behind on oxygen, continuing on to the top with the rest of the team. He'd never have embarked on such a trip if he'd suspected she had Marfan syndrome.

'How long have you known?' he asked her, stroking her hair in the chilly kitchen.

'Not too long before I met you.'

She had known all this time?

She raised her head, appreciating that all of this was a shock to him by the look in her eyes.

'With Mum dying so suddenly of a heart attack, it was always something I meant to get checked out. I wanted to know if I was at risk.'

That was Alison. Practical as ever.

77

'I did my research and I went to Raymond Grogan,' she explained. 'That's when I found out.' She paused. 'You and I have a lot to thank Raymond for, actually.' A slow smile spread across her face.

'Really?' He didn't feel like smiling.

'Really,' she confirmed. 'We wouldn't be together but for Raymond Grogan. There'd be no *us*. That's how I became interested in the whole area of cardiac health, you see. That's how I got involved in fundraising for children with heart defects. How do you think I came to be at that fundraising lunch where we first met?'

Luke had never thought about it before. The reason for Alison being at that lunch. He was aware he had social limitations. He understood facts and evidence and worked with what people told him. He knew, however, there were also clues on a social level that he was unaware of. He and Alison could listen to the same conversation, but could draw different inferences. His based on facts and evidence, hers based on the same, but complemented by body language and other signals that passed him by.

'So I take it you're not a candidate for an aortic root replacement?' he asked.

'No,' Alison replied. 'My condition isn't severe enough for that. Raymond Grogan said it could be managed by lifestyle choices.'

The guy was a leading European authority and if he considered the risks acceptable for Alison to continue without a replacement, Luke would have to be content with that. His thoughts turned to her frenetic lifestyle. The fundraising, the public speaking, her endeavours to support his career. Since their return home, there was talk of setting up a PR firm with her friend and neighbour, Roddy Gilligan. And more worrying – her hunting. How on earth could hunting be deemed a safe activity with her condition?

'Your hunting, Alison?' he ventured. 'What about the hunting? Jesus, when I think you went halfway up Kilimanjaro as well—'

'Stop right there, Luke.'

He was startled by her sharpness.

'Do you realise how many times I wanted to tell you about this?' She looked at him intently. 'This is precisely why I didn't.' Her voice softened. 'I didn't tell you when we started going out together because I didn't want you looking at me as if I were a patient. I can't live my life wrapped in cotton wool. That would be a death sentence to me. I have to do the things that make me happy. If not, I might as well be dead.' Her eyes pleaded for understanding.

'But, Alison—'

'No buts, Luke. I'm careful. I do not take unnecessary risks.'

Unnecessary risks.

The phrase concentrated his thoughts. She had crystallised the issue. Pregnancy was an unnecessary risk. Of immediate concern was her contraceptive choice. His mind was racing. Alison was taking the contraceptive pill. He'd never queried what type of pill she was on before.

'But the pill?'

'It's progestin only. Don't worry.'

That was something at least. Pills containing oestrogen could lead to blood clots which could be fatal for a Marfan patient. Luke was still unhappy. Progestin-only pills had a higher failure rate. Alison could still fall pregnant. He'd had no idea they'd been playing Russian roulette the past few years.

'You know what, Alison? I really think it would be a good idea for me to come along to your next appointment with Grogan.'

'No, Luke, you're not doing that.' Alison shook her head. 'Look, you've already acknowledged that Grogan is an authority on the syndrome, right? You come along with me and I know what you're like. You're going to ask all these questions in that abrasive way you do sometimes. The guy is going to feel you don't trust his judgement. You'll end up undermining the relationship I have with him, make things awkward. I am perfectly happy with the care I'm getting.'

He considered her point reluctantly.

'Look, I know it's tricky,' she went on, 'but these things can be managed. I just need to be extra careful when I get pregnant. Blood pressure checks, aortic scans and suchlike.'

'No.'

It was Alison's turn to look startled.

'I don't want you going through all that,' he said. He'd already thought ahead. 'Regardless of what Raymond Grogan says, the risks are not acceptable to *me*. It's too much pressure on your heart.' He didn't want to frighten her but he knew an aortic tear was possible.

'But—'

'Look, Alison, I know this sucks. It's total shit. It's not fair. But we have a lot going for us. We can still have a good life together. We don't have to be like everybody else.'

Even as he spoke, his words sounded hollow. There was no getting away from it. It was devastating news. It was sinking in that he and Alison would never have children together. It wasn't like he'd ever spent huge amounts of time thinking about it. But it was there in the back of his mind. Something he was looking forward to. Building forts in the sand like he did as a kid with his own dad. One of the happiest memories he had in the short time he'd had with the man. Building dens and treehouses. Playing soccer in the garden. Now this. It was crushing.

'I feel truly awful about this,' Alison whispered. 'I know I've let you down.' Her eyes were pools of hurt. 'You'd be such a brilliant dad. You deserve more.'

'It's not your fault,' Luke said flatly.

Silence followed.

He couldn't think of anything positive to add. 'I'd probably be one of those dads that forgets about his kids and leaves them behind in the supermarket,' he joked eventually. 'We're probably better off just you and me.' He tried to sound convincing.

'You're only saying that to make me feel better, but thanks.' Alison looked at him gratefully. 'It's just that I always imagined us having kids. I know we're good together, but it could be even better. It's just, you know . . . I feel like things won't be complete without a family. I think I'll always feel like I am missing out on something.'

She put her shoes back on and got to her feet. They both fell into silence again, Luke busy thinking, Alison fixing a dinner plate for Cornelius. He understood Alison's fears around not telling him sooner. She was afraid he'd cramp her style. Yet he couldn't help but feel a gnawing, nameless feeling. Keeping him in the dark that long didn't sit well with him.

Shouldn't she have told him before they got married? Why had she not trusted him? Was she afraid he'd lose interest? Or in her sanguine fashion did she really imagine it wouldn't be a problem? There were endless questions but it didn't change a thing. They were where they were. All the same, he couldn't help but wish she'd handled it a bit differently.

The smell of cooking gradually filled the kitchen. He followed her with his eyes as she went to the Aga, checking on the pie for dinner. Since Cornelius had his heart attack, home cooking was arriving in steady batches from the homes of Crow Hall labourers. The old man also had a steady stream of well-wishers. Luke found himself longing more and more for a place of his own.

He watched as Alison cut a large slice of meat pie and arranged it on a plate with steaming turnip and potatoes. Fetching a tray and a heavy crystal glass, she poured a generous glass of Cornelius's favourite red. Despite the heart attack, Cornelius showed little sign of cutting back.

'Can you get the door?' Alison asked. 'I want Dad to eat before Harry Halvey arrives.'

Harry Halvey was an assistant police commissioner.

Luke went to the door. 'There are ways and means, Alison.'

She looked at him curiously, her sombre eyes burning intensely.

'Ways and means,' he repeated, holding the creaky door.

She smiled wanly, then, pulling her shoulders back, she headed through the passageway. Luke watched, listening to her humming her way, her footsteps echoing on the tiles. She was an ace at putting on a brave face.

'See you in the morning, Ali,' he called out. He was heading on to a nightshift. The timing of the bombshell couldn't have been worse.

'Have a good night, darling,' she shouted back.

After what she'd told him, he thought that most unlikely.

Luke opened his eyes. From underneath his bushy eyebrows, Terence studied him. It was a few moments before the therapist ventured any comment on what he'd heard.

'Well, Luke, your recall is remarkable. You paint a vivid picture of what was obviously a distressing time for you.'

'What you might call a spanner in the works.' Luke smiled wryly. 'We humans are a right cantankerous lot. We never know what we want until someone tells us we can't have it. And then we want it right away.'

'True indeed.'

'It was only after Alison's disclosure that I realised just how much I wanted a family. I guess I always thought that when I had a child of my own, I'd recreate the perfect childhood, the one I'd wanted. Not the one I had . . .'

'Oh?'

Luke shook his head. 'I have to say I've no idea why I brought that up. What am I doing talking about my childhood? This is ridiculous. What on earth does that have to do with anything?'

'It's a process.' Terence smiled. 'A bit like peeling back layers of an onion. Bit by bit before getting to the core. I think we've covered enough for today, though. Let's pick it up again at our next session. All right with you?'

Luke nodded. He was happy to pause this visit to his past. He remembered the dark nights before he was sent to board at St Aloysius School for Boys. Staring up at the bedroom ceiling in Aunt Christine's house, wondering whether Mum and Dad could see him from wherever it was they'd gone to. He and Wendy were kids when their parents vanished overnight from their lives.

Ways and Means

'Would you like me to bring you something up from the canteen? I'm going down shortly.' Fran was busy cutting dead leaves from the office plants on the windowsill. 'A sandwich maybe? The ploughman's lunch?'

'No, thanks.' Luke was fairly sure any ploughman worth his salt wouldn't deign to choose the limp, cello-wrapped offering in the hospital canteen. 'I'm heading out in a bit. I'll get something then.'

'Just thought I'd ask,' said Fran with a knowing expression.

Though she never enquired directly, Luke reckoned Fran suspected he was visiting Terence Black during the day. The therapy sessions were more or less continuous with Terence kindly accommodating Luke in a lunchtime slot. Luke didn't confirm Fran's suspicions. He had to remain discreet.

On the eight-minute journey to Terence's office that lunchtime, Luke prepared himself for what he was about to disclose. He thought back to his childhood. The one that came to an end at the tender age of five. Five and a half to be exact. Wendy had been ten.

He remembered his mother bending to kiss him. 'Be good for Aunt Christine,' she said. 'She's not used to children. I'll bring you back some fizzy snakes and cola bottles.'

Luke had loved those long strings of jelly and the way they'd sparkle on his tongue. The jelly cola bottles were the next best thing to Coke. He wasn't allowed fizzy drinks. Mum said they made him crazy.

He remembered being in the garden at Aunt Christine's, his dad slinging him a football. His dad was wearing a jacket with a red flower stuck in it. 'Get some practice, son,' he said. 'We'll play keepie-uppie when I come back.'

Luke kept his side of the bargain. He kept out of Aunt Christine's way. He and Wendy stayed outside in the garden as much as they could. They made a fort at the back behind the greenhouse. And he practised keepie-uppie like he promised. Dad was going to have a hard time beating twenty-three minutes.

It puzzled him when Mum and Dad didn't return the following day as promised. Or the day after that either. He'd had no idea that weddings took that long. He was missing school into the bargain. Mum wouldn't be too pleased about that. And when he asked the adults where his mum and dad were, no one would give him an answer. Well, not one that made sense anyway. It was all very odd. He couldn't understand it.

Wendy wouldn't talk to him either. She went very weird and wouldn't come out to play in their cool fort in the garden. She stayed in a bedroom under the covers with a book. And Aunt Christine spent all her time whispering on the phone in the hall. He had to go off and play by himself. He got up to twenty-seven minutes in keepie-uppie.

Everyone was acting strangely. He was sure Wendy must know something. She was older. People often told her stuff they wouldn't tell him. He knew that because she'd get a look on her face. She had that look now.

'When are Mum and Dad coming back, Wendy?' he asked for the gazillionth time.

Then eventually, instead of ignoring him like all the times before, she looked him straight in the eye. He could tell she'd been crying.

'They're gone to heaven,' she said.

'Oh,' he said, knowing that was somewhere good. 'But when will they be back?' Wendy still hadn't answered his question.

'I just told you, they're gone to heaven.'

Though he asked repeatedly every day for a week, no one could give him a straight answer. Not long after that, they went to church. Everyone there said nice things about his mum and dad. He remembered thinking it was such a shame they weren't there to hear it. Afterwards they went to a hotel. He was allowed to have a Coke. He remembered thinking his mum would be really mad when she found out about that. No one else seemed to care too much.

It must have been months afterwards when he first heard the words 'car crash'. Maybe they'd mentioned those scary words back in the beginning. There used to be a time when he was good at blocking stuff out.

There was a smell of packet soup in Terence's office. Luke recognised it from his student days. It had a malodorous, powdery, oniony, smell. He shouldn't complain. The therapist was forfeiting his lunch break to accommodate him. The waiting area had been empty, as was the reception desk. It was just the two of them.

Terence was about to sit down in his seat with his cup of soup when he stopped. 'I didn't think to ask . . . would you like a cup of soup?'

'I've eaten, thanks,' lied Luke. The smell was making him gag.

'Good. Good. I can never think when I'm hungry.' Terence sat, setting the cup in front of him. He peered at his notepad. 'Last time, you spoke about "ways and means" if I recall correctly? Shall we take it up from there?'

'That's right.' Luke nodded, settling back. 'After finding out about the Marfan's, I felt that I had to do something about Alison. There was no way I could risk her getting pregnant.'

He recalled the feelings of responsibility and of dread. How could he forgive himself if anything were to happen to her? He couldn't leave things to chance. Alison was using a contraceptive pill but it had a higher failure rate than the combined pill that she couldn't take. Apart from being sure-fire passion killers, condoms were too risky.

It had taken Luke a long week of agonising. No matter how he dissected the problem, he could find only one solution. He didn't like it. Not one bit. It seemed so drastic and he worried that he might experience regret and by then it would be too late.

He didn't know anyone else who'd done it. Not anyone who had admitted to it at least. It wasn't exactly the sort of thing you crowed about from the rooftops. And he certainly didn't want to discuss it with anyone, least of all his colleagues. It was a private matter, between him and Alison. No one else's business.

Being on nightshift at that time meant he saw very little of Alison, which was just as well. He wanted to make this decision on his own. He didn't want her trying to dissuade him. If he revealed what he was thinking she might try to change his mind, and as often happened he might easily find himself agreeing with her. This was something he had to do on his own. He'd go to Dublin. He'd tell Fran he was attending a conference. He didn't want anyone in St Matthew's finding out.

Three weeks after finding out about Alison's Marfan syndrome, Luke found himself walking into a private clinic in South County Dublin. He felt clammy and squeamish. When he left again a few hours later, he felt a mixture of relief and sadness. He also felt very bloody sore. He would, however, no longer have to worry about Alison falling pregnant. Weighing it all up, the vasectomy had been the only way to go.

'That was a brave decision, if you don't mind me saying so.'

Wisps of steam curled up from Terence's soup, which had remained untouched these past few minutes. The therapist had crossed his legs, his usual rosy colour deserting him. Talk of the vasectomy had left him looking squeamish.

'In the circumstances, I really didn't see that I had much option. That was the easy part.'

Terence directed him to continue.

'After the vasectomy,' said Luke, whereupon Terence winced again, 'I had to set my mind to dealing with the trickier part of our problem.'

Sensitive to Alison's feelings, Luke would wait until the time was right. To his surprise, it was Alison who broached the subject.

'How about adopting?' she asked one evening after Cornelius had retired to bed.

'Really? You'd be up for that?'

He was quietly delighted.

'Of course. Why not? But we haven't got a hope here at home. No one gives their children up for adoption here these days. We'd have to look abroad, somewhere like Russia.'

And so they embarked on the process. Social workers warned them it would be invasive, long and difficult. They were cautioned that many couples ended up abandoning the adoption process, unable to deal with the added strain on what might already be a strained relationship. Against all this, Alison remained undaunted. The more barriers that were put in their way, the more she enjoyed tearing them down.

The initial meetings with the social workers were interrogations. As if the social work department was seeking a flaw or chink in their relationship or in their backgrounds to hamper them adopting. Unlike Alison, who was unperturbed by this, Luke became uneasy. He proceeded carefully, treating each personal question with the utmost caution.

Alison arranged things so that any disruption to his rosters would be minimised. The social worker met them at Luke's office at times that were convenient to Luke. Alison didn't want the process to interfere with his work.

Wherever possible, he let Alison do the talking. He listened closely as she made their case. They were an educated couple. They had means. They had a stable relationship. They could offer a child a wonderful life. Work had already started on their new home on the shores of Lough Carberry. Then, much to his surprise, the proposed adoption was met with a resistance from unexpected quarters.

'Your sister, Wendy?' Terence ventured.

'Oh God, no. Wendy was delighted at the prospect. But you're right. It was someone close to home.'

Luke shuddered as he recounted what had happened.

'So what class of a foreigner will it be?' asked Cornelius Thompson one Saturday morning, a frown on his brow.

'I don't know yet,' Alison answered.

She was hosing a horsebox out in the yard. Luke was having an early morning cup of tea before heading off to check progress on the new build. He was looking forward to having their own home, to there being just the two of them. And hopefully, soon, three of them.

'This child . . . it's not going to be one of those . . . one of those . . .' Cornelius again directed this at Alison. Luke often found himself invisible in their conversations.

'One of those what, Cornelius?' Luke asked.

'You know, Alison . . .' Cornelius ignored him. 'It's not going to be one of those . . . one of those indigents. Not one of those *darkies* now, is it?'

'Dad!'

Water sprayed everywhere as Alison dropped the hose. To Luke's astonishment, she burst out laughing.

'For goodness' sake, Dad. In this day and age! You can't possibly go around using language like that or saying stuff like that. It's racist.'

Cornelius threw the dregs of his tea on the cobbled ground. 'Now, Alison. You know me. I speak my mind. I can't have a coloured child kicking about here with the Thompson name.'

Alison was giggling.

'Well, that's certainly not going to happen for a start, Cornelius,' Luke said sharply. Heart attack or no heart attack, Cornelius was not getting away with that. 'Any child that Alison and I choose to adopt – whatever colour – will *not* be taking the Thompson name. The child will be taking the Forde surname.'

The clatter of hooves abruptly sounded in the yard, the heated exchange interrupted by Roddy Gilligan's arrival on horseback. In an instant, Cornelius's bullishness disappeared.

'Here to take my lovely daughter for a well-earned gallop?' He patted Roddy's mount.

'If you fancy, Alison?' Roddy shouted to her across the yard.

Alison nodded enthusiastically.

'You coming too, Luke?' This was more of an afterthought on Roddy's part.

'Things to do,' Luke replied. He'd rather stab himself in the eyeballs. The guy was an arse. 'Have to check on the new house. We're expecting a delivery of glass panels. Then I'm heading to the hospital.'

'Right you are,' said Roddy.

Luke made a lingering display of kissing Alison full on the mouth.

'We'll talk about all this later,' he said, 'when I get home this evening.'

Cornelius brushed past Luke on his way back to the house.

'Enjoy the ride,' he said to his daughter. 'I doubt that Gilligan is shooting blanks,' he muttered, looking at Luke.

Luke stared at the retreating bulk of his father-in-law. Alison blushed. How could she have shared news of the vasectomy with her father? That stuff was personal, something between husband and wife. Not for wider consumption, no matter how close she was to her father.

Cornelius should be grateful to Luke. He certainly hadn't expected mocking jibes for his trouble. At that point Luke began to suspect that Cornelius only knew half the story. As familiarity took hold, Luke became more and more unsure about his father-in-law. Alison indulged the man. She doted on him, and Luke had to be careful not to be seen to drive a wedge between them. That said, there was no way on earth he was allowing Cornelius to meddle in their adoption.

During the pre-assessment, Luke and Alison became painfully acquainted with the anomalies and problems with bilateral adoption treaties with other countries. Many countries that were open to adoption had signed the Hague Convention, a treaty supposed to minimise exposure to corruption in the adoption process and to stop money changing hands.

Other countries such as Russia with large state orphanages weren't bound by the Hague Convention. Luke couldn't help but feel dispirited by the stories of other couples in their support group. Most couples had been waiting years to clear the legal requirements. But, miraculously, within a few months Luke and Alison found themselves in the company of other prospective parents on a plane bound for Moscow.

As other adopters headed for Belorussky train station to complete their journeys to orphanages many miles away, Luke and Alison were met by a shiny black diplomatic car to take them to their nearby orphanage.

Despite all Luke's efforts to keep Cornelius at arm's length, he couldn't help but feel the hand of his father-in-law tinkering with the process. When he queried Alison about their preferential treatment, she explained that Cornelius had made some overtures to his Irish trade contacts in Moscow. Luke could no longer delude himself that luck had featured in the process.

Only as they sped through the grey Moscow streets did Luke begin to appreciate the full weight of the Thompson political machine. With a shiver of disgust, he thought back to Cornelius's parting words.

'Do you know what my father-in-law said to Alison and I before we left for Russia?' Luke asked Terence.

'I have no idea,' Terence answered. 'But I'm guessing it wasn't complimentary.'

'Don't bring home a dud,' he said. 'Don't bring home a dud.'

Terence raised an eyebrow. 'A racist, to boot, your father-in-law?'

'Racist is one of the kinder epithets I'd attribute to Cornelius Thompson,' Luke replied. 'I'll tell you why.' He could hear office employees returning from lunch and, seen through the Venetian blinds, cars were pulling up outside.

'If you don't mind, I'd prefer if we kept on track and spoke about the adoption.' Terence drained his soup. 'We can come back to Cornelius if you like, at a later stage.'

Luke was happy to agree. He'd already prepared what he would say. Though it had all happened fifteen years ago, he remembered the first day in the Russian orphanage with razor clarity. He closed his eyes and cast his mind back.

The Chosen One

Luke was standing watching a bundle in the folds of a grey coat, crouched in a corner of the open-air yard of the orphanage. The little girl was playing on her own, making shapes with stones. Alison was beside Luke, her gloved hand in his, and he could feel her shiver in the raw winter air. They'd already seen three children and the supervisor was introducing a fourth to them.

'This is Raisa. Say hello to Dr and Mrs Forde, Raisa.'

Appraising children in an open yard like this lacked dignity. As with the three other children they had seen, Alison went down on one knee to make eye contact. This time, Alison turned her head and looked up at Luke with raised eyebrows. The child's eyes were azure blue and she had the makings of a dimple if only she would smile. Alison smoothed her hand over the child's blonde hair. 'Raisa, what a lovely name,' she said.

They were watched by huddles of other children. Luke took in their guarded looks. Another sweep of the yard confirmed his suspicions. He and Alison were being presented with children who were free from any physical defects. Psychological problems were not as obvious. Those type of problems would manifest later, long after any adoption was completed.

'Raisa has a lovely voice,' the supervisor said. She then said something in Russian. Raisa opened her mouth and started to sing. It sounded like a lullaby. 'Oh, her poor little teeth,' said Alison softly. Luke had also noticed the decay.

As Raisa sang, Luke became aware of someone moving towards them. It was the girl who'd been playing with the stones in the corner. At a guess, she was three years old or four. With poor nutrition, it was difficult to tell. Two lank curtains of dark hair hung on either side of her thin face.

'Yes?' said the supervisor impatiently.

Alison got to her feet, her hand resting on Raisa's head as she stared at the intruder.

The dark-haired child edged closer and pointed to the undone lace on her old-fashioned shoe that looked much too large for her foot. The supervisor clicked her tongue and muttered as she bent to do the lace.

'*Niet.*' The dark-haired child pulled her foot away. She pointed to Luke. Then she pointed to the lace once more. Luke realised that the little girl with the purposeful face and the oversized coat didn't want the supervisor to do up her lace. She wanted Luke to do it. The supervisor shook her head. She was not amused.

'This is how I do it.' Luke fell to one knee and recited:

> Build a tee pee,
> come inside,
> close it tight so we can hide,
> over the mountain,
> and around we go,
> here's my arrow,
> and here's my bow.

The rhyme tripped from his tongue before he even had time to think. Where he'd come by it he couldn't recall, but this little girl had triggered his memory and the rhyme popped out. Now at eye level, he could see that one of her eyes had a squint.

'*Spasiba*,' said the child.

Luke guessed she was thanking him. He stood up.

'You're welcome,' he replied.

He hoped the little girl would understand what he meant from his tone. He'd signed up to do classes in basic Russian but he and Alison had found themselves in Russia sooner than expected. The child slipped her hand into her pocket and took it out in a fist. Unfurling her fingers, she examined the stones in the cup of her hand and with a look of fierce concentration, she carefully picked out a pebble.

It was ringed with three white concentric circles. She presented it to Luke. It was by far the prettiest pebble in her palm. Then she turned and skipped back to her corner, stopping twice on her journey to look over her shoulder at Luke.

'What a strange little girl,' said Alison.

Raisa was still standing beside her, looking blankly into the distance.

'That one . . .' The supervisor shook her head. 'I don't know what she was thinking. Nina Yelena knows how to do her laces. She's one of the cleverest ones here.'

Back in their Moscow hotel room, Luke found it difficult to enjoy the luxury hotel that Cornelius's contact had arranged. Five miles away, 180 children were living a bleak and spartan existence in an orphanage.

He lay on the bed, glazing over as he stared at a basic Russian phrasebook. Alison was in the bathroom talking animatedly on the phone. She was talking loudly. The bathroom door was ajar.

'. . . a little girl, Dad. We thought that would be best . . . yes . . . yes, I know that.'

A little girl. *They* thought it would be best. Really? Luke couldn't recall any such conversation. His ears pricked up even more.

'She's three-and-a-half they think. Yeah – they're not sure of the exact birth date but that's not unusual here. Way beyond the nappy stage.' Alison laughed. 'She's a beautiful little girl. What's that?'

Alison laughed again.

'No, Dad. Of course not. No, she doesn't look Mongolian or Chinese or have slanty eyes in any way.'

Luke bristled.

'She's got the most beautiful eyes . . . yes . . . big bright blue eyes. And blonde hair. What's that? The line is bad . . . yeah, yeah, Dad – don't worry – you'll love her. We're going back for another visit tomorrow. Just to become more familiar and to explain the process to her and what will be happening next. What's that? Oh, sure, the hotel is great, yes . . . so handy to have a driver. You must thank Seanie Higgins for us. He did a great job. Just a pity about the five-month thing . . . I know, I know. Yes, yes of course I will. Her name? Oh, didn't I say? No, no – it's really easy to pronounce. Her name's Raisa.'

So that was it.

Without so much as a word or any form of consultation, Alison had made a decision. There'd been no discussion with Luke. He'd eavesdropped and she'd probably discuss it with him later, after she had her bath. But he was seething. Why would she choose to share her thoughts first with Cornelius on something that would change their married life for ever?

Recounting the events to Terence rekindled the feelings of anger and frustration he'd felt at the time.

'What I'm hearing from you is that it was hard to stomach

Cornelius being kept in the loop. Is that right?' The therapist lifted his tie to inspect the soup stains. He frowned.

'It got on my wick,' Luke confirmed. 'It felt like my father-in-law was always there lurking in the background in a creepy, medieval kind of way. Like those heads of families who used to demand to see the bedsheets after a wedding to satisfy themselves that the marriage had been consummated.'

Terence shook his head.

Luke continued. 'Up until that time in Russia I guess I never understood how much Alison looked to Cornelius for guidance. I had to up my game to deal with that.'

'Tell me some more.' Terence checked the clock. 'We have time.'

Luke took a sip of water. He went back to the Moscow hotel room. To the conversation he'd had with Alison.

'Ah, that's better,' Alison said, reappearing from the bathroom, her hair newly washed, dressed in a bathrobe. 'I just had to scrub the depressing smell of that awful orphanage away.' She patted her hair with a white fluffy towel.

While she'd finished in the bathroom, Luke had had time to consider. He'd play the longer game. He wouldn't let on that he'd overheard her conversation with Cornelius.

'It's a grim life for those poor kids,' he agreed.

The children he'd encountered in Tanzania and Thailand suffered equal deprivation, but were somehow sunnier in their outlook. He wondered if his view was coloured by the bleakness of the Russian winter, thinking poverty and deprivation possibly more tolerable under a hot sky.

'It seems wrong with all we have that we're only taking a single child to a better life,' he mused aloud.

'You're not suggesting that we adopt more than one?'

There was a note of alarm in Alison's voice.

'I think we'll see how we get on with one child before we turn into the Waltons.' He laughed. 'However connected your father's contact is here in Moscow, I doubt even he could rustle up a second set of declaration papers.'

'That's true enough.'

Alison undid her robe and turned to admire herself in the full-length mirror.

'Pity he can't get them to waive that five-month wait though,' she said, sighing.

'It's going to be tough.'

Luke appreciated that it was going to be difficult for all of them. Him, Alison, and their new child.

'Like consumer protection, I guess.' Alison slinked into tight-fitting jeans. 'In case you choose the wrong child in the heat of the moment, I suppose.'

'What?'

He looked at her, askance.

'I mean you could arrive home and think differently about the child you thought you wanted.' She pulled a cashmere sweater over her head, smoothing it approvingly over her flat stomach. 'I know the waiting period is in case a Russian family may want to adopt the same child as you,' she added. 'But you could always think of it as a cooling-off period.'

'This isn't a fridge-freezer or a flatscreen TV we're talking about here, Alison.'

'No, of course not,' she said briskly. 'I know that. I'm really excited about it all, aren't you?'

'I'm apprehensive, if the truth be told,' he said. 'And we need to let the orphanage know in the morning which child we want to see again tomorrow afternoon.'

'Well, that's an easy one, isn't it?' Alison smacked her lips together, having applied a slick of red gloss.

'It is.'

The time had come to set his plan in motion.

A knock sounded on Terence's door. Luke stopped talking and looked at Terence. The therapist's face creased. He turned his eyes to the door waiting for another knock to come. When it did he got to his feet with a look of apology. The door ajar, Luke heard the receptionist saying the next client had arrived and had been waiting some time.

He got to his feet. 'It's OK, Terence, we'll continue this later . . .'

Terence looked over his shoulder. 'You're sure? It's not really where I'd like to leave things.'

'I'm positive.'

'All right, if you're comfortable with it. We'll do lunchtime tomorrow or the day after. Whatever suits.'

Pinky Promise

It was three more days before Luke made it back to Terence's office. Not because events conspired against him. The delay was deliberate. Luke was loath to establish any discernible patterns of behaviour through leaving the hospital at the same time every day. He sensed his movements were being watched.

'Sorry we were cut short last time,' Terence apologised, knocking against the rubber plant in the rattan container as he made his way to his chair, notebook in hand.

'Not at all. I appreciate you squeezing me in,' said Luke. 'Just as well I headed back to the hospital when I did the last day. A colleague was called to a family emergency and I had to step in.'

'OK, so where were we?' Terence checked his notes. 'Ah, yes. You were telling me how you'd agreed on the child you wished to adopt.'

'Not quite.'

'Oh?'

Even now, as Luke recalled what happened, it gave him satisfaction. He closed his eyes. He travelled back to fifteen years ago. To Moscow.

'What do you think – Raisa Forde or Raisa Forde-Thompson?' Alison was dabbing perfume on her wrists in the hotel room.

'Neither.'

She turned to him, surprised.

'What do you mean? I saw the way you looked at her. She was the prettiest child there by far. So many of those poor unfortunates are odd-looking in some way. Come on, Luke. I know you liked her too.'

'It's not a beauty contest, Alison. Remember all our prep sessions. All the hazards and difficulties that arise because of a lack of bonding from infancy, trauma, poor nutrition—'

'Oh sure, I know her teeth are bad. That's not a big problem, we can always get those fixed. And maybe she's a bit short-sighted . . .'

'That's not why her eyes look like that. I'm glad you noticed it, though. That poor child's eyes are like that because she hasn't been socialised enough. Didn't you notice how she didn't make eye contact with anyone? She wasn't capable of doing so. If I'm not mistaken, there are psychological problems there as well. I'm not for one moment saying that we shouldn't adopt her because of that, but we both need to be sure what we're taking on here. We won't know the full extent of any difficulty until she's back at home with us. But if that's something you want to take on, Alison, I'll support you one hundred per cent.'

Alison sat on the edge of the bed, the weight of his words sinking in, a frown forming on her forehead. He continued on while he had her attention.

'Contrast Raisa's behaviour with that little girl who of her own accord, without any prompting, made her way over to us.'

'The little snotty creature in that dreadful coat?'

'The child with the undone shoelace, yes.'

'But that child isn't even on the list.'

Luke smiled at this.

'Considering all the strings that have been pulled to get us this far, I'm sure that won't prove a problem. Surely you noticed how engaged that little girl was with her surroundings? How curious she was? She'd pick up English in no time. You heard the supervisor saying she was one of the clever ones. Imagine all the fun we could have.'

'You think?' Alison looked dubious. 'I know it sounds shallow, but good Lord, she's not one bit photogenic. And what a horrible squint the poor child has.'

'As you said, all things that can be easily fixed. A correctional eye patch, a good haircut. But psychological damage, that's not my area.'

He felt awful saying this but he knew what he had to do to get her to change her mind.

'Yeah, I see what you are saying . . .'

'Maybe when we return to the orphanage tomorrow, we should at least ask to see Nina Yelena's profile.'

'Who?' Alison arched her eyebrows.

'Nina Yelena. That was what the supervisor called her, you didn't hear?'

'I didn't notice,' said Alison flatly. She cleared her throat. 'All right. I know we don't want to take on a situation we can't manage. And perhaps I was a bit hasty . . . It's just that, well, I felt a connection, you know.'

'I know.'

Luke had felt it too. But not with the pretty blonde-haired child. He'd felt it with the child swimming in a winter coat far too big for her. The child in the ill-fitting shoes, with the bad hair and the squint in her eye. He felt it with Nina.

A flurry of phone calls took place between Seanie Higgins and Alison, and Nina Yelena's name made it on to the list of children approved for upcoming adoption. In this endeavour, Seanie

Higgins took a wide interpretation of his role as diplomatic trade ambassador.

It was uncomfortable territory for Luke. He didn't ask questions, preferring instead the comfort of ignorance. Before they'd left for Moscow, their preparatory group had looked at them in wonder on learning that they had been cleared for adoption. Luke and Alison had received the paperwork to proceed, ahead of many other couples, some of whom had been waiting for years.

Over the next three days, Luke and Alison were driven to the orphanage to spend time alone with Nina. Alison brought the play kit she'd packed to help them get to know their prospective child and have some fun.

In a see-through Ziplock bag she'd packed playing cards with cartoon characters, a small draughtsboard and draughts, some coloured paper and crayons, and two Ladybird books, *Cinderella* and *Sleeping Beauty*.

Alison demonstrated how the game of draughts worked by playing first with Luke. Every time Alison took one of Luke's draughts, she whooped. He pretended to be upset. Nina looked from one to the other ponderously at first, not quite sure what to make of the interaction. Luke then took some of Alison's draughts. He winked and smiled at Nina. She soon figured out the game.

It came to Nina's turn to play against Luke. As she studied the board, Alison held the child's hair back from her eyes, toying with it, as if figuring how best to improve her hairstyle. Alison angled her head this way and that, examining Nina. She smiled at Luke when she caught him looking. Nina squealed with delight when Luke let her win her first game of draughts.

Nina pointed at Alison, signalling that it was her turn to play. The second game ended much more quickly, Nina's response not quite as ebullient as before. Alison won. Luke shook his head, laughing at his wife's competitive streak.

The Ladybird books were an instant hit. Nina's eyes devoured the pages, her blunt fingers rubbing over Cinderella's ballgown. As Luke read to her aloud, her eyes moved from him to the pages and back again. Though the child didn't understand a word, she looked enthralled. When Luke came to the last page of the colourful storybook, he closed the hardback cover with a satisfied smile.

'So, Nina Yelena, what do you make of that for a story?'

The little girl clapped her hands and uttered something Luke didn't understand. He looked at the supervisor who sat behind them on a stiff-back chair in the green-walled room.

'Again,' said the supervisor. 'She wants you to read it again.'

Luke smiled at Nina.

'Really? You want me to read it again?'

She nodded vigorously.

Alison smiled at Luke. 'Go ahead,' she said as she took her mobile phone out of her bag.

This time when Luke came to the page where the handsome prince awakens and rescues the sleeping girl, Nina pointed a squat little finger to the prince. Then she pointed to Luke. He threw back his head and laughed. He decided to play along. He liked being compared to a prince.

'And Alison . . .?'

He pointed to Alison. She was busy texting. Nina took the book from him. She started to turn the pages. Then she stopped. She pointed at Cinderella's stepmother and then she looked at Alison. Luke could understand it. Alison's hair was dark, she wore red nail varnish, and her lips were glossy red. But there the similarity ended.

He looked at Nina and raised his eyebrows. He spotted something else he liked. Mischief. There was a glint in her eyes and one corner of her mouth turned up. She was having a joke at his expense. With an inward chuckle, he shook his head. He moved her finger away from the wicked queen. Amusing as the incident was, he was glad Alison hadn't noticed.

Two days later, with all the paperwork in place, he and Alison were due to fly back home. They'd taken lots of photos. Nina smiling broadly on Alison's knee. Nina smiling as Alison hugged her. The photos of Luke and Nina not quite so good.

Luke found the idea of waiting for five months difficult enough to accept without having to explain it to a little child, three-and-a-half years old. Nina sat with wide eyes and listened closely as the supervisor explained that her new mummy and daddy would return to the orphanage in five months' time.

Through the supervisor, Luke explained that they were building a brand new home specially for her, all made out of glass blocks. He sketched a picture of what their new house would look like and gave it to her. Just before he left, he bent down to hug her. He whispered softly in her ear, 'I'm very glad you chose me to be your daddy. And I'll be back for you very soon . . . Pinky promise?'

She looked at him, confused. He took her little finger, entwining it around his own.

'There, Nina, just like that.' He smiled. 'Now it's a promise that can't ever be broken. Never ever. No matter what.'

'Pinky promise,' she repeated, not sure what it meant but from the look in her eyes she understood it was something very important.

'See you soon, sweetie,' said Alison. She blew Nina a kiss and waved.

'The next five months are going to be difficult,' Luke said back in the car.

'I know,' said Alison, fixing her make-up.

Terence sneezed.

'Excuse me,' he said, pulling a tissue from the box and blowing his nose. 'It's hard to imagine you had your choice of child back then.'

Luke nodded in agreement.

'I think the adoption protocols were very different fifteen years ago,' he told Terence. 'The rules changed on a whim. Russia halted adoptions to the US because of sanctions the US imposed. And they wouldn't allow adoption to countries with same-sex marriage.'

'It sounds like you and Alison were pretty fortunate your adoption story ended happily.'

'Oh, but that's where you're wrong, Terence,' Luke responded. 'It didn't.'

A Time to Share

The night before, Luke had tossed and turned in bed. He'd pictured himself hanging on a rope over a canyon. It was time to make a move. Should he struggle on to the other side, or should he let go and face the consequences? Eventually, he decided what he would do. And it turned out to be the first night in months that the white bird did not come to visit him.

'Did I miss a beat somewhere?'

Terence looked puzzled.

'What I told you about visiting the orphanage,' Luke replied, 'that was only the start of it.'

'Carry on.' The therapist reached for his pen. 'I might take some notes.'

'Well, as you might have gathered, I was smitten,' Luke began, 'by this intense, clever kid we met in Moscow. Flattered I guess that she had chosen me. I clicked with Nina straightaway. But Alison . . . well . . . I guess she was just a little more . . .' he paused, searching for a word, '. . . circumspect, knowing what a change it would be to her life.'

Terence scribbled something.

'I was really dreading the five months before we could return so I got stuck into preparing for exams when we returned home to County Clare. An opening for a consultant's position had come up at St Matthew's University Hospital and I was confident if the panel interview went well, I was in with a chance.'

Terence looked up.

'Alison, she was supportive. She was busy as well. Setting up the Thompson Consulting PR company with her business partner, Roddy Gilligan. And decorating the new house, of course.'

Luke didn't share how Cornelius persisted on joking about the arrival of Putin's lovechild. Luke couldn't wait to move out of Crow Hall and into the Glasshouse, even though the interior designers were still tinkering about their unfinished home.

'Building your own home, changing jobs, and the arrival of a child are all recognised stress points in a person's life,' Terence offered.

'Oh, Alison wasn't stressed by any of that,' Luke responded. 'She was thrilled with the new house.'

She'd even persuaded him to pose with her for the cover of an interiors magazine.

'Everything was going according to plan. Neither of us had any inkling how fucked up it was all going to get.'

The walls of Terence's office suddenly felt like they were moving closer. Luke felt beads of perspiration on his forehead.

'All right, Luke. Take a breath.'

He closed his eyes. He took a moment. 'If I could wind the clock back,' he whispered. 'Wind the clock the whole way back. It all started with that awful dinner party. The one we had in the Glasshouse before the paint had even dried . . .'

Just a small gathering of hospital staff for a casual Friday-night supper, no big deal, Alison said. She'd invited them all without telling him. Now they'd all feel obliged to return the social invite.

Luke could kiss goodbye to at least a further five or six other nights of his precious free time. He'd be forced to make small talk when he'd rather be out on Lough Carberry or fixing up his basement.

The evening was excruciating. His dining companions were his peers, Hugh Smyth and his wife Miriam, Johnny Whelan and his companion who looked no more than sixteen, and two consultants who were tipped to be on the panel to assess candidates for the post of consultant cardiothoracic surgeon. Miriam Smyth drank a little too much and had to be helped to the car at the end of the evening.

There was little subtlety in Alison's efforts to advance Luke's career and he was mortified. Rather than take her to task for what she perceived as being helpful, Luke resolved to be more careful in future in what he told her.

Shortly after the dinner party, he had his panel interview. He left it feeling happy. He was ready and competent for the post. It would be a while before the panel would let him know. There were other candidates for them to see that day. Alison said they were external candidates in the main and she pronounced herself confident the job was his. How Alison came by this information baffled him.

In the meantime, there was another tedious social engagement to get through. Hugh and Miriam Smyth had invited Luke and Alison to their home to celebrate their daughter's first communion. Luke found such occasions a chore, but Alison said it would be helpful to know how to host a kids' party. And so on a Saturday afternoon in May they set out for Hugh's, driving a small Mercedes, one of Cornelius's favourite cars. His father-in-law had many penchants, all of which he indulged.

'Nice view,' Alison remarked as they stopped at the crest of the hill outside Hugh's place. 'Shame about the house.' The house was an awkward, seventies-style, split-level build with large windows. Luke and Alison sat in the car, engine running, as they waited for Miriam to untie the gates. Children raced about the garden and Luke could make out the garish turrets of a bouncy castle.

'Sorry about this,' Miriam called to them as she undid the twine. 'I'm just afraid the smallies might stray onto the road.'

'Electric gates,' Alison shouted. 'That's what you need. I'll give you the name of the guy who did ours. They're just the thing.'

Miriam responded with a lukewarm smile.

'Now, aren't you glad you changed?' Alison whispered to Luke after they'd parked and made their way through swarms of children. 'Told you all the men would be wearing blazers.'

Luke had been perfectly comfortable in his crumpled linen jacket but Alison had insisted.

'Great you could make it, big fella.' Hugh pressed a cold beer into Luke's hand. Cigars poked out of his breast pocket. He was in flying form.

'Cheers.' Luke took the bottle even though he felt it a little early for a beer. 'Johnny coming?'

'Nope. Busy with the new girlfriend.'

'Pity,' said Luke. 'She could have played on the bouncy castle.'

Hugh chuckled. 'She's a bit on the young side, all right.' Bottle in hand, he pointed to the bouncy castle. 'C'mon with me. I have to keep an eye on the kids.'

Luke did as directed, leaving Alison searching out a glass of sparkling water. Moments later, she sidled up to join them on the lawn. On her arm was a gold paper bag with white ribbons. 'What are you two up to?' She linked her free arm through Hugh's.

'Oh, we're just remarking how charming little girls are. Isn't that right, Luke?'

Luke agreed.

Alison gave Hugh a coquettish smile. 'We sure are. Sugar and spice and all things nice. Speaking of which – where's your first communion girl? We have a little gift for her.' Alison held up the bag.

'No little something for me?' Hugh teased.

'Sorry.' Alison jutted out her lower lip, playing along. 'Big boys usually want big toys.'

'Well, that's true,' Hugh agreed. He turned to Luke. 'Remind me to take you to the shed. I've something to show you.'

'Will do.' Luke raised his bottle.

Hugh called into the melee of kids on the bouncy castle. 'Jenny!'

A child in a long white dress emerged from a knot of bouncy children and vaulted onto the grass. Red-faced she skipped up to her father.

'Yes, Dad?' She had a pixie face with button eyes.

'Say hello to Alison and Luke. They've brought you a gift.'

'Hello,' said the child, her interest trained on the gold paper bag.

'What a beautiful dress,' said Alison, handing her the gift. 'You must have had the prettiest dress by far in the church today.'

'My friend Lily had the exact same,' said Jenny, tearing at the wrapping.

'It's hard to have anything unique,' said Miriam, coming to join them with a tray of canapés. 'There must have been at least a hundred kids in the church this morning.' She offered the tray around. 'All the local schools had first communion.'

'Thank you so much,' Jenny gushed. 'It's a lovely picture frame.'

'You're very welcome.' Alison smiled down at the child. 'And guess what, Jenny? We're getting a little girl of our own soon. We're adopting her all the way from Russia, in a few months' time. What do you think of that?'

112

'What's her name?' asked Jenny.

'Nina.'

'Is she pretty?'

'Well, she's clever. When we bring her back, maybe your mum will drive you over so the two of you can play?' Alison looked to Miriam for an answer. 'If it's not too much that is. The roads to our place can be tricky.'

'I'm sure I'll manage,' said Miriam tartly. 'I can go through the Talbot estate.'

'The Talbot estate?' asked Alison.

'Down there.' Miriam pointed to the sprawl of houses bleeding out from the city's edges. 'You go through that housing scheme there and it brings you out at the bottom of Lough Carberry.'

'Oh, is that so?'

'Third turning on the right after you leave our house and follow the signs for Lough Carberry. Easy. No need to bother with dreadful country roads.' Her expression brightened. 'Now,' she said, 'time for a drink, I think. Time to enjoy the celebrations. I'll get someone else to keep an eye on the bouncy castle if you can get the barbeque going, Hugh.' She turned on her heel and marched off in a heady waft of perfume.

Hugh broke the awkward silence. 'Still a bit touchy, I'm afraid. She's pretty embarrassed about what happened.'

'That's understandable.' Alison was sympathetic.

'You know that Woody Allen line from *Annie Hall*, "I'll walk to the kerb from here"?' Hugh checked over his shoulder. 'Well, that's my Miriam.' He grinned. 'Now, I'd better go and light that barbeque or I'll really be in trouble.'

Hugh headed off across the lawn, leaving Luke and Alison alone.

'Alison, what on earth possessed you?' asked Luke as soon as

Hugh was out of earshot. 'I mentioned that accident to you in confidence. Why did you bring it up?'

A few weeks earlier Miriam had skidded off a country road, ending up in the ditch. She had to be rescued by a farmer.

'I suppose it was a bit tactless.' Alison looked sheepish. 'Still, there's no need for Miriam to be so sensitive.'

Luke shook his head. He was relieved to see that when he next spotted their hostess, she seemed to have forgotten all about narrow country roads. She was sharing a laugh with someone and topping up her glass of wine.

With the barbeque billowing smoke, Hugh came looking for Luke. He'd rounded up the other guys and they all headed for the shed, where there was a well-stocked fridge.

'Well, fellas, what do you think?' Hugh asked, handing around more beers.

Hugh was keen to demonstrate the progress he'd made on restoring a dilapidated old VW camper van he'd bought.

'She's looking good,' Luke responded.

Personally, he was more interested in boats than cars. He'd recently purchased a small inflatable with an outboard motor, anticipating taking Nina out on the water when they got her back to Clare.

'I needed another interest,' Hugh muttered to Luke. 'Something that won't get me into trouble with Miriam.'

'She doesn't know, does she?'

'Fuck no,' Hugh whispered, his eyes darting around to check the others. 'What goes on tour, stays on tour, remember?'

'Of course.'

Hugh turned back to the group of guys. 'It's great to have you all here in my man-shed,' he said cheerily. 'Not that I get much time out here. I only get to come out after the kids are fast asleep in bed.'

He pulled a face then turned to Luke.

'You'll know all about that soon, with your new arrival.' He gave Luke a friendly slap on the back.

'Here's hoping.' Luke raised his bottle.

Hugh lit a cigar and offered the other to any takers. No one was interested, and he pretended to be disappointed. Hugh was dedicated to his work, and personable with it. At the hospital, everyone liked him.

'I'm kind of nervous about the adoption,' Luke confessed, opening another beer. 'I'm looking forward to it too, though. You seem more than happy with your gang.'

'Smug is the word I'd use,' came a poke from Hugh's younger brother.

'And why wouldn't I be smug?' said Hugh in riposte. 'My kids are wonderful.'

Hugh's brother turned to Luke. 'See what I mean?'

Luke laughed.

When it came time to head back to the house, the other guys walked ahead. Luke was left sauntering behind with Hugh. 'Alison's a natural with kids,' Hugh said encouragingly. 'It'll all be great, just you wait and see.' He looked at Luke with a glint in his eye. 'I don't know if I mentioned it but my sister, Shirley, and her husband in the States – they adopted a kid last year as well. His swimmers were lazy buggers too.'

Luke stopped. He stared at Hugh, gobsmacked. Why the hell did everyone assume he had a problem with his fertility? And why the hell did they feel obliged to let him know? It amounted to an assault on his masculinity, however unintentional. For all Hugh Smyth bloody knew, Luke could sire a nation. A continent in fact. Luke could probably open his own fucking donor clinic if he so wished.

'Sorry, pal, no offence,' said Hugh, realising he'd overstepped the mark.

Luke opened his mouth to protest, but then he stopped. They'd agreed Alison's condition would remain between the two of them. Their business. No matter how bruised Luke felt, he wouldn't breach that trust. He clamped his mouth, saying nothing more. It was tough but there was nothing for it. His pride would have to suffer.

Back on the patio, smoke continued to billow from the barbeque. Miriam was manoeuvring sausages with one hand and holding a wineglass in the other. Her hair, which had been pinned up, was now loose and she pushed at her fringe as she tried to peer through the smoke.

'I'll do that, Miriam,' said Hugh, taking the tongs. 'Can you get more beers?'

Still smarting from the slight, Luke knocked back his bottle. He stood on the patio looking down over the city. He enjoyed the feel of the cold beer hitting the back of his throat. Out on the lawn, Alison was braiding the hair of Hugh's youngest daughter.

All afternoon, Luke had watched as Alison drifted comfortably around the party. She included adults and children alike, laughing at anecdotes, or slipping to her hunkers to engage a child. Now, hours later, high heels off, she was jumping on the bouncy castle as carefree as the kids. Hugh caught Luke smiling fondly at her.

'What did I tell you?' said Hugh. 'A total natural.' He put an arm around Luke's shoulders trying to smooth over his earlier blunder. 'You'll stay around to watch the match, won't you?'

Ireland would be playing a soccer match that evening.

'Yeah, why not?' said Luke. 'Not sure we're in with a chance though. Think we could be flogging a dead horse.'

'Excuse me, everyone!' Miriam clinked a champagne bottle with a spoon. She was on the patio. She swayed a little. 'Can I have your attention, please?'

Hugh looked at his wife, bemused.

'I know it hasn't been formally announced yet, but seeing as we're all gathered here to celebrate Jenny's communion, we have some other news to share.'

She glanced at Hugh.

His expression changed.

'No, Miriam.' He looked concerned. 'Not now.'

'Don't be silly, Hugh. Everyone'll know next week anyway.'

She began to twist the cork.

'My clever husband has just been offered the post of consultant cardiothoracic surgeon at St Matthew's!'

She popped the cork.

Hugh looked mortified. Luke was gutted. And Alison, well, Alison's face looked like thunder.

The door to Terence's office opened just a crack. 'Sorry to interrupt you. It's just that the dentist's surgery and the solicitors upstairs are all complaining about the noise.' The receptionist directed her gaze at Terence. 'Everyone is phoning, wondering if it's your car again.'

Luke had been so absorbed in telling what had happened at the communion party that he hadn't even noticed the alarm.

'What a nuisance. I'm really sorry.' Blue ink stained Terence's lips and he looked like one of Luke's cardiac patients. He'd been chewing the top of his biro.

'I'll go out and sort it if you like?' Through the half-open door the receptionist held out her hand, uncomfortable that she had interrupted the session.

'Would you? Thanks.' Terence handed her a bunch of keys.

She smiled indulgently before closing the door softly.

Terence pulled a face as he returned to Luke. 'I don't know how she puts up with me. I couldn't manage without her.'

The same thought had occurred to Luke more than once. But in a few short minutes Terence would have more on his mind than a noisy car alarm.

'I just want to say, Terence, that what I'm about to tell you doesn't make for easy listening.'

Outside, the car alarm stopped wailing. Terence looked at Luke, somewhat uncertain.

'That's OK,' he said. 'Go ahead.'

White Bird Falling

Luke had lived that day over and over again in his head. He'd examined over and over again all the things he might have done. All the things he could have done. All the things he should have done. He closed his eyes and began. He was faltering at first, nervous. It all came spooling back in slow motion. Every last horrible detail. Starting with him and Alison in the car. On their way home from that communion party at the Smyths.

'The third turning to the right, isn't that what she said?' Luke looked in the wing mirror, unsure now whether they'd passed one or two turnings. He hadn't intended to drink as much and it would have been bad manners to refuse the champagne. It would have looked like sour grapes.

'Smug bitch,' Alison hissed. 'Did you see the look on Miriam's face?'

'She was happy for her husband. That was all. You'd have been exactly the same.'

If Alison hadn't poked in her nose in the first place they could have been the ones celebrating now. Luke was definitely a more experienced candidate than Hugh.

One mile or two?

They hadn't come this way before. What was it Miriam had

said? His head was foggy and he couldn't recall. They passed a row of houses, national flags hanging from the windows. It was dusk and the road was deserted. Everyone was indoors watching the match.

Luke would have liked to stay at Hugh's to watch it with the guys, as planned, but Alison had wanted to leave. Luke was trying to focus, looking ahead through the fly-flecked windscreen. They should surely have come to that turning for the Talbot estate by now?

'Why the hell do you have to be so fucking gracious all the time?'

Alison shook with anger. The truth was Luke wasn't feeling the slightest bit gracious. But he wasn't stooping to humiliate himself by displaying his disappointment in public.

'It's just the way these things go, Alison. My turn will come.'

The canopy of trees was low, some of the branches almost touching the roof. The verges were in need of attention.

'That's what you said in Edinburgh. That's what you said in London. And now here!' She was shouting.

God, he felt like opening the door, jumping out of the car, and walking home.

'I'm young in my position, you know that. I'm doing well. Another promotion is just a matter of time.'

'But you deserved *this* post.' Her tone more shrill now. 'You've got way more experience than Hugh bloody Smyth. That job should be yours.'

'I'm not suggesting this is the case but Hugh trained under McCarthy, one of the professors on the panel. That may have gone in his favour.' Luke didn't care to say it, but the more he thought about it, the timing of Alison's recent dinner party had been seen for what it was. Canvassing for the position.

He was concentrating, looking for that elusive turning, now doubting the directions they'd been given earlier. Alison wasn't paying attention, blinded as she was with fury. She'd been nursing it these past few hours.

'Hugh Smyth stole that job from right underneath your nose and you don't even care, Luke. Do you?'

Shut up, Alison. Just shut the fuck up.

Luke kept his eyes on the road but from the corner of his eye he could feel her turn to glare at him, the force of her gaze penetrating him.

'Well, do you?' she shouted.

Taking his eyes off the road, he turned to look at her.

Thud!

A whiteness swirled, a somersault – a malformed pirouette against a darkening sky. A sickening sound.

Crash!

A glass cobweb spreads across the windscreen . . . something rolls across smearing it in red. A white mass slides off the bonnet.

He blinks in slow motion . . . the brakes are screeching.

Alison screams.

'Jesus! Jesus Christ!'

The car shudders to a stop.

His neck is stiff. His body tight. His brain races ahead without him. He doesn't want to do this. He knows he has to. Slowly, slowly, he twists his head. It hurts. It throbs. His head is turning, his eyes don't want to see what might be there.

No. Oh no, please God, no . . .

The limbs are awkward . . . unnatural.

Splayed on the road.

He holds his breath. Is there movement? A tiny movement? Down the road he sees something poking out of the ditch.

A bike. Its pink wheel buckled. Time stops. He stares. Absorbing. Processing. Everything goes still. His hand reaches for the door handle, training taking over.

A hand grabs him.

'*No, Luke. No . . .*'

Her grip is tight. But he has a job to do. He can't sit here. He prises Alison's fingers away and wills himself from the car. He is first responder.

The sweet sound of birdsong is jarring. There's no traffic. Nothing but the birds. In the fading light he places one foot in front of the other. He sees something. On the tarmac. A silver tiara. Some of its coloured jewels are missing. He wonders if they were there before the impact, or had the impact knocked them from their sockets?

He wants to run. His legs are heavy. Like lead. They won't let him. A trail of blood pools out from under the white dress.

Click clack.

The sound of high heels comes behind him on the road.

Alison tears past him. He is groggy. Alison reaches her first. There are weights in his shoes. Alison bends to look, her head angling to the right, to the left, then back at Luke. She shakes her head. She straightens. She walks towards him, blocking him, jaw set, eyes hard. He tries to push past her but she stops him. Her nails are digging into his arms.

'She's gone, Luke. She's gone.'

'No . . .'

He tries to free his arm. Her nails are sharp and he feels a sudden warmth. She's drawn blood. He winces.

'There's nothing you can do, Luke. *Think.*'

Pain sears through his arm.

'Out of my way, Alison. Let me—'

'No, Luke. We have to go. Get out of here . . .'

'We can't just—'

'Yes. Yes, we can. We have to.' Her voice is urgent.

'But—'

'What about Nina? *Stop*. Think about this.'

Her eyes are rounds of stone.

'You think we'll be allowed to adopt after this?'

Her words burn into him. He's sobering up.

'Luke, think about this. There's *nothing* we can do . . .'

She shakes her head. She is calm.

'The child is dead, Luke. *Your career . . . you work with children*. Look at you, you've been drinking. You think anyone will want to see you again after knocking down a child? Our little girl is waiting for us in that awful orphanage in Moscow. She will *never* get her mummy and daddy. We promised her we were coming back for her . . . you *promised* her, Luke. I was there. I heard you. Pinky promise, remember?'

The birds sing sweetly into the fading light. His mind is playing tricks. Little Nina appears right in front of him, here on the roadside. He sees her shining eyes, her trust. Her faith that they will return for her. Her little finger entwined in his. The pinky promise.

What should he do?

What can he do?

The child yards away in the white communion dress . . . in her white and blood red dress . . . is dead. There's nothing he can do for her. But Nina?

His training demands he stay here. Civility demands it. Humanity demands it. But in doing so, he'll be inflicting grievous hurt on a trusting child thousands of miles away. Nina is waiting for them. And Alison is right, they will never come. Nina will

123

always wonder what became of the couple who'd promised her a happy life with them. His mind reels back to his Aunt Christine's house. He's five years old.

He's lying in bed wondering why Mum and Dad are spending so long at this bloody wedding. He shouldn't say bloody. Mum doesn't like it. Doesn't Mum have to go to work in the hospital? What about all Dad's patients? Luke isn't the only one waiting for his parents. When are they coming back? Aunt Christine is nice enough but she's no fun. She doesn't know anything about kids. She makes him eat eggy bread. Every night after his prayers he tells himself they'll be home tomorrow. He makes himself believe it. He nearly believes it. But they never come. He has a pain in his tummy.

Is he going to do all this to Nina? His career will be over. Working in paediatric medicine? Not any more. It was the only thing that had defined him until recently. He'd been looking forward to fatherhood. He thinks about little else on his walks in the woods by Lough Carberry. Alison is right. However unthinkable it is to leave the scene, what matters now is Nina.

'A little girl in an orphanage is expecting us in two months' time.' Alison's eyes pierce his. 'Are we going to let her down? Are we?'

Alison is grabbing his sleeve, pulling him back towards the car. He allows her. Stumbling, snatching glances at the child lying in the spreading pool of blood. Her legs are splayed, the bloodied netting of her dress not even affording her the dignity of covering her legs. He wants to go back, to cover the little girl, but Alison is propelling him away.

She takes control, getting into the driver's seat, taking off without so much as a look over her shoulder. He feels sober now. Cold with shock. He knows just how heinous this is. They pick up speed. It is difficult to see with the shattered windscreen. Somehow

Alison finds the elusive turning and they find themselves driving through the Talbot estate without meeting another car.

Luke gawps out the passenger window. Stupefied. Horrified. Everything is surreal. The enormity of what they have done heightened by the eeriness outside. Block after block of housing is deserted, the only signs of life are the flags flapping in the breeze from bedroom windows. The whole country is indoors watching the match.

In the failing light, a lone black dog darts out and chases them for a couple of blocks before retiring. A hunched woman on a Zimmer frame looks as they speed by. Alison drives in silence, ignoring speed limits, stopping only to check a road sign at the junction. A left turn and there are eight more miles to the lough.

Luke sees the dent on the bonnet. He feels a sudden rush of lucidity. *What the hell are they doing? What is he thinking?* He is a medically trained professional. What he is doing is unconscionable.

'*Stop!* Turn around, Alison. NOW. We're going back.'

She ignores him.

'Do you hear me, Alison? I want to go back.'

'Get a grip, Luke. We're nearly there.'

'I mean it . . .'

He grabs the wheel. Suddenly and without warning there is a tinkling sound. Beads of glass spray onto their laps. The windscreen has disintegrated completely.

'Christ!'

Alison brakes, shaking glass from her hands.

She keeps on driving.

'You want to kill us both as well?' she screams. 'Get a grip.'

Exposed to the elements, the wind whips around their faces. The chill wraps itself around his midriff and he starts to shake.

Splinters pierce his trousers. He stares at them. Luke looks up. It dawns on him they are not heading to the Glasshouse as he'd thought.

'Where are we going?' he shouts, the wind taking his breath away.

'To sort this out,' Alison shouts back.

Haunted

A deathly lull had descended on Terence's office. Luke opened his eyes, bracing himself for a reaction.

'Now you know who I am,' he said. 'Not the respectable, charitable, humanitarian everyone thinks,' he prompted.

Was Terence about to reach for his phone? Or would he wait until Luke had left before he called the police?

Silence.

'I've lived with what I've done for all these years. I can't take it any more,' said Luke. 'I need help.'

Still nothing.

Terence's expression was hard to decipher, his eyes inscrutable. Both men surveyed one another, a weighty pocket of silence between them. There was no sound but the low hum of Terence's computer. The therapist displayed no overt signs of shock or any obvious signs of revulsion.

Luke waited. After some time, Terence cleared his throat. 'I'm not too sure what I was expecting you to disclose, but I assumed it was going to be something . . . difficult. What you have just told me is utterly tragic.' He looked at Luke as if he were trying to figure something out. 'Have you told me everything? Is there more to this?'

127

Luke looked down at his hands. Strange. They seemed steady. Inside he was shaking. 'There is,' he said.

'Do you want to tell me?' Terence prompted. 'Do you feel safe to talk about it?'

'Give me a moment.' Luke's throat was dry. He took a long drink of water. He rested the glass back on the table.

'In your own time,' Terence said.

Leaning back and closing his eyes, Luke crawled back to the place where he'd left off.

They were at Crow Hall. Darkness had fallen and it was chilly under the clear sky. Luke could make out the shape of a cat slinking along the walls of the stone outhouses before disappearing around the corner. A harsh glare came from the security lights in the yard. Wearing a blanket and clutching a hipflask, Alison stood at his side. Luke shivered, scant warmth provided by his blazer.

As the machine lurched into action, he felt a deepening horror at the sickening crunch of the compacter. Metal crunching on metal. Cornelius Thompson had launched into action straightaway. They'd get rid of the car immediately. A load of scrap was due to be collected from Crow Hall the following Monday so the evidence would be off the premises inside forty-eight hours.

Cornelius approached the task with such composure and efficiency that Luke had a horrible feeling it may not have been the first time he'd used the compacter to make something disappear. His demeanour was urgent but business-like.

Crows cawed into the dark as Cornelius worked, his brow furrowing in concentration in the yellow glow of the cabin. There was something disturbing about the way he smacked his lips together, a macabre elation, a foulness that sat easily on his face. Luke felt like he'd thrown flesh to a monster.

As the compacter ground to a halt, Alison sighed beside him. She offered him the hipflask. He shook his head. More alcohol was not what he needed. She screwed the top back on and linked his arm.

'This is wrong,' he said. He pulled away from her. They did not deserve the comfort of one another after what they'd done.

'We had no choice,' she said. Tears trickled down her cheeks.

As the yard fell into rural silence, Cornelius made his way towards them, his deerstalker pulled low, concealing his face.

'Inside. Now,' he said. 'You'll stay here tonight.'

Whatever Luke's anguish and reservations, Cornelius didn't want to know. 'We've said all we're going to say about what happened,' said Cornelius. 'From what you tell me, Alison, it sounds like you may not have been seen. Fortunately for you both, I think the whole country was watching the match. And even if it's the case that you were seen, there's no proof now. There's no longer a car. There's no evidence. So this is what we do. *Nothing.* We lie low. We don't mention it, not even among ourselves. Understand?'

They were standing in the dark terrazzo passageway between the kitchen and the drawing room. Luke stared at Cornelius, unable to form an answer, horror-struck by what had happened, aghast at Cornelius's response.

'We understand, Dad. Don't we, Luke?' Alison sniffed. She had mistaken Luke's silence for acceptance.

'No. Sorry, I can't do this.' A wave of revulsion rolled over him. 'I just can't. It's wrong.'

'What are you talking about, man? Let's get a brandy inside you,' said Cornelius. 'You're in shock.'

His father-in-law's acceptance of the situation made it more grotesque. Luke was escorted by the arm into the drawing room and a large brandy thrust into his hand. He sank onto the sofa and stared into the yawning chasm of the empty fireplace. Without a fire, the room was like a crypt.

A white-faced Alison sat in Cornelius's armchair. She also had a brandy in hand. She started to shiver. Cornelius draped her in his lap-rug.

'The longer we wait, the worse this gets,' said Luke. He didn't touch the brandy. He wasn't supping with the devil. He eyed the landline on the writing desk. 'We need to phone the police.'

'Now you listen to me, lad. Think this through.' Cornelius had followed his eyes to the phone. 'What good can come of that? You've run someone over and of course that is tragic. But what's done is done. Think of that child waiting for you in Russia. Are you going to let that poor orphan down?'

Luke sat tortured and silent. Two sets of eyes bored into him, waiting for an answer. He listened to the steady ticking of the ugly, carved grandfather clock in the corner. He said nothing.

Alison knocked back her drink and stood, hugging the rug around her.

'I think I'll have a hot bath and a lie down.'

'You do that, Ali,' said Cornelius. 'You've had a shock. I think one of the bedrooms at the back is made up.'

Alison headed for the door. 'Are you coming, Luke?' she asked in a small voice.

He stared hopelessly into the empty fireplace. 'No.'

The door closed and he was left with Cornelius.

'This is so fucked up,' he said.

Cornelius rounded on him. 'What happened tonight was a terrible, terrible accident. I told you once, not so long ago, that we stick together around here. We especially stick together at Crow Hall.' His eyes crawled up the blackened chimney breast to the carved limestone plaque. It was dated 1624 and bore the

Thompson family crest. 'That's exactly what's going to happen now. What happened was awful. That said, you are not going to bring down this family. If you choose to do that, and if you choose to take my daughter with you, as God is my witness, I'll finish you off altogether. Do you hear me?'

Luke stood, placing the brandy on the coffee table.

'I think I'll head to bed now, Cornelius.'

'Good idea,' said Cornelius, more conciliatory. 'You've had a shock and you're not thinking straight.' His rheumy eyes were hooded. 'Get some rest. And grab hold of yourself, man. All you need to remember is that nothing happened.'

Luke remembered lying on damp-smelling sheets on a lumpy mattress in a back bedroom that no one had slept in for years. The bedroom was at the eastern gable of the house. It had a large open chimney. Each time he rolled into the well in the mattress next to a lavender-scented Alison, he pulled himself away.

He stared at the ceiling, at the brass light-fitting fashioned like a deer's antlers. A stag's head stared at him from a far wall, its dead eyes looking at him. He wondered what the child would look like when they found her? Would her eyes be wide, pupils blown, never again to follow the nearby birds swooping from branch to branch, to see the sun burn as it did tonight, pink and orange as it bowed and dipped below the horizon?

He must have dozed off, and waking with a start, his eyes adjusted to the gloom. He couldn't move. He felt a weight on his chest. There, in the chimney well, was a child in a white pinafore. Was it the ghost of Marigold Piper? The child who'd disappeared centuries earlier? Here, hovering in the membrane between this world and the next? Or was it the ghost of the child he'd just killed? His breath came in panicked bursts. He blinked and she was gone. Had he imagined it? Was he losing his mind?

'Luke . . .'

He was startled back to the present, to the garish fluorescent lights of Terence Black's office. He was tired. Very tired. He tasted the salt of his tears as they moved towards his mouth. He plucked a tissue from the box.

'I think I get some sense of the burden you've been carrying,' Terence opened.

Luke held up his hands. 'Don't worry. I didn't come here looking for absolution or redemption.'

Terence uncrossed his legs. 'I'm not in a position to offer anything like that. I left the priesthood years ago.' He smiled wanly. 'But tell me something.' He leaned in close. 'I know I've asked you this before. I'll ask you again. Do you, Luke Forde, think you are a good person?'

Luke was taken aback.

'How could any sane person think themselves a decent human being after what I've told you?'

'Well, the person I see here before me is a thinking human being,' Terence said softly. 'A caring man who did a terrible thing. Tormented because of what he has done. What I say to you, is this: you can still own up to what happened. At any time. Even now, after all this time. There's a family out there somewhere who want to know what happened to their daughter.'

He paused to study Luke. 'You don't need to do it today, tomorrow, or even next week,' he added. 'Think about it. Weigh it up. You'll arrive at the answer in your own time.'

Terence's computer whirred into the fetid air. There was no judgement in the room. No opprobrium. Most people would be repulsed by Luke's disclosure. And rightly so. Yet Terence's expression remained one of stoic contemplation. He sat calmly, giving Luke space to breathe.

'You have lived with this for a very long time. I feel confident that you will do the right thing. I have some experience of this in a previous life, and I know that life is a long song.'

Luke shook his head. 'I know exactly who I am, what I am,' he said. 'I lost my way a long time ago. For me there's no way back.'

'There's a way back for everyone,' said Terence. 'You've shared enough for today. For now, this remains strictly between us. You might book something with my receptionist outside. Ideally in the next day or two.'

Luke stood up. His legs felt hollow. Despite Terence's hope for his redemption, Luke was headed for damnation. For there was worse to come.

No Worst, There is None

Luke recalled those lurid bulletins as the story broke. The crime reporter painting the scene, lasciviously. Breathless at the tragedy of it all. Titillating the viewers as he led the camera to the police tape on the cordoned road. And all the while, checking back over his shoulder, connecting with the viewer, wetting his lips and panting.

It had been years since Luke had spoken about it. Alison was the only person he could have discussed it with. But it was best not spoken about, she said. Best forgotten as Cornelius had advised.

'I'm glad you decided to follow up on our last session as quickly as you did,' said Terence. 'I've been thinking a lot about what you said, as no doubt you'd expect me to. I imagine you have as well.'

'I have.' Luke took a breath and prepared himself. 'You see after the . . . the accident, things took another turn . . .'

'I'm listening.'

Luke's words came in fits and starts. The clock on the filing cabinet ticked loudly as if wanting to drown him out. He imagined himself like a snake crawling out of his skin and slithering off to hide in the undergrowth.

He was back in Crow Hall. Staring at the TV screen, trembling in the doorway of the library, watching the horror unfold.

Alison and her father were on the sofa. Cornelius had a supporting arm round his daughter. Outside, it was as sunny as the day before. But the library was cold, dust motes floating high above the TV screen. Luke leaned against the dark panelling of the door recess for support.

The crime reporter went through the details of the previous day. First communion day for many in the county. Everyone enjoying the sunshine and looking forward to the prospect of watching the soccer later that evening.

There was footage of children smiling outside churches, boys like young James Bonds and girls in frothy dresses. Happy scenes cut with video of houses decked with flags, bunting draped on trees and hedges. Luke stared at the TV, hypnotised. A live camera panned to the edge of the road, to the wheel of a pink bike in a ditch, forlorn.

'For one family, the twenty-seventh of May is a day they won't forget,' the reporter said. 'A day of celebration that so quickly turned to tragedy.' The reporter stopped to lick his lips. 'Young Maisie had cycled to a neighbour's house. She promised to show her communion dress to the pensioner who was wheelchair-bound. It was Maisie's first time on the main road, her father agreeing to let her cycle as it was quiet with people indoors watching the match.'

The reporter paused, his expression troubled. 'Unfortunately for Maisie, there was someone else using this road last night . . . someone who knocked little Maisie down. Her bike . . .' the reporter angled his head, '. . . as you can see here behind me, was found a good twenty yards away.'

The reporter's eyes squinted in the sunlight as he looked directly at the camera, his voice dropping, affecting greater sincerity. 'Information from the police so far suggests that this tragic incident went unseen. So far, no one has come forward except a young local priest who happened upon the scene. Ironically, the priest had been on his way to administer last rites to a parishioner when he came upon the injured child. Emergency services arrived quickly after that and little Maisie was taken to St Matthew's University Hospital where a trauma team worked into the night trying to save her.' The reporter paused. 'Unfortunately, little Maisie lost her fight for life at six-fifteen this morning.'

Luke gasped. His eyes darted to Alison. She was staring blankly at the TV. Had this even registered with her? The child had *not* been dead, she'd been alive. Alison said the child was dead but she was wrong, she was alive. *ALIVE* . . .

'. . . can contact the incident room on . . .' The reporter was still talking.

Horrified, Luke tried to follow the rest of the report.

'It appears that the injured child lay on the road for some considerable time before discovery. A normally busy road, it would seem that most local people were absorbed with the country's fortunes in the soccer match. And tragically, for little Maisie it would appear that what the medics call the golden hour, was lost.'

Luke felt his knees might buckle. White noise engulfed him. Fear, regret and deep self-loathing screamed inside his skull. To think the child had been *alive*, this was the worst. There could be nothing worse. How would he bear this revelation? What had befallen him? He could have saved her. What had happened to his guiding moral code, 'Do no harm'?

The impact of the accident and his negligence bore down on him. He was guilty of murder. Here he was, a medical professional tasked with administering care to the ill and dying, and he'd knocked down a child, abandoning her to die on the road. He might have saved her; because of his inaction a child was dead.

Why had he taken Alison's word? He should have confirmed her vital signs himself. He thought the child had been killed outright. That was horrendous enough, but this? To think he could have saved her. He would never bear it.

'She was alive, Alison,' he whispered. 'She was alive when we left her. Did you hear what the reporter said? Alive.'

He said it not in accusation, just repeating the fact.

'I think she gets that, Luke.' Cornelius adjusted his glasses and pushed the *off* button on the remote. Alison stared out the window at the horses, her expression unfathomable.

'I could have saved her,' said Luke.

'You don't know that,' came Cornelius's swift reply. The old man creaked to his feet. 'What happened was terrible . . . of course it was. You knocked a child down. It was an accident. Accidents happen.' He shuffled to the drinks cabinet. 'We've been through all of this. There's nothing to be gained from blaming Alison . . . or yourself.' He tugged at a cork.

Luke had never been more certain about anything in his life. It *was* his fault. What he'd done was unforgivable. Even if he could find a way to bear what he had done, he knew that it would stain every waking and sleeping moment for the rest of his life.

Cornelius poured two glasses of cognac. Luke watched him shuffle back across the creaking floorboards and hand one to his daughter. With a steady hand she took the glass.

'I said it last night and I'll say it again. What we do is lay low, keep our cool.' Cornelius sipped his drink. 'You too, Luke,' he added as if suddenly remembering that Luke was part of this. 'We carry on as normal.'

'Normal?'

Luke's incredulity went unremarked as Alison and Cornelius fell into a conversation of their own. Did Cornelius have any idea what *normal* was, Luke asked himself? It wasn't any version of normal that Luke had known. He felt himself sinking deeper and deeper into the mire of Crow Hall. He felt lost.

'Are you OK, Luke? We can stop here if you like?'

'What . . .?' Luke found himself hauled back to the present, staring mindlessly at the rubber plant in the room. He curiously noted how all the leaves bar one had been swept free of dust.

'I can see this disclosure is traumatic . . .'

'It's OK, I'm fine,' he lied.

'Very well, if you're sure. You were talking about you and Alison carrying on as normal,' said Terence encouragingly.

'Normal,' Luke repeated. He shook his head. 'I guess I must have loved Alison once. Or at least the idea of who I thought she was. Back then, like now, she was always full of surprises.'

'Can you elaborate on that?'

'I'll try.'

Luke began.

Alison was sticking to her father's advice. She didn't speak about what happened. In the days that followed, she immersed herself in her new PR business and horse riding. Unlike Alison, Luke was in turmoil. He spent as much time as he could at the hospital, and the time he did spend at home, he spent writing papers. The thrill of moving to the Glasshouse was gone. When an architectural magazine asked if they could come and photograph the house, Alison was excited. Her enthusiasm confounded him. How did she have the capacity to find pleasure in anything?

Then one night, Luke arrived home late from the High Dependency Unit. There had been a suspicion of endocarditis with a patient who'd been fitted with a defibrillator. It hadn't been a patient of Luke's, but he'd stayed, maintaining vigil long after the team assured him they were competent to manage the situation.

The truth was that he was more comfortable in the hospital than at home.

Returning to the Glasshouse and waiting for the gates to open, he could see the house was in darkness. He guessed Alison had gone to bed. She seemed able to sleep. Inside the house, his footsteps echoed off the marble floors and the smell of fresh paint filled his nostrils.

At the rear of the house, through the glass in the garden room, he could see the gently lapping water of the lough reflecting off the walls in the moonlight. The rain from earlier in the day had cleared and it was beautiful, but he couldn't allow himself to be soothed. Anguish was his new companion. Collapsing onto the sofa, he reached for the TV remote.

All day he'd kept busy. But it had been there in his mind all the time, the fact that the funeral was today. He flicked through the channels, searching for the news, hoping in a way not to find it. He skimmed past it at first then backtracked to the local channel. With a knot in his gut, he stared at the screen. The church was overflowing, a large crowd outside, solemn-faced in the rain as they listened to the eulogy on a loudspeaker.

The bulletin reported all sections of society were represented at the funeral. The Mayor was there and the President had sent his aide-de-camp. All decent society was appalled that a child celebrating her first communion had been mown down and left to die on a usually busy road.

Luke stared at the screen. The crowd parted. Four pall-bearers, heads downcast, appeared at the mouth of the church, carrying a coffin. A white coffin. A couple, arms linked and dressed in black, appeared behind.

The parents.

As someone stepped forward to protect them with an umbrella, the mother stumbled and buried her face against the father's shoulder. The crowd gasped. A guard of honour lined the path to the hearse and two rows of children in school uniform wiped their faces as rain and tears streamed down their cheeks. Luke thought his skull would explode. Suddenly, he was rigid. *He couldn't have seen that. He'd imagined it.* His mind was playing tricks. Such a thing would be obscene. Straightening himself, he watched as mourners approached the bereaved couple, shaking hands, moving off, wiping away tears.

And . . . there she was.

His stomach lurched.

It was her.

There was no mistake. There she was. Stepping into their space, bending her head, hugging the bereaved mother.

Alison.

He could hardly believe what he was seeing. His wife's back was to the camera as she lingered a while, then turning, tissue in hand, she patted underneath her eyes. He was aghast. What was she doing?

In the days before the funeral, Luke and Alison had observed their code of silence. There hadn't been a single mention of the accident or the upcoming funeral. He was happy to stay out of Alison's way, much as, he imagined, she was happy to stay out of his, both too upset to face what lay between them. But this? Alison going to the dead child's funeral, paying her respects to the child's parents? It was grotesque.

Turning the TV off, Luke got to his feet. Upstairs, moonlight streamed through the enormous glass rooflight bathing the mezzanine hallway in its soft glow. A sliver of light shone through a crack in the bedroom door. He could hear Alison breathing. He went to the side of the bed and stood looking down at her. She was in a deep sleep.

'Alison?'

No response.

'Alison?' More loudly now.

'What . . .?' She opened her eyes. She pushed herself back on the pillow. 'Jesus! What is it? Why are you staring at me like that?'

'I've just seen the news . . . coverage of the funeral.'

'Yes. And . . .?'

She looked puzzled.

'You were there, Alison. I saw you. On the TV. You actually went to that child's funeral – commiserated with the parents.'

She sat upright.

'Yes, that's right, I did.'

'Can you explain to me why you would do such a thing?'

'Of course I can.'

She spoke slowly as if she were explaining a difficult concept to a child.

'The President's aide-de-camp was going. All the figures in local public life were going. Dad wanted to go too but he had chest pain this morning. Someone had to go to represent him.'

Moonlight had illuminated one side of her face, making her seem ethereal and angel-like; the other side was in shadow. Outside, where the lawn fell away to the shore he noticed a fluttering. Night-time creatures winged by. Bats, he guessed.

'Are you going to stand there and stare at me all night?' she said after a while.

'I could stand here and stare at you for the rest of my life and I'd never understand what you've just done.'

She fell silent, considering his response. Then sliding under the sheet again, she said, 'Come to bed, Luke. It's late. You'll feel differently in the morning.'

But Luke did not join his wife that night. He turned his back on her, not leaving the bedroom door ajar but shutting it firmly behind him. He returned to the lower floor. He swung his legs up on the sofa and covered them with a throw. There he stayed in the moonlight, staring out at the lough until dawn streaked the sky, cold and unforgiving.

'I'm sorry, Luke. Can we pause there a moment?' Terence held up a finger. Sounds outside his office heralded the arrival of another client. 'Let me just check on something.'

As he went out into the hallway, he left the door ajar. Luke could hear him speaking in hushed tones at reception. He tensed. Terence had heard enough. He was probably out there calling for the police.

Diagnosis

Terence re-entered the room. 'I've just asked her to reset my next appointment by half an hour. You've been through a traumatic disclosure. I'd like the chance to put a few things in context for you.'

Luke experienced a sudden surge of panic. This was a delaying tactic, keeping him there until the police arrived. 'There's no need.' He made as if to stand. 'I have to be gone in the next ten minutes. I have a long list back at the hospital.'

'Look, I appreciate you're pressed for time. But I really think you should hear me out, as one professional to another.'

Luke made a quick recalculation. Given Terence's reaction so far, Luke suspected in reality the therapist was unlikely to call the police just yet. It wouldn't be his style. He wanted Luke to come clean on his own terms and he'd already hinted it was in Luke's long-term interests to reveal his part in this nightmare.

Perhaps Luke should stay a little longer. He wasn't in control of himself. He should compose himself before taking off for the hospital. 'Give me a second.' He pulled his mobile from his pocket. He searched for Hugh. They sometimes covered for one another. Maybe he could squeeze in an extra twenty minutes.

Terence waited.

As soon as Luke had finished texting, Terence continued, 'I hear what you've been telling me about Alison and her father, and I'll come to all that later. But for now, I think we both agree that you've been suffering deeply with a post-traumatic stress disorder.'

Luke nodded.

'And if you recall what brought you here to me in the first place, it was your care of a young girl suffering trauma. I'm guessing she too had been in a car accident . . .'

'A hit-and-run,' Luke confirmed. There it was. That awful expression. His mobile pinged. He checked. It was Hugh:

Happy to oblige, if patients happy to settle for little old me of course.

Terence signalled that he should deal with his phone.

Cheers. I owe you.

If Luke's patients had any inkling what he'd done, they'd desert him in droves.

Terence pressed ahead. 'Presumably you've attended other children in similar circumstances since the accident fifteen years ago?' he asked.

'Yes.'

Where was Terence going with this?

'But there was something in particular about this recent accident, something about this recent patient that caused you trauma. There were similarities with what happened fifteen years ago?'

'It wasn't the accident itself,' Luke confessed, 'but the parents' reaction to the hit-and-run that brought it home to me. They couldn't believe that someone could knock their child down and just take off. They couldn't comprehend how someone could leave the scene of an accident . . .' He paused. 'It must have been like that for the parents of the little girl that I . . . that I knocked down all those years ago. It came home to me . . . the enormity of the pain and suffering I had inflicted. It's been with me all this time, it never went away, but to be confronted with it head-on like that . . . it made itself so real to me that night.'

'Would I be right in saying that up until the accident on the twenty-seventh of May fifteen years ago, that you thought yourself a strong person, and you saw yourself in a positive light?'

'Well . . . yes. I'd always derived satisfaction from feeling that I was doing valuable work.'

'That figures.' Terence leaned in, making steeples of his fingers. 'What happened to you is like a shellshock, if you can imagine it like that. A number of assumptions you subconsciously made about yourself have been shattered by this tragedy. Your belief in your own personal invulnerability has been shattered. Your perception of the world as a meaningful place has been destroyed. And thirdly and perhaps most damaging of all – your ability to see yourself in a positive light has been damaged.'

Luke sat back, absorbing what he had heard. 'Yes . . . yes, that's all true,' he said. 'I see what you are saying.'

Terence had summarised his situation perfectly. While Luke had been fumbling about his consciousness trying to articulate these feelings, Terence had come up with an accurate and grim analysis of Luke's mental state. Being able to put into words how he was feeling made Luke feel more in control. For the first time, he felt like someone understood. Forgiveness was not what he was looking for. That was out of the question.

'You're in a profession that seeks to heal and repair people physically,' Terence carried on. 'You enjoy doing good. To heal yourself, you need to rid yourself of this secret. You have made the first step, here, with me. The next step is up to you. What do you want to do next, do you think? What does Luke want?'

Luke had thought about it plenty. He was cautious. 'I need more time.'

'Take all the time you need. You will make the right choice, I know that. And I want you to own that choice.'

Part of Luke hoped that he could somehow reassemble a fractured version of himself. Another part was so tired that he wanted it all to be over. But he couldn't just hand himself in to the police. It wasn't that simple.

And then it came to him. Why not explain to Terence his reluctance to go to the authorities? Why not explain what would happen if he did? Let the therapist decide what was wise. Let him decide if it was worth it.

'Believe me, Terence,' he said, 'I've thought about handing myself in to the police many times. But I'm going to tell you a little story. I'm going to tell you what will happen if *I* do that. Then I'm also going to explain what will happen if *you* do.'

Terence stopped clicking his biro.

'It's not a threat,' Luke spoke softly. 'But you need to know what I'm dealing with. I probably have twenty minutes or so to play with. Do you?'

Terence nodded, looking grave. He checked the clock above the filing cabinet.

'My next appointment isn't until half-past.'

'All right, then . . .'

The time had come to talk about the homecoming.

Daughters

February

'It was nerve-wracking taking Nina out of the orphanage, out of Russia, and back to Ireland for the first time,' Luke said.

'I'm sure it was,' said Terence.

'I remember sitting in the back of the car with Nina, and I remember stopping at the crow-topped pillars to drive up the long avenue to Crow Hall.' He closed his eyes picturing that afternoon.

The gates to the avenue were open. They turned in off the narrow lane. To their right, over the line of hedging, he could see the three large chimney stacks of the former hunting lodge. The hedge obscured the facade of the seventeenth-century house. The place gave Luke the creeps. The single-storey, five-bay lodge had been extended and remodelled over the years. It was an ugly house. Behind the house were the stables and the scrapyard.

Luke's hand tightened on Nina's and he fixed a smile on his face. As they approached they could see everyone waiting on the front porch. A *Welcome* banner was draped across the stone columns on either side of the front door. None of this had been Luke's idea. He'd wanted to take Nina to the Glasshouse, his and Alison's home. Cornelius was turning what should have been a small, intimate, gathering into something resembling a trade delegation. Altogether unfitting and ill-considered for the arrival of a young child with only a few words of English.

'Isn't this sweet?' Alison checked with them in the rear-view mirror.

'Peachy,' said Luke.

'Oh, don't be so sarcastic.'

Alison had been amused by his insistence on sitting in the back with Nina. He was regretting that now, feeling queasy. 'See, Nina.' Alison glanced over her shoulder as she drove. 'Grandpa's organised everyone at Crow Hall to welcome you home.'

'This is Grandpa's home, Nina,' Luke was quick to point out. 'You, me and Mummy have our own home, a short drive from here.'

He wondered how much of the conversation Nina was able to follow. She was nodding, studying his face for clues. She was clever, of that he had no doubt. Since leaving the orphanage, everything was new and foreign to her. He imagined it must be overwhelming. Her face was drawn and white, but in her eyes there burned a curiosity.

When they stopped, she got out eagerly. Alison took her by the hand and escorted her along the waiting line of scrapyard workers. Luke stood back. Cornelius was at the end of the line, watching as Nina dutifully shook each adult hand proffered to her. Her little face was serious. Alison approached Cornelius, looking nervous.

'Nina, this is your grandfather.'

Cornelius stared down over the round of his stomach, as if the child was a foal he was considering buying. Nina looked up. And then she did something unexpected. She pointed a finger just where his shirt strained and separated over his belly. She giggled, a delightful rippling sound, and poked her finger into the well of his belly-button. Cornelius gasped.

'What the . . .'

Everyone burst out laughing. Everyone except Cornelius. He took a humourless step back, aligned the folds of cloth, and tucked his shirt tightly into his trousers. Encouraged by the laughter, Nina tried again. Sensing that Cornelius would react even more unfavourably a second time, Luke scooped her up and hugged her to him.

Cornelius looked like he'd been sucking nettles. Rather than enjoy the innocent humour, he reacted badly. The little girl had humiliated him in front of all his staff. Not the most auspicious start.

'Nina was a plucky kid,' Terence offered.

'Yes, she was,' said Luke. 'Not something that endeared her to her mother.' He fell into silence.

'I shouldn't have interrupted, please carry on.'

Luke picked up. 'Well, a week or so after that there was Nina's naming ceremony. That's when the real fun started.'

Alison had relented on the business of a christening in a church. Luke knew it would only serve as another occasion for Cornelius to hijack. He could picture the pomp, the ceremony, the altar of senior church figures, a congregation of those who owed Cornelius a favour, and those to whom he was indebted. In the end, Luke prevailed. It was a small victory, a rare occurrence.

Though he found lavish occasions a chore, Luke readily engaged in the plans for a naming ceremony. It would be a humanist ceremony held at the Glasshouse, much to Cornelius's disgust. In eschewing a traditional christening, there was a price to be paid. Wendy would be godmother but Roddy Gilligan had to be godfather. Alison insisted. He was one of her longest-standing friends, she said. Gilligan and Wendy, godfather and godmother. It was an odd pairing.

The day of the naming ceremony started well. It was warm. A late September day, the sunlight was honey-yellow before October stripped away the leaves. Nina was agog with all the gifts she'd received. Lego, craft sets, a ballerina music box, and a saddle for a pony from Cornelius. She'd put them in a tidy pile in the corner of the garden room and went outside to skim stones on the lough with his sister, Wendy. Alison was in the house. She was giving Miriam Smyth and Johnny Whelan's girlfriend the grand tour.

Luke left them to it and headed out into the garden. It was all going nicely. Guests chatting on the gently shelving lawn. Kids skimming stones across the water. His inflatable boat was bobbing at the pier. It had aroused some interest. He would take Nina and Hugh Smyth's kids out in it later.

In the weeks leading up to Nina's arrival, Hugh had made several concerned remarks on how Luke seemed withdrawn. Johnny Whelan had taken to slapping Luke on the back, calling him 'Pops', advising him not to let the pre-adoption nerves get to him.

Luke was convinced Hugh knew there was more afoot than pre-adoption nerves. He found it strange that in the days that followed the accident, Hugh had never once mentioned the hit-and-run that had happened a few short miles from his home. He tried not to think about it. Since Nina had arrived, he'd found an occasional smile creep up on him. He'd even felt the odd burst of happiness. Feelings he thought he'd never have again.

'Everything OK?' It was Nicola, Alison's friend from school. 'You look a little sad.'

'Actually, I was thinking about all the people who aren't here to share today,' he said. 'My mum and dad . . . Alison's mother . . .'

'Yeah, that's a shame,' Nicola agreed.

'Both Alison and I have been unfortunate in losing parents.'

'Well, Alison's mum wasn't exactly what you'd call healthy,' Nicola said under her breath. 'That's why Alison was sent away to school. Marguerite wasn't fit for much, poor thing.'

'I know about Alison's mother,' he said.

'What do you make of Alison's dad?' Nicola linked his arm. She directed her attention to Cornelius. He was standing at the water's edge talking to Gilligan.

'We get along just fine.' He was not about to share the inner workings of their relationship with his wife's tipsy friend.

Nicola slurred. 'There's no way you'd be here today if Cornelius didn't think you were up to scratch. None of Alison's boyfriends lasted long.'

'That's teenage flings for you.'

Before she and Luke got together, Alison confessed she'd only had a few brief dalliances at home on holidays from school.

'Still, there's nothing quite like first love, is there?' Nicola looked up at him, a hint of mischief in her eyes. Her pupils were dilated. 'She tell you about hers?'

'Are you sure Alison would want you telling tales?' he cautioned.

She looked doubtful. 'No, I don't suppose she would,' she said, continuing on regardless. 'She didn't want to talk about it back at school. But we all knew she was upset.'

'Oh?' She'd piqued his interest now.

'I never got to the bottom of it.' Nicola's furtive expression changed to one of puzzlement. 'This guy, I think his name was Thomas . . . yeah, yeah, that was it . . . can't remember his surname. Anyway, this guy, he was working as a casual labourer, a stable hand, I think, at Crow Hall. A summer job. He and Alison had this thing together during the school holidays. It was messy, I gather. Lots of fighting and making up. Teenage stuff, like you said. During one of their spats, well, things got a little out of hand, and I'm not exactly sure but I think the guy may have hit her. As you can imagine, Alison's dad went crazy. Apparently he marched the guy out of Crow Hall with a shotgun.'

'Alison never mentioned a thing about it.' Luke was sceptical. He'd already decided he didn't trust Nicola and was beginning to wonder if this was a tall tale.

'The only reason I know anything about it—' she hiccupped, 'is because the police turned up at school.'

'Alison pressed charges?'

'No. Nothing like that.'

Nicola's bloodshot eyes grew larger. 'The reason the police were there was to interview Alison. See, it turned out this Thomas guy, well, he just disappeared after that, and the last place he'd been seen was at Crow Hall.'

This was supposed to be a day of celebration for Nina and Luke had little interest in hearing about his wife's old boyfriends or about odd goings-on at Crow Hall. Heedless of his silence, Nicola rabbited on. 'It was sad for Alison, too, when her mum died. But you know, things always have this way of working out for her.'

'That so?' Luke said tartly.

'Sure.' Nicola's cheeks were red from sun and wine. She waved an expansive arm. 'Alison gets what Alison wants.' There was more than a hint of envy in her tone. 'She has the designer house. A successful business. The good-looking, successful husband. A child. And she got to keep her figure.'

'Keep her figure?' Luke gave a derisory laugh. 'I'm not convinced that's high on Alison's list of priorities.'

'Of course it is . . .' Nicola hiccupped again. 'She always reckoned pregnancy was overrated. Said she never wanted a body-wrecking bump. And Alison got what she'd always wanted. A nice potty-trained four-year-old.'

This woman had no insight whatsoever into Alison's condition nor did she know that a pregnancy would have been unwise. Perhaps deliberately, Alison had never shared her health problems with her friend – if you could even call Nicola a friend. She didn't appear particularly loyal and she was certainly far from discreet.

Luke had endured enough of Nicola and her gossip for now. He freed his arm from hers. 'For the record, Nicola, I'd like to confirm that we're delighted with Nina. My mum and dad would have loved her, and I'm sure Marguerite would have too.' He increased his stride in an effort to shake her off.

Nicola was persistent. She kept up. 'Perhaps it's easier for everyone that Marguerite's not here. For the best . . .'

Luke was not engaging.

'It was cirrhosis that did for Marguerite in the end.'

'I think you're way off there, Nicola,' Luke put her right. Fuck, this woman was annoying. She was hammered. 'Marguerite died of a heart attack.'

'Oh, sure,' she slurred. 'The heart attack finished her off. But the old dear had cirrhosis. Marguerite was an alcoholic – a classic, raging alcoholic. But like you said, you knew all about her, right?'

Luke felt the day was taking a wrong turning. No longer concerned with being polite, he broke away from Nicola, heading back to the house. He'd check if Alison needed any help. He found her in the kitchen, directing the catering staff. In her hand was an antibacterial spray and a cloth.

'Finished the grand tour?' he asked. 'Everything under control?'

'Yes and yes,' she said, looking happy. 'They were most impressed. I sent them outside with a drink while I organise the food.' She sprayed the work surface and rubbed it with the cloth.

'I saw you out there on the lawn with Nicola. She have anything interesting to say?'

'She's pissed so she had plenty to say. I know she's your friend, Alison, but I think she has a loose grip on reality.'

Alison laughed. 'Ah, Nicola's great fun. As she says herself, why tell the truth when you can tell a story?'

Luke was not inclined to agree. 'Will I take the rubbish out?' He pointed to a black refuse sack propped against the wall.

'That's not rubbish. I've just finished bagging Nina's gifts. I'm handing them into the community crèche on Monday.'

'What?' He was astonished.

'Oh, don't look at me like that, Luke. I've left out the music box and the saddle. It's mainly the Lego, and all those craft boxes full of those itty-bitty plastic pieces that are a nightmare to tidy. Anyway, it's far too much stuff for the child. We don't want Nina getting spoiled, do we? The last thing anyone likes is a spoiled child.'

'I hardly think that's going to happen.'

'Even so . . .' Alison continued with her spraying.

Not wanting to argue, Luke headed back outside, resolving to do whatever was needed to rescue the black refuse sack from its fate. He headed down towards the water's edge where Cornelius and Gilligan were still deep in conversation.

The two men stood with their backs to him. They were watching Nina and Wendy who were nearby, skimming stones. Both men had a glass in hand. Luke had been wondering about setting aside his misgivings about Gilligan, especially if he was going to be part of Nina's life. The guy was a prick but perhaps he had redeeming features. If Luke looked hard.

'What do you think? What do you make of those two? The dyke and the duckling.' Cornelius sniggered.

Luke froze.

'That sister of Luke's is a bit on the large side. She wouldn't run well on soft grass.'

'Now, now, Cornelius,' said Gilligan with a snort.

'And God bless us all, I don't think that ugly Russian duckling will ever make a swan. But what about it, if she makes my Alison happy?'

'That's true,' Gilligan simpered.

'What matters of state are you two discussing?' Luke was scathing.

'We're just remarking how happy Alison is today. Isn't that right, Roddy?'

'Er . . . yes. Think I'll get myself a top up.'

Gilligan scurried off, embarrassed they may have been overheard.

'Yourself and Roddy don't see eye to eye, do you?' A sly smile hovered on Cornelius's lips.

'We could,' said Luke, 'if he stood on a biscuit tin.'

'Fair point. He's a bit of a short arse. From good stock though. The Gilligans have been round here as long as the Thompsons. And you know what they say,' Cornelius's eyes glinted, 'the best of goods come in small parcels.'

'As does poison,' Luke said drily.

Cornelius chuckled. 'I thought you said something about organising a tug-of-war for the children?'

'I'll round them up in a while. Wendy and Nina seem happy enough for the moment.'

Luke waved at a figure who appeared on the lawn.

'Who's that?' asked Cornelius.

'Johnny Whelan, a colleague.'

'Jaysus, that lad wouldn't be any good to pull a rope. He's all scrawn. Wouldn't pull the socks off a dead man.' Cornelius set his glass on the grass, straightened himself, and pulled a cigar from his breast pocket. 'You seem taken with the child,' he said, lighting up.

'I am.'

Cornelius glanced furtively over his shoulder.

'I trust you've kept your mouth shut. You've not been blabbing to anyone about that little incident a few months back?'

Luke stared.

'I haven't said a thing.'

'Good.' Cornelius exhaled a pungent cloud of smoke.

'You shouldn't smoke,' said Luke.

'I'll be dead soon enough.'

Luke consoled himself with that thought.

'A word in your ear,' Cornelius lowered his voice. 'Just in case you're ever tempted to shoot your mouth off, remember this. We both have daughters now. I'd hate to see Alison upset by any loose talk.' His expression darkened. His mouth was hard. 'As I'm equally sure you'd hate to see anything happen to upset that nice wee girl over there. So, take care. I'm just saying, that's all.' His eyes were pools of menace.

It took Luke some seconds to reply. 'You're some bad bastard.'

Cornelius smiled. 'It's taken you until now to figure that one out? Alison said you were smart. What took you so long?'

In recounting the exchange, Luke had been following Terence's expression closely.

'You've given me a fair chunk to think over here today,' said Terence, eventually. He made a steeple of his fingers. 'I'd like you to make another appointment, but give it a few days. I need to absorb all of this.'

'Of course.'

156

Terence would now have to weigh the consequences of going to the police. Luke was glad he'd told him everything. Well, nearly everything. It just might be enough to guarantee his silence.

An Alternative Truth

Luke was on edge. Though he felt confident Terence would alert him if he was going to the authorities, sightings of police cars outside the emergency department broke him into a sweat. And only yesterday, Fran had advised him in her disapproving manner that there was someone waiting to see him, and not a patient, she added darkly. Preparing for the worst, he'd been relieved and pleasantly surprised to find it wasn't the police to take him off for questioning.

Terence usually opened a session without preamble. Today was different. He perused his notes, rubbed his chin, and glanced at Luke surreptitiously. Luke waited, taking in the surroundings of the now familiar office, noting how there was still one leaf on the rubber plant that remained coated in dust. Not the kind of thing that would have escaped Fran's sharp eye.

'Is there a problem?' Luke asked.

Terence cleared his throat. 'I've been looking over my notes,' he said. 'In the light of what you told me in our last session, I wonder if we might revisit a few little details? There are a few things that remain unclear for me. I wonder if I can bring you back to the day of the communion party in your colleague's house?'

Luke's shoulders slumped.

'I know it's traumatic, but if I can just ask you to go back to that afternoon, to before the accident?'

'I've told you everything. I've been totally honest.'

'I'm not disputing that. And some of it in remarkable detail, even down to remembering the blazer that you were wearing. But sometimes memory is not reliable. Memories change. I just think it would be helpful if we could bring that level of focus, of detail, to other parts of your account. You were under severe stress as you recounted to me what happened the first time. It may seem pedantic, I know, but I want to make sure that we've unlocked everything that happened that day.'

'OK,' said Luke warily. It seemed like going over painful ground unnecessarily. He grudgingly began.

It was a forensic process. Terence questioned his recall at every juncture. Asking him could he remember sounds in the background at certain moments, if he could recall smells, tastes, sensations. Things proceeded in this vein for some time before Terence signalled him to stop.

'Just there. Stop right there. I want to ask you a question now. And think carefully before you answer.'

'I'll do my best,' Luke said, baffled.

The question itself was straightforward, but it stopped Luke in his tracks. A noise like a thunderbolt went off inside his head. He shivered as if a draught had suddenly entered the room. He took a breath and closed his eyes, concentrating.

He cast his mind back.

Was this possible? What Terence was suggesting? Luke had been certain of it all up until a moment ago. He trawled his memory frame by frame. Backwards. Forwards. Freezing on certain moments.

In the end, there was no need for Luke to say anything. Terence had tracked his expressions. He had the answer to the question he had asked. Both men sat and stared at one another for some considerable time. Luke was chilled to his core.

Now

Crow Hall

Saturday 13 April

Frantic, Luke flipped open the glove compartment. His phone was vibrating. It slithered over the car manuals like a snake. He grabbed it as a call rang off.

Ten missed calls.

Engine running, he dialled Nina.

Straight to voicemail.

He tried again.

Still no answer.

He'd try Alison.

You have reached the voicemail of Minister Alison Forde-Thompson. Please leave a message. Alternatively, you can try the constituency office.

He'd try Cornelius.

'Ah, Luke, it's yourself.'

The old bastard had his television voice on. There was the sound of chatter in the background. Strangely too, the sound of barking dogs.

'Have you seen the paper?' Luke asked, breathless.

'We've seen the notice.' The old man sounded cagey. 'I don't know what to say—' He broke off, talking to someone in the background. 'Look, it's bedlam here. The best thing is to come up.'

The line went dead. Cornelius was gone. Luke wound down the window as he reversed. Sophie was standing at the front door.

'I'm heading to Crow Hall,' he shouted. 'There's no answer from Nina.'

'Drive carefully,' she called.

Twelve miles to Crow Hall.

Little Nina. Five years old. Her earnest face. Kneeling at her doll's house, alive and crawling with caterpillars. Alison going crazy. Bad girl, Nina. She was never one for dolls.

Nina, older now, watching him through curtains of dark hair as he inspected an agar plate she'd cultured in the fridge. Again, Alison complaining. Hell, Nina. Not where we keep food. The child behind her round glasses, staring from him to her mother. Trying to figure out what it was that she'd done wrong this time.

Nina scratching her scalp. Alison eyeing her warily. A scene that spools back in painful detail:

Alison is icy. 'Didn't I warn you about what would happen if you came home from school with nits again? I'm done with washing my hair in that stinking lotion.'

'It's not my fault,' Nina says, looking sheepish. 'It's Laurie Hogan who sits in front of me.'

'I don't care. It's coming off. Every last strand.'

'Don't be ridiculous, Alison,' Luke intervenes. 'She can't go into school with no hair.'

'She can, and what's more we'll be saying she did it for charity. Might as well reap some benefit.'

He leaves for St Matthew's shrugging off what he sees as an idle threat. Returning the following morning, he is aghast to see Alison has followed through.

'Look what she did,' a bald and tearful Nina says.

'Stop blubbing, child,' says Alison. 'It's not like it was great hair.'

Nina looks at her mother. 'Sometimes I think you are a horrible lady. Sometimes I think you should have left me in the orphanage.'

'Believe me, Nina, I wanted to. It's not like you were my choice.'

Teenage Nina. Her quiet pursuit for meaning. Her habit of keeping him company, silent, as he worked on papers. Her dubious dress sense. Fake-tan stains over her bedroom, all over the cream linen sofa. Hissy fits from Alison.

Incoming call.

Luke's eyes darted to the touchscreen. It was Fran, his secretary. She'd probably seen the *Herald*. He'd let the call ring out. She'd be distraught. He couldn't deal with Fran just now.

Two more miles.

He was on High Shore Road. With steep drops and corkscrew bends, he wouldn't normally choose this way. He raced past the Fog Catcher Inn. Below him, Creasy's Gully was thick with rhododendrons. He tore past the old workhouse, past the famine graveyard. The roads beneath the Range Rover were slippery. He hit a *Flood* sign, sending it skidding across the road. Wrestling with the steering he avoided a pole. Mud sprayed up all over an election poster. His wife's one-eyed, half-mouthed face looked down on him:

A name you can trust. Your voice in Government. Vote Alison Forde-Thompson.

Much of her face was eaten by the weather and what remained was airbrushed. Posters at this side of the lough had never been taken down, their edges curling and blistering in the rain.

When he reached the crow-topped pillars, he was forced to slow. The gates were open. He turned in off the narrow lane in a screech of tyres, tearing up the avenue.

Around a bend of beech hedging, he met a scene that stunned him. Horseboxes were parked on the verges and packs of yelping dogs circled the lawn. He had to drop a gear for riders. They glared at him from their mounts. Luke glared back.

Pulling up outside the house, he jumped from the car and raced across the gravel up the steps. He crashed against the great oak door. The smell of damp and polish hit him in the entrance hall. He hurried towards the voices coming from the drawing room, his footsteps echoing eerily off the terrazzo floor.

Alison rushed towards him. 'Luke, there you are . . .' She was wearing riding boots and jodhpurs.

'You've seen this?' He held up the rolled-up paper. 'What the hell's going on outside?' He pointed the paper towards the window.

'Steady.' Cornelius leaned against the trophy cabinet, phone in hand.

Luke focused on Alison.

'You've spoken to Nina?' he asked. 'This is a hoax, right?'

'It's OK, Dad.' Alison turned to her father. 'Luke's upset. We all are.' She turned to Luke. 'I'm sure Nina's fine. We've been on to the *Herald* and they're adamant the protocols for inserting a death notice were observed. They've apologised and said they're looking into it.'

'That's it? They've apologised?'

'Well, no, obviously not.' She put a hand on her hip. 'Dad's on to JC just now.'

'Jesus Christ?'

Was he really expected to know who all their cronies were?

She raised an eyebrow. 'No. But close. Johnny Costello – the press liaison officer from Dad's party days. If anyone can find out how this happened, JC can.'

'You seem surprisingly calm about this.'

166

'Of course I'm not calm.' Her eyes grew wide. 'What makes you think—'

'I don't know what to think. All I know is this is sick.'

'I was just about to call you. You were next on the list.'

He was Nina's father, and he was *next* on the list?

'Have you even spoken to Nina?' he asked again. 'Does she know? I called but no answer.'

'I couldn't say.' Alison shrugged. 'You're the one she talks to.'

'Are you telling me you haven't contacted her since you dropped her off?'

'You saw what she was like.' Nina hadn't even waved as Alison had whisked her away. 'Should we fill her in?' She cleaned her boot of imaginary dust.

'Of course we should. We need to know that she's OK. She's going to hear about it some other way if we don't speak to her. It's bound to find its way onto Facebook or something else.'

'There's no need to go off like a dog with a mallet up its arse.' Cornelius's cheeks billowed in and out, like sails catching the wind. 'Alison's only thinking of the girl.'

'Let me try her again.' Luke dialled. Straight to voicemail. He was racked with guilt. Though he'd called and left voicemails, she hadn't taken his calls or phoned him back since that day. And all the while he'd been trying to claw his way out of the dark pit that had become his world. 'You haven't explained why that lot are here.' He nodded towards the window.

'It's the last hunt of the season,' said Alison. 'It's late this year but so many meets were cancelled because of the weather. Roddy said to meet here for eleven, then to head onto his land. It's not as flooded there. Everyone had arrived before I knew about *that*.' She pointed at the paper. 'But don't worry, Roddy's taking care of things.' She rubbed her hands together. 'Now back to this nasty business. Dad won't be much longer. Come here by the fire.' She took Luke by the arm as if cajoling a fractious child.

Cornelius had moved to the writing desk. He was still on the phone, his backside spilling over the edges of the chair.

'A drink?' Alison offered. 'You're shaken.'

'I'm driving.' The springs on the leather sofa squeaked as he sat down.

'That's JC in the picture then.' Cornelius stood. He slid his glasses down, letting them dangle on the chain outside his neck scarf. 'The old codger owes me. If there's one thing I know about JC, he has connections. Being a shirt-lifter can have its advantages, I suppose.' He perched himself on the armrest next to Alison. 'Don't worry, Ali.' He rubbed her hand, indulgently. 'We'll find out how this happened.'

'We handle this ourselves?' She looked up at her father.

'I think so, Ali.' He smoothed the wrinkles of his flannel shirt over his belly.

'Excuse me?' said Luke.

'Yes, Professor?'

There was a time Luke had found this form of address amusing, but the time for that had long since passed. 'It strikes me that neither of you is asking the right question.'

Cornelius and Alison tilted their heads, their faux attention choreographed to perfection.

'*Who* has something to gain by printing something like this?' asked Luke. '*Whose* interests does it serve?'

Alison and Cornelius exchanged glances. The question hung like words on a gibbet.

'*Who* indeed?' Cornelius blinked.

'Let's wait and see what JC comes back with,' said Alison. 'And you, Luke, you'll try and make light of this to Nina? Dress it up as some kind of prank?'

The delegation as usual was seamless.

'I would have thought that was more in your line.'

The drawing room was airless. They waited in silence, each with their own thoughts. The old man's phone rang, breaking the silence.

'Ah, JC, good man.' Cornelius shot a look at Alison. 'Back with the usual alacrity.'

Taking this as a cue, Alison stood and stretched herself, cat-like. She linked Luke's arm.

'I'll walk you to the door.'

The Thompsons were finished with him.

'It's just as well I didn't go today,' Alison remarked. 'It wouldn't have looked clever, me out with the hunt, when I should really be dealing with the floods.'

Rain was falling steadily over the churned-up grass as they stepped from the entrance hall to the porch outside. Alison walked him to the car.

'Still seeing Sylvie?' she asked casually.

'I've told you before. It's not Sylvie. Her name is Sophie – Sophie Ellingham.'

'So you did. Sorry.' She touched his arm. 'We need to work together on this. Agreed? You track Nina down. Let her know and play it down. I'll put something together for social media. I need to kill this before it becomes a story.'

'That's what's important here?'

She just didn't get it. She gave him a puzzled look, opened her mouth as if to say something, then shut it again.

'Don't be difficult, Luke.'

He stared her in the eye, piercing her with a look.

169

'You know, don't you? Or at least you suspect?'

She hesitated. She looked at him. Blinking. Saying nothing. Not wanting to incriminate herself.

'You know what all of this is about.'

He was on to something.

'Listen, why don't you just follow things up from your end, Luke? And Dad and I will tidy things up here.'

He'd heard those words before. The blue vein that ran up the side of her neck pulsed steadily. She knew her words had struck a chord, that they echoed down those murky corridors to a place they'd been before.

'We'll be in touch,' she said. Her lips brushed his cheek. She smelled of soap, shampoo and toothpaste. She smelled scrubbed clean.

Pulling away from the house, he could feel the long hard stare of Cornelius Thompson from the drawing-room window.

Out on the laneway, the water ran fast in the gullies, a jaundiced foam bubbled on the surface. Did Alison know more than she was saying? And if so, should he probe? The chatter in his head was building. His temples throbbed. He felt a migraine brewing. He couldn't handle a setback now. The panic and despair. He'd spent enough time in therapy already.

Deniability. Plausibility. Culpability.

The rhyming words tripped off his silent tongue. And just like goldfish, they swam round and round his head.

The Curse

Back out on the open road, Luke pressed his foot to the floor. He needed distance between himself and Crow Hall. He wished this incessant rain would stop. He wished the heavy sky would lift. His head filled with dark thoughts. Crow Hall always did that to him. A Stygian gloom would descend on him any time he went there.

The house had a bad history that had started with a game of hide-and-seek. When Crow Hall was being extended in 1812, a local child named Marigold Piper went missing. She and her companions had been playing hide-and-seek in a field close by. When she failed to return home that evening to her cottage on the grounds, a search party from the town had set out to look for her.

They searched for Marigold for a full eight days. The search party grew with volunteers joining from towns and villages all over County Clare. But little Marigold was never found. Years later, it was rumoured that the child must have fallen asleep while hiding, and that stonemasons had unwittingly buried her into the new wall at the eastern gable of Crow Hall.

Isaac Thompson, the owner at the time, dismissed the rumours, refusing to tear down his expensive cut-stone wall. Local folklore had it that, at night, Marigold's ghost could be seen feeling its way along the narrow passageways looking for a way out. People said

Marigold had put a curse on all those who ever dwelled in the old hunting lodge. When children on the estate misbehaved they were threatened with the ghost of Marigold Piper, a threat that Cornelius had used on Nina.

Conversations would dry up whenever Luke walked into a room in Crow Hall. Nina had noticed too. When she was little, she complained that when she walked into the drawing room or the kitchen, people would turn to stare. Luke and Nina were the blow-ins. Unlike most of the staff that lived on the grounds or in cottages bordering the estate. They were the interlopers.

Crow Hall had been home to four generations of Thompsons. It reeked of subterfuge and mystery, of dark hatchings and whispered exchanges. At night the old building creaked and groaned, straining to contain its secrets.

Five miles down the road, Luke pulled into a local beauty spot, a car park with a view of Lough Carberry. Finding the number he wanted, he dialled. He waited. He was trying to calculate what time it would be there. It took a few seconds for the ringtone to sound. He waited. She picked up immediately.

'Hello?'

'Wendy, it's me.'

'Everything OK?' His sister sounded frosty.

'Something strange has happened. I need to talk to Nina.'

'She's not here.'

His stomach did a flip. 'Do you know where she is?'

'She left us last week.' Wendy now owned a bar with her girlfriend, Toni, in downtown Sydney. 'She went off travelling in the bush. You haven't talked to her?'

'No.' He tried not to panic. 'I tried ringing her mobile earlier. I'm guessing she has an Australian number by now. She hasn't contacted Alison or I since she left.'

'I guessed there was a problem there all right. She didn't want to talk about it,' Wendy's tone grew cooler. 'She's pretty messed up over something.'

'I know that. I need to talk to her. How can I track her down?'

He could hear her breathing. Thinking. *Christ*. He didn't have time for his sister being all judgemental right now.

'Hang on,' Wendy said. 'She gave me a number before she left. She took off with a bunch of English kids she met at the bar. In some kind of combi van. You could try that but you don't always get a signal out in the bush.'

He took down the number and filled his sister in on the events of the morning.

'That's sick, Luke. That's really going to freak her out.'

'I know, I know. I'll figure it out later. Right now, I need to talk to her. To be honest, I just want her home.'

He hung up and dialled the number Wendy gave him. Again he waited.

'Who's this?' came a whispered reply.

'Nina?'

'Dad, is that you?'

'Nina, thank God you're OK—'

'What do you mean? What's going on?'

'Everything's fine. We need to talk.'

'Just a minute. Everyone's asleep . . .'

There were muffled sounds. Sounds of doors opening and shutting. The sound of footsteps.

'All right, I'm outside. If you're ringing to apologise, forget it. Don't expect me to forgive you, Dad. You just stood by. You didn't stop her.'

'Before we get on to that, are you OK? Something kind of silly has happened here. Some kind of prank.'

He made as light of the death notice as possible, saying that while it was in the worst possible taste, it was likely some fool's idea of a joke. Probably some political opponent of Alison or an old adversary of Cornelius. Luke explained that there would be a printed apology, that they were following it up, and that he didn't want Nina to learn about it on social media or hear it from someone else.

'Read the announcement,' said Nina.

'Are you sure?'

'Just do it, Dad.'

Reluctantly, Luke read out the death notice.

To his astonishment, there followed a snort and then a laugh. A bitter rattle of a laugh.

'It's better than I could have hoped for.'

'What do you mean? I don't understand.'

'"*Beloved* only daughter of Alison Forde-Thompson", I couldn't have hoped for better if I were actually dead.'

'Ah Nina, come on,' he said softly. 'Your mother loves you. You know she does.'

'You think? Let's not kid ourselves, Dad. She thinks I was behind all the carry-on at home. You and I both know you're the only one that loved me.' She paused. 'Where are you?'

'In the car. I'm heading home from Crow Hall.' Her words were hurting. All he'd wanted was for them to be a normal family. 'The roads are terrible. Rain and floods.'

'Listen, Dad, I need to go. Drive safely and call me when you know some more.'

'I will. Bye for now, Nina. Love you.'

Back home, Luke was greeted by the dog pressing his face against the glass of the front door. 'I know you miss her too,' he said, once inside. He bent to stroke the animal. No response. The sound of high heels clacked on the marble floor. It was Sophie, searching his face for clues.

'It's OK, Soph. Nina's OK, thank God.'

'Where is she now?'

'She's travelling in the bush. She headed out from Sydney with some new friends. I've just spoken to her. She's fine.'

'You poor, poor thing. You must be so relieved.'

She put her arms around him and held him tightly. He was comforted by her embrace. Sophie hadn't met Nina yet and Luke hadn't told her why she was sent away. As far as Sophie knew, Nina's departure had been voluntary. Best to keep things simple.

'You're shaking like mad.'

Holding his hand, Sophie guided him down the hallway, past the photos of smiling dark-skinned children, through the kitchen, on to the garden room. The stove was lit. A medical journal was open at the page containing his photo. It looked like she'd been reading about him. She guided him towards the window seat. Duffy followed as far as the doorway but didn't come in.

'Tell me what's going on.'

'I still don't know,' he faltered. 'Alison and her dad are dealing with the announcement in the paper.'

'What did they have to say about it?' She stroked his hand and it felt soothing.

'The paper said that as far as they know, they didn't do anything wrong. They're looking into it. And Alison and Cornelius have some crony of Cornelius's, some press liaison guy, on the case.'

'Are you going to take it to the police?' she asked.

He didn't answer.

'Surely this is an offence of some kind?'

'You know what? Right now, I don't care. I think I'll let the great Thompson machine take care of it. Alison and Cornelius are on it. And they're more than capable.'

'Really?' Sophie looked worried. 'I would have thought that was something for the police? A criminal matter?'

'It may well be. If so, I've no doubt that Alison will take care of that. Alison and her father have hunted with some of the best legal counsel in the country.'

She raised her eyebrows. 'And how was the minister?'

Happily, Sophie hadn't had the dubious pleasure of meeting Luke's wife.

'In command as usual,' he replied. 'Alison loves a good crisis.'

'But *you*?' Sophie asked. 'How do you feel about it all? What's going on in that clever head of yours?'

He looked into her eyes, felt the warmth of her hand, her concern, and it gave him comfort. 'This whole thing is very unsettling . . . freaky.' He paused. 'I just couldn't bring myself to imagine . . .'

Unable to continue, the words were left unsaid, suspended in the air.

Sophie squeezed his hand.

'You really can't imagine,' he tried again. 'You just can't . . . when you have a child . . .' He stopped, not wanting to dwell on it.

'No, I don't suppose I can.' Sophie was divorced and she didn't have children.

'Nina means the world to you, doesn't she?' she said softly.

He nodded. The events of the morning had crystallised his thinking. 'She's my everything.'

Sophie withdrew her hand, falling silent. When next he glanced at her, she was staring into the distance, a hurt expression on her face. It struck him just how clumsy he'd been. He'd offended her.

176

'Of course, I have to say that you, the gorgeous Sophie, have been a very welcome and unexpected addition to my world.'

'I should be flattered, I guess.' She turned to him. 'Having access to the select world of the legendary Luke Forde.'

'You sure should.'

He teased a smile from her. He didn't like to see her upset. She was good for him. She was there when he needed her. She listened. She asked him how he felt. She cared about his feelings. Maybe in the early days with Alison it had been like that. If so, he couldn't remember. He wasn't immune to the attentions of women and until recently he'd soldiered on in his marriage, burying himself in his work. He didn't need complications and Sophie made things easy.

'Everything seems to be OK. Leave it for now. Let's do something fun,' she said, trying to lift his spirits. 'It hasn't exactly been the weekend we'd planned. What do you fancy doing for the rest of the day?'

He stared out at the rain coming down in sheets. A walk was out of the question. He hadn't been cycling in weeks. Sophie wasn't the outdoor type, preferring the gym and kickboxing. She looked fit in her sweater, casual jeans and boots. He looked playfully at the ceiling indicating the bedroom. It seemed as good an idea as any.

'After what's happened today I'm surprised you have the energy.'

'For you, Sophie, I keep a reserve. How about finishing *Breakfast at Tiffany's*?'

Sophie smiled. Alison never had the patience to kick back to watch old movies. Maybe they could salvage something from this awful day after all. Sophie took him by the hand and led him up the slatted stairs.

A wraparound window dominated the master bedroom. It had views up the lough towards the hills and down the lough towards the town. On a clear day, the room felt like an eagle's nest. And at night, the lights of the city sparkled in the distance.

Setting his phone on the bedside locker, he edged as casually as he could towards the window and he scanned outside. He double-checked. All was good. The scrawl on the boathouse wall couldn't be seen from here. He exhaled. He could relax. For now.

Breakfast at Tiffany's

By the time he returned from the bathroom, Sophie was under the covers. She'd retracted the TV from the end of the bed and was in her underwear, hugging her knees. She fiddled with the remote, trying to find the point where they'd stopped watching. Luke hopped in beside her. He could watch Audrey Hepburn for ever. The beautiful bones of her gamine face, her doll-like figure, that voice.

Eyes on the screen, he slipped his hand between her thighs.

'Wait.' Sophie reached across him, her warm skin brushing his face, and she opened the bedside drawer. He held his breath. He had found this unusual at first. There'd been nothing like this with Alison. He watched, mesmerised.

Sophie pulled the black silk from the drawer and smoothed it out slowly and deliberately. Climbing astride him, she leaned over until he could feel her breath hot on his neck. Her concentration was absolute. She was moving trancelike.

She lifted his head, securing the scarf with a knot, then guided him inside her, swiftly, almost roughly. She moved rhythmically at first, slow, then fast and faster. He listened to her breath, rapid, rasping. Restricted by the tightness of the silk, he struggled for air. He gasped suddenly, stung by the sharpness of her teeth. As her nails dug into him, she gave out a cry. He also cried out – in pleasure and in pain. He felt her slide down beside him.

The room fell silent. Still blindfolded, he turned on his side to touch her. He couldn't reach her, and pulling off the scarf, he saw she'd turned her back. Resting on an arm, he watched her. She was staring out at the water, tears trickling down her cheeks. He felt deep satisfaction that he could bring such tears of pleasure to her. He leaned back on the pillow, savouring the experience.

She suddenly sat up and pointed. 'See there, the tops of the turbines turning where the hill dips . . .' Embarrassed, she was trying to direct attention away from herself. He found it endearing and felt drawn close to her.

'We're going to see a lot more if Zephyr get their way.'

Putting her feet on the bed, she pulled her knees towards her. 'Big boys always get their way. After my divorce I thought about coming out here to the lough. I'm glad I decided to stay in the city, especially now they're going to trash the place with those turbines.'

Luke's eyes flicked over her. How flat her stomach was. She pulled the sheet around her, covering herself as if embarrassed by his gaze. She hugged it tightly.

'I remember looking at a few old cottages, fixer-uppers. But I had the strangest feeling that the estate agent didn't actually want me to buy anything. Even when I went for a browse around the town, it felt like people were looking at me, sizing me up. It was weird. Unsettling.'

It made perfect sense to Luke. Anyone that wasn't born and raised in this Clare townland was treated with suspicion. The agent, Seth Quigley, was a childhood hunting pal of Alison's. Luke suspected that the suitability of newcomers to Lough Carberry was being screened through Crow Hall. Like Japanese knotweed, the Thompson reach was silent and pervasive.

'Those poor families up that hill – they won't get a wink of sleep with the growl of turbines,' Sophie said.

'I never had you down as an activist, Sophie. You're not going to go all political on me? I've had enough of that over the last while.'

Her brow furrowed. 'I don't like to see little people trampled on, that's all.' She stood, heading to the bathroom. 'Don't worry, I'm not going to go all Greenpeace on you. There's only room for one Lucy Considine.'

The warm glow of intimacy instantly receded. The unease that had briefly left him now settled back around him. He didn't give a toss about Lucy Considine. The activist could tear through town buck-naked for all he cared, as long as her son, Sebastian, stayed the hell away from Luke and his family. It would have been better for everyone if Sebastian Considine had never turned up. Luke could kick himself, he should have taken care of things sooner. He'd been distracted, he'd let things go too far.

There came a click and the hum of the shower. Luke lay on the bed, brooding, his arm behind his head. It stung a little where Sophie had broken the skin. He didn't want to embarrass her by drawing attention to it.

'The farmers up there are kidding themselves if they think they're in line for any payoff from Zephyr Energy,' Sophie called out. 'Social media has it that Roddy Gilligan will be the one to benefit. The turbines are going onto his estate.'

'Ah, the weasel Gilligan. You know who he is, don't you?' Luke shouted. 'He's Alison's business partner and—'

'Friend with benefits?' Sophie called from the shower.

'You got it right in a oner.'

It was the first time they'd broached the subject of the shambles of his marriage. Luke liked that Sophie didn't pry. He'd asked her only once about her ex. Not out of any curiosity but because he imagined it was expected of him.

'I don't really see much point in talking about any of that,' she'd said. 'I don't ask about your wife, do I?'

He imagined Sophie and her husband had been able to work through their divorce quietly and in private. He doubted he'd be afforded any such privacy. He'd be in the spotlight. Journalists crawling all over him. Poking their noses in. The prospect sent shivers up his spine.

'Stay to the end?' he asked as she emerged from the shower. Audrey Hepburn's eyes were batting child-like on the screen.

'I'm sorry, I need to get back. I have to feed the cat. It's time for his injection too. I've left the shower running if you want to hop in.'

'Thanks.'

Upstaged by a cat. Luke had always thought that cats were self-sufficient. But if Sophie needed an excuse to leave, he wouldn't challenge her. She'd probably had enough of his troubles.

'Maybe you could swing by the hospital again during the week?' he suggested after his shower.

'Yeah, sure.' She smiled up at him. 'You know it's no mean feat getting past that secretary of yours. She's quite a piece of work.'

'You're not talking about dear old Fran?'

'Dear old Fran?' Still smiling, Sophie raised her eyebrows. 'I was there the other day, standing right in front of her when she put that call through to you.'

'Oh yeah?'

'Last Wednesday?' Sophie continued. 'When I drove the whole way over to the hospital in case you might be free for lunch?'

He shook his head. It didn't ring a bell.

'She picked up the phone to you and said, "*That woman* is here again!"'

'Oh, that . . .'

He had the good sense to stop himself from smiling. Fran often overstepped the mark, out of what he imagined was some kind of misguided maternal instinct.

'Ah sure, that's just the way she is. If it's any consolation, she calls Alison "Eva Perón".'

'Well, that's a whole load better than "that woman".' Sophie wasn't smiling any more. 'Who the heck does Fran think she is? She's not a surgeon. Scowling away at everyone, hammering like the hounds of hell on her keyboard, watering all her creepy spider plants with that creepy little watering can.'

Duffy pricked up his ears from where he was lying near the doorway. He could sense the change in mood. He growled.

'All right, boy,' Luke soothed him. It was the first time he'd seen Sophie properly angry. Fran had clearly rattled her. 'You know what? I'll have a word,' he said seriously. 'You're right, that is bad form.'

Sophie's expression mellowed. Alison had always been unfazed by Fran. Alison and Fran circled one another. As a kid, Nina used to do a brilliant impression of her mother saying, 'I'm here to see my husband – *on personal business*.' Nina would pretend to be Alison, looking Fran up and down. Luke had creased up laughing at her. But Sophie was a different person to Alison. More sensitive, less robust. Which was part of her charm and one of the reasons Luke had felt drawn to her.

'I wouldn't dream of treating anyone like that. I'd lose my job on the spot if I did that.' Sophie went to the window. Her eyes scrunched up, as if she were examining something. For one horrible moment Luke worried she'd spotted something he'd missed outside.

'You know if it doesn't stop raining soon, sink holes are going to open in your garden,' she said.

Relieved, he leaned across to the chest of drawers, pulling out a fresh T-shirt and boxer shorts. He stood and dressed. Stepping over the dog, he followed Sophie down the stairs to the front door.

'You don't think I'm heartless for leaving?' She looked up at him, fluttering her lashes, doing an Audrey Hepburn impression.

'Not at all.' He smiled.

'You feeling OK about Nina now?'

'I'll relax when she gets home. Don't you worry about me, Soph. Go back and feed your cat. I'll crack on here. I've got a paper to write.'

'The one about prosthetic valves?' She stood on her toes to kiss him.

'The very one.'

Front door open and keys in hand, she looked up at him admiringly.

'All those brains. That intellect,' she said. 'I'd love to see inside that head.'

Luke said nothing. Of one thing he was certain. Sophie would definitely *not* like to see the inside of his head.

'Call you later,' she shouted as she walked across the gravel to her car.

Letting his smile drop, Luke closed the door, walked across the hallway, and opened the heavy swing door to his basement.

A New Normal

Fran's immediate reaction to the death announcement in the *Herald* was to get the police involved. Returning to his desk from his ward round on Monday morning, Luke found Fran in a highly agitated state.

'This is no joke, Luke.'

'You don't hear me laughing,' he responded.

'The police need to be told about this. Dear Lord, a death notice . . .' Her voice was brittle.

Fran had helped out with Nina a lot when she was a kid. Luke needed to set her mind at rest.

'Don't worry. Alison and her father are looking into it.' The now familiar words tripped off his tongue.

The problem was that Fran didn't trust the Thompsons.

'Infuriating,' she hissed. She vented displeasure, clattering paper trays and desk tidies around her desk. Luke suspected what she was really annoyed about was his willingness to let Cornelius and Alison handle the incident.

'What's the problem?' He'd indulge her if only to shut her up.

'Bloody cleaners,' she fumed. 'They'd annoy a nation. I've warned them plenty not to go anywhere near my desk.'

Fran bundled a sheaf of headed notepaper, lining up the edges.

She was like a nettle. 'Nothing's ever where I leave it. I finally found the practice credit card and that file you were looking for. I was about to cancel the card when I found it here under a pile of paper.' She looked at him, eyes like flint. 'I don't want any of those cleaners near my desk. God knows where half of them are from. I wouldn't trust them as far as I could throw them.'

Luke often wondered if Fran trusted anyone. Given that she was already spitting bullets, he shouldn't let the opportunity pass. He might as well have a word with her about her attitude to Sophie.

'Do I get the sense that you're not too fond of Sophie either?'

She stared at him blankly at first. He imagined she was fomenting a response.

'She's just a secretary, you know.'

'Who is?' He affected innocence.

'Sophie Ellingham.'

'Ah Fran, that's not fair. There's no "just" about it. You're a secretary yourself. And a good one too.'

She slammed the lid of the photocopier. Fran lunched once a month with the other medical secretaries in the region. Luke reckoned their gossip alone could power a wind farm.

'I'm guessing your investigations didn't turn up that Sophie is also qualified as a nurse?' He stared Fran in the eye. 'An accomplished woman, I'd say.' Fran needed to be put back in her place. She was becoming difficult to manage. Her face darkened and she moved stiffly to the waste bin.

'I hear she kickboxes. I mean, what kind of carry-on is that for a lady? She's not your type, Luke. And forgive me for saying, but she's not really in your league.'

Despite the intrusion into his personal life, he burst out laughing.

'I like her, Fran. I'm a grown man. I'm well able to look after myself.' Adopting a slightly more serious tone, he looked her kindly in the face. 'I make my own decisions, Fran. And there's no need for any further background checks into my private life.'

She squeezed the empty packaging into a ball. 'Your marriage is none of my business,' she said frostily.

'That's something we can agree on.'

'But if you are looking for that sort of thing you could do worse than that nice Doctor Mellowes. She's really sweet. I've seen the way she looks at you.'

He thought he'd seen her sizing him up. Sweet was right. Sweet enough for diabetes.

'I have nothing but a professional interest in Amanda Mellowes,' he said firmly.

'Or that lovely Doctor Kelly,' Fran persisted.

Mary-Ann Kelly? Fran had to be joking.

'And that's all I'm going to say about the matter,' said Fran.

'That's good to hear,' responded Luke. 'I'll be back in twenty minutes if anyone's looking for me.'

He needed to gather his thoughts, alone. On advice from Terence, Luke was setting aside more time for himself, taking more breaks in the consultants' sitting room on the top floor of the cardiac surgery unit. Staff knew not to bother him there. He was trying to establish healthy patterns of behaviour but his new routine had been disrupted by the events of this past weekend.

He had a long stretch ahead of him in Outpatients and he felt peckish. He needed something to eat before heading down. He went to the fridge, then settled himself in an armchair. He thought back to Fran's conversation. He'd really have to curb her interest in his private life. He never let anyone else speak to him the way she did. Weighing it all up, it was a reasonable price to pay for diverting her attention away from talk of the police.

The door to the staff room opened. It was Dominic Walsh, a fellow consultant.

'Hi there, Luke.'

'Hey, Dom. How's tricks?'

'Good now. Can't complain.'

Dominic headed to the fridge. He opened the door.

'Fuck's sake. Who keeps swiping my yogurt?'

'Serious? Again?' said Luke. 'That is bad form.'

'See anyone else in here?'

'Sorry, Dom.' Luke scratched his head. 'Although, come to think of it, I may have seen a cleaner leaving.'

They weren't supposed to be in here but why not blame the cleaners? Fran always did.

'Down to that poxy canteen again,' Dominic moaned. 'I could eat a scabby horse.'

Luke could well believe it.

Dom waddled towards the door but Luke waited for it to shut before standing up. He pulled an empty yogurt carton from his pocket and lobbed it into the waste bin. Dominic should take more care. Luke had learned early in life that if you didn't want people to find your stuff, you had to hide it well. A lesson hard-learned at St Aloysius School for Boys. Anyway, he was doing Dom a favour. The guy could do with cutting back. He'd been piling on the pounds.

The Package

Luke was on his way to the postal depot in the city. He was in a hurry. A fortnight had passed since the death notice. A fortnight, too, since he'd painted over the scrawl on the boathouse. He'd locked both episodes into the jam-packed room in the back of his mind and thought instead of Nina. Not long now until she was back. He'd relax when she got home.

The docket advised if the parcel wasn't collected within three days it would be returned to sender. He checked the time on the dashboard. The depot shut in fifteen minutes. The car gave a low purr as it picked up speed. It smelled of wet dog, earth-rich and pungent. A smell he liked. It reminded him of the outdoors. In spite of that, he'd get Fran to organise a valet. Sophie didn't like the smell.

Racing along the country roads, he slaked muck against the verges. He'd swing by Sophie's in the city after he collected the parcel. Her cat had taken a turn for the worse and she was staying home this weekend. He was aggrieved the animal was interfering with his love life.

As he walked into the depot, a woman in a blue uniform squinted up at the clock as if to suggest he'd made it just in time. He handed her the docket.

189

'You have ID?'

Damn.

He'd left his hospital badge on the dashboard.

'I'll just go and get it—'

'Oh, never mind. I trust you. You have an honest face.'

'So I've been told.' That always made him smile.

'Here you go.' The postal worker slid a cardboard box across the counter towards him. He wrapped his arms around the box and headed for the door.

'Wait a minute . . .'

He turned slowly.

'I saw you a few months ago. You're the doctor on the telly, the one that—'

'That's right,' he cut her short, discomfort lingering about the documentary.

Alison had convinced him to do it. She said it would raise awareness about the programmes for which he had volunteered. It would encourage others to follow suit. When the programme aired, he'd been surprised to see it also contained footage of Alison and the charities of which she was patron. The screening had been timely for her – the day she had announced she was running for election.

The postal worker came out from behind the counter and ushered him to the door in a hurry to lock up. 'You take care now, doctor,' she said.

He was curious about what was in the box, not recalling any online orders. It felt heavy and filled the cradle of his arms, and for a moment he wondered if he'd indulged himself online after a late-night whiskey. With only Duffy at home for company, it was entirely possible he'd clicked the *buy* button on that website.

He returned to the car where he'd parked on double yellows

just outside the depot gates. Balancing the box, he fumbled for his clump of keys, pointing with the remote and clicking to open the boot. It opened, thankfully. The locks were acting up.

He bent and laid the box on the dog blanket. Splatters of rain trickled down his back. Using the heavy basement key, he scored through the sealing tape. The cardboard casing separated. Underneath, he spied a layer of bubble-wrap and Styrofoam. Was it a gift? It was a long time since anyone had bought him a present.

Snapping through the Sellotape, the object had an odd but vaguely familiar hexagonal form. Something fashioned from black and shiny lacquered wood. He breathed in the moisture-laden air. A raindrop found its way under his sleeve and shimmied down his arm. He stood, indecisive. Realising he'd been holding his breath, he exhaled. He reached for the metal clasp. About to open it, he stopped. He'd check the despatch notice first.

It was in a plastic pocket. Wiping it dry, he tried to read it. Some of it was in capital letters and in the contents section he was able to make out the words 'tinned goods'. Apart from that, the sender's scrawl was indecipherable. Curious. He shrugged. He shoved the note into his pocket and returned to open the clasp.

It was the smell that got to him first. He recoiled. He covered his nose and mouth. It was putrid. Rancid. He gagged. He took a step away, repulsed by the open unseeing eye staring up at him. The mouth was stuffed with rubber tubing. The lips set in a macabre half smile.

Luke had come across countless gruesome sights. He wasn't squeamish. But this – this was grotesque. Half the doll's head was missing, half its body under wraps. He guessed the smell was coming from a bag of matter taped to the head. The bag was punctured, the contents seeping over a satin pillow and into a white satin coverlet.

He searched inside the car for a pen. There was one in the door pocket. He grabbed it. He'd need a tissue too. He reached for the pack on the dashboard. Covering his mouth with a tissue, he lifted the elasticated satin with the pen. Holding his breath, he peered underneath. There was something shiny and metallic. Like a badge. It was taped to the doll's stomach in a small plastic package.

As he poked to try to free it, he jumped back, noticing the bag of matter on the head was moving. Looking closely, he could see it was full of maggots. Writhing maggots.

He wanted to shut the lid. But first he had to see what was taped to the stomach. This time he applied more force. He flicked it free. It spun high into the air and landed on the road. Trembling, he went to fetch it and he leaned back against his car to examine it. It appeared to be nothing more than a plain metal tag. He turned it over. He went cold.

My Lady's Chamber

He wasn't sure if he had the right bungalow. It sat on the edge of a housing scheme. He'd only been here in the dark before. Then he spotted her small red Polo. It was parked at the side of the house. A line of washing hung underneath the tin roof of an open shed. In the top-right corner of the garden he could see the rusted stumps of what was once a greenhouse. Sheltering from the rain underneath the porch, he pushed the bell.

Shifting his weight from one foot to the other, Luke rang the bell a second time. He thought he detected movement, the twitch of a curtain perhaps. When Sophie didn't come, he pulled out his phone and dialled her number. She answered immediately.

'Oh, Luke . . .' She sounded out of breath.

'I'm at your front door.' He was beginning to regret not phoning first but he wasn't thinking straight. After the shock of the doll, he wanted to talk to someone. 'I know we agreed to give this weekend a miss, but I needed to come into the city. Maybe this isn't convenient . . .'

'No, not at all. I was just in the middle of . . . it's perfectly fine, just a minute.'

She answered the door in sweat pants with her hair tied up. She looked distracted, and for a moment Luke pushed aside his own distress.

'What's the matter?'

'It's Fidget. He's ill. He was sick all night.'

She directed him into the kitchen. Luke looked at the wretched creature huddled in the basket next to the radiator.

'Poor thing.'

He approached the basket and bent down.

'You've had him at the vet?'

'Several times. It's a tumour.'

The animal went into spasm as if to confirm its sickly state.

'You're very fond of him, aren't you?' he asked, making for a kitchen chair.

She didn't reply. The answer lay on the washing line outside. Apart from a duvet cover, it was pegged with the cat's soft playthings.

'Tea or coffee?' she asked. 'I'm mortified . . . the place is such a tip.'

She was flustered, different to the first time he'd been here. There'd been no unease or inhibition that night. They'd both had several cocktails beforehand in the bar near St Matthew's.

A potted plant sat on the windowsill. On the wall was a calendar with cats. By the kitchen table underneath the plastic wall clock was a large wooden crucifix. It was a simple home. Fran's unwelcome words with all their snobbish prejudice echoed in his head, 'She's not for the likes of you.'

'Coffee, please. Remind me where the bathroom is?'

He was still queasy and wanted to splash water on his face. He headed to the door. 'This way? We'd both had a bit to drink the last time I was here.' He grinned.

'Just a second.' She abandoned the kettle. 'I haven't got round to cleaning down there just yet.'

She whizzed past him into the hallway. There followed a succession of doors being shut.

'It's not a hospital audit, Soph. I only want to use the bathroom.' He laughed and followed her into the hallway.

'Oh, I know.' She laughed as well. 'I'm not normally so behind with my housework. Just with Fidget being sick.'

She stepped over the hoover and pointed to the bathroom.

'There you go. I'll get that coffee now. One sugar, right?'

'One sugar,' he confirmed.

He was careful to put the toilet seat back down when he'd finished. Turning on the tap to wash his hands, he looked at the bathroom shelves lined with cosmetics and feminine toiletries. He thought back to his first night here.

She'd surprised him, that night in the bar. With her guarded, professional exterior he'd never have thought it. He'd been surprised when she'd taken his hand, and placed it under the wool of her fitted grey office skirt. She'd slid it up her thigh so he could feel the buttons of her suspender belt, and she'd danced her tongue around his ear. She'd whispered that they should get a taxi back to hers.

It was the first time he'd been unfaithful to Alison. Not because he owed the woman any loyalty but because no one had ever intrigued him so. They'd stumbled out of the taxi, giggling and hanging on to one another. Sophie had borrowed the long navy wool coat Alison had bought for him, saying it made him look distinguished. Inside the house, he remembered swaying down the hallway. That transition from bungalow to bordello.

Lights were switched off and candles lit on the bedside lockers and dressing table. Waxy smells of mandarin and lime. The awkward conversation about contraception over, she slipped the condoms back into the bedside drawer. She examined the vasectomy scars and pushed him back on the pillow.

He watched her in the flickering light, catching glimpses of

195

her pleasure. Her eyes closed as he moved his hands over her shoulders and down her arms. She shuddered. Her breathing grew shallow and she stilled. 'Hold it there,' she whispered, grabbing his wrists.

She forced his arms behind his head. His heart was beating wildly. Alison had never made him feel this. For all he knew at that moment, Alison was with Gilligan. He didn't care. He saw her now as sexless, fired by desires completely alien to his own.

'Wait.' Sophie reached for something behind. He gasped, startled at first, then filled with expectation and excitement. She brushed against his cheek as she reached across to fasten a handcuff to the bedpost. He lay there entranced as she secured his wrist.

'Hurry,' he urged. He couldn't wait much longer. 'Hush,' she said, and nipped his shoulder with her teeth. She took her time as she secured his other wrist. Getting off the bed, she pulled open a dressing-table drawer. Looking coquettishly over her shoulder, she smiled. He felt a tiny prickle of alarm. She turned around in slow deliberation, raising a questioning eyebrow. His eyes travelled to the object in her hand. Her expression changed and she climbed on top of him once more.

'Lift your head,' she commanded.

He obeyed. Pulling a pillowslip over his head, she laid his head against the pillow. For a few brief seconds he was claustrophobic. He wasn't sure about this. She started to move, moaning. When the first lash came, it took his breath away. Shocked, he drew in sharply, the fabric of the pillowslip sticking to his lips. As he flailed to free himself, she brought the switch down across his chest.

'You like that?' She panted and whipped again. It hurt but as she continued to move with him he felt his pleasure heighten until he could no longer control himself. His body relaxed and he was spent. Still the lashes rained down, across the arms, across his chest. He called out in pain, exhorting her to stop.

'Sorry, sorry . . .' she gasped, coming to a stop. She tugged off the pillowcase and he was able to breathe freely. Embarrassment flooded her and she covered her nakedness with the pillowcase.

'That was . . . that was . . .' He was lost for words.

'You enjoyed it.'

He laughed then. A great belly laugh at the earnestness of the role play. 'I don't know,' he said, as if he were considering the matter. 'We'll have to try again later, to make sure.'

She laughed then too. 'I'm going to the bathroom.' She got up, wrapping the sheet around her as she left.

Sex with Alison had been a hasty affair. Something to service a need, rather than something to savour and enjoy. Alison demanded nothing more than an animalistic interaction much like a stallion covering a mare. No intimacy, passion or excitement.

With this woman it was different. As his relationship with Sophie developed and deepened, Luke abandoned himself to whatever games she cared to conjure up. The role play he found intriguing. He allowed himself to be blindfolded, cuffed, caressed and whipped, never knowing what might come next.

With the tap in full flow, he washed his hands with care. He allowed the liquid soap to seep into the creases of his skin. He wanted to cleanse away any residue from the hideous casket that now sat in the boot of his car. He looked in the mirror and checked his appearance. Nothing betrayed the shock he'd had, save for a twitch above his eye. He turned off the tap, folded the towel on the handrail, opened the bathroom door, and headed back down the hallway, back to Sophie in the kitchen.

'Tuna sandwich with your coffee?' she asked.

'Yeah, sure.' Regular meals helped with his migraines. They had become fewer the more he engaged with Terence Black.

Sophie opened a cupboard. She stood on her tiptoes. The cans on the top shelf all had pictures of cats.

'I sincerely hope that *is* tuna,' Luke joked.

'I've made that mistake before, opening tins without looking!' She laughed. Reaching for a can on the bottom shelf, she set to and made sandwiches. She cut the crusts off and handed him a plate.

'I'm quite the charwoman today,' she said. 'You've caught me in all my cleaning glory.'

'You look great,' he countered. It wouldn't take long to get those sweat pants off, he thought.

'Why, Luke Forde, I do believe that's the first compliment you've paid me.'

'No? Really?' He felt sure he'd articulated his admiration for her. He'd be more attentive from now on. He'd never had to consciously flatter or pursue a woman before. All the females in his life had chosen him.

Biting into the sandwich, he allowed his eyes to wander around the kitchen. A pile of folded towels sat on the work surface. A collection of boxes and a syringe also sat on the surface. Medication for the cat. A tea set lay draining on the draining board. Too small to be of any practical use.

Sophie followed his gaze. 'Collecting tea sets is a hobby. Childish, I know.'

'Some of us have pleasures not everyone would understand,' he said.

He felt himself drawn closer to this woman who provided a welcome distraction from all the gruelling sessions with Terence. He made a mental note to seek a gift to add to her collection. His eyes drifted beyond Sophie's shoulder to an open shelving unit, coming to rest on a photo frame. It showed a younger-looking Sophie, a man's arm around her shoulder. His arm was muscled and bulky and he was wearing a sombrero.

'Me and Kevin,' she offered, glancing over her shoulder. 'On honeymoon in Majorca. At a bullfight.'

He took another bite of his sandwich. He was surprisingly hungry.

'You think it's weird, don't you? Keeping a photo of my ex like that.'

'What would I know?' He was hardly qualified to comment. Few couples could have a relationship as strange as his and Alison's.

'Kevin worked at the hydroelectric station on the river.' She wiped some crumbs from her mouth. 'He was a part-time car mechanic too.'

Luke hoped he wasn't prying. But Sophie seemed content to talk.

'There were good times. Before it got messy. I prefer to remember the good times.'

'Is Kevin still around?'

'He moved away after the divorce and we lost touch. I wish him well, wherever he is.'

It was as frank an exchange as they'd ever had about her ex. If he and Alison were to divorce, would Alison be as generous? He doubted it. Not that the subject had ever arisen. Luke appreciated Sophie's sensitivity in not poking about the innards of his marriage. She made things easy. She never brought up separation or legal proceedings, in no rush to regularise their relationship in any way.

A sickly sound came from the cat, hunched in his basket. Sophie sprang from her chair and crouched at the animal's side.

She craned her neck, looking at the clock on the wall. 'It's nearly time. I can give him another shot.'

Luke watched as she tenderly injected the syringe into the cat. The animal stiffened then relaxed with a whimper.

'How old is he?' he asked gently.

'Eighteen this year.' Her eyes were wet.

'Is he in much pain?'

'I really hope not. The injections seem to help.'

'Have you considered . . . do you think it might be kinder—'

'No,' she said firmly, making it clear that this was not something she wanted to talk about. 'I'm too fond of him. I don't know how I'll bear it when he goes.'

He hadn't meant to be insensitive, and he sensed a shift in the atmosphere between them. Things were not going according to plan.

'Of course. I understand completely. I get it. It's just—'

'I couldn't put him to sleep. He's only just started the injections. I need to give it time. He deserves the chance.'

Turning her back to him, she went to the sink.

'I'm sorry, Sophie. I'm not really thinking clearly.' He hadn't realised the depth of Sophie's attachment to the animal. 'The oddest thing just happened. I don't know what to make of it.'

'Yeah?' she answered flatly, her thoughts clearly on the cat.

'I got a note to collect a parcel from the post office.'

She turned around, drying the miniature tea set with a tea towel.

'Come and see,' he said. 'Outside, in the car.'

The Doll

Pulling on a raincoat Sophie followed Luke to the car. The boot opened like the curtains on some ghoulish stage play.

'That looks like a . . . a *coffin*?' She clutched at the folds of her unzipped coat.

As Luke opened the casket, Sophie gripped his arm with one hand, the other flying to cover her mouth. Luke found the sight just as repugnant the second time around. Sophie stared. Her eyes were fixed, unblinking, absorbing the coffin and the doll that lay inside. Reaching in, he closed the lid, sealing off the noxious stench.

'What the hell is that?'

'I know, it's disgusting.'

Sophie shuddered. 'It looks like an effigy of some kind. And what was that taped to its head? Was it supposed to be brain matter?'

He closed the boot. 'Let's get out of the rain.' He clicked the key fob. The doors refused to lock. Nothing was going his way. Back inside, Sophie leaned against a kitchen counter. She turned to Luke.

'Who sent you this? More to the point, why?'

Luke shook his head and shrugged. 'This was in the casket.' He showed her the metal tag.

Sophie stared at the tag in his hand. '*RIP Nina Forde-Thompson,*' she whispered. She looked at Luke. 'What's all this about? You must have some idea.'

He shook his head. 'Someone has gone to a lot of effort. First the death notice, now this. I don't know what to make of it,' he answered carefully. 'It's scaring me, to be honest.'

'Of course it is,' said Sophie gently. 'But you know that Nina's OK. I mean, you've spoken to her and everything?'

She took the metal tag.

'I have, but even so . . .'

Despite their efforts, Alison and Cornelius's investigations so far had come up empty. They were none the wiser about the announcements in the *Herald*.

'Well, one thing is obvious to me,' said Sophie, handing the tag back.

'It is?'

'Someone's got it in for you or your family.'

'I think that much is clear. But the question is, why? And where is all this going? For the moment, Nina is safe in Australia, but what if someone's intent on causing her real harm?'

Sophie looked at him. 'I think the police have to be told. But what are your thoughts?' she asked. 'What's going on in your head?'

Luke didn't answer. He was thinking hard.

'You are going to take this to the police, aren't you?'

'Probably, I don't know.'

From the basket came a plaintive whimper. It sounded like the cat's medication was wearing off. Another whimper followed.

Sophie rushed to the basket and sank to comfort the animal.

'Soph, I'll leave you to it. We can talk later,' Luke said quietly. 'I need to think this through.' Opening the back door, he pulled up his collar and headed back out into the rain.

* * *

Half an hour later, he pulled up outside Crow Hall. Gilligan's two-seater was parked at the house next to Cornelius's Jaguar. Alison's car was nowhere to be seen. Luke guessed it was round the side. Alison spent more time at Crow Hall than her constituency office. The draughty house always drew her back. It was in her marrow. These days, she rarely bothered to return Luke's calls or texts.

He flung his car door open, letting it wallop against Gilligan's vehicle. Getting out, he examined the dent. 'Oops,' he muttered. He headed for the front door and let himself in.

Cornelius and Gilligan were in the kitchen. They were leaning over the table. A flustered Cornelius slurped at a cup of coffee. He was jabbing at a sheet of paper.

'I think that would be better sited here . . .'

Both men looked up as Luke's footsteps sounded on the flagstones.

'If it isn't the professor,' declared Cornelius. A button on his shirt had popped. His cheeks were like a veiny jellyfish.

'Where's Alison?' asked Luke.

'I'm fine, thanks for asking. My daughter's in the yard, helping Sly.'

Luke headed for the back kitchen.

'It's busy out there,' Cornelius warned. 'I had to call the lads in on a Saturday. I'd ordered five extra loads.' He held up five fat fingers.

Crow Hall labourers had been distributing sandbags to flood sites all around the lough. There had been no public talk of any profit to Cornelius from this enterprise. Such talk would be considered disloyal.

Every Christmas Cornelius threw a lavish party for the staff and their families at Crow Hall. No expense was spared. Outside caterers were hired and the large library would fill with sounds of laughter, carol singing and backslapping. In return, Cornelius was invited to every funeral and christening for miles around the county.

Luke edged past the men as he headed for the back kitchen and the exit to the yard. He snatched a glance at the plans draped across the table.

'I think we're done here, Cornelius, old pal,' Gilligan said nervously.

'Ordnance survey?' Luke enquired. 'Or turbine locations?'

Luke recognised the tiny symbols and the Zephyr Energy logo.

Gilligan grappled to fold the expanse of paper.

'You stand to do quite well out of Zephyr, Roddy, by all accounts. All the turbines on your land, if the proposal goes ahead? A nice little earner every year. A nice little *windfall*.'

'You're not here to cause trouble, are you?' Cornelius eyeballed Luke.

Luke squared his shoulders and looked directly at Gilligan.

'The only thing I want here is a word with my wife.'

He couldn't care less that Gilligan was probably screwing his wife, but he damn well wanted the guy to be uncomfortable about it.

'Off outside, so.' Cornelius dismissed him as he laid strips of bacon on a baking tray.

'That dent on your car will set you back a bit, Roddy. I don't know if you've noticed it but someone's given it a right gouge.' Luke left the two men to it.

In the yard, he was greeted by the sight of crushed metal segregated into heaps for collection by recycling operators. He took in the multicoloured accordions of crushed cars, the white goods and mounds of aluminium sheeting. The large compactor was silent.

The rest of the yard was busy. A truck idled by a pile of rusted metal radiators.

He spotted Alison. She was chatting to the driver of the truck, an umbrella in one hand, the other on her hip. The guy in the truck grinned down at her. Sly Hegarty. She handed Sly a piece of paper. He saluted, revved the diesel engine and lumbered off out of the yard, the back of his truck loaded with sandbags. Luke watched as she headed across the yard to talk to three young lads loading up another truck. They greeted her warmly.

'Alison!' Luke shouted.

She looked around and raised her arm in acknowledgement. She started across the yard.

'What a nice surprise,' she gushed. 'You came to visit.' She kissed him on the cheek.

'Not a social call, Alison.'

The charm evaporated. 'So I see from the look on your face. More trouble? Nina again?' She raised a hand directing him not to answer. 'Of course it is.'

'Come with me.'

Alison wasn't easily shocked. Despite that, Luke noticed her flinch as she examined the contents of the casket.

'Any ideas?' he asked her.

No answer. He studied her face for clues.

'Give me a moment,' she said. 'I need to think.'

He walked with her back to the yard.

'Hey, lads!' She shouted across at the youths loading the sandbags. 'Take a break. Get something to eat back in the house.'

She turned to Luke. 'What on earth is Dad up to? He said he was making sandwiches ages ago. I don't know why he insists on doing them himself – makes him feel more involved, I guess . . .'

'He's in there, all right, poring over some map with Gilligan.'

Alison shook her head. 'Jesus, I don't understand why he's so upset about this. There'll be two turbines on the boundary with Roddy's estate. We won't be bothered by either of them here at the house.'

Luke couldn't care less if Alison and Cornelius were kept awake all night. In fact, he hoped they were.

'So what do you make of the casket?' he prompted again.

'Well, I don't think we need to involve anyone else, if that's what you mean.' She looked over her shoulder. The yard had emptied and it was only the two of them.

'No? Maybe Cornelius's connections aren't what they used to be. Your contacts haven't dug up much on the death notices. And now this.'

'I'm pretty sure I know who's behind it.' Alison pursed her lips. 'In fact, that little creation in the boot of your car bears all the hallmarks.'

'Of who?'

The rain plinked on her umbrella as she spoke. And when she told him, it made sense.

'I'll deal with it,' he said.

'You're sure you're up to it?'

'I'm sure.' He turned to go, then hesitated. 'Just one thing. Answer me this. I've always wondered – why on earth didn't you just marry Gilligan in the first place?'

'Roddy?' She looked at him in surprise. 'But I can have Roddy any time. Now where would be the challenge in that?'

Luke shook his head. He was glad to leave the yard.

Encampment

Luke wasn't sure if he could find it again. As he swerved to avoid a flood, he heard the casket thud in the back of the Range Rover. He was a mile outside the town, concentrating hard, looking for the opening to a small side road along the hedgerow. He'd been here once before. He remembered a long-haired shaggy dog staring wildly at him as it barked into the night. The animal had been tied to a fraying length of rope.

There it was. He turned and followed the boreen to a small clearing housing two metal structures – a mobile home and a smaller caravan dovetailing it at a right angle. The mobile home was speckled with orange rust. Luke skidded to a stop on the mud outside.

He sat for a moment, allowing his eyes to take in the site. Perhaps in sunshine or on a dry day the place might exude some kind of romance. Not today. A bare wicker sofa bereft of cushions leaned against the mobile home. Above, the branches of a twisted tree reached down to touch the roof. Outside the mobile home was a length of blue rope but no sign of a dog.

The rain was easing. Through jagged tracks of water on the windscreen, he watched the door to the mobile home open a sliver. He waited. It opened a fraction more. Unfastening his seatbelt, he stepped out of the car. The mud was slippery underfoot. Someone peered through the crack in the door and the barking started. Furious, spitting, snarling. Luke kept on walking.

'Put that animal on a leash,' he shouted.

The door to the mobile home slammed shut. A second later a woman appeared, gripping the dog by the collar. The animal was muzzled. Luke stood in the drizzle while the woman fixed the animal's collar to the length of rope.

'I admire your neck.' Lucy Considine swung around to face him. Her eyes were flashing. 'Have you come to apologise?'

Apologise? Was she serious?

'Where's your son?' Luke asked calmly.

'My son wants nothing to do with you or your family ever again.'

Luke stared. The feeling was mutual, though he had no idea why the woman was so aggrieved. The dog was spinning on the rope, throwing the full force of its body into every bark. Luke sloshed through the muck and banged on the door of the smaller caravan.

'Open up!'

Lucy Considine approached. Mud oozed between her toes in her open sandals.

'He's asleep.'

It was the middle of the day and this useless lump was still asleep?

'I don't care.' Luke thumped louder.

The door swung open.

'What the . . .?' Sebastian shielded his eyes against the daylight, his torso covered in scars. Luke got the whiff of cannabis. He wanted to throttle this stoner's scrawny neck, to land a punch in the plain of his belly.

'Get some shoes,' he ordered. 'I have something to show you.'

'We got the message, man. Piss off and leave us alone.'

'Now!' Luke shouted.

Lucy Considine stepped away and studied Luke as if considering him for the first time. 'People like you and your wife think you're different, don't you?' she said. 'You think this country is your playground. That you can take whatever you want, do whatever you want, use the law as you want.'

Luke said nothing. He waited for Sebastian to step out of the caravan in his unlaced work boots and a crumpled T-shirt. He was smoking a cigarette.

'Well?' He looked at Luke.

'This way.'

Luke walked around to the back of the car. Sebastian followed behind, blowing smoke in Luke's direction. For the third time that day, Luke unveiled the contents of the boot and of the casket. He watched for Sebastian's reaction.

'Well, fuck me sideways. What's that?' Sebastian stepped back and broke into laughter. 'Hey, I kind of like it though,' he said. 'It packs a punch. Why are you showing it to me?'

Lucy had backed away and she was holding a hand over her mouth. Their performances were convincing but Luke wasn't fooled. He pulled the metal tag with Nina's name from his pocket.

'This mean anything?' He looked from one to the other.

'Seriously?' asked Sebastian. 'This is a nice little project you've got here, but I'm afraid I can't lay claim to this one. No, sir. This is not my work.' He blew a smoke ring into the air.

Lucy Considine said nothing, as Luke expected. She would stand by her son.

'Are you telling the truth, Sebastian?' Luke hated having the guy's name in his mouth. It had a taste of something rotten.

'Really, Doc. It's class. But you're not putting this on me.'

'Funny that,' Luke replied. 'Because it's just a bit too similar to all the other stunts you've pulled – my wife's election posters and that latest crap you pulled outside her constituency office in town. All a bit extreme. You see, Sebastian, I think this is exactly the kind of stunt you'd pull. It has the hallmarks of a sick and twisted mind. You have issues, pal.'

In his latest stunt, using red graffiti spray, Sebastian had scrawled *Murdering Bitch* on the window of Alison's constituency office. The one displaying her clinic times and her photo. He then arranged himself on a fake animal fur outside the office, slashing his chest again. This time, he went the extra mile. He slit his wrists. Carefully, precisely, in a way designed not to bleed out quickly, just enough to be dramatic. This all took place at a busy lunchtime, ensuring he wouldn't bleed out alone. Sebastian's timing guaranteed him a sizeable audience by the time the ambulance arrived.

It was clear to Luke that Sebastian had chosen Nina to get close to Alison. To use that access to highlight his aversion to bloodsports. Guys like Sebastian needed a cause to define them. They were nothing without a cause. Of course, there was always the possibility that it had been a team effort. That Sebastian had been his mother's willing pawn.

'You want to talk about issues, Doctor Forde?' Sebastian grinned. 'Well, maybe you should look a little closer to home.' He craned his neck to blow a smoke ring. 'I don't think your little girl digs her parents or her home life. And she sure has issues with that bitch mother of hers. You know what? It wouldn't surprise me if Nina had sent this—'

'You little prick!' Luke took a step towards him.

'Stop!' Lucy stepped between Luke and her son.

'You're really pathetic, you know that?' Luke called out over her shoulder, 'That crap you wrote on our boathouse – fucking childish.'

'I don't know what you're on, man, but I've no idea what you're talking about.'

Luke suddenly felt strange. He knew what was happening to him. He recognised the symptoms. He started to perspire, his heart began to race, and his mouth went dry. He was finding it hard to focus. He sucked in a lungful of air, waited for the rush to subside, and tried to crush the growing swell of anxiety. Terence had helped him to cope with such episodes. What the hell was he thinking anyhow? Squaring off to this stoner in his ramshackle dwelling on the side of the road?

'I think I can settle this,' said Lucy.

'Yeah?' said Luke, taking a step away.

'How and when did you get this . . . this thing?' Lucy jabbed a finger towards the casket.

'I received a note during the week to collect it at the parcel depot in the city. I collected it earlier on today. Why?'

'OK. So that means whoever posted it, must have posted it earlier on this week.'

'I suppose.'

'Well then, there's your answer,' Lucy said. 'It couldn't have been Sebastian. He only got home last night.'

'What do you mean?'

'Sebastian's been in prison these past two months. No need to pretend you didn't know.'

Prison?

It was the first Luke had heard of this.

Mafia

The inside of the mobile home was surprisingly comfortable. Tidy even. Luke didn't know what he'd been expecting but the organised space was not unlike Alison's constituency office. A mound of neatly stacked papers sat on the table next to an open laptop. A reel of postage stamps sat on top of a pile of envelopes next to a pot of recently brewed coffee. The open space smelled of warm bread. Underwear dried on an electric radiator. He felt himself redden as Lucy caught him looking.

'Want some?' She pointed to the coffee pot. 'I expect it's still hot.'

'Thank you.' He'd seen no way of figuring out what had happened other than accepting the offer to enter her mobile home.

'Milk?'

'Please.'

She poured from a china jug. 'You accept my son couldn't have done this?' She handed him the mug. 'And you're not going to make any more trouble for us?'

'Lucy, all I want to do is put an end to whatever this is. I have no interest in making trouble for anyone. I have a busy job. Your son being in prison, that's nothing to do with me.'

'Doctor Forde, please don't take me for a fool.'

'It's Luke, please. And what do you mean by that?'

'All right then, Luke. Pretending you don't know – at the very least that's insulting.'

Seeing his confusion, she explained, 'OK, then. Maybe it's nothing to do with you directly. But there's your wife.'

The coffee scalded the back of his throat.

'Your wife had Sebastian put away on a drugs conviction. Look around you . . . does it look like we're growing on an industrial scale? Does it? Well, what do you think?'

She pointed to a tiny corrugated outhouse at the rear of the mobile home. It was hidden from view of the main road. Luke spotted a white cable running from Sebastian's caravan into the shed through a gap under the corrugated roof.

'Someone neither of us ever heard of gave a statement to Joe Hegarty in the town,' said Lucy. 'Joseph Hegarty, the policeman.'

Luke said nothing.

'A statement intended to show intent of sale and supply,' Lucy continued. 'I don't use myself. Doesn't agree with me. And Sebastian has never sold anyone drugs in his life.

Luke's mind was stuck back on that name, *Joseph Hegarty*. He'd heard the name before. He couldn't swear but he was pretty sure that Joseph was a brother of Sly Hegarty, the foreman of the scrapyard at Crow Hall.

'Do you know how many MS sufferers live around the lough?'

Luke shook his head. He rarely engaged in local gossip.

'Sebastian has supplied cannabis to MS sufferers from time to time, but I assure you that no money ever changed hands. That's not what we're about.' Lucy once again looked aggrieved. 'You can tell your wife, Sebastian won't be anywhere near your precious daughter again. Neither of you need to worry about that.' She was showing signs of mounting anger. 'You know, I'd heard rumours about the Crow Hall mafia out here at the lough. And stupid me, I laughed it off. Don't be ridiculous, I told myself. Well, I can tell you something now, I won't laugh again.'

Luke pulled his collar closer round his neck. *The Crow Hall mafia.* An expression he'd once scoffed at too.

'A bit heavy-handed, don't you think?' Lucy looked at him coolly now, her anger passing. 'A quiet word would have done it. But no. Your wife wanted her pound of flesh. Seven weeks in that place, Sebastian got. And a criminal record to boot. A somewhat unbalanced response. Disproportionate, I'd say.'

To have a charge of 'unbalanced' levelled at anyone from the mother of Sebastian Considine was quite something. If the arrogant prick got more than he'd bargained for, he might consider his actions a little more. It would cool his jets.

Lucy continued. 'I've no idea who's responsible for that exhibit out there in your car,' she said. 'I'd say there's no end to the list of enemies the Thompsons could have. I'm sure you won't have to look too far to find your perpetrator. But don't go bringing this to our door. This has nothing to do with me or Sebastian.'

Luke felt he was taking up a lot of room in the confined space. He felt as if the walls of the caravan were starting to close in. Outside, the rain was drumming fiercely on the roof and his head began to throb.

'Thanks for the coffee.' He stood to leave.

'Don't worry, Doctor Forde. Sebastian won't go anywhere near your daughter again.' Lucy held open the rusting door.

Luke stepped out onto the squelching mud.

'Just one more thing,' said Lucy. 'You can tell your wife and her friends that I won't be dropping my objections to the wind turbines. After what she's done, I'm more determined than ever to stop it. Mafia or no mafia, I will stand up to this.'

Back in the car, Luke felt dejected. The adrenaline that had fuelled his journey to this side of the lough was spent. He'd been falsely buoyed, thinking himself about to solve the happenings of the last couple of weeks. He was furious with Alison. Why had she suggested it was Sebastian who was behind the stunt with the casket and the death notice in the paper? She would have known that Sebastian was in prison. And it was most unlikely he'd orchestrated all of this from prison. He punched the touchscreen for Alison's number.

'Luke,' she answered promptly.

'What are you playing at, Alison?'

'What's the matter? I don't understand . . .'

'Like hell you don't. You just allowed me to tear off half-cocked to the Considines' place and bawl them out for this sick stunt, when you knew all along that it wasn't true because you had that stoner, Sebastian, thrown in jail on some drugs charge. He got out last night.'

'Well, I'm not quite sure how I was supposed to know—'

'Stop. Stop this bullshit now. I confronted them and accused them of sending the coffin and the doll thing. As you can guess, Lucy Considine didn't take that too well. So, if you hoped to warn them off, your little plan backfired. Lucy Considine is more determined than ever to object to the extension of the wind turbines. And I don't imagine your furry friend, Gilligan, will be too pleased with that.'

Luke hung up. The hammering in his head grew louder. He was more confused than ever. The explanations he'd been looking for had been whipped away. Someone was toying with him. Someone was playing this game with him. If it wasn't the Considines, who was it?

Home Alone

Luke arrived back from his altercation with the Considines all fired up. He had work to do. Where had he left the lump hammer? He knew he had it recently. Perhaps it was in the toolbox with the accessories for the cruiser. He headed for the boathouse.

Opening the door at the end of the glass corridor, he was alarmed to see that there were now only three steps free of water. The others were submerged. Driving around the countryside earlier, he'd tuned in to local radio. Reports told that upriver, they were opening weirs to alleviate the flooding. The farmers around Lough Carberry had taken to the airwaves. They were incensed. They argued that the floodwaters were being pushed downstream towards them. Luke reckoned they were right.

In the boathouse, he located the toolbox but couldn't find the hammer. He racked his brains trying to think when he had last used it. Heaving the toolbox back onto its shelf, he headed back to the house. Opening the door to the kitchen, he had a brainwave. It was coming back to him now.

His footsteps were brisk in the marble hallway as he headed for the basement. Fumbling with his keys, he unlocked the door and headed down. There it was . . . poking out from underneath the tattered cardboard box of videotapes he was in the middle of destroying. He'd get back to that at a later stage. For now, all he wanted was to destroy that casket in the car.

He knew the casket was evidence, he knew he should keep it, he knew he should probably share it with the police. But he also knew he wasn't going to do any of that. Lump hammer in hand, he went back up the basement stairs, and headed out the front door to where the car was parked. He opened the dog-run to let Duffy out first.

The casket was surprisingly difficult to smash. Every time the hammer came down, splinters went flying. The dog threw back his hairy head and barked thinking it all a game. Worry tunnelled holes in Luke. This was a game for which he was ill-equipped, knowing neither the rules of engagement, nor his opponents. As soon as he finished, he disposed of the splintered box in the household wheelie bin and went inside. The dog followed.

Luke opened a cupboard looking for dog food. 'You know what, Duffy? I sent Nina off, thinking things would settle down. It's beginning to look like I was wrong.' The dog wagged his tail at the mention of Nina's name. The animal was far more concerned, however, with the tin of food that Luke was opening. He set Duffy's bowl down in the garden room and, returning to the kitchen, he opened a tin of soup for himself, not bothering to heat it up. He went back to the garden room and slumped onto the sofa. Tin in hand, he ate the cold tomato soup, looking out at the rain sliding down the windows.

Melancholia took hold on him. He cast his eyes over the open-plan room, the steel columns, the glass roof, the double-height walls. The white of the walls was broken only by Alison's show-jumping rosettes. The pared-back look had all the warmth of an industrial warehouse.

When Nina had started school, she'd sticky-taped paintings to the kitchen walls. Luke later found them crumpled and discarded in the kitchen bin. They disturbed the cleanness of the walls, Alison said. Luke retrieved the tea-stained paintings, smoothed them out, and put them in a plastic folder. Fran had put them up in his consulting rooms.

Over the dog's wet odour Luke now noticed another smell. Furniture wax. The house had been cleaned in the last few days. There was only a light layer of dog hair around the house and the periodicals he brought home but rarely read were stacked neatly in the magazine rack.

The cupboards were well stocked and there was a supply of luxury-brand ready meals in the fridge. Walking through the hall on his way in, he'd passed an assortment of suits, scarves and a raincoat, all wrapped in plastic sheeting from the dry-cleaner.

Alison no longer lived with Luke, but she understood the benefits of looking like she did. Despite spending her time at Crow Hall, she continued to manage domestic affairs at the Glasshouse. She took care of the dry-cleaning and the grocery shopping. Not personally, of course. She'd arranged a cleaning lady to come twice a week to do the household chores and do the groceries. Luke couldn't see a reason to complain. It made his life easier, and it all took place without any input from him. He departed the house in the morning, leaving behind the detritus of living, and came back to a clean but empty home.

When he checked the postbox, he'd find post addressed to Alison. She was clever like that. She knew the value of having mail delivered here. She understood the value of providing the postman with a managed view of their lives. The postman saw letters from Inland Revenue, the bank, letters for health screening or from solicitors. There was a wealth of information to be gleaned from a sealed envelope.

And when she called in person, Alison marked up the calendar with reminders for dental appointments and her heart check-ups with Raymond Grogan. She knew how to keep up appearances. Family values, or at least the pretence of family values, mattered to her constituents.

Luke couldn't picture how he figured in Alison's long-term plans. He decided to bide his time and play along. But it was difficult to see how the Thompsons would let him leave their clutches. They were unlikely to set him free, knowing what he knew.

He was as congenial as he could muster. He made himself amenable to Alison's wishes. He texted convenient times for her to drop by to collect her post or dry-cleaning. The texts served another purpose. He could avoid any embarrassment should he have company in the Glasshouse.

These past few months he'd made a lot of progress with Terence. Opening up and considering his next steps. The events of recent weeks, however, had put all that in jeopardy. With the scrawl on the boathouse wall, the death notice and now the doll in the casket, it was a lot to deal with. He felt he was on the verge of a setback.

It was affecting his relationship with Sophie. He'd seen the look on her face when he'd shown her that horrible casket. He had sensed suspicion. He'd noticed her snatched sidelong glances wondering what he'd been up to. Wondering what he'd done to invite such darkness into his life. He didn't want to scare her off. She'd been good for him these past few months. He was more settled and he was getting out more. They'd been to two shows in Dublin and *The Book of Mormon* in London. More than he'd ever done with Alison.

Making love to Sophie was unpredictable and exhilarating. There were times he'd prefer she didn't cover his face and eyes but it was a small price to pay. She liked it like that. She was easy company, and always took care to ask him his thoughts and how he was feeling. He thought back to how useless he'd been this morning when talking about her cat. Reaching for his mobile, he dialled and waited. He was about to hang up when she answered.

'Yes?'

She sounded throaty.

'It's me, Soph,' he said. 'I'm just ringing to see how the cat is . . . and to apologise for sharing all that weird stuff with you earlier. I shouldn't be bothering you with any of this.'

'Fidget's dead.'

'Oh no.'

'He passed away not long after you left. So that's it.'

Her voice sounded flat. Hoarse. As if she'd been crying.

'I'm so sorry, Sophie. Give me half an hour and I'll be over.'

Silence.

'Sophie? Are you there?'

He thought he could hear a sob.

'Don't take this the wrong way, Luke. But I'd rather be on my own for now.'

'Of course, I understand. I know this must be hard.'

She tried to respond but her voice sounded strange and strangled.

Luke didn't know what more to say. He waited for her to say something.

'I'll call you when I'm ready,' she said.

The line went dead.

In Memoriam

'You must be looking forward to seeing Nina,' said Fran, checking the razor pleats of her navy skirt. 'I'm dying to hear all about her trip.' She sat down at her desk.

Weeks earlier, Fran had waved a postcard in front of Luke as if it were a prize. It was from Australia. She'd Sellotaped it to the filing cabinet. Nina and Fran were close. Fran had helped out with Nina's homework when she was a kid and she took her to the optician or the dentist when he couldn't. Alison was always busy campaigning for every child except her own.

'It'll be great to have Nina home,' he said, ignoring the worry gnawing away at him. He was checking through emails, sitting at his desk.

'Loads has happened since she left.' Fran wore a sly expression on her face. 'With that awful death notice for a start. It's not the same home she left.' She made a pretence of tackling the mail tray. Getting up, she placed a manila envelope marked 'personal' on his desk. 'Yes indeed, I expect things will take a bit of getting used to.'

'How so, Fran?'

'Well, with your new lady friend and all – I do hope Nina won't feel left out. But you'd never know, maybe they could go to kick-boxing together.'

Luke pulled his car keys from his pocket and lobbed them across the room onto Fran's desk.

Fran jumped.

'The key fob isn't working. I can't lock the car doors. Can you sort it?'

'The car is booked in for a service next week . . .' She was taken aback. 'But yes, of course, I'll bring it forward if you like.'

'Never mind. It can wait a week,' he snapped.

Heading to her desk, he reached across and snatched the keys. He wasn't having any more of her wisecracks. When Nina met Sophie, he knew she'd like her, and he knew, or hoped, that Nina would not feel threatened by his new relationship.

'Did you confirm my availability for the Chicago transplant conference in the autumn?'

'Yes.' Fran was looking beyond Luke, over his shoulder. Luke hadn't heard the door open but he felt the presence of someone standing behind him. He felt a rush of embarrassment at what must have sounded like his bad-tempered, churlish behaviour.

'Thank you,' he said in a kinder voice, looking over his shoulder to see who it was.

Hugh Smyth. Luke had no idea how long he'd been there.

'Hugh,' he said, 'didn't see you there, my man.'

'You're busy.' Hugh was already halfway out the door. 'Catch you again.' And he was gone.

'Ready for your patients now?' Fran asked smugly, happy that his rudeness had been witnessed.

'Wheel them in.'

Fran was making her way to the door to the waiting room when she stopped. 'Oh, before I forget,' she said, 'Johnny Whelan dropped in just before you got here. He was wondering if you were still on for tonight?' She looked at him in question.

'Said to text him and Hugh Smyth – that you'd know what it was about.'

Shit.

He'd completely forgotten. Probably why Hugh had called in. Luke bowed his head making it clear the conversation was over.

'I'll send in your patients,' Fran said in her receptionist voice. 'You know,' she delayed, her hand on the door jamb. 'There's something about him.'

'Who?'

The woman never knew when to put a sock in it. Could she not just do the job he paid her for?

'Johnny Whelan. Something odd.'

'Let's just get on with my patients.'

He had forgotten about tonight's arrangement with Hugh and Johnny. He wasn't prepared. He hadn't edited the video yet. He hadn't been in the basement much since Nina left. And there wasn't any beer. He'd have to stop at the off licence when he finished up today.

All of this meant he couldn't call on Sophie. Damn. He'd been considering dropping by her place. She hadn't returned his phone calls and she wasn't answering the landline at her work. He'd sent a bouquet of flowers to her house, but so far she hadn't acknowledged them.

She was still clearly upset about the cat. He didn't like Sophie ignoring him. He missed her. The way she made him feel. Good and wholesome. The way he liked to feel. When her eyes searched his, she saw the conscientious doctor, the father who missed his child, the lover. When she cupped his face and her eyes plumbed his, she did not see a weak man, a man who had lost his way. Tomorrow, he resolved. He'd drop by the office tomorrow. Or stop by her house at least.

Luke's appointments ran late that afternoon. It was after seven when he pulled out of the hospital car park, the sky dark with rain. He set the wipers to full speed. A mile up the dual carriageway, he pulled into the retail complex to buy some craft beers. Hugh Smyth liked his craft beer.

Purchase complete, he headed back out onto the carriageway away from the city, taking care to follow the detour signs for the lough. And still it rained. It pummelled down, sloshing down the windscreen, hopping off the tarmac. He was sick to the back teeth of this weather. If he heard the word 'unprecedented' once more he'd scream. Roads were closing all the time. He hoped the guys would make it to the Glasshouse without much bother.

Hugh would be fine. He could take the shortcut from his place through that housing estate out to the lough. The roads should be OK there. Luke's mind began to wander. His trousers were sticking to his legs where the rain had wet them. He shivered. In his mind's eye he could picture that housing estate. Gripping the wheel, he willed the pictures from his mind.

There was Johnny. Luke wasn't sure where Johnny lived these days. Always moving from one bachelor pad to another. Floods, hail or snow, Johnny would turn up. He wouldn't miss it. He enjoyed these nights more than the rest of them.

Luke turned on the radio. Some guy from the Inland Waterways was advising about measures being taken to control the water levels in the catchment areas upstream from the lough. Levels there had increased by 50 centimetres in the last forty-eight hours and the hydroelectric station was approaching capacity. Only another 50 cubic metres of floodwater could be accommodated. After that, the remaining floodwater would have to be diverted through the weir and it would be difficult to predict the rise in the level of the lough. This news was broken by the sound of Luke's mobile ringing.

'Luke?'

Fran sounded panicked.

'I'm sorry but I have to ask you to come back.'

'Louise Troy is the consultant on call tonight, Fran. Not me.'

'Not to the ward, Luke. To your consulting rooms.'

Luke pulled into the hard shoulder and put his hazard lights on.

'What is it, Fran?'

'When you get here,' she replied. 'I'd rather not say while you're driving.'

Luke entered the hospital by the outpatient consulting rooms. The corridor was quiet save for the low hum of a cleaner using an electric floor polisher. His hurried footsteps echoed off the lime-green walls. He was texting, cancelling the evening's arrangements with Johnny and Hugh. The guys would be unhappy about this.

There was only the light from Fran's desk lamp as he walked into the outer office. She was sitting at her desk.

'What is it? What's going on?' he asked.

She lifted a manila envelope from where it was sitting on her lap, placed it on the desk, and moved it towards him.

'This,' she said.

The same A4 envelope she'd left on his desk earlier, marked 'personal'.

Swallowing, he looked inside.

Bookmarks?

He took one out. He stared. A photograph above several lines of verse. He'd seen that photograph before. It was taken the night Alison won the election. The three of them together. Luke, Alison and Nina. Alison had liked it and put it on the console table in the hallway at the Glasshouse. He recognised the verse below the photo as Yeats. 'The Lake Isle of Innisfree'. And above the photo:

In memoriam, Nina Forde-Thompson. Gone but never forgotten.

'I didn't know what to do,' Fran said quietly. 'I opened it after you left. Then I called you.'

So, this game wasn't over.

'It was marked "personal". Why did you open it?'

Her eyes widened.

'You've never said anything before. I always open things for you marked "personal".'

'From now on, don't.'

'What's all this about, Luke? Shouldn't you call the police?'

'This is nothing to do with you, Fran. Forget about it.'

He had his suspicions.

'But—'

'But nothing, Fran.' He towered over her desk. 'You don't want to get involved in this. Believe me.'

Personal Effects

'It's great to see you. I was chatting to Wendy earlier. She loved having you in Sydney.'

Luke was in the car in St Matthew's car park on a video call to Nina. It gave him some comfort that she was taking his calls again these past two weeks. He held his phone close up. Nina was looking tanned and healthy. He didn't tell her about the memoriam cards. He hadn't mentioned them to anyone and he was staying out of Fran's way as much as possible.

'Wendy's really cool. Toni too,' said Nina. Her speech and mouth were out of synch. 'It's nice to be around people who treat you like an adult.'

He let it slide.

'Can you do something for me, Dad? Tell Mum I won't be doing Politics and History at college.'

'Really? Well, believe it or not, I've only seen Mum a handful of times since you left. She's in Dublin most of the week. She's busy with a select committee on energy.'

'Not wind energy by any chance?' Nina pulled a face.

'Got it in one.'

It was time to declare his change in situation. Given that he'd already dropped Sophie into conversation a good few times, Nina had probably figured things out for herself. Still, it was best to spell things out clearly. Nina was aware the marriage had been thinly held together. Giving voice to it would simply acknowledge that it was time for them all to move on.

'To be honest, Nina, Mum has more or less moved out of the house. Even when she's back in Clare, she spends most of her time at Crow Hall.'

Nina responded straightaway. 'I can't say that comes as a big surprise. I could never picture how the two of you ended up together to start with. I guess she's up there with Grandpa and Groper Gilligan calling in and fawning all over her?'

'I imagine so.'

'Well, I've no intention of being her little accessory any more. Just because she paid money for me doesn't mean she owns me.'

Cornelius, the bastard, had told her once that her mother had paid a lot of money to the orphanage for her.

'Of course it doesn't,' said Luke.

'So here's my news. I'm going to be going to catering college.'

Luke had to stop himself from laughing. A cook Nina was not.

'That's fantastic news,' he said. He didn't care as long as she was happy and didn't hook up with any more nutjobs. 'You know the woman I've mentioned a few times – Sophie?'

'Yeah . . . I kind of guessed you were having a thing,' she said cautiously.

'Well, you're right and Sophie's lovely, you'll like her . . . and of course she's dying to meet you. She wants to cook dinner for the three of us when you get back.'

'Oh right.'

'She suggested next Thursday when you fly back to Ireland, but I said you'd be jet-lagged. Maybe sometime the following week though?'

'Thursday's fine with me, Dad. I'm coming in to Heathrow first, spending a couple of days with friends in London before coming home.'

'Well, if you're sure. That'd be great.'

Nina giggled. 'I can't wait to meet the woman who'd put herself between you and Mum. One more thing – I'd prefer if Mum wasn't the one to collect me from the airport.'

He'd anticipated this. 'I'll do my best. Have a safe journey home, pet.'

'Will do, Dad. Love you.'

Nina hung up.

She seemed indifferent at the prospect of meeting Sophie. When he'd first mentioned her on the phone, Nina had asked very few questions. That was normal enough, wasn't it? Teenagers were self-absorbed. While Nina might be indifferent, he suspected Sophie was nervous at the prospect of meeting his daughter. Normal enough, too.

He'd been upset about Sophie's withdrawal from him after her cat had died. It had felt like an overreaction, as if it were somehow his fault. Whatever it was, it was water under the bridge now. Given their most recent night together he was confident their relationship had weathered its first chill.

The role play had been intense. Maybe a little too intense. He shifted in the driver's seat. His back was still tender. It was two nights ago. Under his shirt he bore deep welts from a riding crop that Sophie had picked up from the hallway.

With a few minutes to spare before leaving the car and heading into the hospital, it was an opportunity to give her a call and fill her in.

'Everything all right?' Sophie answered.

He was usually too busy to call her during the day.

229

'Sure. Everything's fine,' he said. 'I was talking to Nina just now. Thought I'd phone to say how much she's looking forward to meeting you.'

'Well, I'm looking forward to meeting the golden child.'

For one brief moment he worried she might be jealous.

'What night is it again?' she asked cheerily.

'You'd mentioned Thursday. Her first night home. If that's still all right with you?'

'But won't her mother want to see her on her first night home?'

'She'll see Nina the following day or so. I'd hoped the break might have done them both good. Things are still a bit . . . well . . . still a bit strained between them.'

'That's a pity.'

'There are two of them in it. Nina can be difficult too. Are you OK to come out to the house this weekend?'

'I'd love to but I'm away with some girlfriends. By the way, I do realise I have been a bit off lately. Sorry.'

'No need to apologise. I'm sure you'll make it up to me.'

'We'll see.' She chuckled.

'Look, if you're not around this weekend, I might as well work. I'll see if a colleague will swap shifts. That way I'll have more time with Nina when she gets back.'

'Good idea.'

'How about I collect Nina, then swing by yours to get you? Her flight's in from Heathrow around five. We can head up to the lough together.'

'I'll make something we can heat up when we get to yours. Something special. Vegetarian, I guess?'

'Yes.'

A pause.

'Will you miss me this weekend?'

'Of course. I was kind of looking forward to . . . to . . .'

'Shagging my brains out?'

'Ah, the eloquent Ms Ellingham.'

'You want to now, don't you?' Her voice was husky.

'I can't deny I feel a certain stirring in the glove compartment.'
He looked furtively in the wing mirror but there was no one else
in the rainy car park.

'You have no idea what I'd like to do to you.'

'Tell me. What would you like to do?'

The voice in his head told him this was absurd. Ludicrous.
Sitting in his car in the hospital car park talking like this. But
sense had deserted him. He'd never done this with his wife. Alison
got turned on by crises and how to manage them.

Sophie whispered, 'I'd love to rip your clothes off with my bare
hands . . .'

'And?'

'To cuff you. Tight.'

'And then?'

'Tie your feet together with my black silk scarf. Blindfold
you. And when you're waiting, desperate, then . . .' She paused,
her voice hoarse, 'that's when you'd feel it. Just a little at first . . .
nothing much . . . a short swish.'

This was one of her things. He was shocked the first time it
had happened, it had taken his breath away. Sex with Sophie was
something unknown, sometimes dangerous, always exciting. Lust
and a sense of being alive colliding into one. Before Sophie, he'd
never done anything like this and, though he found it weird at
first, he went along with it.

'I'd whip you harder . . .' Sophie giggled.

In an instant his desire evaporated. He'd spotted something.
His eyes were trained on the rear-view mirror.

231

'Got to go.' He hung up.

Slowly, slowly, he turned.

He reached across the seat. He swallowed. He recognised it. One of the blue plastic hospital bags used to package personal effects. It wasn't his, and it hadn't been there this morning when he'd driven to the hospital. It was tied with a knot at the top. It was bulky. Cautiously, he lifted it onto the passenger seat beside him, the blue plastic making a crinkling sound. It was printed with black block lettering:

HOSPITAL PROPERTY

He undid the knot and looked inside. He saw clothing. He reached in and pulled out something. Something pink. He held it up. Not a true pink. It had once been white. A T-shirt that had absorbed colour from the sodden clothes beneath. The clothes had a smell he recognised. The ferrous smell of blood.

Luke stared at the T-shirt. He'd seen one similar to this before. One like this had caused a pile of trouble. It was printed across the chest with *BAN THE HUNT* and it had a fox motif. He pulled his latex gloves out of the pocket of his white coat and put them on. He delved into the blue bag again.

Out came jeans, a pair of socks, a flowery bra, and a pair of panties. He laid them carefully across the plastic bag. All were soaked in blood. He surveyed the clothes. Then he spotted something, the outline of something he'd missed. Something small. Poking the garments aside, he put his hand back inside the bag. He pulled out a small white card:

Property of Nina Forde-Thompson (Deceased)

He pushed open the car door and breathed. He had to process this. Leaving the door open, he turned again to look at the blood-soaked clothes, scrutinising them. Nina had a T-shirt like this. But was this hers? And the jeans? How could he know? They had

232

been ripped intentionally. It was the design. Looking closer, he spotted writing in several places between the blood. *Ban the hunt.* It was Nina's handwriting. These were Nina's clothes. Luke placed the clothes back in the bag and secured the top with a knot.

Anyone could have had access to his car. He hadn't been able to lock it for weeks. Fran had just reminded him to drop the car off at the garage on his way to the hospital the following morning. She'd arranged a replacement car for the day.

Making his way across the wet car park, he looked up at the windows of the four-storey cardiac surgery unit. Consulting rooms, waiting rooms and offices all had a full view of the car park. Craning his neck, he made out Fran's collection of potted plants up against a window. He scanned the rest of the building. His eyes registered movement. Had someone stepped back from a different window? Had someone up there been watching him as he'd bundled the blue plastic hospital bag into the back of his car? He shuddered as drops of rain hit his face. He felt powerless. He was no closer to figuring out whoever was orchestrating any of this.

Back in his office, Fran was busy at her computer. She didn't look up as he entered.

'They're looking for you,' she said. 'I've been trying to get you. Your mobile was busy.'

'Who's looking for me?'

'The third-year Med students. It's your round this afternoon.'

'Oh, yes . . .'

'Hugh Smyth was in looking for you too.'

'I'll catch him later.'

He hesitated.

'You didn't put something in my car earlier?' he asked. 'No one asked you to put anything in it?'

Fran looked up at him, alert.

'No, why?' Her eyes scoured his face. She was like a hawk.

'Oh, nothing.'

He could feel her eyes boring a hole in his back as he closed the door behind him.

Fire

Over the weekend Luke had to deal with parents who were angry that their child couldn't be accommodated in paediatric ICU. Management had closed it for the weekend and the girl was obliged to take a bed with middle-aged men in the stepdown coronary care unit. Being busy meant Luke had less time to dwell on the blood-soaked clothing that had been placed on the back seat of his car.

By the time he crawled into bed on Saturday night he was shattered. A short time later, he was woken by the sound of sirens coming across the lough. It had taken a while to get back to sleep. He headed back to St Matthew's on Sunday, planning to take the dog for a walk when he got home that evening. With Nina gone, the poor animal was penned up for stretches at a time. Nina would be home soon but he was full of trepidation. Was it even safe for her to return?

He'd thought about suggesting she stay in Australia a while longer. But he couldn't think of any reasonable way to explain things without frightening her. He'd shared nothing with her beyond the death notice in the paper. If she was aware of all that had happened, he felt sure she'd no longer find it amusing.

He would call at Crow Hall on the way home from the hospital. He hadn't mentioned the memoriam cards or the bag of

Nina's blood-soaked clothes to Alison. There was, however, stuff Alison needed to know.

'To what do we owe the honour?' Cornelius greeted Luke in the hallway that evening. The hall was damp with drying boots and rainwear. 'Still flogging rain? I've never seen the like. I was just saying to Alison there's no point in sending Hegarty down to do the Glasshouse lawn. In this wet, the ride-on would only churn the grass.' He turned and headed towards the drawing room. Luke followed.

Luke had passed Sly Hegarty on the front porch on his way in. Sly was in his work clothes and he'd smelled of wet wool and chemicals.

Cornelius turned the doorknob and entered the drawing room. Though May, a fire smouldered in the hearth, and there, legs sprawled out by the burning logs was Roddy Gilligan. Alison was stretched out on the sofa, her stockinged feet in Roddy's lap, working on a laptop. Two Irish coffees rested on the burnished metal coffee table.

'How's it going, Luke?' asked Gilligan, more boldly than he would have done before. 'Anything strange?'

'Apart from you cosying up here with my wife, nothing more than usual.'

Gilligan reddened. Alison pulled her feet towards her.

'In top form this evening, so I see, Luke.' Cornelius enjoyed nothing more than a fractious exchange between the two men.

'Roddy's bringing me up to date on what's happening on the local farms,' said Alison.

'So it would appear.'

'The Jeffries place is under water,' Alison carried on. 'Crow Hall lads had to help winch his cattle that got stuck in the floods, isn't that right, Dad?'

'That's right,' said Cornelius, with a nod of satisfaction. 'I warned him to move them to higher ground, but you know Jeffries, he's a stubborn old bullock.'

'No more stubborn than you, Dad.'

Alison looked fondly at her father.

'Now, now,' said Cornelius. 'I just hope they appreciate all you're doing for them, Alison. That's all.'

'What exactly are you doing for them?' Luke was curious.

'There'll have to be compensation, won't there?' said Alison. 'This flooding is unprecedented. Thousands of acres are under water, properties are destroyed, cattle drowned. I'm making representations to our people in Brussels to investigate compensation. It's a head-wreck. I could have done without this at the beginning of my period of office.'

Luke doubted that things could have worked out any better. What better way to deflect any criticism of her stance on the wind farm than to be a conduit for compensation? It was a disaster that served the Thompson grace-and-favour system well. They'd supply sandbags at a cost. They'd rescue cattle. And with Alison as minister, they'd look after compensation.

When the time came, Luke had no doubt that any favours to Jeffries and other landowners would be called in. All those that had been helped would be in debt to the Thompsons of Crow Hall. Which was how they liked it.

'At least it's a distraction from your setbacks on the wind farm.' Luke couldn't resist.

Alison looked up from her laptop. 'Oh, I imagine any hold-ups there will soon be over.'

Luke doubted that. Lucy Considine had been adamant.

'You haven't heard?' Alison's eyes grew wide.

'Heard what?'

'Those awful caravans the Considines were living in – they burned down last night. Thank God they weren't in them. I imagine Miss Considine will have more on her mind than wind farms at the moment. You must have heard the sound of all those sirens coming across the lough last night?'

Luke looked from Alison to Gilligan. Was that a smirk on Gilligan's lips?

Luke pulled his shoulders back. 'Delightful as it is to see you, I only called to remind you all that Nina will be home this week.'

'Is that so?' said Cornelius. 'Let's hope that they've managed to put some manners on the girl out there.'

Luke glared at him.

'It's OK, Dad. I'm sure Nina will have got her act together now.'

'Well, the girl might be better off staying in Australia. There's a lot of opportunity out there. I'm just saying—'

'OK, Dad.' Alison was looking warily at Luke.

Cornelius shrugged and slurped his coffee, a sloppy cream moustache forming on his lips. He looked with rheumy eyes over his glass, eyes straying to Gilligan. He cleared his throat. 'All I'm saying is that the girl was never one of us.'

Gilligan bowed his head. Luke then realised what the old bastard meant. He had wanted a grandchild all right. Not knowing his daughter's heart condition, he had hoped for a grandchild bred from Gilligan and his daughter.

'Nina will be staying with me when she comes home.'

All three heads turned to look at Luke. It was time to leave. There was something unholy about this house. The dank lair of an evil old man. If Luke never set another foot in the place again, he'd be happy.

'Nina plans to go to catering college,' said Luke. 'She won't be doing Politics and History at university.'

Alison opened her mouth.

'I support that decision,' Luke said firmly. 'Just to let you know, I'm collecting her on Thursday. She'll be spending her first night home with me. If any of you want to see her, she'll be at the Glasshouse.'

'Teeth in a zip,' said Alison. Her smile was cold. 'I expected nothing less.'

'What you expect or do not expect is no longer any concern of mine, Alison. And you know what?' Luke paused. 'Someone like you should never have had children,' he said calmly. 'You're a fucking dreadful mother.'

Gilligan spewed his drink.

Alison stared.

'I'd watch myself if I were you, lad,' said Cornelius.

Luke let the front door slam as he went back out to the car. As he reversed, he took pleasure in churning up the lawn. How much longer would he and Alison have to limp along in their festering marriage? He longed to be free of her, her father and Crow Hall. It flummoxed him why Alison, businesslike and practical in all her dealings, had not suggested putting a legal end to the marriage. This was no oversight. Deliberate in all things, there had to be a reason.

As he headed for home in the pummelling rain, he considered her possible motives. Perhaps the Thompsons still didn't trust him. They needed to keep him close. Despite Cornelius's threat all those years ago, did they think he'd break ranks with what he knew and take that risk?

Or was it something more simple? Alison was a politician, after all. She'd aligned herself with Luke's success to get herself elected. Perhaps she didn't want to be associated with messy extramarital affairs. Perhaps she wanted to avoid a scandal.

The Thompsons and their coterie filled their days with scheming, their conversation never direct but laced with nuance in a parlance of their own. Nina would wither in such company. Or worse, but not unthinkable, she'd adapt to become like them. He didn't want Nina anywhere near Crow Hall.

Nina had asked once why Grandpa never answered her questions. Perturbed, Luke had challenged Cornelius. 'Sure I never know who the girl is talking to,' Cornelius responded. 'With one eye looking east and the other west, how's a man to know?' Even now it made Luke angry.

A few miles from Crow Hall, an oncoming vehicle swung out from its side of the road straight into Luke's path.

What the . . .!

Yanking the wheel, Luke swerved, and came to a shuddering halt, right on the edge of the ditch that ran along the roadside. He snapped his gaze to the wing mirror in time to see the vehicle as it rounded a bend. It was a truck laden with sandbags, its lights full-on in the rain. Righting himself in his seat, Luke adjusted the gears, revved the engine and reversed the Range Rover out into the open road.

The sky brightened in a strange colour and a fork of lightning flashed, followed by a clap of thunder. In the light, he saw a reason why the truck may have swerved. A pothole in the road. But did it need to swerve so wildly, and did it have to cross to Luke's side of the road?

Wondering who might have been driving, his thoughts turned to Sly. Something struck him. He thought back to earlier, to when he'd passed Sly on the porch. To that smell of wet wool and chemicals. Thinking about it now, he realised what the chemical smell was. It had an unmistakable smell. The distinctive smell of petrol.

He thought back to the sound of sirens coming across the lough last night.

Cameras

As Luke waited for the front gates to open, he could hear the dog barking. The rain had spluttered to drizzle and the thunder had rumbled off into the distance. Parking up, he headed for the dog-run. He'd bring the animal inside to calm him down.

'It's OK, little fella,' he said. 'I'm here now.'

As he reached to open the dog-run, he saw the chicken wire was warped where Duffy had been pulling at it. Bursting through, the dog raced to the front gates, tore down the lawn out to the water's edge, yelping and growling and sniffing at the ground. He threw back his head and barked into the sky.

'Here, boy!' Luke turned the key in the front door. He entered the house, keying the alarm code by the door. The dog appeared, snarling on the step outside. He looked into the hallway with a growl.

Luke bent to coax him in, catching him by the collar. The animal's nose was bloody, cut and chaffed from the chicken wire. Luke dropped to his haunches for a closer look. But the animal wouldn't settle. Luke straightened and pulled the reluctant animal into the house.

A quick scan of the hall confirmed nothing untoward. He tossed his raincoat onto the coat stand. The dog continued to growl. The light outside was starting to fail and Luke reached to turn on a hall lamp, which Alison had insisted was fashionable.

Something was wrong. Nothing obvious, but something felt not right. Luke headed for the kitchen, propping up a photo frame that had fallen over on the console table. The dog padded behind him, sniffing. There was a clean smell. Detergent, spray polish, bleach – no cooking smells, just the sterile smell of loneliness. At first glance, everything seemed in order.

The dog yelped.

Luke jumped. 'What is it, what do you see?' He proceeded from the kitchen into the garden room. He stared at the wall in front of him, over his left shoulder, then his right, and scanned those walls as well. He went from room to room. It was the same in the study and the dining room. Every family photograph, or rather every photograph that included Nina, was turned face down, or turned to face the wall. The same sight met him in every room he checked. Holding his breath, he turned the photographs around, one by one.

There was the large one of Alison and Nina accepting a cheque for a charity raising funds for African children whose sight was in danger. One of Nina wearing a spider outfit at a fundraiser. The forced smile. The one on the desk in the study of Nina next to Cornelius making a donation to a retirement home for police officers. And in the dining room, one of Nina and Cornelius at the inaugural Thompson bursary for Planning Law.

Back in the garden room, Luke felt anger as he righted the frame on the mantelpiece above the stove. It was a photograph of Nina sitting on his knee in the orphanage in Russia. Whoever had done this had slammed the frame so hard they had broken the glass.

'Hello?' he called. His voice sounded alien. High-pitched. Constricted.

Silence.

The dog cocked his head. His ears twitched, listening. If there had been anyone in the house, the motion sensors would have triggered the alarm. The alarm had been on when Luke had entered, so it followed that whoever had been here knew the code.

He'd check upstairs. From the landing he could see his bedroom door was open. His eyes scanned the space for anything unusual. He couldn't remember if he had left the door open or not. He walked softly towards the door, stopped and pushed it gently.

There, laid out flat on the bed was a suit. A tailored black jacket, tailored trousers, a black tie, stark against the whiteness of the shirt. And placed neatly on top, a pair of black shoes. A funeral suit.

He carried on to Nina's room. Her bedroom door was open wide. He reached inside and turned on the light. He held his breath. There was nothing immediately out of place in her room.

He was about to continue when he noticed her wardrobe door was slid open, just a little. He went in to the room and pulled the door fully open. There on the floor was a puddle of clothes, jeans, dungarees, T-shirts, jackets. They'd fallen from hangers onto the floor.

His eyes were pulled to her chest of drawers. Looking more closely now, he saw the top drawer jutting out slightly, proud of the others. He pulled it open and checked inside. It was Nina's underwear drawer. The clothes in the blue hospital bag had been taken from here, straight from Nina's room.

Someone was coming and going freely in his home. He had to secure his home, and quickly. The first thing he'd have to do was change the alarm codes. Luke glanced at the dog. 'Come on, little fella.' He moved towards the stairs. 'What say you and I head downstairs and see what we can tell from the security cameras?'

The dog looked up at him, trusting eyes searching his face. He could sense Luke's anxiety. He sniffed each step as he followed Luke down the stairs.

The security cameras had been installed primarily to deter prowlers from interfering with Luke's boat. One camera was positioned outside the garden room, trained on the boathouse. A second camera was positioned inside the boathouse. And a third camera was placed just inside the porch recess at the front door. It was trained on the front gates in the driveway.

It was possible that the intruder had arrived by boat, but it was more probable that he or she had gained access from the front of the house. Inside the house, Luke had a laptop in the kitchen he used to flip between the cameras. He pulled up a chair and sat. The feeds were live and he would have to rewind.

On camera one, he could see the shoreline and the boathouse at the far end of the lawn. The lough water had risen and foamy waves licked the edge of the grass where there had never been water before. On camera two, inside the boathouse, the cruiser bobbed up and down. The water was high. Now only two steps remained visible above the churning water.

There was a problem with camera three. Instead of the view Luke expected of the driveway and the gates at the front perimeter, all he could see was veiny marble. He was looking down at the front step in the porch. He got to his feet. Outside the front door, he looked up to study the camera. It had been moved. It was now angled to face the ground. He stood there looking, thinking. Duffy sat back on his haunches looking from the camera to Luke and back again.

'You know who did this, don't you, boy?'

The dog pricked up his ears and looked at him solemnly. It had been a state-of-the-art security system when it was first installed.

Luke and Alison had been advised on the system by Dickie Traynor, a security specialist who'd provided security advice for Cornelius when Cornelius had been a government minister.

The cameras could be adjusted manually or remotely using software. When building at the Glasshouse was nearing completion, before the site was secure, Alison and Luke moved in some furniture and personal items before moving in themselves. Dickie had configured the system so the cameras at the Glasshouse could be monitored from Crow Hall. Perhaps this facility had never been disabled.

Luke went back indoors and sniffed. *There it was again.* Detergent and furniture polish. The only smells in the house these past few months. Whoever was cleaning the house was heavy-handed on the cleaning agents.

'Jesus. Am I really that stupid?' He stopped in his tracks. 'What an idiot.'

He pulled his phone from his trouser pocket and scrolled. She picked up on the second ring.

'I assume you're ringing to say sorry.' Her tone was cold.

'Who was in the Glasshouse today, Alison?'

'I don't know what you—'

'You can cut the bullshit now. Who was here? Who do you have coming in to clean the place?'

She drew a sharp breath.

'Myra,' came her cautious reply. 'Why? What's the problem?'

'And who is Myra?'

'Luke, there's no need to be—'

'It's a simple question.'

He could hear her breathing.

'She's the cleaning lady.'

'No kidding.'

Another pause. He waited.

'She cleans here at Crow Hall and she does a bit for Roddy.'

She cleaned for Gilligan, did she?

'Did you arrange for her to come to the Glasshouse today?'

'No . . . no, at least I don't think so. Today is Sunday, Luke. I'm pretty sure I asked her to go on Friday. Why? What's she done?'

'I'm asking you one more time, who exactly is Myra?'

'I've told you,' her words were slow and deliberate, 'Myra's a hard-working cleaning lady. Salt-of-the-earth. You know her husband, Sly Hegarty.'

'Hegarty? Your father's henchman?'

'Well, if you must put it like that.'

Luke hung up.

This was worse than he thought. Myra Hegarty had been free to wander around the Glasshouse, his home. Free to study all the nooks and crannies of his personal life. Free to feed whatever titbits she saw fit back to her husband, Sly, and from there to Cornelius at Crow Hall.

He often left stuff lying around at home. Unlike in his hospital rooms. Receipts, diary entries, scribbled notes or tickets could be discarded on a bedside locker. The innocuous debris from a coat or trouser pocket could easily be used to piece together a view of his daily activities and reported back to Crow Hall. At least he'd kept the basement locked.

He thought back to what was on his bedside locker. Lance Armstrong's *It's Not About the Bike*, a phone charger and a few business cards. Among them the card of Terence Black, Psychotherapist and Counsellor.

Suspect Device

'Give Nina my love,' said Fran.

'I will.' Luke grabbed his raincoat from the coat stand.

Fran was standing at the office window. 'She'll want to turn straight around and head right back to the sun when she sees it here.' She looked out miserably at the car park. 'Just look at that rain. Look at all those potholes down there.' The rain had opened fissures in the tarmac.

'See you Monday, Fran.' Luke opened the door to leave.

Fran turned around. 'You're sure you want that security company calling to you tomorrow, Nina's first day home?'

'Certain.' He looked at his watch. 'Now, I have to go.'

As he headed for the lift, his brow furrowed. Fran was curious about why he was upgrading the security system at the Glasshouse. So far he'd managed to sidestep her none-too-subtle interrogations.

He'd cleared away some stuff in anticipation of the engineers' arrival. The basement had been a mess and he'd used the opportunity to do some filing. There were also those videotapes from the early days, the viewing quality poor in comparison to today's high-definition imagery. He used to discard sensitive material in the compactors at Crow Hall. But using the hospital incinerator for personal use could raise eyebrows. It was time to look for a different solution. He'd ask Johnny and Hugh how they got rid of stuff.

His thoughts returned to the business of the alarm as he waited for the lift. His home had been violated and he felt differently about being there. It didn't quite feel like *his* any longer. He wasn't taking any more chances. The alarm system was only one of a number of things he was changing. He'd informed Alison that from now on he no longer required the services of Sly Hegarty or his wife, Myra. He'd gone further, saying that in fact he no longer required the services of anyone from Crow Hall.

Stepping into the lift, he avoided eye contact with the other occupants. He checked the time. He was running late. But would make it as long as traffic was light. First out of the lift, he bowed his head as he headed for the exit. Once outside, he made briskly for the car, weaving a path through the puddles.

His heart sank as soon as he spotted his car. Every window of the Range Rover was plastered in lime-green stickers saying: *YOU ARE ILLEGALLY PARKED*. All over the front windscreen, the rear windscreen and each of the side windows. Security was trying to humiliate car-park users into observing the rules by using the most lurid stickers they could source. Hold on. He wasn't illegally parked, was he? He'd fallen foul of the wardens before. Since then, he was careful to park in his own reserved space, the one he always used. Something must have changed and perhaps he'd missed an email.

The stickers were a nightmare to peel off. The adhesive used was designed for maximum annoyance. This was a job for the ice scraper. He opened the passenger door. At least the fob was working again. He reached in to the glove compartment for an ice-scraper and set to work. It took fifteen minutes with rain sliding down the back of his neck before he managed to clear enough to see through the front and side windows. He didn't bother with the rear window.

Jumping into the car he started the engine. He checked the time on the dashboard. Dealing with Amanda Mellowes had taken longer than he'd thought. He could still smell that cloying perfume she wore. She had a habit of standing too close to him. Fran had suggested Amanda check with him before proceeding with a course of action for a child with Down's syndrome who had breathing difficulties. Why medical staff would take a blind bit of notice of Fran was beyond him. Amanda was a senior reg and some of the questions she'd put to him were frankly ridiculous. The doctor was more than qualified to answer them for herself. Now he was going to be late. Turning on the radio, he pulled out of the car park.

'Weather chiefs have upgraded their weather warning for certain counties to a Status Red.'

Excellent. More rain.

'A prediction of 90 millimetres of rainfall accumulation is expected in parts of the country overnight. The warning for this severe weather event is valid from 3 p.m. this afternoon right up until 3 a.m. on Saturday.'

Seriously?

When was it going to stop?

'Unprecedented flooding in parts of the catchment area of the longest river in the country is continuing in what the National Emergency Coordination Group has described as a "once in a lifetime flood situation". Landowners and small-town dwellers on the lower reaches of the river are incensed at the behaviour of the Water Authorities on the upper lakes. They stand accused of pandering to the concerns of business interests in the larger towns further up the river system. This from Independent minister Alison Forde-Thompson, whom we interviewed earlier today . . .'

Luke turned up the volume.

'Farmers in my constituency have said another ten thousand acres of land have been covered by water over the weekend. These farmers want the Department of Agriculture to defer inspections in flooded areas and to go ahead with EU farm payments before the end of the week . . .'

Alison sounded competent and confident.

'And Minister, what do you say to those people who are worried that by this time tomorrow their homes could be under water if the Office of Public Works goes ahead with their proposal to open the sluice gates at the top of the river to alleviate flooding there?'

Alison responded immediately:

'Well, Brian, as you know, the river system feeds into the top of Lough Carberry and feeds out into the lower river by the narrow channels at the hydroelectric station and the weir. If all the sluices are opened further up the system, there is a greater volume of water in the lough resulting in the unprecedented flooding that we've seen. The maximum capacity of the hydroelectric station is four hundred cubic meters per second and the remaining water flows over the weir.'

'Yes, Minister, but as I asked, what can you say to those people who are worried?'

'As my constituents are well aware, Brian, the Thompsons will always stand shoulder to shoulder with them. I'm a lough resident myself and I can tell you it's most alarming when you see that water coming closer and closer to your home. I've been affected personally by this, so I know what I'm talking about here and I can assure—'

Luke switched stations. Her too-smooth voice was grating in his ears. Rain sluiced down the windscreen. He increased the wiper settings and turned his fog lights on. He was making time. He might not be disastrously late.

'—and now to finish our round-up of more local news. Initial reports from Health and Safety experts at the site of a blaze that

destroyed the temporary dwelling of environmental activist Lucy Considine at Dromafooka, suggest that an unattended chip pan may have been the cause of the fire. The Considine family is said to be moving out of the area, alleging a campaign of intimidation. An invitation to the family by this programme to clarify their position was turned down, and as of going to air the Considines remained unavailable for comment.'

The airwaves were doing nothing to soothe Luke's mood. He changed frequency again, this time selecting a classic hits show. They were playing 'It's Raining Men'. Some joker at the station had a sense of humour. Luke checked his calls. Nothing more from Nina since she'd boarded. He smiled as he re-read her last message:

Yay. Got the window. Ignoring the weirdo coming on to me in the next seat. Dying to see u. xxx.

Nina always had to have the window seat. As a kid during school holidays when Alison was busy, and Alison was always busy, he took her abroad to conferences with him. She'd sit with puzzle books and listen to him speak in vast conference halls. She preferred that to staying in the Glasshouse with a babysitter or rattling around Crow Hall with Cornelius.

Arriving at the airport, Luke skidded to a stop at the short-term car park. He checked a flight scanner. The London flight had landed. He grabbed his umbrella, hoping to make it to Arrivals before Nina passed through. He got there, out of breath.

As he stood there, he registered something rare. A happy anticipation. He couldn't wait to throw his arms around his daughter. He checked the Arrivals board. Her flight had landed fifteen minutes earlier. It was the only flight in the last half hour. Passengers were coming through. She should be easy to spot among businesspeople dressed in suits and heels. Each time the doors into the Customs Hall parted, Luke rocked onto his toes, straining to catch a glimpse of her. The flow of passengers slowed to a trickle. Any moment now.

He pulled his phone from his pocket to check for messages. Nothing. Looking up, he felt a poke of excitement. A girl with long dark hair was looking back over her shoulder, sleeves rolled up, a tattoo covering most of the skin on her forearm. Was Nina sporting a tattoo? Excellent stuff. Alison would be livid. The girl turned around. Disappointed, he saw it wasn't her.

Five more minutes passed by. Another handful of passengers with small children came through the doors. He felt a growing disquiet. Maybe she'd been stopped by Customs. He could imagine how that might happen. He hadn't seen her in months but he could picture how she might look. Bedraggled, hair falling into her face, dark circles under her eyes. Being stopped was something she would relish. It would appeal to her inner rebel.

For the third time, he took his phone out of his pocket to check if she was trying to contact him. Nothing. He became aware of a sudden shift in atmosphere. An unseen crackle of tension. Something was going on behind him. He could hear the sound of running and a sudden commotion. Airport police swarmed onto the concourse. There were four of them, all in hi-vis vests. And a robot. Airport personnel ushered people towards the doors with a sense of urgency. In seconds, the concourse had all but emptied.

'Can you come this way, please, sir?'

Luke felt a hand guiding him towards the door, away from the robot, away from the police who were standing at a distance. Away from the lone suitcase that was standing in the middle of the now empty floor. Even as he was being guided away, he recognised the suitcase, the stickers plastered all over it. He craned his neck over his shoulder. He couldn't tear his eyes away. He kept staring at the stickers. *Ban Fox Hunting*. It was Nina's suitcase.

Taken

The security office was cramped. It smelled of sweaty feet and damp. As soon as Luke disclosed his knowledge of the suitcase and who he was, he was whisked off to the security office next to the Customs Hall. Surrounded by the four airport police, he sat, eyes glued to a monitor, and watched a controlled explosion of Nina's suitcase. He tried to process what was happening.

'Do you know where my daughter is?' he asked. 'I have no idea what this is about.' He scrutinised the stony faces of the airport police for clues. 'I don't understand why you had to destroy the suitcase.'

'Your daughter came in on a flight from Heathrow, right?'

'I believe so, yes. Where is she now?'

'And she entered the UK earlier in the week on a flight from Sydney?'

'Again, I think so. That was certainly her plan. Why? What's going on?'

'Has your daughter ever had any connections with extremism?'

'What?'

'Can you take a look at the screen here, sir? No, no . . . the one on the top right, yes, there . . . this is footage from thirty minutes ago.'

The scrawny policeman with the hard eyes pulled his chair closer and pointed at the grainy images.

'Just there.' He pointed to someone on the screen.

It was Nina. She was dishevelled. She was wearing a short jacket, the collar up, hair half inside the collar, half out. Sweat prickled his palms. He watched as she pushed her glasses up her nose, looking around expectantly. She was looking for him. She was dragging her suitcase behind her.

A man with a briefcase cut across her, almost tripping her up. He turned to her and said something. Luke guessed he was apologising. Nina smiled, accepting the apology. Luke watched closely, the only sound in the small office coming from the policemen breathing heavily as they also followed Nina's movements on screen. She was making her way beyond the steel handrails and out onto the concourse. She was looking, searching. Standing on the tips of her toes.

He should have been there. If he'd been on time—

'Look at this,' the policeman pointed.

Luke watched as Nina let the suitcase go and rifled in her denim jacket. She took out her phone and looked at it. Her expression was hard to decipher. The picture quality was poor. She looked agitated and was scanning the hall, running a hand distractedly through her hair.

Looking back to the phone, her manner changed and she broke into a run, forgetting all about the suitcase. His adrenaline surged as he tracked her through the crowd and followed her to the exit. His heart was pounding and blood whooshed in his ears as he watched her race through the sliding doors to the rain outside.

In the room, the four policemen remained silent. They were watching him, waiting, looking to see how he'd react.

He shook his head and looked at them.

'Where is she now? Where is my daughter?'

Two hard eyes bored into him. 'We don't know,' said the scrawny policeman. 'The exterior camera in that location has been damaged by—'

The door opened. Luke turned to look. A woman in army fatigues half-leaned into the overcrowded room and bent to whisper in the scrawny policeman's ear. The policeman nodded, expressionless. The woman backed discreetly out of the room. Luke raised an expectant eyebrow.

'As I was saying, Mr Forde . . . what was I saying . . . oh, yes . . .' The policeman faltered. 'Well, it would appear that there was nothing to be unduly concerned about with the suitcase.'

'Really? But I just saw the robot blow it up.'

'We have protocols, sir. And given the current climate,' he shrugged, 'we can't take chances. You understand.'

'What about my daughter?'

'As I said, sir. There are protocols. We've checked things out and it appears that your daughter isn't a person of interest at this time.'

The policeman's eyes narrowed as he spoke, suggesting a lingering suspicion about what had unfolded.

'You're free to go, sir.'

Luke stood and steadied himself.

'Thank you,' he said, realising how absurd that sounded. But he had no words for the situation.

He left through the door to the Customs Hall. Evidence of the explosion was being cleared away. People were still clearly uneasy as they began to reappear in the Arrivals Hall.

Proceeding briskly to the exit in Nina's footsteps, he traced the route that she had taken. He stopped outside and scanned the drop-off area and the car park for any sign. People were scurrying to and from their cars shielded by umbrellas. There was no trace of Nina. She had disappeared into the rain.

He stood, rain seeping onto his skin across his shoulders. He could hang around here hoping for a sighting, but deep down he knew that she was gone. Back in the car, he plugged his mobile in to charge. He tried to think. He tried to imagine what could have shocked her into running off like that, into abandoning her suitcase. He was starting to get cold. His wet shirt stuck to his skin and he couldn't stop shivering.

He tried her again.

'Hi, this is Nina Forde. Please leave a message.'

Her happy voice was jarring. In normal circumstances, Luke would have been amused that she'd dropped the 'Thompson' from her surname.

He tried another number.

'You have reached the voicemail of Minister Alison Forde-Thompson. If your call is about assistance for a flood-related matter, please call—'

He hung up. He turned on the ignition. The time on the dash read 19:20. More than an hour after he'd arranged to collect Sophie. He should call her.

No answer.

He waited a minute and dialled again. Still no answer. Was she annoyed he was late? It seemed unlikely.

His mobile pinged, a message from Sophie:

Hi, Nina's here with me. Safe and sound. Says you didn't show? V agitated. Fill you in when you get here.

He had never been so delighted to see a text. He called Sophie right back. She didn't answer so he left a voicemail:

'Hi, Soph. I'm on my way. It was pretty chaotic at the airport. I'm leaving there just now. I'll see you shortly.'

Revving the engine he pulled out of the short-term car park. Wipers on, headlights on, he took off, heading for the city. He couldn't work out how Nina had ended up with Sophie, but he'd find out soon enough. The main thing was she was safe. He couldn't wait to see her.

The light was poor as he pulled into Sophie's front yard. It wasn't quite 8 p.m. but in the rain it was hard to see. He'd expected to see lights on, but from the front, the bungalow appeared to be unlit.

He drove around the side. No lights there either. And no sign of her car. That was strange. Walking around the back, he knocked on a window pane on the back door. He stood on the step waiting for an answer. A neighbouring dog barked at the disturbance. He knocked again. More vigorously this time. A second dog joined in the barking. The evening air thickened with yelps and snarls.

Edging towards the kitchen window, he stood on his toes trying to see in over the high sill. The blind was halfway down. All he could see were jars of herbs, the same miniature tea set he had seen previously, and what looked like a necklace. No, wait. A set of rosary beads. And on the kitchen table sat an open tool-box. There was no one here. He'd have to phone her.

Returning to the car, he opened the door, put the umbrella down and shook off the water. He looked down the garden as he did so and his eyes caught sight of something out of place. Walking the short distance over the grass, he stood, finding himself staring down at what looked like a mound of recently dug earth staked with a cross.

He walked around the cross, the mucky grass, the ground making a sucking, squelching sound at his feet. He stopped. He examined the mound. One or two tufts of grass were beginning to take over the new soil. On one end was a small cross made of wood. Carved into the wood was the word, *Fidget*.

Luke knelt, extending a finger to the neck collar that hung around the simple cross. The animal was not long dead, but already the leather was beginning to rot in the wet. The name disk, however, was intact and he turned it over in his hand. The shock was instant.

My name is Fidget Sweetman. If found please call 0888 56455.

He stood and stumbled towards the house.

Breaking and Entering

He stood in the quiet of the kitchen. Listening. Broken glass had skittered all across the floor. He squinted as if in doing so he might hear better. There was no alarm. No footsteps. No sound except the steady ticking of the clock above the cooker, next to the crucifix.

His raincoat sleeve and the shirt underneath had ripped. Blood stained the fabric. There were splinters of glass in the wound where he'd gashed himself breaking in through the back door. It hurt. The pain kept him focused.

An empty cat basket sat in the corner next to the fridge. Kitchen utensils were set on a draining rack next to the sink – a frying pan, some saucepans, a wooden spoon. The work surface was tidy and a cookbook was propped open on a stand. The recipe said Potato Pie. There was the recent smell of cooking. The smell of baking herbs and garlic.

He needed proof. Where would she keep her post? He imagined she filed bills, kept receipts and categorised everything. She was a tidy, organised person. He needed a utility bill, a payslip, a personal letter, a credit card bill. Anything. Anything to prove that he was wrong. He wanted to be wrong.

He pulled open a drawer. Tea towels. Another drawer. Cello-wrap and lining for cat litter. He bent down to pull at the lower drawer, not caring that it came crashing out all over the floor. No sign of any correspondence. He'd try the other rooms.

He entered the hallway and listened. The hallway was dark with no natural light. He flicked a light switch. All the doors leading from the hallway were shut except for one. Sophie's bedroom door at the end. It was open.

He proceeded down the hall. He pushed it wide open. Clothes and hangers were strewn across the bed. The same bed where they'd lain together. Wardrobe doors stood open. She'd cleared most of her clothes.

He stepped back into the hallway. He tried the doorway on the left. It was locked. Above the doorframe was a small hook with a key. He reached up, took the key and cautiously opened the door. The room was in gloom. Unnaturally dark. Heavy curtains were drawn. He flicked the light switch.

The shock hit him first in the chest like a punch. It was small, the room mainly taken up with a single bed. There was a Disney poster, *101 Dalmatians*. The bed was dressed with a pink duvet and on the bed was a number of soft toys, carefully arranged. He recognised them.

These were the toys he'd seen hanging on the line the day he'd called unannounced. The day he'd collected that hideous parcel from the post depot. The toys he assumed were Fidget's playthings. Above the bed in cross-stitched lettering was a wall hanging. *Maisie's Room.*

The bedroom was pristine, a shrine. He edged around the bed to the small white dressing table. Plastic necklaces were draped over a wing of the mirror. There was a photograph on the table. A battery-operated candle flickered in front of it.

The photograph showed a sunny day. Sophie smiling, her

husband Kevin in short sleeves, between them both a young girl of about seven or eight, wearing a white dress with a full skirt. On her head, a tiara. The metal frame was engraved, *My First Communion Day*. The light from the candle cast a ghostly light on the long-dead child.

Luke stepped back and forced himself to the wardrobe. He opened it. Inside, clothes hung neatly from a rail. Sets of school pinafores, casual clothes and dresses. Small shoes and training shoes were in a neat line underneath. He shut it gently. He returned to the door and turned off the light. Locking the room, he placed the key back on the hook above the doorframe. He had come face to face with his crime.

Something struck him. Those rusted stumps in the garden that he'd assumed were the remnants of a greenhouse – were they the remains of a garden swing? And Sophie's tea set? Had that too belonged to a child?

He tried the next door to the left. It opened into a sitting room. It was small. He'd never been in there before. There was an open fireplace and a TV. There was a sofa and an armchair and a roll-top writing desk. And on the mantelpiece was a photograph of a child holding a kitten. Above her head was a banner reading *Welcome Fidget*.

He made for the roll-top desk. Inside were pigeonholes with letters. He pulled out a wad. There was a credit card bill addressed to a Ms Sophie Ellingham. An electricity bill. That too addressed to Ms Sophie Ellingham. He pulled a selection from another pigeonhole. Older letters, personal and yellowed. Handwritten. All addressed to a Mr and Mrs Sweetman. A name he would never forget. He tried the drawer beneath but it jammed. He shoved it home before yanking it again.

The drawer was packed with cards. Sympathy cards. He read one. Then another. And another. All the same. Each one extending condolences to Kevin and Sophie on the loss of their daughter, Maisie. Cold evidence of the devastation he had wreaked.

Luke was standing in the home of Sophie Sweetman. Once the childhood home of Maisie Sweetman. The child who on her first communion day, a day of celebration, had gone for a ride on her bicycle. The child Luke had abandoned on a deserted road, fifteen years ago. He had no idea how long he stood there before his phone rang. He pulled it from his pocket.

It was her.

Sophie.

'Hello?' he answered.

'Luke, you said you were on the way ages ago. Where are you?'

'I thought you meant to come to yours.'

'You're at *mine*?'

'Yes.' He paused. Then more deliberately, 'I'm in the house.'

A pause.

'How did you get in? Where are you now?'

'I broke the glass in your back door. I'm in the kitchen but I've been all through the house. I know who you are, Sophie.'

Silence.

'Where are you?' he asked.

In the background was the sound of barking.

'At the Glasshouse. I have a key, remember?'

Of course she had a key. He'd given it to her before their third date. She had the alarm code too.

More barking.

He heard a shout. A cry of distress. His grip tightened on the phone.

'I promised you a special dinner on Nina's return, didn't I?' Sophie said softly.

His knees went weak.

262

'Nina's there with you?'

'I said so in my text. And Luke, one more thing . . .'

'Yes?'

'We're looking forward to seeing you. But come alone.'

Out of Hours

He checked the dashboard: 20:15. Terence would have left the office hours ago. He had given Luke a mobile number back in the early days, anticipating he might want to talk out of hours.

'Luke, how are you?' Terence sounded as if he was eating. 'Everything OK?'

'No.'

'I see . . . what can I do to help?'

'What do you know about Sophie?'

'Sophie? You mean Sophie Ellingham, my secretary?'

'Yes.'

'Why do you ask?'

'It's important, Terence. I haven't got much time. I don't suppose you know that Sophie and I have been seeing each other?'

There was a pause. This was one disclosure he had felt the therapist didn't need to know. The one thing he hadn't shared with Terence during his sessions.

'No, Luke. I did not.' Terence sounded unhappy to hear this, just like Luke thought he might be. 'When did this start?'

'It's a recent thing. I don't have time to go into it at the moment. And I know now I've made a huge mistake. Can you tell me what you know about her?'

'I sense from your voice that you're agitated, Luke. Are you driving?'

'It's OK. I have you on hands-free.'

'Listen, do you want to meet at the office?'

'No. There isn't time . . . this is really very important. How did Sophie come to be your secretary?'

He could hear Terence breathing, thinking.

'She's been with me for years . . .' Terence began, unsure. 'She worked for my predecessor, Tom Slater. He had the practice before me. She attended him for some counselling and then I believe he took her on as his secretary sometime later.'

'And when you took over the practice, you asked Sophie to stay on?'

'That's right.'

'Do you know why Sophie was attending Tom Slater?'

'I don't think that would be ethical of me to say,' he said after a few seconds. 'I took Sophie on as a secretary, not a client.'

'Look, I'm not asking you to breach a confidence here. But if you have any idea at all, can you give me a rough pointer? It's really very important.'

'I suppose she did speak openly about it afterwards . . .' Terence sounded unsure.

'*Please*, I really need to know.'

'I think it may have been something to do with her divorce.'

'OK. And you've always known her as Sophie Ellingham?'

'Yes, why?'

'You've never known her as Sophie Sweetman?'

'What's all this about, Luke?'

'Please, just answer me.'

He could hear Terence breathing.

'That's correct,' he said, slowly. 'I've always known her as

265

Sophie Ellingham. That was her maiden name. I think she mentioned that she'd gone back to her maiden name after the divorce.'

'This is a disaster, Terence. A complete disaster. Do you think the woman could be dangerous?'

'Dangerous?'

'Sophie Ellingham is Sophie Sweetman. They're the same person.'

Terence took a few moments to digest this.

'I don't see why any of this is a problem.'

'OK. I'll spell it out. Sophie Sweetman is Maisie Sweetman's mother.'

'And Maisie Sweetman is . . .?'

'Maisie Sweetman was the child . . . the child killed in the hit-and-run.'

There it was. Luke had said it aloud. He'd voiced those words. *Hit-and-run.* He'd said her name aloud. *Maisie Sweetman.* Even in the painful honesty of his sessions with Terence, he'd never used her name before. He'd called her 'the child', as if in not naming her, he might somehow distance himself from what he'd done.

'Good God,' said Terence softly. 'How do you know this?'

Luke ignored the question. 'Did you ever tell Sophie why I was attending you?'

'Of course not. Did you?'

'No. Not the real reason. I think she assumed it was down to my marriage falling apart. And she didn't ask. Did she have access to my notes?'

'Let's think . . .' said Terence. 'In all our sessions you never mentioned this child's name. Even if you had, it's not something I would record. It wouldn't be relevant to the therapy.' He paused. 'I jot down the odd thought or doodle as it occurs to me

266

throughout a session. And I might do a mind map and revisit it as a client's sessions progress.'

'What do you do with those notes?'

'Some are purely for the duration of the session. Those, I put in a box for shredding. The notes I want to revisit, I usually give to Sophie to file. And if I record notes on a Dictaphone, I get her to transcribe them to a Word document.'

'So, you never recorded any specific information about the . . . the accident? You wouldn't have recorded that it was a . . . a hit-and-run?' Luke had a gagging reflex as he uttered the words again.

This time around Terence was slow to respond.

'The honest answer is that I don't know. I may have done. But even if I had, they would have gone into a box for shredding on the same day.'

'And you do that yourself, the shredding?'

'Generally, yes.'

This didn't sound good. Luke knew how disorganised Terence could be.

'Off the top of my head, there's nothing specifically linking you to the accident,' Terence added.

'I don't know how, but I think you're wrong, Terence. Sophie has taken Nina. She's holding her at my house. I'm on my way there now.'

Now We Can Start

From the road above, Luke could make out pools of light coming from the direction of the kitchen in the Glasshouse. Oddly too, he could see the lights on in the glass corridor between the house and the boathouse. Swinging into the drive, he saw Sophie's car parked at the front door. He was startled to also see Alison's soft-top BMW.

Jumping down from the car, he ran for the door, squeezing the housekeys in his fist. The rain soaked through him in seconds. As he passed Sophie's car, he noticed suitcases and travel bags in the back.

At the door, he cupped his hands around his eyes and peered through the glass side panels. The hallway lay in gloom. Some light seeped through from the back of the house. All was eerily quiet. He put the key in the lock. As quietly as he could, he turned the key. Listening, he held his breath before pushing against the door.

Without warning, he found himself on the floor. He couldn't breathe. The kick to his groin had been delivered with devastating force. He twisted to his knees. He barely had time to register what was happening before he was kicked again, this time the kick was delivered between his shoulder blades. He crumpled to the floor, disabled. His scalp burned as someone grabbed a fistful of hair and pushed his face into the marble floor.

He was stunned. He felt someone grab his wrists. He was powerless. Whoever it was, was working fast, behind him now, wordless. He winced at the force of the knee on his back. He felt breathing on his neck, panting.

'Jesus,' he moaned. 'What the—'

'Quiet,' she said.

He recognised the voice. It was Sophie.

He felt something hard cutting into his wrists. She pulled even tighter. He wondered did she mean to break the skin.

'Get up.'

'I can't,' he mumbled. Waves of nausea washed over him.

'Try.'

The pain was too much. He rolled onto his side and curled his knees towards him.

'Luke?' a panicked voice called out. 'Is that you?'

Alison.

She sounded terrified. He'd never heard her like that before. Craning his neck, he could see her sitting at the kitchen table. From the position of her body, he could tell she was tied up, her arms behind her at an unnatural angle.

'Where's Nina?' he asked.

From the hall, Luke could see the laptop open on the table, the screen facing Alison. He guessed they had been watching the driveway camera, waiting for him to arrive.

'Come on,' said Sophie, less roughly this time. 'Time to join your wife. Happy families. I took the liberty of inviting her to join us for dinner. An invitation she clearly couldn't refuse.'

'You'll need to help me up.'

'Knees first . . .' Sophie pushed him into a kneeling position.

'One foot on the ground . . . yes, like that . . . then the other. There we go.'

Luke could now see Sophie. Her hair was tied up and she was dressed in black. A black zip-up Lycra jacket. Black Lycra leggings. Black runners.

'Sorry,' she said. She sounded oddly sincere, as if pained by the assault she'd just inflicted on him. 'The force was necessary,' she added, a hardness closing in across her face.

'Where's Nina?' he asked shakily.

'Come to the table,' she commanded. She guided him by the arm.

'Is Nina here?'

She ignored him. 'You must eat.'

The thought of eating made him feel even more nauseous. His head was thumping and his groin throbbed. The scene was surreal. The domesticity so completely at odds with Sophie's violent behaviour. The smell of hot food assailed him.

'Here, next to your wife . . .' Sophie pointed.

Alison's eyes bulged. He sat clumsily, trying not to lose his balance as he collapsed onto the chair. Alison stared. They were separated by only a few feet. He felt the weight of her glare accusing him as she shook her head from side to side.

'What in God's name are you involved in?' she hissed.

He let the question go unanswered. He was trying to focus. He looked groggily at Sophie as she calmly zipped open a pocket in her jacket to take out a handful of long black tie-wraps. She drew up briskly behind him.

He could hear her breath. He twisted his head to see what she was doing, watching as she secured his wrists to the spokes of the chair. He grimaced as a second plastic bracelet cut into his skin. She pulled the tie-wrap even tighter.

270

'Christ!' he cried.

'Good,' came Sophie's satisfied response. He could feel her breath hot against his neck. She got to her feet. 'Now we can start.'

She walked purposefully back to the other side of the table. It had been laid with two place settings. One for Alison and the other for Luke. They watched in silence as Sophie plated up a dish for Luke from the casserole in the centre of the table.

Putting the lid back on the casserole, Sophie sat and put her hands in her lap. She was unruffled, expressionless. It was a Sophie that Luke didn't recognise. His eyes flitted around the room. He glanced at the laptop on the table and saw that it was indeed covering the driveway.

'Where's Nina?' he asked again. He tried to mask his fear.

'All in good time.'

'And the dog? Where's the dog?'

'He's a noisy creature.' She picked up a spare fork. 'He's in your basement.'

He must have left it open last time he'd been down. He'd been distracted looking for the lump hammer.

Sophie scooped up a forkful of stew from Luke's plate. She held it to his lips across the narrow table.

'I'm not hungry.'

'You'll need to keep your strength up. You must eat. Come on, open.'

The prongs of the fork jabbed his lips and, gagging, he opened his mouth.

'Now eat.'

He forced himself to swallow. One forkful, followed by another.

'I can't,' he protested.

'You can,' said Sophie sternly. 'I know what it's like to be told to eat when you're not hungry.' She looked from Alison to Luke.

Her expression was grave. 'I know what it's like to feel sick in every bone of your body, to be shaking inside with fear and anger, and then have people telling you to eat.'

Her voice was brittle and her eyes hard glass pebbles.

She stood up, studying them both, and said, 'I think it's time.'

She reached for the laptop, turning it towards her. 'Let's see what's on the cameras, shall we?'

She tapped briefly on the keyboard before turning the laptop back to face Luke and Alison.

'Sadly, I know what's on this one. There's no need for me to look.'

At first, Luke couldn't figure out what he was looking at. He squinted his eyes, improving his focus. It looked like a buoy, bouncing on the surface of the water by the steps in the boathouse. He squinted some more.

Alison was first to register what they were watching. As Luke processed the blurry image, the breath left his body.

The Boathouse

It was Nina. He could clearly make out her head in the water. She was in the boathouse. He guessed she was standing on the bottom step, and from the position of her arms he also guessed that she was tied up to the handrail by the boathouse steps. Her head flailed from side to side as the water washed above her shoulders. Luke watched in horror. He could see her fear.

Sophie shifted in her chair. An odd expression on her face, looking almost sad. Her eyes darted from Luke to Alison.

'Cruel, isn't it, to see your child like that?' She picked up her fork.

Luke's eyes darted from the laptop screen to Sophie. He spotted a shake in her hand. She steadied it by clenching the fork until her knuckles went white. She scooped another mouthful.

'Open up,' she instructed Alison.

'Stop this now,' said Alison. 'Before it goes too far.'

'I know how you feel.' Sophie studied her. 'You don't feel like eating, do you? You're not even hungry. But, eat you must.'

Alison's eyes widened as Sophie jabbed the laden fork against her mouth.

'I want you both to know I derive no pleasure from this.' Sophie directed her gaze at Luke. 'It's what people said as we waited for news. They thought they were being kind. "Eat," they said. "Keep your strength up. You'll need your strength for later."'

'I have no idea what you're talking about.' Alison spluttered food from her mouth. Particles landed on the table.

'You don't recognise me, do you?' said Sophie.

Alison studied her. 'No.' She was cautious. She shook her head. 'I meet scores of people every day. I shake lots of hands. I don't recognise you. Should I?'

'You shook my hand once. Quite a while ago now. Fifteen years ago, in fact. You looked into my eyes and told me how sorry you were.'

Alison looked at her blankly.

'No? Doesn't ring a bell? I can't say I'm all that surprised. I suppose I don't really expect you'd remember me from fifteen years ago. You must look into a thousand faces and say stuff like that a million times over and never mean one word of it.'

Sophie's delivery was slow and deliberate.

'You told me how sorry you were for my loss, that your father wasn't well and couldn't come to my child's funeral, and how much he wanted to be there. He sent his condolences, you said. You took my hands, and you cried with me. You shook my husband's hand too. Remember now?'

The colour drained from Alison's face.

'You lost a child?' Alison looked for confirmation.

'My child was killed,' said Sophie. 'Murdered.'

'I'm sorry, I still don't see . . .'

'My seven-year-old child was killed on the day of her first communion. She was playing on her bike and she was mown down on a quiet road and left for dead. Ploughed into and left with internal injuries, cut and bleeding into her white dress. A hit-and-run.'

274

Alison went very still.

'I remember that now . . . so sad.'

Sophie's eyes were locked on Alison. 'She was seven.'

'Her name was Mary . . .?'

'You can't even remember her name?'

'I'm sorry – I thought it was Mary.'

'Her name was Maisie – Maisie Sweetman. And it was your car that mowed her down and killed her. You murdered her.'

Alison looked up at Sophie. 'I think you've made a horrible mistake here.'

'Don't play the innocent with me.' Sophie was calm. 'I *know* what happened. You know too. People like you never pay for their mistakes. People like you get away with everything – even killing a child.'

Alison opened her mouth to protest.

Sophie dismissed her. 'Spare me. Luke's already confessed. Appears he had a crisis of conscience after all this time. Had to dump the burden he's been humping around all these years. He owned up to Terence Black.'

'Who?'

'I work for Terence. I guess Luke never mentioned he was seeing a therapist?'

'You're talking nonsense.'

'So he never mentioned it then. You two never shared much, except maybe . . .' She broke off, glancing at the laptop before quickly looking away.

'For pity's sake,' pleaded Luke, 'let Nina go. Untie her before it's too late. None of this has anything to do with her.'

Nina was arching her head, trying to escape the waves that were splashing against her face. Her long hair swirled and eddied on the water's surface. Luke tried not think how cold the water would be. The longer she was in, the more her core temperature would drop. He had no idea how long she'd been in already.

'You can't mean to do this. This isn't you, Sophie. You're a good person. Let her go.' He tried again.

'You only have yourselves to blame,' she said. 'You're the ones who brought Nina into this when you knocked my daughter down fifteen years ago. On the twenty-seventh of May to be precise. That's how I caught you, Luke.' She stared at him. 'It was the date that caught my eye.'

Luke stared back blankly at her, waiting for her to explain.

'It must have been around your third session, when Terence left the box for shredding on his desk. I thought I'd help him by doing it. It was only by chance that I even glanced at those pages.' She paused. 'He's a great one to scribble and doodle.'

Luke's mind was racing, desperately trying to think of a way to get her to let Nina go.

'I thought I was imagining things at first.' Sophie traced a carrot about the plate. 'It seemed like such a coincidence. There I am, feeding sheets into the shredder, when I see a date, the twenty-seventh of May. I was curious, given that's the day Maisie was killed. Terence had drawn a stick figure in a bubble. It looked like a fairy or a butterfly to me. Next to it, he'd scribbled the words "First Communion". And then the words "hit and run". You can imagine the impact that had.'

She looked from Luke to Alison.

'Of course, it might have been coincidence. Unlikely. But I had to be sure. So I got the key for the filing cabinet. I studied your folder, Luke,' she paused, her expression black. 'Terence's notes showed that you'd been drinking . . . that you and your wife were looking for a shortcut home through the Talbot Estate when you were involved in an accident. An accident.'

The word was like poison in her mouth.

'He'd written down that you did not check the victim, that you made no interventions and that you were suffering a delayed reaction – a post-traumatic stress disorder.' She spat the words as if they caused her distaste.

'Sophie—'

'Don't interrupt! I realised of course that it was Maisie. I realised that the man coming to my place of work, attending my employer for counselling, was none other than the man who had killed my child. Can you imagine how that felt?'

Images from the moment of impact flashed through his mind. And on the screen, in the here and now, he was witnessing his own child dying right in front of him.

'Horrendous . . . devastating . . .' he stumbled over the words, knowing no response would be adequate.

'What is it that you want here, Sophie?' Though petrified, Alison managed to sound businesslike. 'Compensation?'

Luke turned. 'Alison—'

'Compensation?' Sophie cut across him. 'You think I can be compensated for the killing of my daughter?'

'I don't think that at all,' said Alison, quietly. 'What happened to your daughter . . . to Maisie . . . was a tragedy. A terrible, terrible accident.'

'An *accident*? There you go. That word again.' Sophie was incredulous. 'Don't try that on me.' She pointed with the fork. 'My daughter was mown down and you and your husband left her for dead. There was nothing *accidental* about that.'

She pointed at Luke.

'It's your behaviour I really don't understand. Over these past few months, I've tried. It was why I needed to get close to you in the first place. I had to understand how any of this could happen.

277

You spend your day saving lives, helping children. Something inside you made you want to work with children. I've tried to get inside your head. What kind of a doctor are you? What kind of a *man* are you?'

Luke was staring into the abyss. Soon, he'd have the deaths of two children on his hands. He had to make Sophie understand that he'd believed her child to be dead when the car had driven away.

'I thought—'

'I know exactly what you thought. You feared for your careers. You were a successful couple. Alison was the face of so many children's charities, and you, Luke, were a respected children's doctor. I understand all that, I do really.' Her tone was icy, full of hate. 'The political system, the judicial system, they protect people like you.'

'I think I have some idea of how you feel,' said Luke. 'Please, Sophie, I'm begging you to leave Nina out of this.'

'You know how I feel? I've lost everything. Even Maisie's cat. As long as Fidget was alive, I always felt that some part of Maisie lived on. I doubt you know how I feel. Tonight, however, I'm going to remedy that.' She drew in a deep breath. 'Tonight, I'm going to give you both a little insight into how I felt back then.'

'Jesus, Sophie! Nina's going to drown. Just look at what you're doing. Look!'

Nina wouldn't last much longer. The wind was whipping up, the water level continued to rise. The cruiser was rocking side to side.

'I don't need to look,' she said. 'I know exactly how this feels. This is for you.'

'I'll do whatever you want,' he implored her. 'Please let Nina go.'

'Begging doesn't work, Luke. That night, fifteen years ago, I tried making all kinds of bargains with God. I don't know what I did to deserve what happened but God didn't hear me that night, the night Maisie lay in hospital. "It's in God's hands now" – that's what everyone said to us that night. Friends, family, the trauma team. And I prayed and prayed. I prayed so hard I nearly bled. It didn't matter. Maisie died.' She paused. 'But who knows?' she added, shrugging. 'God may listen to you tonight. We'll find out soon.'

'What do you mean?' Luke struggled for control.

'Whatever happens out there to Nina tonight will not be my doing. I'm not the one who decides. I'm just an instrument in all of this. People told me I had to accept what happened to Maisie. That acceptance was part of the grieving process. A priest told me not to look for reasons. That it was somehow part of God's great plan.'

'This is all about revenge?' asked Alison.

'I see I'm going to have to spell it out.' Sophie took a breath. 'This is not about revenge although I was of course consumed by that for years.' She broke off and looked at Luke. 'You need to know how it was for me and my husband that night. You need to know what it felt like. You need to feel every moment of that torment too. You need to know what you've done to me, what you've taken from me. What happened to my daughter was an act of God. Tonight, one way or the other, what happens to your daughter will also be an act of God.'

Sophie checked from Luke to Alison.

'As we've been hearing from the insurance companies, all this flooding is an act of God. That's when the idea came to me. That's when it struck me that the time was now. This way, I can show you what I experienced fifteen years ago.'

'What do you mean?' Alison whispered.

'It's simple. Today the sluice gates were opened further up the river to help alleviate flooding up in the midlands. The levels here have been rising ever since. Just how far they rise remains to be seen. Your daughter is out there in the water, cuffed to the wall. If God wills it, the waters will rise enough for Him to take her, just like He took Maisie. If it's not her time, He may spare her. Either way, we'll find out soon.'

Feel My Pain

Staying in control was the only way Luke could get Nina out of this. He knew he had to think of something. The water was continuing to rise, slapping angrily around Nina's face as she fought to keep her head above the waves. Hypothermia would set in soon. He willed her to fight on. She was tiring, her situation grave.

Sophie caught his eye. 'I used our special handcuffs.'

She had cuffed his daughter to the handrail with the handcuffs she'd used for their sex games? It was grotesque.

'I see from your expression, it offends you.'

'What's she talking about?' Alison's voice was small.

'It's my experience that your husband enjoys a bit of role play. He likes blindfolds, wearing a hood. He likes to be cuffed to the bedpost when—'

'Please! Spare me.'

'It's something I would have liked to have been spared myself. Do you really imagine I wanted to get into bed with my daughter's killer?'

'So why did you?' asked Luke. 'I never forced myself on you.'

'"Why?" you ask. Because I had to get to know you. Because I had to get inside your head. For my sanity I needed to understand how a man dedicated to saving lives could behave as monstrously as you did.'

She stopped. She leaned across the table.

'I did it because I had to get close to you. So I could understand you. So I could *kill* you.'

The air crackled with tension.

'Kill me then,' he said. For the first time since this ordeal began, Luke felt a glimmer of hope. There might be a way to save his daughter. 'No one would blame you. Free Nina, then do whatever you want with me. What happened has nothing to do with her.'

'That's not what all of this is about. Don't you see? Why would I put you out of your misery? No one put me out of mine. I want you to walk in my shoes. For a while at least.'

'I understand,' he tried again. 'I do, really. But think of the satisfaction you'd have in taking my life.' He angled his head, indicating a knife on the table.

'If I wanted I could take all your lives.'

'Stop,' Alison pleaded. 'This is insane.'

'I agree. What you did to me was also insane.' Sophie turned to Luke. 'That day in Terence's office, when I found out who you were – I decided what to do. I was going to get you into my bed and I was going to kill you. That was my original intention. Before that I was going to make you hurt.'

Sophie stood. She gathered the knives and forks. She settled them in pairs across each plate. She looked at Luke and shuddered.

'I had my doubts about whether I could physically go through with it all. The revulsion I felt for you was so . . . so completely overwhelming. The thought of Maisie's killer near me in that way, it made me ill. I was sure you'd see my loathing, that I wouldn't be able to hide it. I didn't realise how much I'd need to drink before I could bring myself to touch you. So I got wasted.' She spoke mechanically. 'I thought I might be able to do it if I didn't have to look at your face. I couldn't hide my revulsion. So I made you wear the hoods and eye masks.' Her voice lowered. 'I whipped you that first night, remember? I wanted to flay you, to tear the skin from your back, and your thighs, your chest . . . but something told me it wasn't right. That the pleasure of killing you would be short-lived. Because you would not *feel* any more, you would be nothing, you would not *exist*. You would never know the pain I felt. The only way I could get relief was for you to experience what it was like for me and Kevin.'

She cleared her throat.

'It meant continuing our relationship. I'd have to continue sleeping with you. There were times I almost gave up. My head would explode at the hideousness of it all. Every muscle, every sinew in my body would scream in disgust. Afterwards, I'd have to rush to the bathroom to clean myself. I so nearly gave in to the urge to strangle you. I had to try not to keep pulling the knot and choking you. So very hard.'

Alison looked stunned. Luke felt numb.

Sophie looked from him to Alison, to the laptop. 'I knew what I must do. I had to reconstruct a hell like mine, especially for you.' Two spots of colour appeared on her cheeks. 'By the way you're looking at the screen, I'd say I've done my job.'

'You have.' Luke was desperate. 'For pity's sake, end this now. You're not a murderer. Don't let my actions turn you into one. Nina's going to drown . . . don't do this.'

The spots on Sophie's cheeks stained a deeper red.

'I set all this up so you could take the same journey you forced me to. It's your pain I want to witness, not Nina's. I want you to call out to God in desperation. I want *you* to feel a pain so strong that you feel your insides have ruptured. I want *you* to feel the agony that only a parent can feel. I want *you* to make all manner of bargains with God to spare your child. And I want *you* to have to endure. Above all else, I want that. Because that is what *you* made me do. Endure.'

'I know what I did was unforgiveable.' He felt hope ebbing away. 'Please, bring this to an end.'

'Don't worry. It's nearly over. And it's true what you say, I'm not a murderer. All of this is in God's hands. If the waters start to subside, I'll take that as a sign. I'll release Nina. What you're witnessing here is the final act.' Sophie paused as if reflecting on something. 'I'm glad I didn't take your life that night, Luke. Watching you go through all the stages these past few months has been cathartic. Replicating what I went through. It was difficult to get them all in sequence. I did the best I could. And I gave you a warning, which was more than I got—'

'A warning?'

'The message on your boathouse? *"Guilty"*. I'm assuming you saw that, although you never said.'

'That was you?'

'Of course. And the funeral announcement. That should have come much later. But I had to take my chances when I could.'

'So, it was you who placed the death notice in the paper,' Alison whispered. 'The *Herald* couldn't explain it.'

'It was me.'

Luke didn't take his eyes from the screen. He had to stay with Nina. Brown murky foam was slapping up against her cheeks.

'That was easy,' Sophie continued. 'When Maisie was small I couldn't get work as a nurse so I worked part-time at the *Herald*, accounts and invoicing. I could still access their system so I could arrange the death notice without leaving a trace.' She turned to Luke. 'The announcement about the closure of your private rooms

284

was more challenging. I borrowed headed notepaper and a credit card from your office. Tricky under the watchful eye of that bitch, Fran. In the end, a spilled coffee got her out of the room for a while. It's quite something to see your child's death notice in the paper, isn't it?'

Bits and pieces of that horrendous morning came back to him. Sophie's concern as he'd read the paper. Her eyes searching his. The way she'd examined his face. He'd mistaken it all for empathy.

'You can close your mouth now, Luke,' said Sophie. 'I have to say your reaction surprised me that day. High-tailing it off to Crow Hall. You didn't know who to suspect, who to trust, did you?'

She turned to Alison, who hadn't said a word.

'What dysfunctional relationships you all have,' she said. 'None of you trust one another, do you? Although, from the little I know of you, I can see why Luke wouldn't trust a snake like you or your father. Lie with dogs and you'll get fleas.'

'You need help,' said Alison. 'We can help you.'

'No, my dear,' said Sophie calmly. 'You're the ones who need help. The ones who are sick. You're the ones who put Maisie in hospital. Tubes down her throat, a fractured skull, open head wounds. Do you have any idea how horrific that is?'

'That thing I collected at the post office?' asked Luke. 'That revolting casket . . . that was you as well?'

Sophie's face changed. 'It genuinely upset me to do that.' She was solemn. 'It brought everything back. I had to do it. How else were you ever going to understand what you had done? It was only a doll. But I hope you experienced a little of what I felt. I had to watch my living, breathing child turn into a cold, waxen carcass.'

'And the memoriam cards. The bag of clothes . . .' Luke was making all the diabolical connections.

'All me.' Sophie nodded. 'It's quite a thing to see your child's bloodied clothes stuffed into a plastic bag. Did you know that her beautiful white dress was ripped right up the middle? They'd had to cut her out of it. I heard you complaining about problems with your car locks. So I took a chance that the door would open. Tell me, how was it, seeing a bag of your daughter's clothes, all bloody and torn to shreds?'

'Why did you never tell me any of this, Luke?' asked Alison.

Out of the corner of his eye, Luke saw Sophie leaning back, watching them intently.

He turned to Alison. 'I never told you because I didn't know who was behind it,' he said. 'When I found out it couldn't have been Sebastian Considine because he was in prison, I figured that it could have been you.'

'*Me?* Are you mad?'

Luke spoke, keeping his eyes on the laptop. 'I thought it could be you, with your father, and possibly Gilligan, playing mind games. It's the sort of crap Cornelius would get up to. I thought maybe you were looking for a way to unnerve me . . . to discredit me. I know stuff. I knew Cornelius didn't trust me. I thought he maybe found out I was seeing a therapist and thinking of handing myself in. I thought it could be a warning.'

'Oh my, what a family,' Sophie said softly.

Tears ran down Alison's cheeks and her nose began to run.

'Stop snivelling. I have tissues here somewhere. Now where are they?'

She picked up her handbag and put it on the kitchen table. She rummaged around the bag. Suddenly, she turned it upside down. Luke jumped as the contents scattered all across the table. Among the tie-wraps, a tube of lipstick drum-rolled eerily across the table towards him, slipping off the edge and clattering onto the hard floor.

There was something else. A roll of stickers. The sickly lime green colour was hard to miss. He could make out the letters *ILLEGALLY PAR*. He drew a sharp breath.

'This came in handy,' Sophie looked at Luke. 'The public was parking in spaces reserved for Terence's practice. Some people have no respect when it comes to parking spaces.'

Luke glanced back at the laptop. He couldn't see Nina.

'She's gone under. Jesus Christ, Sophie, have pity. You don't really mean to do this!'

A jagged pain seared through his temples. His vision blurred. He pulled and yanked at his restraints, feeling a burning where they cut into his wrists. He felt a warm trickle of blood run down his fingers. It wasn't any use. Sophie walked around to glance at the laptop. As she turned, Luke spotted movement. What was that? Had he been mistaken? She was there. It was Nina. There she was again, dark snakes of hair swirling over her face. She was still alive.

Sophie returned to the chair and sat. 'You know that Kevin didn't own a suit? Or at least not a formal one that he could wear to Maisie's funeral. Apart from our wedding I'd never seen him in one and he hired that. As Maisie lay in the hospital morgue, we went into the city. The assistants in the shop fussed, adjusting lapels, straightening trouser legs, telling him how smart he looked. You should have seen their faces when he told them he was burying his child.' She gave a mirthless smile.

The missing pieces were slotting into their horrendous homes. This warm, attractive woman, in whose company he had felt appreciated, had chiselled a way into his heart. But everything she'd said, everything she'd done, was a deceit. A cold, exacting plan to wreak revenge.

A profound feeling of despair and sadness descended on him. Nina was going to drown. There was nothing more he could say.

He squeezed his eyes shut, giving himself up to the inevitable. He hoped it would be quick. He wanted Nina to give herself up to the waves. He wanted her agony to come to an end.

'Would Kevin want you to do this on Maisie's account?' he tried one last time. 'Does he even know what you are doing?'

The doorbell pierced the silence. Sophie jumped up from the chair. She pulled the laptop towards her and tapped the keyboard. She was looking at the front-door camera. A shadow crossed her face. She stood and headed to the hall.

The Truth

Luke twisted his head to see. Sophie was at the front door. She hesitated. There came the sound of the door clicking open. Luke couldn't see who was there.

'Sophie . . .'

A moan of pain. A body hitting the floor.

'Sorry.'

Sophie was astride the figure, whose raincoat was lying on the floor. There came the sound of scuffling. Whoever it was had been surprised and overpowered. Luke turned away, no longer able to suffer his screaming neck muscles.

Whoever was on the floor was no good any more. He knew the voice. A pleasant voice. A soothing voice. He'd heard it many times before. He glanced at Alison. Her cheeks bled with mascara where tears had found a gully down her cheeks. It felt odd to see her vulnerable.

Sophie reappeared, steering the hunched-over figure towards the table.

'Over there,' she commanded.

Terence Black.

He was buckled over, groaning, his wrists tied behind him. A slight man, he would have been easier to overpower than

Luke. Sophie guided him onto the chair on the other side of Luke. Sitting down, he looked up from under his rain-soaked fringe. He was ashen.

'You OK?' Luke asked.

'I'm so sorry—' Terence began. His body spasmed as if he might throw up. His attention was diverted to the laptop on the table. Confused, his eyes widened and they filled with horror.

Sophie moved her chair to the end of the table so that Terence, Luke and Alison sat in a row with an unobstructed view as they faced the laptop. Nina was drowning right in front of them. The rising water slapped about her head and between very few waves was she managing to draw any air.

'That's Nina?' Terence whispered as he looked at the screen.

'Yes,' Sophie confirmed. 'That's Nina.'

'This is your doing?'

'Yes, it is.'

'You don't *really* want to do this, Sophie, do you?'

There it was. That soothing voice that Luke had come to know so well. Luke's distress was too acute to let him speak. Compelled to witness his daughter's death was beyond what he could do. Still she fought. She spluttered and spat. Luke no longer wanted her to resist. He wanted it to be over. He wanted Nina to escape her torment. He closed his eyes, willing her to succumb. He was in a pit. Every second an eternity. He couldn't watch, yet how could he abandon Nina to leave this world alone? He forced his eyes to open. He was her father. He would have to keep vigil.

'Sophie. Sophie, look at me,' Terence tried to reason. 'Whatever this is, you've made your point.'

'I find it's helping, Terence. I find it cathartic. You of all people should understand that. I know you know exactly what this man did fifteen years ago. But did you know that the child was my daughter?'

'I only learned that an hour or so ago and I'm truly sorry,' Terence said gently. 'Sophie, just what exactly is it that you think Luke did?'

'You want me to give you a step-by-step?' she asked coolly.

'That might be helpful.'

Sophie pushed back her chair and stood. She looked at Terence, appearing to think. 'All right then, have it your way.' She began to walk around the table. 'On May the twenty-seventh fifteen years ago – a beautiful, sunny day – a bunch of kids all over County Clare woke up excited about their first communion. My daughter Maisie just so happened to be one of those excited children.' Luke heard her footsteps coming to a stop behind him.

The footsteps recommenced. 'On the same day, Doctor Luke Forde here, along with his wife Alison, also sitting here, attended a party to celebrate the first communion of another child. Luke Forde,' with a wave of her arm she indicated to Luke, 'was drinking at this party.' Sophie stopped her pacing. She rested her eyes on Terence, then Luke and on to Alison. Her expression hardened.

'Later that evening, my little girl went out for a spin on her bike. But unbeknownst to Maisie, Luke Forde had taken to the road in his car. He had left the party and he was taking a shortcut home – a route through the Talbot estate that passes close to my home. The home I used to live in with Maisie and my husband, Kevin.' She paused and looked directly at Luke. 'Doctor Luke Forde was drunk. Not fit to be behind the wheel. But that didn't stop him driving.' There was steely venom in her voice.

'On Doctor Forde's way home to his fancy house with his fancy wife he ploughed straight into a little girl. He drove into her, knocked her off her bike and sent her flying. My little girl. But the neighbourhood was quiet that night. Ireland was playing on the television. What a stroke of luck for Luke and Alison that no one was around to see what had happened. So what does the good doctor do?' Sophie recommenced her walkabout. 'Does he rush to her aid? Does he administer CPR? Does he phone an ambulance?' She stops again. Behind him. 'No. The good doctor does none of those things. He leaves her there. He leaves my Maisie lying there. He takes off and abandons the scene of the accident. He drives off. A doctor. He didn't even try to save her. *A doctor, for God's sake.* And that, Terence, is exactly what Luke did.'

'OK, Sophie. Listen very carefully,' said Terence calmly. 'Do you trust me?'

Luke heard the hesitation in her voice. She returned to her chair and sat, considering the question.

'I suppose so . . . yes.'

'Right, then. I'm going to tell you a story and you'll have to concentrate. Here's what really happened that night,' he took a breath, 'and Luke, please step in if there's something I'm missing.'

Terence's words came quickly at first, slipping over one another in a cascade. 'You're right, Sophie. Luke had been drinking that day. And just like you said, Luke was in the car that hit Maisie. But here's where you're mistaken.' He paused, his expression grave. 'Luke was in the car all right; however, there's a "but" here. It's a big "but", and a critical "but" . . .' He stopped again. Luke wrenched his eyes away from the laptop. The therapist was making sure he had Sophie's full attention before going on. Sophie's gaze was locked on to Terence with intense concentration. Satisfied, Terence proceeded. 'Contrary to what you believe, Luke is not the sort to get behind the wheel when he's been drinking. Neither did he get behind the wheel the day your daughter died. Luke was in the car, as I said . . . *but* Luke was in the passenger seat.' Terence stopped a moment and then said very deliberately, 'The person driving the car that day was not Luke. It was Alison . . .'

Luke turned to Sophie as she absorbed these words. Her eyes narrowed in momentary suspicion and confusion, wondering if she were somehow being tricked. Could this be true? Alison had been the one driving the car?

Luke now turned to look at his wife and witnessed a flicker of alarm. Alison opened her mouth to protest.

'But—'

'But what, Alison?' said Luke. 'You thought I couldn't recall everything that happened properly? Yeah, you're right. I wasn't able to, at least not until Terence took me step by step through the events of the day of the accident. You always behaved as if I had been the driver. But it was always odd. I could never remember getting behind the wheel. I always assumed it was because I didn't want to. Because I'd been drinking. Because of the accident itself. It was that old Mercedes of your father's, remember? His favourite. The one that only you and he were allowed to drive. Yet both you and your father led me to believe that I had been the one driving.'

When the truth had revealed itself that day in Terence's office, Luke was shocked. But rather than challenge Alison with the truth, he'd thought it safer to keep his mouth shut. If Alison was capable of that, it was clear she was capable of anything.

'I'm so sorry, Luke.' Alison's lip trembled.

'No, you're not. You don't even know the meaning of the word, Alison. You really don't.'

Luke glanced at Sophie. Would it make a jot of difference to her that he had not been the one behind the wheel? Terence said nothing, allowing the impact of the words to percolate the room.

'No . . .' Sophie shook her head slowly.

293

'It's true,' said Terence. 'I'm telling you the truth of what happened. This all unfolded during one of our later sessions.'

Luke had only ever allowed himself scant comfort that he had not been the one driving. It was relevant but it was immaterial to what happened to Maisie Sweetman. In the end, it was his inaction that had killed the child.

Sophie was now off-balance. A fog of confusion spread across her face. 'Is this true?' She looked at Alison.

Alison's eyes bulged. She nodded.

Sophie shook her head and turned again to Terence. 'But Luke didn't go to help her, he didn't even try to save her . . .'

She turned to Luke with eyes that burned.

'You know why?' Terence asked, calmly. 'Because his wife got to the scene first.'

Terence nodded in Alison's direction. Alison was no longer crying. Her eyes were flashing with alarm.

Terence had Sophie's attention now. 'Alison ran back to Luke, convincing him all was lost, that it was already too late, there was nothing he could do. Alison convinced him that Maisie was killed outright. That she was dead already.'

'He should have checked . . .'

'Of course he should. In any other circumstances, he would have. But he'd been drinking. And with the shock of the accident, he wasn't thinking clearly.'

'Even if he believed Maisie was dead, how could he just leave her there? How? To save his precious reputation and the so-called reputation of the Thompson family, that's how.'

'*No, Sophie.*' Terence was gentle but emphatic. 'Luke was thinking of something more important than his reputation. Something that meant more to him than his career. I genuinely believe that. Luke held the future of another little girl in his hands. A little child

294

waiting for him in an orphanage half a world away in Russia. Nina's adopted – you knew that, right?'

'Yes . . .' she faltered.

'Well, Luke and Alison met Nina five or six months before the accident. He made a promise to a three-year-old little girl that he'd be back for her.' Terence held up a hand. 'Put aside your pre-conceptions for a second. Imagine the horrific situation he found himself in – one child he absolutely believes to be dead – and another child he's made a promise to, who waits for him in an orphanage . . . what should he do? It's a terrible, terrible choice but one he must make.'

Sophie was listening.

'His judgement is clouded by shock and alcohol,' Terence continued. 'He has to make a decision and quickly. He chooses not to ruin the life of another child. In order to do that, he has to leave the scene of the accident. I'm not asking you to excuse what he did, Sophie, or to forgive what he did, but he is not the cold-blooded monster you think. If he was, do you think he would have been coming to me to find some peace for what he'd done? This has been tormenting him for years. He is not an ogre. He is a normal person who did a very bad thing. He made the only decision he felt was open to him. And you, Sophie, you are not a bad person either. But this – whatever you think you're doing here – this is very wrong. Please, please stop this before it's too late.'

Sophie's chest rose and fell. She stared at Luke. A vein pulsed at her temple. She blinked. A storm of emotion swept wildly across her face like clouds across moorland. Luke swallowed. He waited. Having harboured years of hate, was Sophie capable of considering anything in mitigation?

She began. 'Any decent human being with any shred of decency in them wouldn't just leave a child there . . . dead or not . . . they

295

just wouldn't. It's barbaric. It's evil . . . and a doctor at that. He's a respected doctor, for God's sake. Look at him.' She spat out the words. 'The whole world thinks he's a saint. It makes me sick.'

'It makes him sick too, Sophie. Why do you think he can't sleep at night? Why do you think he has nightmares?'

'He still has his daughter.'

'Not for much longer if we don't end this madness now. You are doing this in cold blood, Sophie. Do you think if Maisie were here today she'd want you to do this on her behalf? Do you think this would make her proud?'

'Don't you dare. Don't you bloody dare bring Maisie into this.' Sophie's face had gone white. Her voice shook. Her eyes blinked furiously and she bit her trembling lower lip. Luke's heart skipped a beat. He dared to hope Terence was getting through.

'There was only a few years between them,' Terence said. 'It's possible they could have been friends, had Maisie lived. Nina and Maisie might even have shared the same interests, liked the same music or books. They might have gone InterRailing together.'

Sophie flinched.

'You're visiting the sins of her parents on an innocent kid. Nina never asked for any of this.' Terence was trying his damnedest.

'I know, but—'

'All you are doing is making this worse. Believe me, Sophie, none of this will make you feel any better. There are other ways to deal with how you feel apart from drowning an innocent girl.'

'Other ways,' Sophie echoed.

Her face suddenly changed. She stood up. Her chair toppled and she reached out to stop it falling. She shut the laptop. Luke could no longer see what was happening. He couldn't see Nina.

'Look at me.' She directed her attention to Alison. 'So this is true? You were driving the car that day? *You* knocked Maisie down?'

Alison's eyes were frantic. Her mouth opened and closed like a fish but no words came out.

'Is this *true*? And is it the case that you told Luke that Maisie was dead when she wasn't?'

'I . . . I made a mistake . . . I didn't know . . . I was in shock too. She appeared out of nowhere.' Sophie grabbed the knife from the table. 'It was an accident, believe me. Please, oh please . . .'

Sophie moved behind Alison. She freed her from the chair.

'Stand,' she barked.

Unsteady, Alison got to her feet. With Alison's wrists still secured behind her back, Sophie shoved her out of the kitchen.

'What are you doing? Where are we going?'

'The boathouse.'

'No, please . . . let me go. What are you going to do? It was an accident. You must believe that – a tragic accident.'

There came the opening groan of the heavy door to the glass corridor.

'Move,' ordered Sophie.

The door clanged shut. All went silent.

You're a Doctor

Luke willed them speedily to the boathouse.

Terence was shaking. 'It's going to be OK,' he said. 'She'll let her go.' The man looked like hell. A stain of sweat had seeped out from his armpits, darkening the cotton of his pale blue shirt. He wore a tie from earlier in the day. 'Nina's going to be OK.'

What was happening in the boathouse? Was Sophie going to free Nina? And what were her plans for Alison? Sophie had a knife. It was chilling the way she'd looked at Alison, shoving her through the door like that.

He listened for approaching footsteps. They were going to come back to the house, weren't they? He thought about the cruiser tied up in the boathouse. Seconds went by. Still he listened. Still nothing.

Underneath Terence's eyes had taken on a blue-black hue. In fact, his entire face had gone a strange colour. A cardiac event was all Luke needed. He looked away. He could only concentrate on Nina. With hands still tied to the back of the chair, he balled his fists, digging his nails into his palms. His thoughts turned to what he'd need to treat Nina. He'd heat her core up slowly. She'd be fine.

Terence stared into his lap. 'This is hell. I never in a million years—'

'Did you call the police before you came?'

'No, I didn't. I'd no idea how grave the situation was. I knew it was bad, but I expected to be able to deal with it. If I'd had any inkling . . . Sophie's always been such a level-headed person.' He shook his head.

What was keeping them? They should be back by now.

Luke stared at the cover of the laptop as if by force of will he might prise it open. Second after interminable second, he waited. He tapped his feet. His stomach was clenched rock solid. In his dark imaginings, upsetting images flashed on and off.

'It's going to be OK,' said Terence again, talking into his lap.

Nina had to hang on. Stress hormones were key to keeping her alive. She couldn't relax. Luke reckoned the water temperature in the lough at this time of year would be around 10 °C. Not as harsh as winter temperatures. Nina's body mass and the clothes she was wearing were factors weighing in her favour.

There came the sound of a door opening and Luke heard spluttering. Lots of spluttering. Terence whispered under his breath. It sounded like 'Thank God.'

Luke watched as Nina was half-dragged, half-supported, across the kitchen floor. Her dripping arms draped over Sophie and Alison's shoulders. Alison was wet from head to foot. Her wrists were no longer bound with a tie-wrap.

Luke's spirit soared. The two women manoeuvred Nina past the kitchen table and onto the sofa in the garden room. Her long hair was matted with algae and bits of brackish matter.

'I'm f-f . . . freezing.' Her teeth chattered through her purple lips.

He felt a burst of elation. That was good. Her temperature

299

wasn't so low it muted a shivering response. Fear ebbed away. Each new pulse of adrenaline buoyed him up.

'A duvet, we need a duvet,' he instructed, taking control. 'Scissors too. We need to cut those clothes off.'

Sophie set the knife down. She got on her knees to loosen Nina's trainers.

'Untie me,' Luke directed. 'You'll need my help.'

Sophie turned her head. She held his gaze, contemplating his request. Her eyes shifted to Alison, who had returned from the kitchen with scissors. Sophie looked again at Luke. She was weighing everything up, calculating risk.

'All I want to do is take care of Nina,' he reassured her.

'You!' barked Sophie, switching her attention to Alison. 'Stay there. Not another step.'

Alison stopped in her tracks. In her right hand was the pair of scissors. Her hand shook.

'Put those scissors down and kick them across to me.'

Alison did as she was asked. The scissors skated across the floor, landing close to Sophie. Picking up the knife in one hand, Sophie reached to grab the scissors with the other. She stood up. She eyeballed Alison. Alison flinched and retreated.

'Get back to your chair.'

Sophie followed, moving behind Alison's chair to secure her wrists once again. Then she reached down and cut the tie-wraps holding Luke in place. His wrists were sore and bloodied. He stood, aware his calves and shins had pins and needles, and made immediately for the sofa. He sank to his knees by Nina's side.

'I'll get a duvet,' said Sophie.

'Also get towels and a hot-water bottle from her room.'

Luke set to work with the scissors. It was easy to cut through

Nina's cotton skirt. The sodden T-shirt was more tricky. 'That's great, Nina. Keep it up. The more you shiver the better.'

Sophie returned with a duvet and towels. He dried Nina's hair and face with a towel.

'There's a first-aid box in the larder cupboard. Can you get that?'

Nina was warming. If he'd been in St Matthew's, he'd have asked for warm internal saline for her bladder and warm IV fluids.

'Here.' Sophie set the first-aid box on the floor beside him. She didn't let go of the knife in her other hand.

'The duvet?' he requested, pulling off Nina's trainers.

Together they manoeuvred Nina so they could separate her from her clothes, at the same time drying and wrapping the duvet around her for warmth. Luke raised her now bare feet onto the sofa.

'Shouldn't you put her in a hot bath?' Terence hadn't spoken for some time. He was shocked.

'No,' said Luke.

'Not even a basin of hot water for her feet?'

'We need to do this slowly. To warm her core first. Don't worry. I'm on it.'

He gently tucked a shivering Nina in the duvet. He then proceeded to wrap her head in a towel turban. Taking the thermometer from the first-aid box, he placed it in her ear: 32 °C. Moderate hypothermia. He could treat her here. She didn't need to be in hospital.

Fifteen minutes later he spooned chicken soup into her. The hot-water bottle lay over the duvet on her stomach. When she spotted the Winnie-the-Pooh cover she attempted a smile. Her colour was improving.

As he knelt, monitoring her, he noticed her expression change.

She pressed her head back into the sofa, as if she were afraid. Sophie was standing right behind him.

'Nina's glasses.' She handed them to him.

'You're scaring her.' He perched the glasses on Nina's nose before securing them gently over her ears. She blinked a few times before closing her eyes. Warmth was creeping into her hands. Sophie drew closer.

'What are you doing?' Luke flinched.

'I got it wrong, Nina,' she said softly. 'And for that I'm sorry.'

'Not now,' said Luke, under his breath. 'She's confused.'

'I want you to know that what I did, I did to punish your father, to make him understand what he took from me. Instead, I find out that it was your mother. I want you to know I hold no grudge against you.'

Sophie looked over her shoulder and then back to Nina. 'I am sorry you have such a monster for a mother.'

Nina opened her eyes. 'What? What's she . . . she t-t-talking about, Dad?'

'Nothing. It's nothing,' he soothed. 'I'll explain later.'

Nina closed her eyes.

'Please, just go, Sophie,' he said.

'Don't worry. I am.' She turned to Terence. 'You and I need to talk. Not now, later.'

'Sophie, you need help,' Terence said. 'Anyone would in . . . in your situation. You need to talk to someone. Certainly after . . . after what nearly happened here today.'

'You're right, Terence. I do need help. I'll get to that. There are one or two things I need to do first.'

'Dad, I feel weird.'

Luke switched his attention back to Nina. He heard the front door bang shut. He listened. There was no sound of a car starting up.

302

Had she gone? And then it came, the spin of gravel on the driveway and the welcome sound of Sophie's car driving off.

Luke swung into action. He untied Alison and Terence. He suggested Alison take a shower to warm up. She stumbled out of the room.

'Terence, how are you? Do you feel OK?'

'I think so . . .' he replied. 'Probably in shock. Feel a little strange.'

'Lie up on the other sofa. Rest a little. I'll get some tea. I'm going to suggest that you stay here tonight.'

Terence nodded.

'Is there something you can tell your wife?'

Terence nodded again, sitting back into the sofa.

'There you go.' Luke handed Terence his mobile phone before checking once again on Nina. Her lips were changing from blue to red. He took her temperature. It was on the way up.

It wasn't long before Alison reappeared back downstairs after her shower. Her hair was washed and blow-dried. She wore a slick of lipstick.

She looked around cautiously as if Sophie might be lurking. 'She has gone, hasn't she?'

'She's gone,' Luke confirmed.

Alison edged towards the sofa.

'You feeling a little better, sweetie? What a fright you gave us all.'

Nina's eyes fluttered.

'That woman is deranged,' Alison lowered her voice. 'Bat-shit crazy.'

Nina straightened up. 'Where's Duffy?'

'I forgot all about him.' Luke was delighted she was recovering. 'He must still be in the basement.'

God only knew what havoc the animal had wreaked down there. Luke turned to Alison. 'Keep an eye on Nina while I fetch the dog, will you?'

'Don't be long.'

'I'm just going to the basement.'

'I need to get back to Crow Hall.'

'For God's sake, Alison,' Luke hissed. 'You're not going to stay here with us?'

'I need to talk to Dad. I don't know what to think, Luke. That woman is crazy and as long as she's out there, she's a danger to every one of us. Dad will know what to do.'

'I doubt you'll get back to Crow Hall tonight. The roads up there are closed.'

'I'll take the High Shore Road. The police will let me through. I promised Dad I'd be back.' Alison sat to give Nina a hug. 'You're going to be just fine, sweetie. I'm leaving shortly but I'll be back first thing in the morning to check on you. We've all had a terrible ordeal but your dad has the situation under control. He is a doctor after all.'

Goodbye, Sweet Daughter

Luke blew his nose. The sound echoed off the marble pillars, the terrazzo floors and the high-domed ceiling of the cathedral. He felt the eyes of a thousand mourners boring into his back. They were here for a spectacle and Cornelius would make sure they got it. The most elaborate of funeral rites would be observed.

Sitting in the front pew, Luke's eyes welled up. He dabbed at his red and swollen lids. He felt a hand on his leg. It was Wendy. She gave him a look of concern. She'd taken a non-stop flight to Heathrow. Her connecting flight to Ireland landed two hours ago. Luke told Wendy only what she needed to know. Nothing about the ordeal with Sophie.

'All right there, mate?' she whispered. She patted his leg.

'The pollen,' he said, his voice choking.

There were lilies everywhere. He'd never seen so many. He'd never seen quite so many clergy on an altar either. He'd counted sixteen priests, two bishops and a cardinal. All had queued to sympathise with him before proceeding to the altar. Luke had stopped trying to find the right words. He resigned himself to a nod as he shook their hands. 'You're in shock,' some said. 'Like us all,' more added.

A sound system had been set up for the overspill outside. The

305

cathedral couldn't hold them all. There were Nina's friends from school. They were trying really hard. They'd been a good support, arriving at the Glasshouse not long after the news had broken.

There were the labourers and their families from Crow Hall. And, of course, a big crowd from Dublin. Cornelius's and Alison's political associates. Stiff-faced men in ill-fitting raincoats. Women with heavy make-up. There were also Alison's friends from the Scarigell Hunt and representatives from the charities she sat on. Hugh Smyth and Johnny Whelan sat a few rows back. Their concern was touching. Next to them sat Fran. All three were there for Luke.

He was moved by the attendance of Celine and Matthew Rogerson, a couple that he and Alison had met through adoption preparation classes. They always asked about Nina's progress and always sent a card on her birthday.

The Glasshouse was awash with cards. He'd read some. Most remained unopened. He couldn't bring himself to read them. Along with mounds of cards was a stack of newspapers, all running with the same headline:

Family Reunion Ends in Tragedy.

Aided by a walking stick, Cornelius shuffled towards the lectern. Luke tensed. Wendy squeezed his hand. Cornelius had insisted on a eulogy though he was advised against it. He'd assumed the role of chief mourner, wearing long black tails. He looked like a sad old crow.

He cleared his throat. 'My son-in-law has asked that I say a few words . . .' What was Cornelius playing at? The old man peered over the top of his reading glasses, scanning the congregation. 'So, please bear with me.'

Luke had suggested no such thing. All he wanted to do was make it through the funeral. To get it over with.

'It's a terrible, terrible thing for any man to have to bury a daughter,' began Cornelius. 'It isn't natural.'

Luke closed his eyes and bowed his head. Wendy squeezed his hand more tightly. Around him, he could sense women looking in bags in search of hankies.

'In the short time she was here with us, she brought so much joy and light to those around her,' Cornelius said.

Luke winced.

'The time we have together goes so quickly,' Cornelius continued. 'In the blink of an eye. It feels like only yesterday that we were here in this very church for the christening. Many of you here were also in the church that day. And what a hell of a party we had back at Crow Hall. Her mother was so proud—'

Cornelius broke off, directing his gaze at the photo on top of the coffin.

'She'd accomplished much. But she had so much yet to give. It seems cruel and senseless that she was taken from us now when she had so much life—' His voice cracked. 'She was a devoted daughter . . .' He couldn't continue.

All along the pew, heads turned to Luke in sympathy. He squirmed. If he could get up and sneak out, he'd gladly do so. Listening to Cornelius talk about his precious daughter was scarcely bearable.

Cornelius pulled himself together. 'Her untimely passing is a loss to all the children's charities she worked with,' he said. 'To all her constituents she worked tirelessly for with warmth and fervour. She is an irreplaceable loss to our extended family at Crow Hall, and of course to her former business partner, Roddy Gilligan . . .'

He broke off to retrieve a handkerchief from his breast pocket.

Nina whispered in Luke's ear. 'Is Grandpa going to mention *us* at all?'

'I'm sure he will,' Luke replied.

The old man had better give Nina a mention at least. Luke put his arm around her shoulder.

Cornelius resumed. 'I think we all agree that Alison was a rare breed in politics. She was selfless. Unlike many of us who go into the game in good faith, a lot of old-timers like myself, we become disillusioned, we become cynical. Alison was none of those things. Nothing was too much for her constituents. Since the election, she'd been spending a lot of time up at Crow Hall with me.'

'And Groper Gilligan,' muttered Nina, under her breath.

'She leaned on me for advice. The two of us would stay up into the small hours, figuring out what could be done to help the suffering of farmers and householders affected by the floods. Alison worried for them. She went on many a sandbag delivery with my foreman, Sly Hegarty, down there.' He nodded his head in Sly's direction. 'As you know, Alison was never one to shy away from work.'

'A proper Mother Teresa,' Wendy whispered.

Suppressing a giggle, Nina hid her face in a tissue and pretended to sob. After the ordeal she'd suffered, Luke was relieved to see she hadn't lost her sense of humour.

'Alison's special gift lay with children,' Cornelius was hitting his stride. 'Kids seemed to gravitate towards her. And after she and Luke got married, well . . . and I know it was a source of great sadness to her . . . it was difficult when children didn't come along.' Cornelius stopped to dab his eyes.

What the hell? A ripple of unease cascaded through the pews. Luke's face burned. How dare Cornelius use the occasion of Alison's funeral to humiliate him. Wendy looked at Luke, dismayed.

'But Alison was made of grit and got on with things. I'm sure Nina feels as proud to have had Alison as a mother as I was to have her as a daughter.'

Cornelius eyeballed Nina. She bowed her head.

'Alison was always loyal and she was always kind. It was typical that once she'd welcomed Nina home from her travels, she wanted to get on with sorting out the floods. She was on her way back to Crow Hall to discuss disaster relief with me last Thursday.'

The lie that had tripped off Luke's tongue to the police that Friday morning made its way to Cornelius later.

'Most of the roads were closed but that wasn't going to stop my Alison. She set out for the High Shore Road.' He shrugged. 'Sadly, Luke couldn't convince her to wait until the morning.'

Luke bristled. How dare the old bastard blame him?

'I'm sorry . . .' Cornelius's voice wavered as he succumbed to a fit of shaking. A bishop took a tentative step in his direction. But Cornelius rallied. 'There's so much more that I wanted to say but I promised I would keep it brief.' He scanned the congregation. 'I'd like to invite you all to Crow Hall for refreshments after we put Alison to rest alongside her dear departed mother, Marguerite. For those of you that don't know the way, Roddy Gilligan will be handing out directions at the back of the cathedral.'

Wendy gasped and looked at Luke. Protocol suggested the funeral reception should be at the Glasshouse, at the home of the grieving widower. Cornelius's wishes trumped convention. Luke had been ignored in any funeral planning, learning of the arrangements through a funeral notice in the newspaper, just like any member of the public. Neither he nor Nina had been consulted, their wishes an irrelevance.

Luke wouldn't give Cornelius the satisfaction of making a scene. He was withered from his father-in-law's shenanigans.

When his anger subsided, it struck him that in fact the arrangements suited him quite well. He didn't have it in him to host a reception, or to make hypocritical small-talk about the wife he had grown to loathe. He was also distrustful of some of the mourners.

Alison had fostered genuine affection in some. More were looking for an angle, a connection to exploit. Cornelius and Gilligan were welcome to their conniving milieu. Luke wanted nothing more than to slip home with Nina and Wendy. To get away from this charade. But he would have to attend Crow Hall for a short while to thank his colleagues for attending.

He wasn't looking forward to that. There'd be Fran to contend with for a start. She radiated suspicion. She'd been desperate to call out to the Glasshouse the afternoon the news had broken. Despite her nosiness, Luke knew her urge to call was due mainly to her long-standing affection for Nina.

'That poor little lamb,' she said, 'what a homecoming. Are you sure I can't be any help? I can do sandwiches and tea for callers.' He'd stood firm. 'Thanks, Fran, but the police are calling again.' Unfortunately for him, he'd chosen the wrong thing to say. It made Fran even more curious. He had to resort to very firm words to dissuade her from calling. With her razor-sharp eyes, Fran might spot things the police had not.

When the police had first called that Friday morning, Nina had been ghostly in the folds of her dressing gown. They were not to know that hours before, Nina had been hypothermic. It had been a slow process to raise her temperature without a drop in blood pressure. Neither did they notice Nina pulling the dressing-gown sleeves over her hands to cover the marks made by the handcuffs. They didn't notice the discoloration on Luke's wrists from the tie-wraps either.

Luke was careful with his clothing. If he'd been in hospital scrubs, the abrasions and bruising would have required an explanation. By the time his compassionate leave was up, any residual discoloration should draw little if any attention.

Cornelius stepped away from the lectern, off the altar, and leaned on his stick. His colour was poor. Returning to the pew, he stopped by the coffin. The congregation held its breath. Kissing a finger, Cornelius laid it on the photo of Alison. They'd been unable to have an open coffin because of the state of her remains.

'Goodbye, sweet daughter,' he said. He shuffled awkwardly back to his seat. Sitting down, he made a sound like a pocket of air being released.

'All right, Grandpa?' Nina leaned forward and whispered along the pew. Luke wondered why she bothered. She never received a scintilla of affection from him.

'Hmph,' came his reply.

Mourners approached the altar with symbols and stories of Alison's life. Luke hardly recognised the woman they described. It wasn't the woman he had married. His mind started to wander. He wondered how he was going to get through the next few days. He was longing to get back to work. He wanted some routine.

'Dad.'

He felt a nudge.

'Dad.'

Another nudge, more insistent.

'And so now we must take leave of our sister, Alison, in the sure and certain hope that we will meet again one day,' the voice on the altar said mournfully.

'Stand up, Dad.'

The congregation was on its feet. Alison's coffin was being shouldered by Sly Hegarty and labourers from Crow Hall. The

311

pall-bearers began the awkward procession down the central aisle, like a lumbering woodlouse. Cornelius edged in first behind the coffin. Luke and Nina moved along the pew to follow with Wendy close behind.

'Who's that supporting Cornelius?' whispered Wendy.

'Roddy Gilligan,' said Nina.

'I didn't recognise the guy,' said Wendy. 'It's years since I saw him. My, he looks shifty.'

It angered Luke to walk behind Cornelius and Gilligan, knowing half the parish had to know the rumours about Alison and Gilligan. He felt humiliated, as if he were being paraded as a cuckold.

A large crowd awaited as they emerged into the sunlight. It was the first time it had stopped raining in weeks. The sky was no longer a blanket of dishwater grey. Further pomp awaited. Luke groaned inside. A guard of honour was waiting for the coffin. Members of the Scarigell Hunt. Luke estimated it to be fifty-strong, buttoned, tucked and smoothed into black hunting coats, breeches, boots and caps.

The press was out in force. As Luke's eyes flitted through the crowds, there was a spray of camera flashes. He wanted this to be over. The aping pretence of playing the grieving but errant husband. He'd been discreet, but he suspected there were also people aware of his affair with Sophie.

His mind started to play tricks. He thought he saw her. For one split second he'd thought it was Sophie. There, on the edge of the crowd, in a peach-toned raincoat. The face he'd imagined had melted away. He let his breath out. Linking Nina and Wendy, he headed for the car.

Family Tragedy

'What dreadful people!' Wendy was sitting in the back as Luke drove out past the crow-topped pillars on their way back to the Glasshouse.

'Well, I felt like stabbing needles in my eyes.' Nina turned around in the passenger seat to face her aunt.

'It must be awful to bury your daughter,' Wendy continued. 'And I should feel sorry for Cornelius. But all I can do is feel sorry for you, Luke. That you've had to suffer that man and those goons he keeps for company.'

'What about me?' Nina was indignant too. 'When I was a kid I hated going to Crow Hall. The way they all looked at me, like I was a freak.'

Wendy laughed. 'After the people I saw in there today, you're the normal one.'

'Too right. I remember once as a kid, I was on the wall between the yard and the back fields, with my sketch pad, minding my own business, when I felt a jab in the back. It was that lump, Sly Hegarty with that big leery face of his. He was poking me with the handle of a yard brush, thinking it was funny. When I went in and complained to Grandpa, he told me they must have no sense of humour where I came from.'

'The man's an arse,' said Wendy, 'there's no two ways about it. I know he's your grandpa and all . . .'

'Yeah, though he's never exactly been thrilled about that now, has he? I remember another time when I'd stopped eating meat. He cooked up liver and kidneys. He sat down to eat them right in front of me, red juice running all down his chin.'

'As I said, he's a prize arse. I plain never liked the man.'

'It's OK, Wendy. I don't much like him either. I just try because he's my grandpa.'

'The man's a buffoon,' Luke chipped in.

Nina turned around and set to tugging off her boots. She leaned back in the passenger seat and put her odd-socked feet on the dashboard. 'Mm . . . buffoon.' She rolled the word around her mouth, trying it out for size. 'I like that. A prize arse and a buffoon.'

For the next few miles they travelled along the country road in companionable silence. The gullies bubbled brown, running fast with water, but there'd been no more rain. All three looked out over the fields, reflecting on the strangeness of the day.

All around them, neighbours, political cronies, ex-colleagues, charity workers and the hunting set had sniffed, cried and cleared their throats. Not once had Nina parted with a tear. Not today, not yesterday or once since Alison's death. Luke didn't wish any further trauma on his daughter, she'd suffered ordeal enough. But he couldn't help but feel how unnatural it was that, in her lifetime, Alison could inspire such little affection in her only child.

Watching over Nina the night they'd taken her from the water, Luke had tried to picture how events might play out. Not once in his wild imaginings did he anticipate what would follow.

Terence had left the house the following morning. He and

Luke had agreed that Terence would take no immediate action about what had happened, that they would discuss it later, and decide how to handle it then.

Not long after Terence had left, the buzzer had sounded at the gate. Only then did Luke remember the alarm company, Sentry Systems, had been due to call. He pressed the button to open the gates. To his surprise, when he opened the door, he was met by two policemen.

He'd assumed that Terence had changed his mind or that Sophie had alerted them. It had always been a possibility. He was prepared for full disclosure. 'You'd better come in.' He'd directed the police to the garden room. Nina was on a sofa buried in his dressing gown.

When the police explained why they were there, and what had happened to Alison, Luke was speechless. He'd been bracing himself to tell them about the hit-and-run. He was not prepared for this. Nina stared blankly at the policemen. After they'd left, Luke rang to cancel the alarm company. He made two mugs of strong black tea with sugar.

'This is unbelievable,' he said. 'I can't get my head around it.' He handed a mug to Nina. 'I'm so very, very sorry.'

'It's not your fault, Dad.' Her voice was dull and brittle.

She sipped at the syrupy tea, then blew on it. They sat for a long time, side by side, staring out at the lough. They didn't speak and there were no tears.

'I'd love to say I'm going to miss her,' Nina volunteered, eventually. 'But I really don't think that I will.'

They were the saddest words Luke had ever heard. Nina had tried to love her mother. He thought back to the many times she'd sought her mother's approval. She must have felt affection once, to even try. Sadly, Luke could remember few occasions when that approval had been forthcoming. Like a plant starved of sunlight, any love that Nina had for her mother had curled at the edges and withered away.

'You know what I think, Dad?' Nina was sanguine. 'For years I was an unwanted accessory that Mum had tired of. She just didn't know what to do with me.'

Luke could not find any words for a rebuttal. Nina put her mug down with a shrug. She'd turned to the window. The incursion of the lough was slowly receding, leaving a murky residue on the lawn.

Arriving back at the Glasshouse, Wendy wanted to unpack and freshen up. Her suitcase sat in the hall where she'd left it earlier.

'You remember where everything is?' asked Luke.

Wendy nodded.

'I'll put on one of the dinners that Fran left. We'll eat in a bit.'

Luke wasn't hungry but it would make them feel human to sit around a table together. To salvage some normality. Nina went to fetch Duffy from the dog-run. The animal had played his part in Nina's recovery that awful night.

As soon as Luke had opened the basement door, the dog had burst out in a frenzy, bounding up the stairs. Sensing something was wrong, he'd snuggled in to Nina tightly, sharing his body heat with her. It provided the gradual warmth she'd needed. Every now and then, he'd looked up at her to check her progress. He'd wriggled closer and licked her face.

Luke's appreciation for Duffy was tempered by what had met him in the basement. He surveyed the damage with dismay. In the time he'd been locked up, Duffy had pulled the place apart. The den was destroyed. The animal had ripped the leather on the

L-shaped sofa. He'd chewed through the table-tennis net. The table itself was scored with claw marks.

The old videotapes Luke had set aside for secure disposal were scattered across the floor. *RHD/Study 4521/ Tanzania/ Prevention Prog.* read the scrawled handwriting on one spine. *Balloon Valvuloplasty/Ho Chi Min/WHO RHD prog ref:a32* read another. Most of the cassettes were videos of workshops he'd delivered. Some were of procedures he'd performed in remote areas. They had formed the basis of a training programme he'd put together with Hugh and Johnny. They'd worked together on a joint venture between St Matthew's University Hospital and Thai Region 3 Children's Clinic. Thankfully, most were now committed to computer.

With the upset of recent months, Luke hadn't finished editing stuff from their earlier Thailand trips. He'd hoped to share it with the guys before things had spun out of control. There was material for a lecture on 'Task Shifting in the Developing World'. Reallocating clinical tasks to health workers with fewer qualifications was controversial. Luke had been looking forward to sharing his experiences with the World Heart Congress in Osaka later in the year.

Whatever happened about Osaka, it seemed unlikely that Luke would make this year's trip to Thailand. Every year he expected Hugh to be the one to pull out, expecting him to balk at forfeiting a family holiday in favour of the programme. And if Miriam ever found out about his misadventure in Railay Beach, he'd never be allowed to go again.

Unknown to Miriam, after they finished work in Thai Unit 3, Hugh went rock climbing in Railay Beach. Freestyle rock climbing, without ropes. As she was fond of recounting, she and Hugh had children on the condition he gave up dangerous sport.

Away from home, Hugh wavered. Last year he'd taken a tumble. Luckily, he wasn't that high when it happened. He'd landed on soft sand but Luke and Johnny were sworn to secrecy.

Typically by this time of year, Luke, Hugh and Johnny would be organised. They'd have had their night in his basement. It was usually a laugh, the night fuelled by beer, curry and lots of banter. The three of them would plan their trip.

It took Luke a good three hours to make good the damage that Duffy had done. He gathered up eighteen tapes. He knotted the black bin liner and looked at it, thinking. Why not use St Matthew's incinerator? The videos were hospital-related after all. They were not personal material, so it was hardly an abuse of hospital facilities.

The chicken and broccoli bake was ready when Wendy reappeared with a newspaper in hand. She sat at the table, next to Nina, who was typing with both thumbs on her phone. Considering what she'd been through, Nina seemed to be doing OK. Luke didn't allow himself to dwell on how differently things might have turned out if Terence hadn't called that night. He hadn't told anyone Terence had even been here. He didn't want to draw the man any deeper into the murky goings-on of Crow Hall.

Wendy smoothed out the paper. 'Looks like Alison made the front page of all the papers by what I can see out there on the hall table. Let's see what this one says.' Lowering her glasses from the top of her head, she set them on her nose, moved aside the cutlery that Nina had set, and smoothed the newspaper across the table. Clearing her throat, she started.

'Family reunion ends in tragedy,' she read aloud. 'Flood-hit communities the length and breadth of lakeside counties are reeling at the tragic news that they have lost one of their most popular ministerial representatives in years. In a cruel irony, Independent minister, Alison Forde-Thompson, met her untimely death late Thursday night – an apparent victim of the flooding – the effects of which she'd worked tirelessly to mitigate in recent weeks.'

Wendy stopped and looked over the rim of her glasses. 'Setting the tone for sainthood,' she said. Nina looked up from her phone and nodded in agreement.

Wendy continued:

'On Thursday night last, residents of High Shore Road reported hearing an explosion sometime close to 10.45 p.m. Other residents reported seeing flames and plumes of smoke and alerted the fire services. Given the severe weather conditions that night, the flames were short-lived and without an exact location the already stretched fire brigade were unable to locate the source of the explosion. It was only when daylight broke in the early hours of the following morning that a local farmer noticed what appeared to be the burnt-out shell of a car. It was at the bottom of a gully on the notoriously treacherous bend on High Shore Road. With that section of road already under water, initial investigations suggest that the car lost control on the bend, ploughing its way through a crash barrier already unstable with the rains. The car tumbled unhindered to the bottom of the two-hundred foot gully . . .'

Wendy broke off and looked at Luke.

'Don't you just love the way they use that phrase "the car lost control" – like the car had a mind of its own? Alison always did drive way too fast, didn't she?' Wendy shook her head.

'Tragically, Minister Forde-Thompson had just finished a family dinner to celebrate her daughter's return home. The young woman had returned earlier that day from a gap-holiday in Australia.'

Wendy looked up again. 'Seriously, Luke, I don't get why Alison couldn't have stayed here with you both on Nina's first night home. Why did she have to leave and take herself off to creepy Crow Hall?'

'I thought you might ask that,' Luke replied.

Full Disclosure

'A lot of things happened that night.'

Luke sat down.

Wendy gave him her full attention. 'Go on then. Tell me. The two of you are giving me the creeps the way you're looking at me.'

Luke began. 'To understand what happened here that night, I have to tell you another story. And that story started back fifteen years ago.' He snatched a glance at Nina. 'I know we've been through this. But it may not hurt you to hear it again.'

'That's all right, Dad.' Nina looked up from her phone.

Six nights earlier, as Nina hugged her hot-water bottle, Luke had attempted to account for Sophie's actions. Given Nina's ordeal that night, he had no idea how much she'd taken in. Since then, he'd caught her looking strangely at him, always when she thought he wasn't looking. He had yet to hear her judgement on what he'd done.

As succinctly as he could, he started by telling Wendy that he'd been attending a therapist. He recounted how he'd been in a hit-and-run in which a young child, Maisie Sweetman, had been killed. He explained that Alison had been the driver of the car. Wendy tensed with shock.

He trotted out the wretched details. He explained his reason for not owning up to the crime. Namely, his fear that Nina's adoption would fall through. He said this as much for Nina's ears as Wendy's. He wanted more than anything for Nina to understand his actions.

'Oh my God, Luke.' Wendy sat back. 'I had no idea.'

'What happened wasn't just Alison's doing,' he added quickly. 'I should have checked the child. I should have called an ambulance. I should have called the police.'

'I know. I hear you. But I also know that Alison could be a difficult woman.'

'Oh, she was,' said Nina, quietly. 'And she never loved me. I wasn't what she wanted. Maybe she tried, I don't know . . .' She broke off.

'It was nothing to do with you, Nina,' said Wendy, firmly. 'You were a gorgeous, smart, funny little girl when you arrived from Russia. Anyone would have been delighted to be your mother. I know I would.'

'I dunno about that, Wendy. I was a bit of a geek.'

'But geeks are cool, right?' Wendy lifted her hand to high-five her niece.

Nina reached to return it.

Wendy gripped Nina's arm. 'What happened to your wrist?'

Nina looked to Luke for guidance.

'I'm getting to that.' He wanted to get this over with.

He described arriving at the airport, with Nina nowhere to be seen, how her abandoned suitcase had sparked a security alert.

Wendy's jaw fell.

'When I landed from Heathrow, I got a text,' Nina explained. 'It said . . .' She reached for her phone and started to search.

322

'Yeah, here it is: "Sophie here (your dad's friend), outside at pick-up zone B. Red VW Polo. Your dad in an accident. Critical. Come quick."'

Luke had no recollection of giving Nina's number to Sophie. He had no reason to. But he'd often left his phone on the bedside locker. Sophie had ample opportunity to look at it any time he was in the shower.

Nina looked at Wendy. 'Well, as soon as I saw the message,' she said, 'I was like completely freaked out, as you can imagine. I tore to the exit. I forgot all about the suitcase. When I get to the pick-up zone, I see this red car there, waiting. It's at the front of the queue. There's this really serious-looking woman inside. She's waving at me and she leans across to open the passenger door. She takes off before I've even shut it properly. By the way she's driving, I'm guessing that things are really bad. She says she's really sorry to meet me like this. She's jabbering on saying something about the boathouse and an accident with the cruiser.' Nina took a breath. 'I'm even more freaked out when we get back here. There's no one around. Dad's car is gone. Mum's not here. There's no sign of emergency services. Sophie tells me they had come by the water and to come down with her to the boathouse. I'm like really spooked, but I'm thinking Dad said really nice stuff about this woman and she seemed genuinely upset herself . . .'

Nina shrugged and pulled a face.

'Anyway, I follow her. But down in the boathouse there's no one around. I knew then I'd made a mistake. That something was off. Then next thing I know, something hits me from behind, I buckle, Sophie is pushing me down the steps into the water, she's clamping something on to my wrists, and next thing I'm locked to the handrail, up to my neck in water.'

She stopped, suddenly breathless from an awareness of the danger she'd been in.

'You've got to be kidding me.' Wendy turned to Luke. 'This really happened?'

'Yes. This really happened.' He checked Nina, reckoning she'd had enough for now. 'That's fine, Nina,' he said. 'I can take it from here. Unbeknown to me, Sophie was the girl's mother.'

'Sophie did all of this out of revenge?' Wendy asked when Luke had finished the story. 'This whole macabre ordeal was old testament eye-for-an-eye, tooth-for-a-tooth?'

'Well, yes and no. I don't really think Sophie wanted Nina to . . . to . . .' He hesitated. 'I don't think she wanted to be responsible for that. The way she told it, it wasn't down to her. Whatever would happen would be down to God. It was all in His hands.'

'So the woman is some kind of Jesus freak?'

'Not that either. I think it was more like her wanting me to endure all that she'd endured.'

'OK.' Wendy nodded. 'I kind of get that twisted logic. But at the end of the day, what happened is a crime.'

'I know. I get that too. Completely.'

'And I'm guessing you can't involve the police without incriminating yourself?'

'There you have it.' Luke nodded. 'Should Sophie decide to involve the police, she would also end up incriminating herself.'

'At the same time, the woman is too dangerous to be left out there unchallenged,' said Wendy.

'Oh, I don't think she's a danger any more.' Luke flashed his sister a look. He didn't want Nina feeling scared. 'I don't feel any particular need to see Sophie arrested. The woman has been through enough in life already. And like you say, if I did contact the police, it would mean me explaining everything about the hit-and-run. To compound that, one I didn't report. I believe I can offer more in the way of redemption as a doctor than I ever could serving some prison sentence.'

Wendy looked unconvinced. 'But with the right lawyer, and given that you were not the driver, isn't it more likely that you'd be looking at a suspended sentence?'

Luke didn't want to take that chance. What if he had to go to prison? Nina would be alone. He shook his head. 'It's unlikely I'd still be able to practise. And even if I was, who would want to work with me? Anyway, it's not just that. What's the point in going to the police if Sophie no longer poses a threat?'

'I don't know how you can say that with such conviction.' Wendy shook her head. 'How do you know the woman is no harm?'

'Because of this.' He pulled an envelope from his pocket. He had read and re-read the handwritten letter inside. 'I found it in the postbox.'

Wendy took the envelope and withdrew the folded sheet of paper.

'Will I read it out loud?'

'If you like.' Luke nodded. 'Nina should hear it too.'

Dear Luke,
  I hope this letter finds Nina well
and recovering. I had hoped that God
wouldn't take her as He took my Maisie.
In the end, things worked out for you,
if not for me. I know how strange that
sounds given what I have done. From
the little I saw she seems a good person.

Please explain to her everything that happened and why. Nina seems like a nice kid — hardly a kid really. She's a young woman. Please explain that it was nothing personal on my part.

As for you, I hated you blindly from the first moment I figured out who you were. But as we got to know one another, it got really hard. Especially as I always knew what I was going to do.

In the first year after the accident, with the help of the grief support group I still attend, I managed to get out of bed each day. My husband Kevin didn't. He couldn't even bear to look at any photographs of her around the house. He always blamed himself for staying in to watch the football on the telly that night and not keeping an eye on Maisie as he normally did. He blamed himself. That turned to depression, then divorce, and he died by suicide a few years later.

I always thought that you had been the one driving the car that killed Maisie. And I know now why you felt you couldn't come forward. I'm writing to tell you that I understand. And although I'm not there yet, I hope that maybe someday I can forgive you. I want to do this as much for me as for you. Deep down I suspect you are a good person. That is not an easy thing for me to say.

I must also sympathise with you on your wife. On her death firstly, but, if I'm being honest here — which I am — on having had to live with such a person for most of your adult life. God may not have taken Nina that night, but it seems God saw fit to call on Alison instead. Who knows what God has in store for her father, Cornelius Thompson?

I am leaving Terence. I suspect this is beyond even his capacity for forgiveness. For me, it's time for a new start. Just in case you're in any doubt, you and Nina have nothing to fear from me. My aim was never to cause Nina harm. My aim was to make you feel the pain that I had felt.

In the same way that I understand what you did, Luke, I hope that one day you'll also understand my actions.

Sophie

'I don't know,' said Wendy, settling the letter back into its folds. 'I'm not so sure I could rest easy knowing that she's out there.'

'It's all going to be fine,' Luke said firmly. 'Wait and see.' What else could he say? He could hardly say he too was gripped by a nagging unease. He'd looked back at the security footage from that night at the Glasshouse. Watching Sophie leave the house, watching her glide between her own car and Alison's, before disappearing from view behind Alison's car. What was she doing? It was impossible to tell from the grainy images. The light was poor and it was sheeting rain. He had his doubts. His own private doubts.

'Yeah, you're probably right, Luke. Everything will be fine.' Wendy back-tracked, thankfully.

'I think so too,' Nina said. 'What happened that night in the boathouse was the scariest thing that's ever happened in my life. All I can think is that Sophie loved her daughter so much and was unbalanced by her death.' She turned to Luke. 'And I can understand why Dad did what he did. He did it for me. You're a good man, Dad.'

Luke looked at his daughter, awash with gratitude. What he didn't share with his sister or his daughter was his sense of loss. How he missed what he thought he'd had with Sophie. Discovering what existed between them both was nothing but a grand deceit left him feeling sad and very foolish.

Neither Luke, Wendy nor Nina ate more than a few mouthfuls of food, content just to sit at the table making small talk. Trying to feel normal. Wendy talked about Toni's plans to extend the bar in Sydney. She suggested that Nina and Luke join them in Australia for Christmas later in the year. Though there were frequent lulls in conversation, none were filled with any mention of Alison or her passing.

'Anyone fancy coming down to the basement?' asked Luke as they cleared away the table.

'You've still got that old ping-pong table?' Wendy asked.

'Of course he has.' Nina laughed. 'Dad's ridiculously

competitive. He was in a total huff when I beat him before I went to Australia.'

'Not true.' With a half smile, Luke denied the charge.

'Aw, Dad, you know it is.'

Nina turned to Wendy. 'When Dad's buddies from the hospital come over, they have these tournaments and Dad always has to win.'

'I don't know what she's talking about,' said Luke with exaggerated innocence.

Wendy grinned. 'Tell me about it. He was exactly like that when we were kids. Do you remember, Luke, when we were in primary together – the three-legged races? How you always wanted us to win?'

'I didn't care about winning as long as we beat Teddy and Henry Sullivan.'

'God,' said Wendy, laughing. 'I haven't thought about them in years – what a pair of wankers they were.'

Nina giggled.

'Someone's mobile's ringing,' shouted Wendy, as she loaded the dishwasher.

'Mine, I think,' said Luke.

He went out to the coat stand. He pulled his ringing phone from the pocket of his coat.

Roddy Gilligan.

He'd had a belly-full of Gilligan at the funeral today. What did that weasel want now?

'Roddy, hi,' he answered.

'Umm, I'm sorry to bother you like this,' Roddy said. 'But I'm afraid I've got some, umm, more bad news . . .'

'Oh?'

'Yeah. I'm still at Crow Hall. It's Cornelius. We were just

shooting the breeze about the wind turbines and stuff . . . I was just trying to distract him really, that was all. Anyway, we've had to call an ambulance. I'm not sure, Luke, but it's looking very much like the old boy's had a stroke.'

Myths and Truths

Cornelius spent the first three days in the High Dependency Unit. The prognosis was poor. The stroke had been massive. But in true Thompson fashion, Cornelius clung on. He was transferred to the Stroke Rehabilitation Unit at St Matthew's. His deficits were many. He had suffered a left hemisphere stroke. He had no power in his right arm, his speech was garbled and he was wheelchair-bound.

The old man displayed little emotion when Luke dropped by. There were no outward signs of welcome. His rheumy eyes blinked in and out of synch and he studied Luke with caution. Whether he had difficulty in recognising Luke, or whether a natural distrust had kicked in, it was hard to tell.

Back at the Glasshouse, Wendy had decided to stay on indefinitely. She asserted that Toni was perfectly capable of running the bar in Sydney on her own. In snatches of overheard conversation, Luke was amused to hear her dispense advice to Toni. Wendy had a habit of shouting at the laptop screen.

Luke was interested to meet the woman who could cope with his sister's bossiness. He'd see her at Christmas when they went to Sydney. Wendy said the sunshine would be good for him. These days everyone was at pains to tell Luke what was good for him.

Neighbours, friends and colleagues all subscribed to the notion that Luke had enjoyed a happy marriage. In their eyes, he was bereft. Even those who knew Alison and Gilligan had enjoyed more than business dealings preferred to disregard the truth. They trotted out their condolences. Acknowledgement of any estrangement between Alison and Luke would have proved too awkward. It was easier to draw on protocols used for dealing with a grieving spouse.

In the weeks following Alison's death, Luke played along with the charade, looking mournful and shaking hands. He hated every minute of it. He balked at the faux sincerity of an overly squeezed hand and the intrusive, sympathetic locking of the eyes.

Luke was beset by an urge to declare his feelings. *I fell out of love with Alison a long time back*, he longed to confess. *I found it hard to even like her, and I doubt that I shall miss her*, he wanted to say. He imagined in the unlikely event of any such utterances, they would be dismissed and ignored. Everyone loved the illusion of the successful couple that Alison had created. No one wanted to shatter the image of the Crow Hall Camelot.

Luke had plenty to do after the funeral. There were phone calls for a start. Alison's accident had attracted lots of media coverage. He expected her Marfan's specialist, Raymond Grogan, would be aware of her death. Even so, he thought it courteous to phone and cancel her quarterly check-ups. It annoyed him when his own patients missed appointments that others would gladly fill. He readied himself for forthcoming expressions of sympathy.

'Doctor Grogan's rooms,' came the frosty greeting.

'I'm ringing to cancel my late wife's quarterly check-ups with Doctor Grogan.'

'Oh, I see.' A little softer now.

'Yes. She died last month.'

'I'm very sorry to hear that. Can you give me your wife's name?'

'Alison Forde-Thompson.'

'OK . . . if you could just bear with me a second.'

'Sure.'

He listened to the gentle breathing on the other end of the line.

'I'm sorry,' the woman apologised, 'but I don't seem to have a record of anyone with that name at this practice. Is it possible she went by another name?'

Then he remembered. Alison had been with Grogan for years. She would have used her maiden name.

'She probably went by Alison Thompson, her maiden name.'

More breathing followed.

'Again, I'm sorry, but I'm not seeing anyone by that name on our database either.'

'Can you hold the line a second, please?' he asked. 'I want to check on something.'

'Yes, of course.'

Phone in hand, Luke went to the equestrian calendar in the kitchen. He flicked through every three months. As he thought, the appointments were regular. As far as May this year, the eighteenth of every third month was circled with the letters RG.

'I've just checked my wife's calendar. If you check your diary, I think you'll find she attended on the eighteenth every third month.'

He waited.

'I'm really sorry but I can categorically tell you that no one of that name has attended this practice on those dates for the past year.'

Luke stared unseeing at the calendar.

'I see,' he said slowly. 'There appears to be some confusion. Thank you for your help.'

'No problem. Thank you for your call.'

It seemed impossible. Yet there was only one possible explanation he could think of. It looked like Alison's old school friend, Nicola, had been telling the truth. And yet it seemed so shallow, so selfish, so vain, that he had difficulty accepting it. He cast his mind back to the conversation he'd had many years earlier, the day of Nina's welcoming ceremony. That September afternoon in the garden at the Glasshouse.

He'd thought Nicola absurd for suggesting Alison had never wanted to ruin her figure by getting pregnant. That Alison would prefer to have a child that was potty-trained. That Alison always got what she wanted. Remarks he'd attributed to begrudgery at the time.

He tried to grasp the enormity of what this meant. For eighteen years the woman he had married had masqueraded as a Marfan's sufferer. She had created the Marfan's myth. For sure, Alison had physical traits that could be construed as outward indicators of the syndrome. Luke had been suggestible and had embraced the deceit. What was it Alison used to say? 'I can create myths and I can make ugly truths go away.'

Something occurred to him now. The initials R and G. Roddy Gilligan. The same initials as Raymond Grogan. Was Roddy Gilligan the RG that Alison would meet every few months in Dublin? A lovers' assignation? Would she have been so bold as to mark that in the calendar, taking delight in duping Luke? His head hurt to think about it all.

He looked at his watch. 11.05 a.m. He made for the drinks cabinet. He unlocked the walnut door, racked out the recessed tray, and set out a crystal tumbler. He ripped the seal on a rare malt that Hugh had gifted him. He filled the tumbler to the top. Raising the tumbler to his lips, he swallowed. The amber liquid burned his throat, his oesophagus, and finally hit his trembling stomach. He wanted to feel something, anything, other than what he felt now.

When Wendy and Nina returned from their shopping trip late that afternoon, they found him passed out on the sofa. There was a blanket over him when he woke. Duffy had climbed onto the sofa and was at his feet. The tumbler and the half-empty whiskey bottle had been cleared away. Neither Wendy nor Nina queried him about the episode. He was grateful for that. He wasn't going to talk about it to them or anyone. It was all too monstrous.

In the weeks that followed, the weather improved. It got warmer and it was now possible to walk outside on the Glasshouse lawn without sinking ankle deep. Summer was on the way. Luke needed to put alternative arrangements in place for someone to cut the grass.

Early one morning, with a rare few minutes to spare before heading off to the hospital, he sat at the kitchen table, laptop open, and searched for a gardening service. An alert suddenly popped up on his screen:

Body found during wind-farm groundworks.

Diggers

Luke clicked on the alert:

Yesterday afternoon on the shores of Lough Carberry, engineers from Zephyr Energy made a gruesome discovery. While conducting groundworks for wind turbines they found what appear to be the remains of a body. The works were taking place close to Crow Hall. The body was discovered at a depth of five feet, on the border of two local estates. One of the estates belongs to Roddy Gilligan and the other to Senator Cornelius Thompson.

Police were called immediately and they preserved the site. A state pathologist is currently at the scene where she is conducting a preliminary investigation. There is some speculation that the body could be that of casual labourer Thomas Delahunty who disappeared twenty-eight years ago.

Thomas was raised in a state care home along with his sister. The eighteen-year-old youth spent a summer working at Crow Hall, disappearing shortly afterwards. Despite ill health, his sister has never given up hope of finding out what happened to her younger brother. 'People said that Thomas was a tearaway. But they never gave him a chance,' she said. 'To me he was just a young lad like any other. He was mad about horses. He had a sense of humour and a cheeky smile. I miss him.'

Locals remain tight-lipped about the find. They are still grieving the loss of their much-loved Minister, Alison Forde-Thompson from Crow Hall, who died in a car accident during the spring floods.

More to follow . . .

Luke stared at the screen and read the news again. He now understood exactly why Cornelius had been so uneasy about the siting of the turbines. He knew there were human remains just beyond the boundary of his land. Cornelius knew, because the bad bastard had put them there himself.

Luke reached for his phone. He called the landline at Crow Hall.

'Hello?'

It was Gilligan.

'Hi, it's Luke. I've just read the news. Just ringing to see how the old man is doing?'

'It's busy today with all the police. We're all pretty shocked, as you can imagine.'

I'll bet you are, thought Luke.

'Do you know anything about it, Roddy? Is it true?'

'I know nothing. Myself and Sly were interviewed earlier this morning and the police are speaking to Cornelius now. But of course I don't think the old boy understands much of what's going on.'

Even in ill health Cornelius was running rings around everyone.

'Has any of the old boy's speech returned?' Luke feigned concern.

'Up to now progress has been pretty slow,' Gilligan replied. 'But he's managing a few more words. I call in most days.'

I bet you do, thought Luke.

'Sly and Myra are in and out a bit as well,' said Gilligan. 'And the old boy seems to be getting on well with the new homecare package.'

'Is that right?' said Luke. He looked at his watch. He should go.

'Yeah. A new agency nurse has moved in to Crow Hall. Cornelius has round-the-clock care now. It's working out well. She seems like a lovely woman. Her name is Sophie.'

Acknowledgements

Heartfelt thanks to my agent Jo Bell for her support, encouragement and sunny guidance. Thanks also to the wider team at Bell Lomax Moreton.

Thank you to Krystyna Green, Rebecca Sheppard, Howard Watson and all at Little, Brown.

Thank you to Elaine Egan and all at Hachette Ireland.

The extent of my copious references to the world of medicine became clear while editing. A million thanks to Clodagh O'Gorman for putting me right on all my sticky-noted queries. And apologies for hijacking you for a lot longer than a quick cup of coffee!

Writing a novel is a solitary business so the good company and encouragement of my friends and family mean everything. Thanks to my early readers, Sarah O'Donoghue and Joanna O'Donoghue. Also to Joanna Leahy, always there to lend a helping hand. Thanks to Jamie and Alasdair – who never fail to make me laugh. The support of other writers is invaluable, and special thanks to Judi Curtin for allowing me to bend her ear on many an occasion.

And finally, thanks to Neil as always. First reader, first editor, first responder (when it's all going pear-shaped). Always my first.

ACKNOWLEDGMENTS